BLUE BANDITS

Blue Bandits

DON MALATESTA

Mallard Cove Publishing

This book is dedicated to my good friend Dave Trefry (1941-2021). We met forty-six years ago and have been good friends ever since. After a distinguished Air Force career, he occupied some of his time by painting. His most recent business card says, "Desert Dave's Designs." When he found out I was writing a novel set in the Sonoran Desert, he volunteered to do the cover art. Thank you, Dave, both for your friendship and the many hours you spent developing just the right scene for the cover of *Blue Bandits*.

This is a work of fiction. Any similarity to actual people, places, or events is coincidental.

Copyright © 2022 by Mallard Cove Publishing, Incorporated, Olympia, Washington, USA

ISBN: 978-1-7369582-3-0

Library of Congress Control Number: 2022942499

All rights reserved. No part of this book may be reproduced in any manner whatsoever without written permission except in the case of brief quotations embodied in critical articles and reviews.

First Printing, September, 2022

Chapter 1

John Martin stood at the wood stove, ignoring the burning match he held, staring at the blinking red light on his answering machine. Had it been blinking three hours ago? Nope, when he and Rex had passed through the kitchen at 5:30 a.m., a few minutes after sunrise, it had still been dark in the house. The light would have stood out like an emergency beacon. The call must have come in while they had been out for their early morning kayak paddle. Despite the cold, he didn't light the fire. The machine demanded his immediate attention. He blamed it on his fighter pilot background. In his business—his former business—a flashing red light meant something had gone terribly wrong.

He blew out the match just before the flame reached his fingertips and tossed the blackened matchstick onto the stove top. Very few of the locals knew he had a phone. Most likely, the caller was someone from his past, someone intruding on his new life. He sighed and pushed the play button. Hank Carter's voice boomed out of the speaker.

Viper, this is Snake. I need you in Tucson today, sixteen hundred, at Customs Service flight ops. It's an emergency. We lost an airplane last week. I've been to the crash site. Can't say much on the phone. Just two words: Blue Bandits. Think about it. There's more but . . . just be there, buddy. I say again, be there.

The machine's fuzzy digital voice announced that the call had come in at 6:40 a.m. It was almost 9:00, he needed a shower, and the next ferry to the mainland wasn't until 11:00. He wasn't going to make it in time. That was unacceptable. He had to answer Hank's call for help. Their relationship, forged during combat missions in two wars, demanded it. John replayed the message, amused that Hank still used their old fighter pilot call signs. How long had they both been retired? The rest of the message bothered him. It was a shock to hear Hank's deep, gravelly, self-assured voice saying, "I need you."

He had to get to Tucson, to that Customs Service building on Davis-Monthan Air Force Base, by 4:00 p.m. and there was only one way to do it. He picked up the telephone, dialed, and waited.

"Olympic Flight Museum, may I help you?"

It was one of the volunteers. He had met her once but couldn't remember her name. She was the widow of a World War II bomber pilot. "Hi. This is John Martin. May I speak to Mr. Rowe?"

"John Martin? Don't you own that cute little silver jet in the hangar? What's it called? I don't know these modern planes at all. To me, you see, anything built after 1945—"

"It's a T-33, an Air Force jet trainer from the fifties. Ma'am, I'm sorry, but I've got some urgent business with the director, Mr. Rowe.

"Oh. Yes, yes, of course. But he won't be in until noon. In fact, I'm the only one here except for a mechanic."

"Is it Whitaker?"

"The mechanic? Well, I don't really—"

"Short, skinny black guy with gray hair?"

"That's the one," she said.

"Can you get him on the phone, please? It's really important."

She set down the phone. John did some quick mental arithmetic. If the weather was good and the winds were favorable, he could make it in two hops. Elko, Nevada would be about halfway and would have less traffic than Reno. He heard muffled voices and the sound of a wrench landing on a workbench. An air compressor chugged in the background.

"Yeah?" Whitaker wasn't polite when he was interrupted.

"Whit, it's John. I've got a problem."

"John?" The mechanic's voice rose half an octave.

He braced himself for a dose of Whitaker's sarcasm.

"Is it really you, John? My favorite pilot from the old days, for whom I sweated and slaved in extreme desert heat to keep your personal F-16 in tip-top shape, and who now lives about ten miles away but never—"

"Cheer up, old buddy. You'll be seeing me in about an hour."

"Ah, bad timing, my friend," Whitaker said. "No can do. The museum is putting on an air show today. I'm assholes and elbows getting these planes ready, including the one you so graciously leased to us. It'll be the star of the—"

"That's why I'm coming down. I've got to pull the T-Bird out of the show."

"Pull it out? You can't do that. It's our only jet!"

"Sorry, but I really need it."

"You need it? What for?"

"I'm going to fly it to Tucson. In about an hour."

Whitaker sputtered. "You? You haven't flown in, what, five years? Rowe won't allow that. The FAA would have his ass for letting you off the ground."

"That's why he's going with me," John said. "He's a flight instructor, right? He can get me current on the first leg. Then I'll drop him off."

"What's the deal? Why such short notice?"

"I've got to meet Hank Carter in Tucson at four this afternoon. It's urgent. I just found out a few minutes ago. The T-Bird is my only hope of getting there on time."

"Urgent, you say? Hell, for that crazy sucker, everything's urgent. Probably needs help opening a can of tuna."

"No, this is different, Whit. He was serious, like in the war. I've got to go." He waited, listening to Whitaker's breathing.

After three noisy breaths, the mechanic said, "Well, if you've gotta go, the T-Bird's definitely ready. But it's set up for the show with only a light fuel load. You want the tip tanks filled?"

"Yeah, I'll need all the gas I can get."

"Okay. By the way, how'd you convince Rowe? This air show is his baby. It'll be the biggest event of 1995. They've got TV news coverage and everything, not to mention that he's really excited about flying the T-Bird."

John swallowed hard. "Ah, he doesn't know about this yet. I need you to tell him and get him in there for an 1100 departure."

"What?"

This time Whitaker's screech was a full octave higher than normal.

"Look, the museum's had my T-Bird for five years and this is the first time I've asked for a favor. Set it up, Whit. I'm short on time and I'm counting on you."

Whitaker's heavy breathing outpaced the beat of the compressor. "Oh, man. You don't know what you're asking."

After ten more seconds of nothing but compressor noise, Whitaker said, "Yeah, okay. I'll talk to Rowe. For old time's sake. For you and Hank. God knows I owe you both."

"Let's not get into all that. We were just friends helping a friend. But there's one more thing. You remember where I live?"

"Anderson Island, right?"

"Send a helicopter to pick me up in thirty minutes. There's a helipad at the island school. The pilot should know it."

"Now wait a—"

John hung up. Whitaker was a good man. Resourceful. The helicopter would be there.

"Rex, old boy," he said, patting the Shepherd on the head, "how'd you like to spend a day or so with Jerry?" Before leaving the kitchen, he erased Hank's message.

Chapter 2

John's microphone wasn't working, so he leaned closer to the chopper pilot and shouted, "Put me down as close as you can to that T-33 at the Flight Museum."

The fuzzy-faced kid looked down at the several airplanes outside the hangar and said, "Uh, which one is that?"

God, that made him feel old. He was being flown around by a pilot too young to recognize a T-Bird. "It's that straight-winged silver jet, with tip tanks. The one with the canopy open."

"Thanks," John said after they were on the ground. "Good job." He handed the pilot a check and two twenties as a tip. He stepped out and reached behind the seat for his gym bag and his olive-drab Air Force-issue helmet bag. After waving goodbye, he crouched to clear the rotor blades and jogged toward the T-Bird. Behind him, the helicopter revved its engine and lugged itself into the air. The rotor wash ruffled his hair and fluttered the sleeves of his leather flying jacket.

It was quiet enough to talk by the time he reached Whitaker, who stood beside the ladder with a greasy rag in his hand. A red-faced Dan Rowe, already strapped into the rear cockpit, glared down at him. He shook hands with Whitaker and slapped him on the back. "Thanks, man. I owe you one."

"No shit."

"How did you get Rowe into the cockpit so fast?"

Whitaker glanced up at Rowe and turned back toward John with a grin. He said, "I told him you'd cancel your $100,000-dollar grant to the museum if he didn't go along."

John winced. "That was dirty pool. I'd never do that."

"I know that, but Rowe doesn't."

"Look, I'm sorry about not keeping in touch," John said. "I've lived like a hermit out there for almost five years but, you know what? I haven't gotten tired of it yet." He reached down and picked up his helmet bag. "I do miss you, though."

"No sweat, man. You got a rough deal. It's about time you got some peace and quiet in your life." He cleared his throat. "The bird's all ready for you."

"Thanks, Whit. It looks beautiful." He expected nothing less from his old crew chief. The forty-four-year-old T-33 looked new, as if it had just come off the assembly line at Lockheed. Its silver wings, tail and cigar-shaped fuselage gleamed so brightly that he had to shade his eyes with one hand. All the painted surfaces—even the insides of the wheel wells—looked fresh and clean. Air Force markings had been faithfully reproduced, probably hand-painted by Whitaker.

He reached out, grabbed Whit's hand, and squeezed it. "Thanks for everything." He pulled on his flying gloves and put one foot on the ladder.

"John?"

"Yeah?"

"You sure you're okay with this? Flying, I mean. What about your back?"

"I'm fine, Whit. Mentally and physically. I've been working out a lot to keep the back muscles strong."

"What do the doctors say?"

John shrugged. "I never talk to them anymore."

"Why does that not surprise me?" Whitaker looked him over from head to toe, as if he were scrutinizing a wing or a fuselage, looking for metal fatigue or cracks. "All right, my man. Looks like you've been keeping yourself in good shape." He grimaced. "Good luck with Mr. Rowe up there."

John raised his eyebrows briefly, shrugged, and climbed up the ladder.

When he reached the top, Rowe snapped at him. "Aren't you even going to do a preflight inspection?"

Oh, boy, what a way to begin the trip. He had only met Rowe twice, once while signing the T-Bird's lease agreement and again at last year's museum fund raiser. The man had a knack for rubbing people the wrong way. He said, "Dan, look down there on the ramp. That's Jim Whitaker, Chief Master Sergeant, United States Air Force, Retired. The best jet mechanic on the face of the earth. He and I go a long way back. If he says this bird is good to go, it's good to go. If you have a problem with that, just hop down there and do your own damn preflight."

Rowe sighed and lifted his helmet off the canopy rail. He shoved it onto his head and pounded the chin strap into place, effectively cutting off conversation.

John let himself down into the narrow front cockpit and sank back against the parachute. He buckled the fittings across his chest and legs, chiding himself for using that kind of language with Rowe. He'd smooth things over after they were airborne. Whitaker unhooked the ladder from the canopy rail and gave him a thumbs-up, which he returned. Just like the old days. He unzipped the helmet bag and pulled out his helmet and oxygen mask. They still fit fine; he had confirmed that before leaving home. It was time to go. Would he remember all the switch positions and procedures to get this old bird airborne?

*   *   *

At about 4,000 feet during the climb-out, John pushed the stick to the right and looked down. The right wingtip, almost vertical now, pointed directly at his apple orchard, his cottage, and his bright red sea kayak on the beach. He missed all those things already and hated to leave. But he would. For Hank.

"Hey! What are you doing?" Rowe called over the intercom. "We're supposed to be on a heading of . . . never mind."

John rolled the T-Bird back to level flight and resumed the assigned heading. "Just taking a look at where I live, Dan." The Island, as true Anderson Islanders called it—as if there were no others in the Sound—was behind him now. So was the slow-paced lifestyle, where time was measured not in seconds but in six-hour-plus tidal cycles. He looked over his shoulder to get a final glimpse of home. He thanked God for this place, a heavily forested island insulated from the outrages of an over-crowded society. His cottage was small, with few amenities, just a single wood-burning stove for both heat and cooking. It was a primitive life, yes. But it had its advantages.

The privacy had helped him adjust. After five years, people had stopped wondering where he came from and what he used to do. They had adopted him, treated him as if he were a native, and let him live in peace.

John faced forward and admired a close-up view of The Mountain. Islanders never used its English-given name of Mount Rainier or its native name, Tahoma. To them—to *us*, he corrected himself—it was The Mountain, 14,411 feet of glacier-clad beauty rising from a lush evergreen forest. Today, thanks to the T-Bird's altitude and a cloudless sky, the view was even more breathtaking than usual. To the south, a truncated Mt. St. Helens, and the more distant sharp peak of Mt. Hood, each with a cap of dazzling white snow, poked up above the horizon.

It was time to make peace with Rowe. The man would have a difficult time remaining grumpy with such beautiful scenery down there. John keyed his microphone. "Nice view."

Rowe didn't answer.

John banked left and right, gently this time, to see the last few miles of Puget Sound's inlets and estuaries before they disappeared under the nose. If Rowe wanted to sulk all the way to Elko, that was okay as long as he signed off his logbook when they landed. Then he'd be legal to press on to Tucson solo, the way God intended pilots to fly. As they passed 10,000 feet, he tightened his oxygen mask against his face, disconnected the low-altitude lanyard on his parachute and checked the engine gauges. The T-Bird was fine. But was he?

He should be euphoric, savoring the feel of the stick in his right hand and the throttle in his left, the tug of a parachute harness on his shoulders and the rubbery taste of air inhaled through an oxygen mask—all things he used to live for. He flexed his hands, squeezing the stick and throttle as if he could milk some enjoyment out of the metal and plastic grips. It didn't work. His passion for living in the air, suppressed for five years, must have atrophied, like a nerve-damaged muscle. Was he a different man now, one who would rather be down there on the Sound, paddling a kayak across smooth waters, listening to nature rather than air traffic control?

* * *

Rowe didn't say a single word until seventy miles from Elko, when John reduced power and pushed the stick forward, lowering the nose for the descent. Ahead was a view not unknown to John, but much different than the lush green forests and bright blue waters of Puget Sound. He was back over the all-too-familiar desert. From this height, the wrinkled, light-brown terrain, crisscrossed by random crevasses of dry streambeds, resembled an elephant's creased and furrowed hide.

"I need to see three landings," Rowe said. "Two touch-and-goes, one full stop."

"Roger that," John said. He didn't bother asking Rowe what type of pattern to fly. For a true fighter pilot, there was only one way to line up for landing. He pushed the throttle forward and accelerated.

"Mind if I ask a personal question?" Rowe said.

"Go ahead and ask. I can't guarantee an answer, though."

"Is what they say about you true?"

"That depends. Who is 'they'? And what do they say?"

"Well," Rowe said, "in the Flight Museum brochure, you're listed as a donor, of course, with 'Lieutenant Colonel, USAF, Retired' after your name. Occasionally a visitor will see that and ask me if you're *the* John Martin, like you're famous or something. I really don't know you, so I asked around. Asked Whitaker, in fact."

"And what did Whit say?"

"He told me to mind my own business, that you moved up to Puget Sound to get some privacy. But I hear things, you know, from other visitors who know military aviation."

"Things?"

"Yeah, things like a promising career cut short when you had to retire under, ah, what someone called 'cloudy circumstances.' Some kind of family tragedy. You drop out of sight for a few years and then turn up on Anderson Island as a millionaire."

John laughed, "Wow, when you put it like that, it does sound intriguing." Rowe hadn't said anything about the charges of attempted murder. Maybe he was being polite. Nosy, but polite.

"Whitaker did finally say that you're a genuine hero. The only fighter pilot to shoot down MiGs in both Vietnam and the Gulf War. Two MiG kills on one mission in 'Nam, he said."

John frowned. So much for Whit's promise to protect his privacy. "Just doing my job," he said. He responded to a few radio instructions from air traffic control, which gave him time to think about how much more to tell Rowe.

"I'd like to hear the MiG stories someday," Rowe said. Also, that story about you bringing a shot-up F-16 back from over Baghdad. According to Whitaker—"

"Excuse me, I've got to check in with the tower." He hoped Rowe would get the hint. Damn that Whitaker! A superb jet mechanic, yes, but he talked too much.

"Quite a story the old guy tells," Rowe said. "He says you were some type of covert operative before you got into the F-4. Wounded in action. Whitaker's dying to know more about all that, you know? But he says you never talk about it. Say, have you ever thought about writing your autobiography? We could market it for you at the Flight Museum!"

"Bad idea, Dan. The story does not have a happy ending." They were fifteen miles from Elko's runway. The descent was working out well despite Rowe's distractions.

Rowe said, "Yeah, yeah, I see. I'm kinda sorry to have brought it up. Seems like you got a raw deal, though. Don't you want the truth to come out?"

"I'd like to keep it all private," John said. "It's all behind me now." He wasn't especially proud of the truth.

"Well, you can't blame a guy for trying," Rowe said. "Always looking for more publicity for the museum. I would've asked you about this long ago, but you never come by."

"No offense, but I'm kind of happy where I am."

"You don't miss flying?"

"Not a bit," John said. "Never think about it anymore. Or hadn't until today, anyway." He looked ahead at Runway 6, now ten miles away, and lowered the T-Bird's nose a bit, refining his descent angle. "Dan, I've got to concentrate on the landing now, okay?"

"Oh. Sure. Sorry."

"Look, Dan, I'm sorry about dragging you away from the museum and pulling the T-Bird out of the show. I'm answering a short notice call from an old flying buddy who's never needed help before. So, it must be pretty serious. And, no matter what that foul-mouthed old coot Whitaker might have told you, I would never cancel my grant to the museum."

"It's all water under the bridge now," Rowe said. "What about my ride home?"

"It's all arranged. All paid for. In fact, I see a shiny, bright white Lear Jet charter parked on the ramp down there. You'll be home by sunset." John leveled off at 1,500 feet above Elko's runway. Two patterns and a full stop landing would use up valuable time. Once free of Rowe and refueled, he'd have to push the little silver jet hard to make it to Tucson on time.

Chapter 3

Carlos Alvarado checked his watch for the tenth time. He should go now. The decoy aircraft would enter US airspace in five minutes. He pushed the throttle full forward into afterburner, which was a waste of fuel. The MiG could easily take off without use of afterburner. He just enjoyed hearing the explosive *Boom!* when it lit off and the resulting kick of acceleration. Alvarado knew it would rattle the crystal chandeliers in his mansion a few hundred meters away and frighten the chickens and pigs in the barnyard. He didn't care. He owned it all: the private airstrip, the custom-built mansion, even the chickens—everything on this large ranch. Four million U.S. dollars, in cash, to purchase the two MiGs? No problem.

The MiG-21 leapt forward with the gusto of a charging attack dog. It accelerated to takeoff speed in less than ten seconds and lifted off with very little coaxing from him. Alvarado raised the landing gear and pushed forward on the stick to keep the jet level, close to the runway. He risked a quick look to his left. Several of his men, those not busy in the sheds processing cocaine and other "product," stood there cheering him on, expecting a show. Who was he, Carlos Alvarado, leader of their cartel and former jet pilot for the Mexican Air Force, to disappoint them? He waved with his throttle hand but didn't look at the men a second time. Accelerating quickly and only a meter or so above the runway, it was wise to keep the eyes forward and his right hand on the stick.

Airspeed was 600 kilometers per hour when he passed the departure end of the runway. *Qué fuerza!* What power! Alvarado pulled the stick back into his lap, grunted like a weightlifter to compensate for the *g*-force and pointed the nose straight up. As airspeed decreased, he relaxed the *g*'s, making a symmetrical vertical turn until the MiG was flat on its back, upside down, two thousand meters above the runway. He rolled upright, completing the Immelmann turn with his nose pointed the opposite direction from that of his takeoff.

He pulled the throttle out of afterburner. The show was over. He looked down to see his wingman, young Enrique Hernandez, begin his takeoff roll. The man was a good pilot but had no fighter experience, so Enrique's takeoff was much more conservative than his own. As Alvarado watched the boy maneuver into his assigned position, he admired the jet's camouflage paint job. His men had painted over the Albanian markings on both MiGs. All that remained were the two large red I.D. numbers painted on the noses. These were traditions and made the aircraft look, well, macho—powerful, fitting weapons for men of their stature. When Enrique was in proper position, Alvarado accelerated to combat speed, 750 kilometers per hour, and headed north. He reached forward and raised the red-guarded switch, arming the guns. If Enrique could stay with him, the kid might learn something today.

*   *   *

Hank Carter perked up when the female controller's voice said, "Sidearm Three, Looking Glass, standby. Possible bogey, Bullseye 180, 40, low."

Looking Glass was this month's call sign for AWACS. He wouldn't want to fly one of those airborne command and control centers—it was too big and had too many people in the crew. But he respected what it could do. Today, that monstrous, billion-dollar, converted Boeing 707 with a giant thirty-foot diameter black radar disc mounted on top was going to vector him to intercept a drug smuggler. Hank guessed that AWACS people liked this drug surveillance stuff. It was something to keep them busy until the politicians could arrange another foreign war.

"Sidearm Three!" the controller shouted. "I've got a target for you! Bogey—"

"Sidearm Three, Looking Glass Zero Five," said a deep male voice.

That was probably her supervisor.

"Cleared to engage," the male voice said.

Hank pushed the microphone button on the yoke and said, "Sidearm Three copies clear to en—"

"Sidearm Three!" the female voice gasped. "Your bogey is Bullseye 160, 25, heading north, low, speed 180!"

"Sidearm Three copies," Hank replied. He wanted to add, "Okay, calm down." She must be new. Oh well, everyone had a right to be nervous on their first intercept. His first one had been a disaster. He would have been shot down over North Vietnam and captured or, worse yet, dead, if it hadn't been for John. That guy had saved his butt, killed both MiGs and got them both safely home—all without breaking a sweat.

He was still using techniques John had taught him so long ago. This time it wasn't over 'Nam or Iraq but the vast khaki-colored Sonoran Desert, 120 miles southwest of Tucson. He wasn't in a jet fighter but a tricked-out Cessna Citation, adapted by the Customs Service for the drug surveillance mission. He wasn't alone in this aircraft, although he would have preferred it that way. He had a co-pilot, a young guy by the name of Jack, and an equipment operator, Julie, in the back. Her job was to operate all the on-board sensors that were supposed to find the drug smugglers.

"Looking Glass, Sidearm Three's departing the orbit, heading south." If the target was dumb enough to land, a Customs Service Blackhawk would swoop down and take them into custody, along with whomever was waiting on the ground to pick up the shipment. He released the radio button and triggered the intercom. "Julie, do you see 'em yet?"

"Negative."

As usual, the fancy stuff wasn't working. Hank stayed at 20,000 feet; that would conserve fuel and keep them out of sight of the target. He would fall back on the basics, on what John had taught him back in their F-4 days—dead reckoning. In later years, John had evolved into calling it TLAR, or That Looks About Right. In other words, an educated guess. Even when they had transitioned to the high-tech F-16 and been christened with call signs—Viper for John and Snake for him—John had preached knowing the basics, the old-fashioned way of flying.

Hank ignored all the sophisticated displays in the cockpit and glanced down at the paper map on his kneeboard. He did some figuring and came up with a plan. Did he have time to explain this plan to Jack? Sure. Maybe the kid could learn something about Situational Awareness. He said, "Jack, what would you do right now?"

"Uh, wait for more info? Wait until Julie gets a radar contact?"

"Bullshit!" Hank said. "We need to move this jet! We need to engage the—" He almost said *enemy*. "—engage the target." Hell, wasn't that what they were, though? Drug runners were the enemy.

"How?" Jack asked.

Hank pushed up the throttles until the indicated airspeed read 250 knots. He asked Jack, "What's our groundspeed?"

As expected, the boy's eyes went toward the cockpit display. Hank reached out and blocked the digital readout with his hand. "No! Don't use the gauges. Use your brain! What's 250 knots indicated in true airspeed or groundspeed?"

"Uh . . . "

"Not down to the gnat's ass, dammit! Just a WAG."

Jack gave him a blank stare.

"A WAG! A guess. A Wild-Assed-Guess!"

Hank felt sorry for the poor kid. This conversation had already consumed about thirty seconds, during which time they had closed the distance to their target by four miles, when you considered the speeds of both his Citation and the target.

"I guess that would be about 300 knots true, so with no wind, that's—"

"Bingo! That's my boy! So, we're going 300 knots groundspeed. Please tell me you can convert that to miles per minute. Quickly!"

"Ah . . ."

"Too slow, dammit! You've got to know this stuff cold. Five miles per minute." Hank took a deep breath while scanning the sky above, below, and both left and right. It was the kid's job to visually scan their right side, from 12 o'clock to six o'clock, but he hadn't moved his head during this whole conversation. Jack was way out of his depth. He'd need to have a training session when they got back on the ground. Which would begin with a tongue-lashing for neglecting the visual lookout doctrine.

"All right, don't worry," Hank said. "We'll talk about this on the ground." He realized he had been ignoring Julie. "Any news back there?"

"No contact yet."

Hank keyed the radio. "Looking Glass, Sidearm Three, status bogey."

"Sidearm Three, your bogey is Bullseye 150, 9, low."

"Sidearm Three."

Hank knew he could do this himself, all alone. But would that teach the other two crewmembers anything? He needed to talk them through it, so they might learn how to catch bad guys the old-fashioned way.

He said, "Listen up. I am going to think out loud. But first, Jack, hack your clock."

Jack pushed the button on the old-fashioned clock on his instrument panel.

Hank continued, "It's simple math, a formula. Speed times time equals distance. Distance first: AWACS just called the bogey nine miles south of Bullseye. We are fifteen miles north of Bullseye. So, we are about twenty-four miles apart. Now for the speeds: It's easier if you convert it to miles per minute. We're going five miles per minute. How fast is the bogey going?"

"Ah, I have no clue," Jack said. "Oh, wait. AWACS said speed was 180."

"Okay, please tell me you can convert that to miles per minute."

After an encouragingly short pause, Jack said, "Three miles per—"

"Correct!" Hank said. "So, we are closing at a combined speed of five plus three, or eight miles per minute. When will we merge with the bogey?"

"Ah . . ."

Hank looked at the clock. Fifty-five seconds had elapsed; he needed to speed this lesson up or they'd miss the bogey, "Son, try to follow me on this, but if I lose you, we'll debrief it later. We started twenty-four miles apart. We will merge at an equal time point when we have traveled some of those twenty-four miles and the bogey has traveled some of it. So, time is the variable, call it t. Our speed times t plus bogey's speed times t equals twenty-four. If you do this in miles per minute, you get $5t$ plus $3t$ equals 24, or $8t$ equals 24. Can you solve that equation?"

Jack said, "Three! Three minutes until merge!"

"Good boy. But that three minutes started back when I began this dissertation. What's your clock say now?"

"One minute, fifty-five seconds."

"Okay, my friend, subtract that from three minutes and you get?"

"One minute, five seconds until merge!" Julie said. "Sorry to break in, but I've been following along."

"Good on you, Julie. Now, where do we look for the bogey?

Jack said, "Ah, if he was southeast of us, and we're going straight south, then it would be off your side, maybe about ten degrees left."

"Excellent! There's hope for you after all. That's where I'm looking right now." Hank paused for a moment as he remembered hearing those same exact words, *"There's hope for you after all,"* spoken by his fighter pilot mentor, whom he would be meeting in an hour or so. Viper would be shocked to learn about evidence of a shootdown and what seemed to be a high-level cover-up of the incident. Despite his untimely exit from the Air Force, Viper still had some powerful connections. Together they'd get those desk jockeys in Washington off their fat asses and make them do something. For now, it was time to catch some bad guys.

Today's Bullseye was a ground reference not marked on any maps except those of the Customs Service. It was an abandoned dirt airstrip at the edge of a dry lake fifty miles southeast of Gila Bend, just northeast of Organ Pipe National Monument and only thirty miles north of the Mexican border. It was easy to spot. The dry lake, shining bright white in the mid-afternoon sunlight, stood out like a beacon. Just south of that was the light-brown runway, which was the same length as the lake was wide, about three thousand feet. It had been used for drug deliveries before. Could he be lucky enough that this was today's destination?

"Julie, get some of your fancy sensors to look around Bullseye," Hank said. "We might have some action there today." He glanced over his right shoulder and noted the position of the sun. He wanted it to be at his back, blinding the eyes of the bogey's pilot, when he rolled in behind him. As soon as he got a tally-ho, he'd swoop down to about 10,000 feet and fall into a surveillance position. He checked the engine and fuel gauges one more time—yes, that was Jack's job, but no self-respecting pilot would trust anyone else to do that. They were all in the green.

Julie said, "I've got a large box truck sitting just east of the runway at Bullseye."

This was going to be good. Some guys waiting for a load of drugs, unaware that they would soon be in handcuffs.

"Sidearm Three, your bogey is Bullseye 160, 5, low," Looking Glass said. "Good hunting."

The controller sounded much more relaxed now. Her job was almost done. By the end of the day, she'd be calling herself a veteran.

"Sidearm Three." He focused on the desert floor. It was times like this that he missed the F-16's heads-up display and all the other magic that made intercepts so easy. In this beast, when the job got up close and personal, it was his eyeballs and his WAG about the bogey's flight path that would have to win the day. If his calculations were correct, the bogey would be coming across that range of small hills just south of Bullseye right about . . . there he was!

He pulled the throttles back and simultaneously rolled the Citation left, almost over on its back, and pulled the nose down toward the desert. "Tally-ho!" he called to Looking Glass. He didn't need to warn Jack or Julie; they knew his style. They would hold on for dear life while he yanked the jet around the sky.

During the dive, he said on the intercom, "Tally on a single bogey, on the nose, five miles, very low."

Jack called out, "Tally!" The kid sounded very pleased with himself.

"Dumb shit," Hank muttered to himself. Jack gave him a worried glance. "No, not you." He pointed at the drug pilot. Oops, the *suspected* drug pilot—innocent until proven guilty and all that crap. "That guy. He's too easy to see." The jerk was flying on the west side of the ridge, in full sun, his aircraft's white paint standing out against the dark hills like a searchlight. He could identify it now; it was a twin-engine Beech Baron, bobbing along just above the Saguaro cacti on the ridge. Its pilot had to be a rookie, and a stupid one at that. Where do they find such men?

". . . Looking Glass . . . contact lost . . . additional targets . . ."

Radio transmissions from Looking Glass were breaking up. No problem. The controller wouldn't be much more help anyway. With the target in sight, he leveled off at 10,000 feet and stayed high, in the bogey's six o'clock position and on the up-sun side. The Baron's pilot wouldn't be expecting him there. *Always be where you're not expected.* That was one of the many lessons Viper had drilled into him on his first combat mission.

The intercept had been easy. He had done hundreds like it in the Air Force. In the Citation or the F-16, the objective was the same: Slide into visual range of the target without being detected. In the F-16, of course, what happened next was to pump a missile up the enemy's tailpipe or close in for a gun kill with the 20-millimeter cannon. No AIM-9 missiles or guns today, Hank lamented. "Just follow 'em, report back, and keep 'em in sight until the helicopter arrives," his boss, Tucson Customs Service Chief Pilot Eric Briggs, had said. "Remember, we can't force them down. We've gotta catch them in the act of unloading drugs. Let the helicopter guys make the arrests." Hank relaxed his grip on the controls and congratulated himself. He was camped out, undetected, at the bogey's six o'clock. This one wouldn't get away.

A small object flashed over the right wing. A bird? But it appeared to have been moving *forward*. Impossible. He twisted in his seat, looking behind and to the right. "Jack, did you see that?"

"What?"

Something punched a hole in the right wing, leaving a momentary puff of smoke and debris before the slipstream carried it away. Orange flame and black smoke erupted from the hole.

"Shit!" Hank could feel the impacts. Solid thumps pounded the wing spar and then the aft fuselage. The control column rattled so hard it almost jumped out of his hand. He slammed the yoke full right and pulled back hard, almost to the aft limit. Too hard—too many g's. He greyed out; his field of vision shrank to a small, colorless, telescope-sized view. If he pulled back any harder, he would black out, or stall the airplane, or both. He gasped for air. When his vision cleared, he saw it was a disaster. His right wing was being blown apart. Worse yet, the trail of impacts would reach the cockpit in less than a second.

Debris and leaking fuel streamed off the wing. The entire right side of the Citation was engulfed in a fireball. Above all that, Hank finally saw the other airplane. It was less than five hundred feet away, its nose in a perfect attack position. He flinched as the cockpit shook violently. When he opened his eyes, the cockpit was splattered with red. Jack slumped in his seat. One side of his face was gone. Poor kid. It was a little late to yell at him for not checking six. Hank tried to grab the controls, but his arms would not work. For the first time in his life, he was helpless.

Chapter 4

John steered the T-33 in a descending arc around the east side of Tucson's Mount Lemmon and glanced inside at the forty-year-old wind-up clock on the instrument panel. It still kept perfect time. He was going to be a few minutes late. He called "Airport in sight" to air traffic control and they cleared him to navigate on his own to Davis-Monthan Air Force Base. Once clear of the high terrain, he pushed the nose down to gain some speed. The T-Bird bounced through pockets of afternoon turbulence, rattling like an old pickup truck on a washboard dirt road, its empty wingtip fuel tanks deflecting up and down with each bump. John reached for the radio dial on the left console and, without looking down to see the numbers, twisted each of the knobs the correct number of clicks for the tower frequency.

His eyes were focused outside the cockpit—above, below, left, right, and even behind—looking for traffic. After a quick glance down at the radio to confirm he had dialed correctly, he keyed the mic. "D-M Tower, this is Lockheed Three-One-One-Juliet Mike, fifteen miles north for landing, information Zulu."

There was no reply, which was worrisome. Maybe Lacy Simmons hadn't passed the word. John turned up the volume to overcome the roar of the 300-knot descent.

"Roger, Juliet Mike, this is Davis-Monthan tower. Be advised we are PPR today. Do you have prior permission to land?"

"Stand by." He unbuckled his chest strap just long enough reach inside his jacket and pull out a piece of paper, then refastened the buckle. "Tower, One Juliet Mike. PPR number is eleven-dash-two."

He leveled off at traffic pattern altitude, accelerated to the desired airspeed, and lined up on a five-mile initial.

Tower said, "One Juliet Mike, report a five-mile . . . never mind, you're in sight. Report base, runway three-zero, right traffic, winds two-niner-zero at ten."

John exhaled and wondered what excuse good old Simmons had dreamed up to authorize a Prior Permission Required number for the T-Bird. Without Simmons's influence, his chances of landing at this busy air base, also home to Hank's Customs Service aviation detachment, would have been zero. Civilian aircraft were rarely cleared to land here.

After overflying the end of the runway at 1,500 feet above the airport, he cranked the T-Bird into a 60-degree right bank and pulled two g's, ending up on downwind. With the throttle set about 55%, he lowered the landing gear and flaps. When the approach end of the runway was 45 degrees behind him, over his right shoulder, he rolled right and lowered the nose, aiming at the approach end of the runway. "One Juliet Mike, base, gear down, full stop."

"One Juliet Mike, cleared to land."

The winds turned out to be a little gusty. John worked hard to put the T-Bird down at the five-hundred-foot marker of Runway 30. It didn't matter that no one was grading his landing or that there were two miles of runway remaining. He wanted everyone to know that this jet was flown by a true fighter pilot, one who subscribed to the credo, *There's nothing more useless than runway behind you.*

During the landing roll, tower asked, "One Juliet Mike, say your parking spot."

"One Juliet Mike is headed for the Aero Club." John could see Simmons waiting for him on the tarmac, next to two Cessna 172s that must belong to the base flying club.

Once parked, he shut off the throttle, pushed the switch to raise the canopy and wriggled out of his parachute harness. He patted the flat-black glare shield over the instrument panel, thanking the T-Bird for a good ride, as if it were a faithful horse about to be unsaddled and sent to the barn. It *had* been a good ride, especially the second hop, up there alone, free of Rowe. Not that Rowe was such a bad guy; in the end, he had been a good sport about the whole unscheduled trip. It was just nice to fly solo. John pushed himself out of the cockpit and hopped onto the wing. He waved to Simmons, sat on the leading edge of the wing, and slid off. His feet hit the ground before the T-Bird's engine had stopped turning and before the ground crew could bring up a ladder. John stretched his back and twisted left and right. After two flights and several two-*g*, fighter-style overhead traffic patterns, he felt great. His legs hadn't tingled at all—well, maybe just a little. At least he wasn't paralyzed. The flight docs had been wrong.

"Hi, Lacy," he said when Simmons walked up. "Thank God I've got friends in high places." He gave his old friend and co-worker a hearty handshake.

"Well, if your idea of high places is airfield manager, who am I to tell you different?"

John grinned. Simmons had never lost his self-effacing Oklahoma drawl and country mannerisms. People often underestimated him until they learned he had served thirty years, retired as Chief Master Sergeant—the Air Force's highest enlisted rank—and now worked a high-paying civilian, civil-service job managing one of the country's largest air bases. He wished he had time for some small talk. "Lacy, thanks a million for getting me in here. Like I said on the phone, I've got a friend over at Customs Service who has some kind of emergency. Can you give me a ride?"

Simmons reached into his pocket, pulled out a set of keys, and tossed them to him. He pointed outside the fence and said, "Take that silver Honda Civic. Just leave the keys under the mat. I'll have Colleen come pick me up."

"Thanks a bunch. I swear I'll spend some quality time with you guys soon, but now I've got to run. Please give Colleen my love." He turned to go.

Simmons gave him a "stop" signal with his right palm. "Whoa, John. It might be a little hard getting in over at Customs Service. One of their planes, a Cessna Citation, just went down."

"Yeah, I know . . . wait." John felt his gut tighten. "What do mean by 'just went down?' The one last week?"

"No, another one. Today. They just rang it out on the crash phone. They're scrambling the rescue helicopter. Why? What's wrong?"

Old Simmons knew him too well. John wasn't going to insult him by making up a story. "That friend I mentioned? He's a Citation pilot. I'd better go."

*   *   *

The youngster with a badge and sidearm was unsympathetic to John's story. "Sorry, sir. Without a Custom's Service ID, I can't let you in. We're at increased security this afternoon."

"Okay, thanks." There was no use arguing. He stepped aside as two grim-faced Customs Service pilots rushed past him into the building. They had Blackhawk helicopter patches on the shoulders of their blue Nomex flight suits. John guessed they were going to fly the Search and Rescue mission. When the double doors swung open, he got a glimpse of the operations center. The two pilots headed directly for a cluster of people near the counter, behind which was a large map of southern Arizona covered in plexiglass.

He did an about-face and walked away from the entrance. The landscaping was new, as was the shiny desert-brown paint on the cinder block walls. Inside a low split-rail fence, several cacti struggled to survive in a sea of low-maintenance rock that looked like coarse brown sandpaper. Years ago, during his years as a fighter pilot at D-M, this area had been grass. He reached Simmons's car, which he had parked in the shade of an old ash tree, turned back toward the building, and had another look. He had to get in there.

A large Coca-Cola truck passed in front of him, blocking his view. It made two right turns and disappeared behind the Customs Service building. John looked down at his worn work boots, faded jeans, and white polo shirt. He could pass as a delivery man. When the guard wasn't looking, he hurried down the access road, following the truck's path. As he rounded the corner at the rear of the building, he saw the driver wheel a cart stacked with soda cases through the rear doors. He waited several seconds to give the driver a head start before he walked up to the side of the truck and picked up two cases of Coke.

John walked through the open doors as if he had been there a hundred times. He was at the end of a long hallway. Thirty feet ahead, the real delivery man turned right and entered what he presumed to be the break room. John followed, saying, "How you doin'?" to several people as he waddled down the hall with his load.

A few steps short of the breakroom door, he turned, confirmed he was alone in the hall and set the two cases down against the wall. He continued to the center of the building and turned right into another corridor. Two people walking line abreast approached him. He made eye contact and said, "hi." Neither person challenged him; they just nodded and squeezed past.

John heard the operations center before he saw it. Telephones rang. Some were answered by clipped, anxious voices; others were ignored. Three people in flight suits stood in front of a chest-high countertop. Two were the Blackhawk pilots he had seen earlier, now with helmets, sidearms and survival vests in hand. The third aviator was a tall, trim, red-haired woman holding a phone to one ear. Behind the counter, a stocky man with crew cut hair, his flight suit sleeves pushed up over his elbows, stood facing the map John had seen earlier. One of his massive hands was wrapped around a microphone.

The day's flying schedule was written in grease pencil on a back-lighted plexiglass board. There was a section for Blackhawks, Citations, and two types of smaller prop jobs. Aircraft numbers and crew members were listed. John moved a few steps to his left so he could see the details for Citations. His mouth went dry when he saw that all the aircraft were accounted for—except Hank's.

"Who the hell are you?" It was the man with the crew cut. His face was red. Before answering, John memorized the information from the schedule. *Sidearm Three. Carter/Armstrong/Newsome. Takeoff, sched/actual: 1300/1300. Landing, sched/actual: 1600/___* No landing time was listed and, from all the long faces at this desk, John was sure there never would be.

"Hey! You in the white shirt. Come here." The three pilots at the counter parted quickly when the man in the crew cut slammed down the microphone and stepped closer. "Who are you?"

John walked up to the counter. Mister Crew Cut, even in his thick-soled flight boots, had to look up at him. His name tag said, *Eric Briggs*. His forearms rippled and his biceps bulged inside the thin material of his flight suit. He acted like the boss, and he looked rough—the type who could take care of himself in a bar room brawl despite his height disadvantage.

"I'm John Martin. Hank Carter's best friend."

Briggs opened his mouth to speak but the radio speaker cut him short.

"Blue Ops, Sidearm Seven."

Briggs lunged for the microphone. "Sidearm Seven, go."

"I'm over the crash site now. 150 for 41 from Gila Bend. It's a Citation, all right. I can see the tail and not much else. Lots of fire."

Briggs said, "Can you see the tail number?"

"Ah, stand by." A few seconds later, the pilot said, "Just the last three digits. Six-Five-Six. It's Sidearm Three."

There was dead silence as Briggs picked up a grease pencil, marked a spot on the map, and picked up the mic. "Okay, Seven, come on home. We'll send the Blackhawk." He stood facing the map, breathing heavily, as if he were a weightlifter preparing for a bench press.

In his military days, John had been in Briggs's shoes all too many times. A jet crashes, killing the pilot. Rescue aircraft are launched. An investigation ensues. But that couldn't happen to Hank, could it? He was indestructible. He'd probably show up on some rancher's front porch and demand a whiskey. John's heart wished for this, but his instinct told him it wasn't going to happen. There were no ejection seats in a Citation.

Briggs made a fist with his right hand and lashed out, punching the "X' on the plexiglass. The impact sounded like a gunshot and made everyone flinch. His fist bounced off the wall map. leaving a foot-long crack in the plastic.

"Dammit!" Briggs shouted. He took two deep breaths before turning around. "You heard it," he said to the Blackhawk pilots. "Wait for the security team, take 'em out there and report back." To the others at the desk he said, "Nothing is released until I say so, understood?" Briggs pointed across the desk.

"You. Martin, is it? How'd you get in here? Never mind, I don't want to know." He stared. "You look like an aviator. Are you?"

John said, "Retired Air Force. Flew with Hank in Vietnam and Iraq. I've got some info that may—"

"Martin, you're ex-military, so you can follow orders. Friend or no friend, I am ordering you out of this building, right now. And if I find out you've told anybody what you saw or heard in here, I'll get your butt thrown in jail so fast your head will swim. Do you read me?"

"Loud and clear."

Briggs pointed at the female pilot and said, "Olsen, you're off duty now, right? Escort Mister Martin out, then go home. You'll get an update later." He turned and stomped into a back office.

The red-haired woman turned to him with a grim face and held out her hand. "Leslie Olsen. I guess we're going out together." She shook his hand firmly before setting off for the front door at a brisk pace.

"I guess so," John said to her back. He wasn't going to get anything out of Briggs and, judging by the man's iron-fisted leadership style, the other pilots wouldn't be too forthcoming if they valued their jobs.

Leslie Olsen was taller than Briggs. About five-ten, John guessed. She took long strides with a fluid, athletic grace. Despite his height advantage, he had to hurry to catch up. As he pulled alongside, she said, "Where's your car?"

John pointed at the Civic and she angled in that direction, walking at a pace that made conversation impossible. She evidently took her escort job seriously. Her head swiveled back and forth as if she were looking for threats. When they reached Simmons's car, she looked back at the front door of the Customs Service building and stared at it for several seconds. She turned around and looked at him.

"Mister Martin, I shouldn't be seen talking to you. Would you mind if we sat in your car for a moment?"

"Sure. It's unlocked." He let her open her own door. She seemed like an independent woman. Feminine—the blue flight suit could not hide that fact—but quite capable of doing things on her own. She had a freckled face that, under better circumstances, he could imagine as cheery and vivacious. Today, something had worn her down. Her cheeks and eyes were red and puffy. She didn't seem like the type of woman who would fall to pieces at the news of a crash. Unless . . . he took another look at her. Was she romantically involved with Hank? Or one of the other two crewmembers?

Once they were seated, John silently complimented her on her choice of location. No one could see them in the shaded car.

Leslie took a deep breath and said, "Before I go any further, you've got to promise me something. If Briggs asks, we never had this conversation, okay?"

"Okay." He couldn't imagine doing Briggs any favors.

"Mister Martin, I was the one who gave Hank his checkout in the Citation. He talked about you but didn't say who you worked for. Why are you here? Do you work for Northern Air Transport?"

The question took John by surprise. Why connect him with Northern Air? She would know, as most government pilots did, of Northern Air's reputation for clandestine operations. And, if she had seen Hank's flight records, which was likely if she had been his Citation instructor, she would know that he came from Northern Air.

"No," he said. "I'm retired Air Force. I live up near Olympia, Washington. Hank called me this morning, but I was out kayaking. He left a message asking for my immediate help and told me to meet him here at 1600 today. If you know Hank, you know he is not the kind of guy that would ask for help from anyone unless something big was happening." John paused. If only he had been home, asleep—like any retired fighter pilot should be—he might have said something to Hank, something that might have kept him alive.

"Exactly who is Hank Carter?" Leslie said.

"What do you mean?"

"I mean, that name. It's got to be fake. And Hank is just . . . different, like he answers to a higher power. Oh, he flies well enough. What I mean is, he seems to have an agenda here. I think he's snooping. Or was, I guess."

"Ms. . . . Officer . . . may I just call you Leslie?"

She nodded.

"Okay. Please call me John. I've known Hank since 1972 and that's his real name. You bet he acts differently than most men, but that's just him. He's a maverick, the kind of guy who would quit a management job at Northern Air and come out to fly drug surveillance in Tucson just because it was more exciting."

Leslie said, "Well, Hank knew something that the rest of us didn't and it was beginning to get on my nerves. It all came to a head last week when Bobby was killed. Hank—"

"Wait." John held up a hand. "Who's Bobby?"

"Bob Olsen." Her eyes reddened and she clenched her jaw. A single tear leaked out of her left eye. "My little brother. A good man and a good pilot. I'm the one who got him the job here and boy, do I regret that." Two more tears dripped down her cheek.

So, Bobby's aircraft was the one that Hank had mentioned. Nothing he could say would help. "I'm very sorry, Leslie."

She stared at her lap for a few seconds; then she raised her head. "Bobby's Citation went down seven days ago. Hank was orbiting in an adjacent area and was first on the scene. After he landed, he went right into Briggs's office, still with his flight gear on, and closed the door. A few minutes later,

Hank stormed out of the office, departed the building, and disappeared for about seven hours. That whole time, I had stayed in ops because, well, I didn't know what else to do. That was my little brother and his crew out there in the desert and I wasn't about to leave until there was news of any survivors or . . . confirmation of . . ."

"Yeah," John said. "I know what you mean. Again, I'm sorry."

"I wanted to go out there, but Briggs vetoed that," she said. "Excuse me, may I use one of those?" She pointed to a small package of tissues on the center console.

"Of course."

She wiped her eyes and nose. "I think Hank drove out to the crash site or commandeered another chopper or something. Next thing I know, Hank was back. He flung open the door to the building, marched into ops, and just about ordered Briggs into his office."

John could only imagine the clash of egos and tempers involved in that exchange.

"The door slammed shut again. But I was right outside, at the desk, right where you first saw me today. I could hear the shouting. It was all Hank. I'm pretty sure I heard him blurt out, 'They shot him out of the sky, Briggs, just like they were at war with us.' It got really quiet in there for several seconds. Next, I heard Briggs's voice but—for a change—he wasn't shouting. I couldn't get what he was saying.

John took several long breaths. "Leslie, are you sure about what Hank said?"

"Totally. I'll never forget it."

"What did Briggs do about it?"

Leslie said, "No idea. Since then, he's been spending a lot of time on the phone with his door closed."

John closed his eyes and tried to digest all this. The whole situation smelled bad. He thought back to Hank's message, in which he had mentioned Blue Bandits. Just hours after Bobby's crash, Hank barges in and mentions a shootdown. Several days later, Hank, the world's second-best pilot, is killed in a "crash." Hell, he was too good to crash. Was it two shootdowns, then? Hank wouldn't have mentioned Blue Bandits unless he had evidence. But where would they come from? A military exercise gone terribly wrong? A sad case of mistaken—

"Hey! I asked you a question."

John said, "Sorry. What?"

"Do you think the two crashes are related?"

"There's only one way to find out," he said. "Go out there and see for myself."

Leslie shook her head. "No way. Once the Blackhawk gets there, they'll establish a security zone and drop off a couple guards. You'll never get in."

He had already figured that out. "I'm going to get there first."

Leslie rolled her eyes. "The Blackhawk's a lot faster than a Honda Civic, John."

"I've got a T-33 down at the Aero Club. With just enough fuel to get to Ajo." He put the key into the ignition. "It was good meeting you. I'd better go." When she didn't open her door, he reached across her legs and did it for her. She didn't budge. The door began to swing closed. He pushed it open again. "Goodbye, Leslie."

Leslie caught the door on its inward swing and pulled it shut. She rammed the seat belt buckle into place as if she were sheathing a sword. "Don't waste your time arguing, John. I've got as big a stake in this as you do. We can sit here and argue about this, in which case the Blackhawk will get there first. Or we can go together."

John narrowed his eyes and studied her face as if she were on the other side of a poker table. Something told him not to bet against her. He started the engine and put the Civic in gear. It was time to fold.

Chapter 5

"How are you doing back there?" John asked over the intercom. At 300 knots, in turbulent desert air, the T-Bird buffeted and bounced like a racehorse at full gallop. He had offered to adjust her parachute harness, but she had declined, saying it would just use up valuable time. He knew she would be uncomfortable with loose straps and with Rowe's oversized helmet.

She said something, but the words were drowned out by the roaring engine and slipstream noise. She sounded like she was yelling from the bottom of Niagara Falls. After a few seconds of silence, her voice came through loud and clear.

"I'm fine," Leslie said. "This oxygen mask is way too big. I have to push it up to my face to shut out the engine noise."

She had climbed the ladder and strapped in like a veteran, which led him to believe she had some military experience. He'd have to ask later. John estimated the ground speed and checked the distance to Ajo. They'd be there in seventeen minutes, if the airplane didn't shake itself to pieces first or run out of gas. There had been no chance to refuel at Davis-Monthan.

"How fast does the Blackhawk cruise?" John asked.

"About one-ten."

"So," John said, "assuming we got a ten-minute head start on the Blackhawk, we're going to have thirty minutes after landing before they catch up to us. Do you know anybody at Ajo who might loan us, or rent us, a car? Better yet, a truck?"

*   *   *

The borrowed pickup truck fish-tailed on the dirt road, scattering pebbles and sand into the desert. John corrected and slowed down. He'd paid the kid at the airport forty bucks for the use of his old truck, but the price might increase if he tore up the tires or banged into something.

Leslie looked up from the aeronautical chart he had loaned her. She said, "Get ready to turn right up there, just past that hill. Should be another dirt road, in worse shape than this one by the symbols I'm reading. But it'll get us close."

A column of smoke had been visible for the last several miles. If they were in luck, the crash site would be a short walk from the road. When the path became little more than two ruts in the desert, he stopped and engaged four wheel drive. They crested a small rise. "Uh-oh," he said.

Two vehicles blocked the road ahead. One was a fire truck, the other a sheriff's patrol car. A deputy was leaning against the roof and talking on the radio. Behind him, on the west side of a gently sloped gully, was the crash site.

Some of the taller bushes were already casting shadows but the wreckage was still in bright sunlight. John looked to his right, out west, at the sun's elevation. They had about an hour of daylight left.

"I can talk my way past him with this," Leslie said, flipping open a black leather case with her Customs Service shield. "But, what about you?'

"Introduce me as FAA. I'll just flash my pilot's license."

He let Leslie do the talking at first but, as soon as the deputy had accepted their presence, he asked the essential question. "Are there any survivors?"

The color drained from the deputy's face. He shook his head. "Nope, afraid not." He nodded toward the firemen, who were shoveling dirt onto the few remaining brush fires. "Once they got the fire under control, EMTs confirmed three fatalities. We were told that's the entire crew, right?"

"Correct," Leslie said. "Did anyone actually see the aircraft crash?"

"No, ma'am. Somebody called in the smoke and fire. I was the first person out here. The fire unit arrived a few minutes later."

Most of the remaining smoke was from brush fires; the aircraft wreckage had already burned itself out or had been extinguished by the firefighters.

John said, "Deputy, we're going to take a look. There's going to be a Customs Service helicopter arriving in—" He checked his watch. "—about ten minutes. Would you mind staying by your radio in case they call in for directions?"

"Yes, sir. I mean, no sir, I won't mind. But, ah—" He glanced at Leslie. "You should know that, er, over there, it's not a pretty sight."

"Okay," John said. "Thank you."

They walked toward the wreckage. The sloping terrain afforded them a bird's-eye view of the debris field.

Once out of earshot from the deputy, John said, "We've only got ten minutes, so we'd better split up. Look for anything out of place. Pieces missing. Damage that may have happened before impact. Strange colors in the metal. I can't tell you exactly, just anything unusual."

"One thing's for sure," Leslie said. "The airplane was not under control when it hit the ground. It came straight down, like it was in a spin. Nothing bounced or skipped. See how all the wreckage is concentrated in one area?"

John pointed at a spot about a hundred yards to the south. "All except that piece. It looks like most of the right wing. Why don't you look at that wing while I go over to the main part?"

She nodded and walked off. That gave him a good excuse to look at the cockpit, something he'd rather do alone. John wondered if it was wise to approach the upside-down, smoldering, half-melted section of forward fuselage. He knew that at least two of the three crewmembers had sidearms. It would ruin his day if one of their rounds cooked off, sending a bullet, or bullets, whizzing around the crash site. It was worth the risk. Hank was in there; his day had been ruined too.

John got down on his hands and knees next to the left side of the cockpit. The metal had crumpled, and the side window had been crushed, leaving just a small opening about the size of a shoe box. The nose of the airplane had landed on a small patch of prickly pear cactus and what looked like a creosote bush. He used his foot to push some pieces of cactus aside, took a deep breath, and knelt.

It was bad. A blackened, grotesquely shriveled figure hung from the upside-down seat, held in place by a charred lap belt and shoulder harness. The shrunken, unrecognizable face seemed to be grinning at him. The co-pilot looked at least as bad. Maybe even worse; half his face was missing. He shuddered and wanted to pull back, to get out of there. Not yet, he told himself. There was something he had to do.

John's hand trembled as he reached in through the small opening. This was not the first crash site he had visited, nor was it the first burned body he had seen. But that was *Hank* in there. No one should have to see their best friend like this. A small, round, embossed key fob hung outside one of Hank's zippered flight suit pockets. John pushed his arm further in, put his hand around the key fob, and yanked hard. It pulled free, snapping the chain. He stood, rubbed soot from one side of the silver dollar-sized disk and read the engraved word:

Snake. John had one just like it in his pocket bearing his call sign. Hank would never let that coin out of his sight, so yes, that was Hank in there. This "Juvat Nickel" was carried by all pilots from the 80th Fighter Squadron—even those who, like Hank and him, had long been reassigned. "Snake, old buddy, this is going to your son," he whispered.

"What should we do with the bodies, sir?"

John flinched. He hadn't heard the firefighter approach. She had a Gila County EMT patch on her shoulder. Had she seen him pull the medallion off Hank's flight suit? He tried to think of something a real investigator would say. "Nothing you can do for him or the other two crew members now. Our full team will be here in a few minutes with more equipment. Let's wait until then to move them."

He couldn't learn anything more from the cockpit; it was too blackened and broken. John brushed sand from his knees and scanned the wreckage. What about the engines? He walked to the aft end of the fuselage, where the engines were mounted. Or had been. Since everything was upside-down, it took some effort to visualize which was the left and right side of this mess. The left engine had broken off and lay next to the fuselage, just forward of the horizontal tail. The intake was half-buried in the sand. He crouched down and looked inside it. Some fan blades were missing; others were bent. Rocks, dirt, and vegetation had been drawn deep into the intake. This engine was still turning at impact.

"Hey John! Come here, please."

Leslie was waving to him and pointing at the large section of right wing. As he walked through the brush and cactus, he counted his steps. Sixty paces, almost two hundred feet, over ground with no visible debris. That piece of wing must have ripped off before impact. He stopped to orient himself. Leslie was two hundred feet south of him. It would be safe to assume that Hank's jet had been traveling north when it lost that piece of wing.

When he got close to Leslie, she pointed the toe of her boot at the wing and said, "Look at this. What do these look like to you?"

He bent down and ran his hand over a large, jagged hole, about an inch in diameter, that had been punched into the thin aluminum skin. There were two more holes further inboard.

"Leslie, these are bullet holes. Large ones, not the work of some rancher armed with a hunting rifle. Notice how the aluminum has been punched in from the outside."

"That's what I thought," she said. "This is all scorched with black soot. Whatever hit this caused a fire. Could it have been an HEI round?"

John bent down and wiped the filmy black soot off one of the holes. It looked like a miniature crater. He rubbed a little harder and saw raw aluminum; the white paint had peeled off around the hole. He carefully ran his finger around the inside of the hole and felt the sharp edges of metal on the inside, splayed out like the petals of a spent rose.

"Does the Citation have a wet wing?" he said.

"Yes," she said. "This part of the wing has a fuel cell."

She was correct; this damage was caused by High Explosive Incendiary rounds. Next, he remembered Hank's words on his answering machine: *Blue Bandits*. Finally, there was what Leslie had overheard Hank shout to Briggs: *They shot him out of the sky. . .*

"C'mon, Leslie, we need to go back up there." He turned and jogged toward the main crash site.

"What? What are you thinking?" Leslie called out to him as she ran through the desert behind him.

They were both out of breath by the time they reached the Citation's fuselage section. This site was no different than others he had seen before. The ground was littered with small pieces of debris, the internal organs of an aircraft that no one outside the factory ever saw—until a crash. Although most were scorched, bent, or smashed, some had survived intact and bore bright mint-colored anti-corrosion paint, as if they had just fallen out of a new parts bin in the warehouse.

The Citation's right side had sustained much greater fire damage. John led the way between the aft fuselage and the severed tail section to get a closer look. The outer half of the right wing was missing. That was the piece they had just seen. The right engine and the fuselage near it were badly burned. He had to crouch down to see the top of the engine cowling, which had popped loose and was hanging by one piece of mangled hinge. There were several large holes in the cowling. They matched the ones in the wing. Punctures from the outside in. Not an engine failure, which would have thrown debris outward.

Leslie leaned over his shoulder. "Talk to me, John. What are you seeing?"

He stood up and pointed to the piece of cowling. "Take a look at that, the piece hanging loose."

"More bullet holes," she said, "punching in from the outside."

"Yep," he said. "Now, reattach it for a second."

John tried to memorize the location of the bullet holes and the orientation of the puckers in the metal so he could get an idea of where to look for engine damage. "Now, let it drop back down." He studied the engine and found two areas of interest. There was nothing to use as a rag except his white shirt. He pulled the shirt out of his jeans and used the bottom to rub the sooty metal in two places.

"What's that? Leslie asked. She pushed the cowling away from the engine and got down on both knees to see the areas he had wiped.

"Those deep pockmarks, Leslie, are evidence of spalling."

"Say again?"

"Spalling. That's not a perfect word, but it will do for now. Impact marks, like craters, made when bullets hit thick metal. Let go of your end, please. Stand back."

When she was clear, he grabbed the piece of cowling and twisted it until the hinge broke. He pulled the four-foot-long piece of metal free of the engine and set it on the ground.

"Leslie, go get the truck. The keys are in it. Say goodbye to the deputy. You'll have to make up some story about why we have to leave. Then drive over here to pick me up. It's pretty flat; the truck should make it easily."

"Are you going to take that cowling?"

"Yeah," He stopped her before she could object. "Hank's phone message said he knew something about your brother's crash. Now Hank's dead. Your brother is dead. So are the rest of their crews. I'm taking my own proof about this one."

She opened her mouth to speak but closed it, nodded slowly, and jogged away. That was a relief. He didn't need her to remind him that tampering with a crash site was a federal crime. So was impersonating an FAA crash investigator. As soon as he found the right people, he was going to shove this evidence down their throats and make them tell him what the hell was going on.

The truck was approaching. When John picked up the cowling, he heard a sound like a large marble rolling off the metal. It thumped onto the ground. A piece of melted aircraft? He looked down. It was a bullet, only slightly deformed, as if it had penetrated the engine cowling and rattled around inside the engine compartment. If this was an HEI round, it could go off at any moment. But, if it hadn't detonated already, it must be a dud. The truck arrived in a cloud of dust. There was no time to examine the bullet; he could hear the unmistakable beat of Blackhawk rotor blades. He put the bullet into his pocket, picked up the piece of cowling, and ran for the truck. Leslie had already opened the passenger door.

She put the truck in gear, gunned the engine, and aimed for the shortest path to the road. It was also the roughest; he had to hold onto the dash with both hands. She glared at him and said, "Here comes the Blackhawk. Didn't you hear it?"

"Yeah, sorry. I found something back there." John saw the chopper crest the hill, its fuselage tilted back, decelerating for landing. "It was worth the extra few seconds." He waited until they had passed the Sheriff's SUV and rejoined the dirt road before he pulled the bullet out of his pocket and showed it to Leslie.

Her eyes lingered on the spent bullet long enough to worry him. "Hey, watch the road."

She corrected back to the center of the narrow road. "Okay, okay." She stole another glance at it and said, "Explain that, please."

"Hold on a second." They were back on the paved road now and the ride was smoother. He brushed dirt from the bullet and rubbed it on his jeans to clean off some soot—until he decided that might be dangerous. Could it detonate from a buildup of static electricity? He didn't want to find out. The base of the projectile was stamped with some markings. John used his fingers to clean more soot from those, then held the bullet up to catch the fading daylight.

"Holy shit," he said.

"What?" The truck bounced when one wheel hit a pothole, forcing Leslie's eyes back on the road.

"This is a Russian 23-millimeter round."

"No way!"

"I'm sure of it," John said. "And I know what fired it. A Gish Twenty-three."

"Gish what? Is that an aircraft?"

"No, it's just a way to pronounce GSh-23 which stands for Grayazev-Shipanov 23, a Russian-made, twin-barreled, 23 mm cannon."

"You can tell all that just from one bullet?"

"I've seen a bullet like this before." He pointed to some Cyrillic markings stamped on the bottom. "At the Air Force Fighter Weapons School, they showed us one of these and told us the markings mean it's made for air-to-air guns, not ground-based Triple-A. That's anti-aircraft artill—"

"I know what Triple-A is. So, that came from an airplane? A Soviet-made fighter?"

"Not just any fighter. I'm betting it came from a MiG-21. In fact, I can narrow it down to one of the later models, probably a MiG-21M, known to us by its NATO designation, Fishbed J."

Leslie lifted her foot off the gas pedal and coasted to a stop on the shoulder. She pulled up the parking brake lever, turned to him and said, "Are you trying to tell me that Hank was gunned by a MiG-21? Bobby too? And how can you be so sure of the aircraft type?"

He'd have to tell her. They were both too deep into this for him to keep secrets. "It's something Hank said in his telephone message, the one that caused me to rush down here. He didn't give details, but he mentioned the words, Blue Bandits. To a fighter pilot, that means—"

"Yeah, I know," she said. "The code word for MiG-21s. And, the day Bobby crashed, remember what I told you Hank shouted to Briggs?"

"It all adds up, doesn't it?" He put the bullet back in his pocket. How Leslie knew about Blue Bandits and Triple-A was a question for later.

She got the truck back on the road. They drove in silence until she turned off the highway onto the access road for the Ajo airport.

"Don't go to the FBO yet," John said. "Go back to that restaurant we just passed. The one near the convenience store. Park there."

Leslie slowed and, after checking behind them, made a U-turn. She spun the rear tires on loose gravel before regaining the asphalt road and speeding back out. She covered the three blocks in ten seconds, parked, and shut off the engine.

"I need to do something with that piece of wreckage in the back. You can't see what I do with it. Do you understand?"

She didn't.

"You're Customs Service and you'll be in deep trouble when they find out we came out here and took a piece of wreckage. The less you know about what I did with it, the better off you'll be. You didn't remove it, you didn't put it in the truck, and didn't notice if there was anything in the pickup's bed. Got it?"

"I won't lie."

"I get that," John said. This made him glad. She was a woman of principle. "Well, at least don't volunteer anything. And prevaricate when you can."

"Do what?"

"Lie without lying. Be vague. Can you at least do that?"

"Huh."

That did not constitute a firm yes or no. She was already prevaricating. "So, wait for me in the restaurant. I'll put—never mind. I'll run a short errand and be right back." He got out of the truck. Leslie did the same.

They looked at one another across the hood of the dusty red pickup.

She said, "I have your word you'll be back?"

"Yes, of course."

She tossed him the keys.

After she disappeared into the restaurant, he drove to the convenience store, hoping they had what he needed.

Chapter 6

Ten minutes later, Leslie parked the truck in front of Ajo's FBO. John gave the kid an extra twenty for all the dust he had put on it. He called in a flight plan to FAA and signed the credit card receipt for the fuel. Although the sky was perfectly clear, he used the FBO's phone to check Tucson's weather. He didn't want to be surprised by high winds or dust storms. The forecast was for clear skies and ten knots of wind out of the east. He made the takeoff. After raising the gear and flaps, he said, "Want to fly?"

"Sure."

"You have the aircraft."

He felt the stick wiggle left and right against his gloved hand. The wings wobbled in response.

"I have the aircraft," Leslie said.

"You're prior Air Force, aren't you?"

"Yes. Eight years."

John asked, "Fighters?"

"How did you know?"

"Well, for one thing, by the way you shook the stick to take control. Also, you know what HEI stands for and what a Blue Bandit is. The kicker was how you used the word "gunned." Only fighter pilots and Old West gunfighters would say that. Everyone else would say, 'gunned down" or, 'shot down.'" He decided not to mention her fighter pilot-style, in-your-face approach to things.

47

"Very perceptive," she said. "Let's see if you can guess what I flew."

John reviewed his choices. When he retired, females had just been assigned to fly the F-15. "Eagles?"

"Nope. F-16s. Same as you and Hank. He told me you guys had flown together—a lot."

Times had certainly changed since he and Hank had flown in an all-male fighter force. "How about that," he said.

"What's the best climb speed for this thing?"

"Use two-eighty until point six Mach, then cruise at point six. We won't be up at altitude that long. By the way, check 29.92 on your altimeter."

"Set."

She leveled off smoothly and, without asking for his help, experimented with a power setting to hold cruise Mach. She only needed one correction to get it right.

Leslie said, "So, what's the story about this jet? Is it yours?"

"Yeah. Believe it or not, I bought it at an IRS auction. Someone couldn't pay their income tax."

"It's in great shape."

"Now it is. At first it needed a lot of work. I only flew it twice, then parked it until I could afford to restore it."

"So, now it's your hobby?"

"Oh, no," he said. "On the contrary, I haven't been in this cockpit, or any other, since my last flight in the F-16, five years ago."

"Why not? Couldn't you have gotten hired by an airline or something?"

"In my book, Leslie, that's not flying. It's like driving a bus. For me, it was the F-16 or nothing."

"I hear you."

She got quiet for a full minute, as if his words had inspired extra reverence for the serenity of single-seat, single-engine flying. He spent that time admiring the darkening sky to the east. A planet and one or two stars were visible, even though sunset was about thirty minutes away. Down below, to the south, the sparsely populated desert terrain began to lose its definition in the shadows. Later, after it got fully dark, the black terrain with isolated twinkling lights from ranches would blend into the equally dark sky, dotted with stars. More than one pilot had gotten disoriented on a clear desert night and mistaken the ground for the sky. Some of those hadn't survived the experience of spatial disorientation.

He looked north and was reassured by the ribbon of Interstate 10 cutting through the desert just north of the small towns of Marana and Avra Valley. Ahead, he could see the dark row of the uninhabited Santa Cruz mountains just west of Tucson. Beyond that was the expansive urban area of Tucson, with lighted streets running up the sloping terrain toward Mount Lemmon.

The intercom clicked. Leslie said, "Now, tell me what we're going to do with that bullet and the piece of wreckage." Her tone had changed from eager pilot to that of an interrogator.

"We?" He turned and looked into the dark rear cockpit, but her face was invisible, obscured by the oxygen mask and reflections off the clear plastic helmet visor. Leslie's helmeted face looked devilish due to the reflected red glow from the rear cockpit flight instruments.

"Yes, we," she said in a voice that burned his ears. "Don't give me any of that, 'But she's a woman' bullshit. Bobby was my brother. If somebody killed him and his crew, no way I'm going to let it get covered up."

John turned to face forward, which caused a brief burning sensation in his lower back. He couldn't blame her for wanting to pursue the killers. In fact, he admired her for it. She had already broken several laws and jeopardized her career as a Customs Service pilot. How could he tell her that she didn't fit into his plan? Hell, he didn't even have a plan. But he didn't want to drag Leslie along on whatever came next—for her own protection as well as his preference to work alone.

He said, "I can't figure out why Customs Service would want to hide a shootdown. Two of them, in fact. By the way, did you get a look at Bobby's crash site?"

"Couldn't get near it. Briggs was the only one they allowed out there. I asked the helicopter crew that took him, but they were very evasive. I wrote that off to being considerate of me, the grieving sister. Of course, based on Hank's late-night visit to Briggs, it's obvious that Hank somehow got access to the site. Later, a team of investigators carted off all the wreckage to Washington."

"Didn't that seem odd?"

"Yes, but Briggs said they were a special team investigating the Citation's airworthiness. It's an old airframe, you know, and we've loaded it up with a lot of very heavy electronic gear and stuck lots of sensor pods onto the fuselage. I've heard that the Service is considering retiring it and going back to the old turboprop, the OV-1 Mohawk, which was retired a year or so ago. Some say that it's much more suitable for running down the slow-movers, the small piston-engine prop jobs."

She was quiet for a few seconds, after which she said, "What do you use for the descent, John?"

They were seventy miles from Tucson. He said, "Sixty-five miles out, make an idle descent at two-fifty. The goal is to be thirty miles out at 10,000 feet AGL and 250 knots.

He gave her time to do the descent calculations. That would keep her busy while he did some thinking. He had three problems, the first of which was to get this overly curious and assertive woman out of his hair. The second was even more difficult: Find out who had killed Hank and all those other people. And the third? Bring the killers to justice.

John watched the throttle move aft in his cockpit as Leslie retarded hers to idle and lowered the nose until Tucson

International's runway was centered in the windscreen. The nose gyrated ever so gently as she trimmed for the descent.

"How come Tucson?" she asked. "Why not back to D-M?"

"Can't get fuel for civilian jets at D-M."

"So, what are we going to do when we land?"

That was a good question. "Let's talk about it when we get on the ground," he said. "You're going to be busy with the landing."

"*I'm* going to land? I've never flown one of these before."

"You're doing fine so far. I'll talk you through it." The approach and landing would keep her busy while he considered a plan.

*   *   *

John unstrapped first and climbed out onto the ladder. Leslie was still unhooking her harness. "Nice landing," he said.

"Thanks, You're a good coach."

She followed him down the ladder, her blue flight suit stretched tight enough to make him look away, which was more than he could say for the ground crewman who had marshalled them into their parking spot. The young man stared shamelessly at her curves and narrow waist until she turned around and faced him. She reached up with both hands and fluffed up her hair, releasing a cascade of red sparkles in the glare of overhead lights. Leslie stared at the man. "Is there a problem?"

"Uh, no, ma'am," the crewman said. His face was now as red as her hair. "No problem at all." He busied himself with installing the landing gear safety pins.

John signed a credit card receipt. He looked up to see a red Ford Explorer pull up and stop just outside the fence. "Looks like the FBO came through for us. Our rental car's already here." He picked up his helmet bag and the black gym bag with a change of clothes and some toiletries, waited for Leslie to join him, and walked toward the gate.

The green-shirted rental car employee returned John's driver's license and credit card. He said, "It's all yours, sir. The gas tank's full. Someone will come by soon to take me back to the terminal."

"Thanks very much," John said. He took the keys, walked to the passenger door, and opened it for Leslie. He walked around to the driver's side, got in, and started the engine.

"Well, where to?" Leslie said.

"I have to see Briggs, but I don't think you should be there. After all, he sent you straight home. So, why don't I take you home?"

"Briggs won't see you, John. He's already thrown you out of there once today."

"He'll see me all right, after he learns that I have these." John reached into the inside pocket of his flight jacket, pulled out a thick envelope and opened it. He pulled out a stack of photos, shuffled through them and handed two to Leslie. "If he doesn't see me, these go to the press, with a graphic description of what I saw out there near Ajo."

She reached up and turned on the reading light. "Instant photos? How'd you—"

"They have disposable instant cameras now. I got one at the convenience store next to the restaurant. I made one set for you, one for me, and one for Briggs." He didn't tell her about the fourth set.

"Nice touch, the ruler next to the bullet. Gives it some perspective."

"Yeah. That ruler cost me an extra eighty-nine cents."

She held the second photo up to catch more of the late-afternoon sunlight. "The holes in the cowling are easy to see. And, again, putting the ruler next to the holes is brilliant. But why give me a set?"

"Just instinct, I guess. In case something happens to me. Now, why don't I take you home?"

"Why not just drop me at my car? It's at Ops, where you're headed anyway."

"Sounds good, as long as you promise to stay away from the building." He didn't want Briggs to get curious about where she'd been.

*   *   *

"It's that white Jeep Cherokee," Leslie said, pointing to the far corner of an almost empty parking lot. "I park it over there because it gets shade in the afternoon." She pointed again, this time at a green pickup in a reserved slot close to the building. "That's Briggs's truck, for all the good that will do you. He's a real by-the-book type of guy. A real company man. You're not going to get anything out of him."

The armed guard, or his replacement, was still at the entrance and appeared to be following their progress toward Leslie's car. John stopped behind the Cherokee and said, "Am I going to have as much trouble getting you out of this car as I did earlier?"

She laughed. Her hair bounced as if she were a model advertising the latest herbal shampoo. He hadn't noticed her perfect smile earlier, probably because it hadn't been much of a day for smiling.

"No, this time, I'm out of here." She reached down, unzipped a leg pocket on her flight suit and pulled out a business card. Using a pen she pulled from the pocket on her sleeve, she wrote something on it. "This is my home number and address. Call me later, no matter what time it is."

"Okay." He held out his hand. She shook it and held on a little longer than he expected. That was okay. They had just shared a gruesome experience and she was probably still reeling from the loss of her brother. Leslie was handling it all pretty well. Under different circumstances, he'd like to know more about her—where she grew up, her family, how she became a pilot—but that kind of exchange was for people in normal social situations. Right now, he just wanted her to go home.

"I'll be in touch soon," he said, apologizing silently to God for the lie.

When she opened her door, he heard a noise. Footsteps, shoe leather on asphalt, heading toward them. Leslie hopped out of the car into a defensive stance. He did the same. A man was running toward them. John recognized the squat wrestler's body, the blue flight suit, and the rolled-up sleeves—Briggs.

By the time John had rushed over to the passenger side, Briggs had pulled up about two feet short of Leslie and was leaning into her like a drill sergeant. Surprisingly, he didn't shout. Without taking his eyes off Leslie, he pointed to the operations building door. "Olsen, get your butt into my office. Now. I'll be there in a minute."

Leslie's chest rose and fell once before she moved off.

Briggs pivoted to face him and assumed a wide stance, with his arms out, elbows bent, as if he were ready to wrestle. John stood out of reach in case he attacked.

"You too, Martin." I'm gonna escort you over to that door." He jerked his thumb over his shoulder in the direction of the building entrance. "You will wait there, under armed guard, until I'm done with Olsen. I swear to God, if you don't cooperate, I will cold-cock you right here, carry your ass over there, and dump you onto the rocks like a sack of potatoes." He snapped out his left arm and hand, with index finger pointing at the Customs Service door. "Go!"

Part of him wanted to make Briggs pay for ordering him around as if he were a misbehaving dog. The time wasn't right for that. He said, "Okay. Just let me get my car keys." He went to the driver's door, opened it and, with one hand, he pulled out the keys. With the other hand, and out of Briggs's sight, he shoved all but one set of pictures under the floor mat.

When they reached the building, Briggs gave the door guard some instructions before going inside. John began pacing up and down the walkway.

"Sorry, sir, but Officer Briggs was very clear. I need you to come over here and stand still. I can't let you leave this area until he calls for you."

John couldn't blame the guard. He was just a kid. Nevertheless, he was a kid armed with a 9-millimeter Beretta automatic. "Don't worry, son. I'm not going anywhere. I need to speak to Briggs. But I really need a drink of water." Next to the front door was a coiled-up garden hose attached to a faucet. He took two steps over to the faucet and turned it on.

"I wouldn't do that, sir."

He let some water run until he was sure it was cool, then bent down and drank for several seconds. Before he shut off the faucet, he asked the guard, "You want some?"

"No thank you."

While he was coiling the hose, the front door opened, and Leslie walked out with Briggs close behind. She stopped in front of him.

"I had to tell the truth, John."

Leslie walked away, leaving him face-to-face with Briggs, who stood, arms folded, biceps and forearm muscles bulging, looking like a short version of Mister Clean from the TV commercials.

"Martin, follow me." Briggs turned and yanked on the handle of the heavy metal door. It flew open as if it were made of balsa wood. The guard caught the door just before it banged into the wall. He raised his eyebrows as John passed as if to say, *It's been nice knowing you. Briggs is going to eat you alive.*

Briggs had disappeared.

"Martin! In here. Now!" Briggs's voice ricocheted off the walls like steel-jacketed bullets off concrete.

John walked through an opening in the operations counter and headed for the office. He stepped through the open door and closed it behind him. Pictures and plaques hung on three of the four walls. Most showed current and past generations of Customs Service aircraft, but one plaque got his attention. It was some sort of award and had a Marine Corps emblem on it. Next to that was a photo of Briggs in full battle gear next to a Blackhawk. Both the man and the machine were dressed for desert warfare.

Briggs sat behind a grey metal government-issue desk. His arms were folded again; his face was as rumpled as his flight suit. He needed a shave. A gold badge and a semiautomatic in a shoulder holster lay in the center of the desk. Briggs unfolded an arm long enough to stab a finger at a chair in front of the desk. "Sit," he said.

As he lowered himself into the chair, John got a look at the name on the badge—Olsen. He had been afraid of this.

Briggs picked up the badge and bounced it in one hand for several seconds. He slammed it onto the desk and said, "Martin, you asshole, because of you I just had to suspend my best pilot and put her under house arrest. What the hell did you think you were doing out there?" He rolled his chair closer and leaned forward, hands flat on the desk. The veins on his forearms bulged. "Give me one good reason why I shouldn't arrest your ass for obstruction of justice."

John reached into his jacket pocket, somewhat amused that the gesture made Briggs stiffen. Did the guy think he was going for a gun? "I'll give you two reasons." He pulled out two photos, slapped them onto the desk and spread them apart, as if he were displaying a winning poker hand. "Number one, these show evidence of a shootdown. Number two, if you arrest me, I've left instructions with a friend to send copies of these to the media, along with my description of what I think happened."

Briggs paid special attention to the picture of the bullet. He said, "Bring these items to me tonight. Otherwise—"

"Otherwise, what? Do you want to see this story and these pictures on Channel Five News tomorrow morning? Look, I'd like to think we're on the same side here. You've lost two airplanes and two crews, apparently to hostile action. One of them happened to be my best friend. We both want the same thing. To find out who did it and make them pay. Can't we work together on this? Share some information?"

Briggs was already shaking his head. "No way. It's a law enforcement matter. You will cooperate or you *will* go to jail."

Leslie was right. Briggs was a company man through and through. There was no use wasting time trying to reason with a robot. John stood up and leaned on the desk with both hands. "Briggs, I am going to walk out of this building, unless you want to try and stop me, and find out what the hell happened to Hank." He did an about-face, walked to the door, and turned the knob.

"Wait."

John let go of the doorknob and turned around.

Briggs rubbed the top of his crew cut with one hand. His facial muscles had softened, making him look a little less like a machine. "There's more I'd like to tell you, Martin, but I can't. My hands are tied. Shit, this thing is way out of my league or yours. It's not a Customs Service show any more. There are national security issues involved. So, unless you'd like to take it up with the President himself, you'd—"

"I may do just that." John opened the door and walked out, leaving an open-mouthed and speechless Briggs behind.

He tried to have some sympathy for the guy. He had just lost six members of his team in seven days. Now, evidently, the investigation was being taken out of his hands.

As he passed the operations desk, he glanced up at the clock above the flying schedule. It was 7:30 p.m. Did Tucson have any flights to D.C at this time of day? The guard looked at him wide-eyed as he hurried past, as if he had expected to see him marched out in leg irons. John hurried over to the Explorer. Leslie's Jeep was gone. He felt sorry for her, but he had no intention of calling her.

He froze. Someone was in the Explorer's passenger seat, slouched low enough to be invisible from a distance. He scanned the area and didn't see any other threats. He moved closer, ready to duck or drop to the ground if threatened. The person waved, beckoning him closer. Shit. The "threat" had curly red hair. Yeah, she was a threat all right. To his sanity. He walked around to the driver's side and opened the door.

"Hurry up and close the door," Leslie whispered. She slid lower in the seat and pointed at the dome light.

He resisted the temptation to slam the door shut. With the door closed and the light out, she seemed to relax. He put both hands on the steering wheel and sighed. "That'll teach me to lock the car."

"Can you please get this thing out of the parking lot so I can straighten up? I'm getting a cramp in my leg."

John started the car, backed out of the parking spot, and headed for the exit. "What did you do with your Jeep?"

"Down the road about a quarter-mile, behind a storage building."

"I'll drop you off there."

Leslie sat up and fastened her seat belt. That worried him. She seemed to be settling in.

"I'm going with you," she said.

"You don't even know where I'm going."

"Oh, yes I do."

How could she? The Explorer's tires hummed on the asphalt. He glanced over at her. She stared back at him without blinking. He looked away and concentrated on following the road.

"Well, not exactly," Leslie said. "I just get the feeling that somehow, some way, you're going to track down whoever shot down Bobby's and Hank's planes. Am I right?"

"What I am going to do is none of your damn business." But that was not correct. "Well, I guess it *is* your business, since your brother and his crew were victims, just like Hank. I'm going to Washington, DC. You obviously can't go. Briggs told me about your suspension and house arrest."

She shrugged, as if to say that didn't matter. "Why Washington?"

"Actually, it was Briggs who gave me the idea. He used national security as an excuse to suppress information about the shootdowns. Then he barked at me to go see the President if I had any objections. I told him I was going to do just that. You should have seen the look on his face."

"You're going to see the President?"

"Well, not the President," John said. "But someone almost as good." He slowed the Explorer and turned down a short driveway leading to the storage building. He stopped behind Leslie's Jeep. "I've really got to go. I've got to check on flights to DC."

"Take me with you," she said.

He shook his head. "No way."

Chapter 7

Leslie opened her eyes and yawned. She rolled onto her back. Her shoulders and neck were itchy. What had happened to her fancy silk sheets? And why could she hear a shower running when she lived alone? Oh. She wasn't at home, snug in her own bed. She was reclined in a spacious first-class seat on an America West Airbus, a redeye flight from Tucson to DC. The muted roar of twin jet engines sounded remarkably like the shower in her townhouse. She felt a hand on her shoulder and sat bolt upright. It was John Martin's hand.

"Sorry to wake you, Leslie." He lifted his hand from her shoulder. "We're in the descent. I figured you might want to . . . might need a bathroom break before the seat belt sign comes back on."

She rubbed a hand over her face, tried but failed to stifle another yawn, and stretched her back and arms. A flight attendant offered her a warm towel, which she used to massage her face. "How long have I been asleep?"

"Almost four hours," he said without looking at her. His eyes were fixed on the laptop that he had pulled out shortly after takeoff. He was hunched forward over the keyboard, squinting, arms tensed, like someone driving too fast in a heavy rainstorm.

"Have you been up this whole time?" she said.

"Yeah. Couldn't sleep. Anyway, I needed to do some research.'

At least he was talking to her now, unlike the tight-jawed cold shoulder he had given her on the way to the airport. John had reacted badly when she had refused to get out of his car—for the second time that day. He struck her as a man who didn't like to lose. Well, neither did she. She couldn't see what he was working on, so she studied his face, his arms, and the rest of him. He was clean-shaven now and smelled of Old Spice. How old was he, anyway? John had to be at least as old as Hank, who was—had been—in his mid-forties. That would explain the grey streaks in his hair and the wrinkles under his eyes. But his body, now clad in a green polo shirt, beige chinos, and brown loafers, was that of a thirty-year-old. Trim and fit, he exuded energy even while at rest, like a crouching tiger.

She, on the other hand, had morning-mouth, messy hair, and was wearing yesterday's sweat-stained and severely wrinkled flight suit. None of that would be appropriate for where they were going. "Excuse me, John. I've got to go freshen up."

"Just one second." He closed the laptop, disconnected the cord to the seatback Airphone, and picked up his cup of coffee. "Can you get that tray table?"

Leslie pushed the table up into its stowed position. Using his elbows, John pushed himself up and stepped into the aisle, holding the laptop in one hand and the coffee in the other.

"Thanks," she said. Once in the aisle, she opened the overhead bin and extracted the small "go" bag that she always kept in her car. She didn't bother with her clunky black flight boots. Leslie padded to the lavatory in her white athletic socks and rumpled flight suit. She felt more like a kid in pajamas than a former fighter pilot and current sworn Customs Service officer. Thank God the other passengers were all asleep and wouldn't see her. It was a major uniform infraction to travel on a commercial jet in a flight suit; she added that to the growing list of her crimes. If Briggs found out about this trip, she could kiss the Customs career goodbye.

She freshened up and changed in record time, but not before a flight attendant had knocked on the door to remind her they were descending for landing. She opened the lavatory door, apologized to the flight attendant, and walked back down the aisle. John didn't see her coming. He was staring at the laptop screen. His face was so close to it that he was bathed in unflattering, ghoulish grey light reflected off the screen.

What was fascinating enough to make him focus this hard? Leslie stepped a little farther down the aisle so she could look over his shoulder. John was studying a grainy black-and white aerial photo. The screen blinked and zoomed in for more detail. It was an airfield surrounded by forest. He clicked a key and the picture dissolved again but returned in even more detail. It showed a row of jet fighters on a concrete apron. Leslie's heart pounded. MiG-21s!

"John?" she whispered. He didn't react, so she touched his shoulder and said, "Excuse me, John."

He flinched. "Oh. Hold on a second. He closed the laptop and repeated the awkward dance with laptop, phone cord, and coffee cup to let her pass.

Leslie sat down and buckled her lap belt. John did the same and, without commenting on her change of clothes, he opened the laptop but oriented it so she couldn't see the screen. He pressed a key and, when the device ceased whirring and clicking, he extracted a diskette from a slot on the left side. He started to close the laptop.

She said, "Wait a minute. Don't close that up yet."

"Ah, why not?"

"Do you want to tell me what you just downloaded?"

His eyes flicked away for a split second. "Nothing special. Just some business from home."

She couldn't suppress a cynical laugh. "Give me a break, John. I saw the aerial photos. I saw the MiGs."

John closed his eyes for one or two seconds before looking at her. "Let me guess. You're not going to leave me alone until I tell you what I found."

She nodded and smiled, trying to make it friendly, rather than a smug, triumphant grin. He was learning not to argue with her.

"Okay," he said, running a hand through his hair. "We'll have to hurry; the flight attendant wants me to stow this." He showed her the screen. "Do you read *Aviation Week*?"

"Only if someone leaves a copy around operations. I'm too cheap to pay for a subscription."

He chuckled. "Me too. Well, I was sitting here trying to figure out how MiGs could get into Arizona. At first, I could come up with only one answer. Let me ask you a silly question. When you flew F-16s, what was your security clearance?"

"Top Secret."

"Okay. Did you ever hear about a program called Constant Peg? By the way, before you answer, you should know the program's still classified."

She hesitated. She could lie, or she could openly talk about a still-secret government program. Hah! She would prevaricate, as John himself had taught her. "Let's just say, on a purely theoretical basis, that if I did know about it, I never got to participate. Did you?"

He said, "No comment. But, speaking theoretically, what are the chances that a Constant Peg MiG would find its way into southern Arizona? Slim, in my opinion. And, even if it had, with all the instrumentation involved with this program—"

"Which neither of us has acknowledged really exists."

"Right. My point is, from what I know of the program, there would be no way in hell a Constant Peg pilot would attack a Customs Service Citation. Those guys are better than that."

"What guys?" she said.

"Hmm. Those highly trained, highly experienced fighter pilots who, ah, who may have volunteered for Constant Peg."

"So," she said, "you know some of them?"

"No comment. Anyway, I just have to rule out the scenario that a Constant Peg aircraft shot down two Citations. So, while you snoozed—you snore occasionally, by the way—I kept searching the World Wide Web. I typed 'MiG-21' into the search function. What popped up was a link to an *Aviation Week* article about the attempted smuggling of MiGs out of Albania."

"You know, I remember seeing that article," Leslie said. "Last winter, wasn't it? But didn't they seize the MiG-21s at some port before they were shipped off? A bunch of corrupt Albanian air force people were arrested."

John nodded. "Yes, but something caught my attention when I read the article." He pointed to the laptop. "It's all here for you to read, but I'll summarize. Two Mig-21s, disassembled and packed in wooden crates, were seized just before they were loaded onto a Cuban freighter bound for, guess where?"

"Mexico?"

"You got it."

Leslie said, "But, if they never made it out of port—"

"I'm getting to that part. The *Aviation Week* article mentioned the name of the Albanian base from which the MiGs were stolen. I downloaded a series of satellite photos—"

"Wait a minute," she said. "You can get satellite photos on the web? Of *Albania*?"

"Yes, believe it or not. For a price, photos are available of almost any place on earth. It's ironic. The ones I downloaded are from Russian satellites that are no longer needed to spy on the US." He tapped the laptop's screen and said, "This is Gjadër, an Albanian fighter base. Very interesting place. A relic of the Cold War. Lots of MiGs hidden in tunnels, deep inside caves. What do you see?"

"Four MiG-21s."

"Exactly. Four MiGs, parked all by themselves next to an isolated hanger, far away from those tunnels and caves I just mentioned. Subsequent photos show the MiGs in various stages of disassembly, then crated up and loaded onto railroad flatcars. One day before the seizure, those same crates showed up on the dock at the Albanian port of Durrës, next to a Cuban ship, the *Cienfuego*."

"Wait," Leslie said. "Four crates or two?"

"Bingo! There were four crates on the dock the night before. But only two seized the next day."

"You think the ship left port with the other two MiGs?"

John shook his head. "I don't think it. I know it. I've got satellite photos of two crated MiG-21s being offloaded from the *Cienfuego* onto railroad cars at its first stop, Tampico, Mexico."

Leslie didn't know where Tampico was, but it didn't matter. If the MiGs went by rail, they could've gone anywhere. "Where'd they go from there?"

"I don't know yet. Couldn't get the train schedules downloaded yet. I should know in a couple minutes unless they make me shut this off for landing."

"Amazing," Leslie said. She wasn't sure if she meant the capabilities of the Internet or the man next to her. John was a little behind the times in web terminology—most people no longer used the term World Wide Web. However, he sure knew how to do web searches. She had assumed John had spent the extra money for first-class tickets because he was rich—Hank had said so—but what he had really needed was the new in-flight dial-up Internet connection, available only in first class from the seat-back Airphone. At first, she had thought he might be some kind of online junkie, addicted to computer games. She now understood that he was just a determined man hunting down some killers. A chime sounded, followed by a flight attendant's announcement of final preparations for landing. John would have to unplug his laptop and shut it down. The captain came on the PA system and announced a 7:15 a.m. arrival time at Washington National—five minutes early—and mentioned overcast skies, light rain, and a temperature of forty-five degrees.

"Just in the nick of time," John said. "The train schedules just downloaded." He shut down the laptop, coiled up the cord, and stowed all that in his gym bag, which he shoved into the space on the floor under the seat in front of him. "I'll have to look at them on the way to the White House."

"The White House," Leslie said. "So, we are really going there?"

"Yes. I have an appointment at 0930."

"You mean, *we* have an appointment at 0930."

"Look, Leslie, as I said back at the airport, back when I had the foolish idea that I could dissuade you from coming along, I only got his answering machine. I made the request to include you, but there's no guarantee that Hardwick will see you. Security is tight there. You knew that before we got on the plane."

"Yeah," she said. "Well, no offense, John, but all this sounds a little over the top. You expect me to believe that you can call up Lynwood Hardwick, the President's National Security Advisor, in the middle of the night and set up a meeting for 0930 the next morning? You know him well enough to do that?"

"He checks his voice mail every morning at 0700 sharp. We're still on pretty good terms. He knows I wouldn't ask this if it weren't important. I'm sure he'll see me—us, I hope—especially since I told him I have new evidence about the Citation crashes."

"Still on pretty good terms?" she said. "Where do you know him from?"

"The Air Force."

"Air Force? I thought you said this guy was a diplomat, or college professor, or something."

"He was both," John said. "But before all that, he was a fighter pilot."

Leslie waited in vain for him to say more. She pretended to enjoy the view from the Airbus, now below the clouds, as it banked left and right, snaking along the Potomac River to avoid the odd-shaped boundary of prohibited airspace surrounding the Lincoln Memorial, the White House, and the Capitol. She wasn't familiar enough with DC to pick out the White House, but she did see the Washington Monument. It was unbelievable to think that, in less than an hour, she would be down there, inside the White House, and not as a tourist. She looked over at John, who was not staring out the window, but looking at her legs.

He said, "Do you always carry clothes like that in your backpack?"

"Oh, this." The simple but elegant black ballet-neck dress, made of wrinkle-resistant rayon and cut just above the knee, often caused heads to turn, especially from people who had seen her only in a baggy flight suit. She fingered the string of pearls around her neck. "I call this my basic black courtroom dress," she said. "In my business, you get some no-notice trips to testify in court. It pays to have decent clothes in your locker. Since I live thirty minutes from D-M, I keep this, some jeans, and some gym clothes in that bag. Will it do?"

"It'll do," he said. "It'll do just fine."

So, he had noticed after all.

Chapter 8

"I'm impressed," Leslie said.

John said, "With the office or the view?"

"Neither. I'm impressed that you're on a first-name basis with the National Security Advisor's secretary."

"Margaret? I've known her for years." He paused to count them but gave up; the answer would make him feel old. "She's been with Hardwick since his days as commander of 5th Air Force in Japan." Margaret had seated them in two chairs facing Hardwick's massive mahogany desk. She had offered tea or coffee and went off to get black tea and milk for Leslie. John had declined; he had exceeded his coffee quota during last night's flight.

While waiting for the tea, John listened patiently while Leslie oohed and aahed about Hardwick's office.

"That desk," she said. "Unless I am sorely mistaken, it's an authentic Chippendale George III library desk. Look at how the wood gleams! Look at those handles! They're originals. That thing is probably over two hundred years old. These chairs we're sitting in? All that ornate carving?" She stood up, tilted her chair back and looked under the seat. "They're Chippendales too, ribbands, also mahogany, of course, and at least as old as the desk. You can tell by the arms—"

"You seem to know a lot about old furniture."

She glared at him.

"I mean, about fine antique furniture."

"That's better," she said.

"So, what's a ribband chair, anyway?"

"In this context, it means chairs whose backs are constructed from hand-carved, interwoven ribbon motifs and moldings. My dad was an antique dealer, so I grew up hearing this kind of talk. He's retired now; so's my mom. She had her own interior decorating service. Speaking of which, this room has great colors. All the dark wood! And these blue seat cushions fit in perfectly with the cream-colored carpet and curtains. And, yes, the view out the windows is nice. A corner office—very impressive." She pointed at the west-facing window. "What's that big building out there?"

"That's the Executive Office Building. It's over a hundred years old and has more than five hundred rooms, all filled with people in the Executive Branch who are trying to save the world."

"My, aren't you cynical." She looked at Hardwick's massive high-backed leather chair and said, "If I were him, I'd move my desk around so I could look out over the White House lawn and park to the north." After a brief pause, she said, "Hardwick was a General?"

"Yes. He was one of my role models and mentors in the Air Force. He flew F-86s in Korea and 105s in Vietnam. Had a good combat record, a good reputation, and a chest full of medals. John pointed at a row of framed photographs displayed on one shelf of a floor-to-ceiling bookcase. "See that picture on the left? That's him and his F-86."

Next to a five-by-seven photo of Hardwick as a college quarterback was a larger black and white picture of a hulking, short-haired black fighter pilot in combat gear, flying helmet tucked under his arm as if it were a football. He was smiling from his perch on the ladder of an F-86 parked between rows of sandbags at a bleak, snow-covered airfield in Korea.

"That's his favorite picture of himself," John said. "He retired as a general, with a PhD in International Relations, and taught at Georgetown. Then he did time in the State Department and the CIA before the President chose him as his National Security Advisor. Our paths have crossed several times; in fact, after I left the Air Force, he tried to recruit me for some special—"

"I knew it!" Leslie said. "See? When we first met, didn't I ask you if you worked for Northern Air Transport? Hank wouldn't talk about it, but everyone knows Northern Air flies clandestine missions for the CIA. I just know you were involved too. That's why you know how to access satellite photos and do all that other spy-type research. And you knew just what to look for out at the crash—"

"I hate to disappoint you, Leslie, but I never worked for the CIA, Northern Air, or anybody like that. I've turned down General Hardwick's offers so often that it's become a joke between us."

"Oh," she said.

"All I ever wanted to do was fly fighters. It took a couple years for Hardwick to understand that."

"What is it that General Hardwick couldn't understand?" said Margaret, holding a tray with Leslie's tea.

"Hi, Margaret. I was just explaining that General Hardwick never quite understood my passion to stay in the cockpit."

"How true." Margaret set the tray on a side table and said, "Please help yourself, Ms. Olsen. I'm afraid it will be a few more minutes until the General can break free."

"That's fine," John said. "But, while we're waiting, is there any way I can get a World Wide Web connection in here?"

"Well . . ." She bent down and said in a conspiratorial voice, "If you don't tell anyone I showed you, you may use the wall jack over by that side table. But you'll need a cable."

"Thanks Margaret! I've got a cable in my bag."

This delay was a lucky break. It would give him time to follow up on where those MiGs ended up. John got the laptop set up and the Cat III cable plugged into the wall. Within a minute he was looking at the schedule for all trains leaving Tampico on the date when the crated MiGs were unloaded. He concentrated on those headed north. There were only two trains of interest. One was a passenger-only train, which he disregarded. The other was a freight train headed north to the city of Chihuahua, where it turned west and connected with the major north-south FerroMex line. As he scrolled through the list of stops, a familiar name flashed into view.

"Hermosillo. Damn," He hadn't meant to say that out loud. Leslie was sure to—

"What did you say?" Leslie asked.

"Nothing. Computer problems," he said. "I'll have to look at this later." John powered off the laptop and disconnected the cord. His hands were trembling. Hermosillo—just a few miles south of Carlos Alvarado's ranch at La Coruba. That had to be where the MiGs went. He'd prove it with more aerial photos. On the other hand, why bother? Hardwick could get one of his clandestine agencies to do that.

He did his best to breathe normally. He tried to focus on the bookcase or the impressionistic painting on the opposite wall, but he couldn't shake the nightmarish image. Carlos Alvarado, the slimy macho ex-Mexican Air Force pilot, heir to the Alvarado drug empire, had managed to pile on one final insult by squeezing the trigger of a MiG-21 and blowing Hank out of the sky. John vowed to be there when they brought Alvarado to justice. He'd accept Hardwick's standing offer to hire on as a "consultant" for aviation-related "special projects." It would be sweet revenge.

"Hello, John? Earth to John? Did you hear me?"

It was Leslie. "Ah, sorry. Say again?"

"I asked you what you think Hardwick will do with the evidence we show him. Will he be able to track down these killers?"

"If he can't, nobody can. Anyway, he's as close as I can get to the top. He zipped the laptop back into its case.

The door opened behind them, and Lynwood Hardwick's deep bass voice filled the room.

"John! It's been too long, son. And this must be Leslie Olsen."

They stood.

Hardwick walked up to Leslie and offered a handshake. "Ms. Olsen, or should I say Officer Olsen, I am truly sorry for your loss."

"Thank you, General. And thanks for meeting with us."

So, Hardwick knew about this. John wondered if that was what the delay had been—Hardwick getting briefed on the Citation losses.

"You're welcome," Hardwick said. He turned to John, shook his hand, and slapped him on the shoulder. "I am deeply sorry for Hank's loss also, as well as the other Customs Service crewmembers. Sit down, please."

Hardwick's hair was no longer a salt and pepper shade but pure white. His face, darker than the mahogany wood of his desk, bore a few new wrinkles under his eyes and on his forehead. The last few years had not been kind to his waistline. He looked more like a bulky lineman than a quarterback. All that aside, the man still projected energy and power. Tucked under his left arm was a thick brown folder with a red and white Top-Secret label. Hardwick walked around his desk, put the folder down, and lowered himself into his chair. The wood creaked under his weight.

John didn't sit. He pulled a computer diskette and two Polaroid photos out of a side pocket on his laptop case. He put them on the desk and slid them halfway across the wide surface toward Hardwick. "Take a look at these, General. And then tell me—" He stopped and glanced at Leslie. "—tell *us*, please, what the hell is going on out in Arizona?"

Hardwick pulled the two photos closer and picked them up one at a time, studying them for several seconds each. "Still like the direct approach, eh, John? Please excuse him, Ms. Olsen. May I call you Leslie?" He didn't wait for a response. "John's a smart son of a . . . gun, but occasionally forgets his manners. I appreciate that you have both lost someone close to you in these accidents, but I assure you—"

"These weren't accidents," Leslie said. "These were *murders*. With all due respect, sir, please answer John's question."

Hardwick's thick eyebrows raised briefly and unevenly, but he seemed more amused than insulted, like a father whose young child had talked back to him for the first time. Leslie's face turned red. John waited for her to apologize, but she just swallowed and set her jaw.

The big man took another look at the photos and picked up the diskette, studying both sides. "Well," he said, looking at John. "You seem to have conducted your own independent investigation, so why don't you tell me what happened?

John said, "Sir, we believe that both Citations were shot down by MiGs. And, with all the resources at your disposal, I can't believe that you don't already know that."

"MiGs." Hardwick rubbed his chin with a hand the same color and almost the same size as a catcher's mitt. He reached inside his suit coat, pulled out a pair of reading glasses and held one of the photos up to the light. He looked at it from several different angles. He repeated the process with the other photo. He put them back on the desk and pointed to one. "You found this bullet in the wreckage? It looks like twenty mike-mike, but bigger and different somehow."

"Good eyes, sir," John said. "It's a 23-millimeter HEI round. The markings on the base indicate it came from a Russian-made fighter."

"No way."

John almost smiled, but this was not a day for smiling. "That's exactly what Leslie said. But there is no doubt in my military mind. That round was fired from a Russian-made fighter, most probably a MiG-21."

Hardwick's eyes widened, making quite a contrast between the whites of his eyes and his dark skin. "That is very interesting news. Sit down, please. Relax. Never mind. Your body language tells me you are not going to relax anytime soon."

John looked down at his clenched fists and tight forearms. He opened his hands, backed up a step and settled into the chair next to Leslie's.

Hardwick put his elbows on the desk, laced his fingers together to form a tent and rested his forehead on it. He closed his eyes. The only sound in the room was the big man's loud nasal breathing. When he opened his eyes, he looked at John and then at Leslie. He reached out and pushed a button on his telephone.

Margaret's voice came over the intercom. "Yes, General?"

"Margaret, please call my wife and tell her I'll be late for our brunch. And, no interruptions, please." He punched off the intercom and leaned back in his chair. "I seem to have underestimated you both. Should have known better, eh, John?"

John shrugged.

"Before I say any more," Hardwick said, "do I have your word it won't go beyond this room?"

"Of course," Leslie said.

"John?'

"I won't repeat anything you tell us here. What I find out for myself, that's another story."

"Fair enough." Hardwick shifted his weight, causing some complaints from the springs in his chair. Look," he said. "I'm going way out on a limb discussing this with you." He pointed toward the Oval Office. "I have been directed, from the highest level, to put a lid on this and keep it on." He glanced at the Polaroid prints. "You are right. Someone shot down the Citations. The question is, who did it and why? Until you showed me this, my—" He paused to draw air quotes with his finger. "—my 'experts' had me convinced it was ground fire."

"Hell, John, are you sure you don't want to come work for me? If you can figure out all this about MiGs so early in the investigation, can't you see how valuable you would be to the national security process?"

"For the umpteenth time, General, although I am sincerely flattered by your confidence in me, the answer is still no."

"Okay," Hardwick said. "I'll give up on that. For now. Let's get back to this crisis." He turned to Leslie. "Leslie, as a Customs Service pilot, you already know this, but bear with me while I explain it to John. Congress has really tied our hands, son. They won't let us use the military to patrol our borders anymore, not after our soldiers accidentally shot that rancher's son. Remember that?"

John shook his head. Leslie nodded.

"For a few months," Hardwick said, "we had Marines and Army troops aggressively patrolling the southern border. It was a dual-purpose mission, immigration, and drugs. There had even been talk of using military aircraft to protect DEA and Customs Service anti-drug operations. All that went down the tubes when a soldier killed a suspected drug smuggler. Sadly, the victim turned out to be an innocent U.S. citizen. Congress pulled their support for the military patrols. They'll never change their minds, especially after some trigger-happy CIA-trained pilots down in South America shot down an unarmed civilian plane carrying missionaries—missionaries, for God's sake, not drug smugglers!"

"I heard about that one," John said.

"But sir," Leslie said. "Won't that all change now that you have new evidence?"

Hardwick picked up the photo of the bullet and studied it from different angles. "About that evidence. I know you, John. You wouldn't come waltzing in here if you weren't sure of your facts. But humor me for a moment. Tell me why you are sure that this came from a MiG? And why are you so sure it's a MiG-21?"

"It began with a phone call from Hank Carter." John told him who Hank was, mentioned his "Blue Bandits" message and everything that had happened since the phone call. God, that had been less than twenty-four hours ago. When he finished, he said to Leslie, "Do you have anything to add?"

"One thing," she said. "The day Bobby—my brother—was shot down, I overheard Hank in Briggs's office. That's Eric Briggs, the Customs Service ops officer. "I heard Hank shout, 'They shot him down, just like they were at war with us.'"

"But you've got no hard evidence of actual MiGs," Hardwick said. He picked up the file folder on his desk, opened it and read for several seconds. He took a second look at the diskette. "Or do you?"

"Yes, sir, we do," John said. "It's all there, on the diskette. He summarized what he had learned on the web. "You've got a copy of everything I've learned, including satellite photos tracing the MiGs across Mexico. I know where they ended up. Hermosillo. It might interest you to know that thirty miles north of Hermosillo, near the town of La Coruba, is a ranch with a jet-capable runway. That ranch is owned by a well-known Mexican drug lord with jet fighter experience in the Mexican air force. Carlos Alvarado." He spat out the last two words.

Hardwick had a good memory, but it was too much to expect he would remember that name. "To refresh your memory, that's—"

"Alvarado?" Hardwick said. "The guy you tried to kill?"

Leslie sat up straight. "Tried to kill?"

"Alvarado's the man responsible for these shootdowns," John said. "I feel it in my gut. Check out all that information on the diskette. Confirm it yourself. Then, when you run an operation to get Alvarado, I want to be in on it. You owe me that."

Hardwick closed his eyes and rubbed the bridge of his nose with two fingers and a thumb. He looked at John and sighed. "There's not going to be an op, John. Not for quite some time."

"What do you mean? The information will check out. Trust me."

"I'm sure it will. But even so, I'm afraid we can't take any action right now."

"That's not good enough, General," Leslie said. "We came in here with proof the Citations were shot down. What else do you want?"

"Leslie, John," Hardwick said, looking at both in sequence. "I won't lie to you. I should, but I won't. I've got too much respect for the crews that died and for you two. Too much respect for the truth. But reality, political reality, changes the big picture. I've been ordered to sit on this one for a little while."

John jumped out of his chair and leaned over Hardwick's desk, his hands squeezing the solid lip as hard as he could. If it broke, Hardwick would deserve it. "Dammit! Sit on it? For a little while? What the hell for?" He was right in Hardwick's face, far too close and far too disrespectful to the man who sits a few doors down from the Oval Office and chairs the National Security Council. He didn't care if he pissed off the entire Federal government. Alvarado was not going to go unpunished —again.

Hardwick said, "Are you finished?"

"Yes, sir." John released his grip on the desk and sat down. He had left marks on the wood. Maybe they would be permanent, reminders to Hardwick that politics was not more important than justice.

"As I was trying to explain," Hardwick said, "this is the situation. We know one or more of the drug cartels have been hurt by the Citation's effectiveness. Emboldened by our wimpy Congress—don't repeat that to *anyone*—they've evidently decided to shoot a couple down and force us to ground them. Which is essentially what has been done, as of this morning."

Hardwick must have seen the surprise on their faces. "Oh, you've been traveling all night and haven't seen the news. Someone—" He inclined his head toward the Oval Office again. "Someone has directed the Customs Service to release a statement that the Citations are obsolete and structurally unsound. Dangerous to fly. After today's flyby at the memorial service for both crews, the Citations will be grounded pending 'further review'".

"Why the cover-up?" John asked.

"Here's the bottom line." Hardwick rapped his knuckles on the Top-Secret folder and spoke from between clenched teeth. "A new president has just been inaugurated in Mexico which, of course, is the most likely haven for those who shot down the Citations. My boss does not want to embarrass this new guy by making the shootdown public. It would portray the Mexican government as weak or ineffective. Needless to say, that also rules out sending our military across the border to kick ass on Mexican soil. Assuming we could find any asses to kick. Pardon my language, Leslie."

"I'm former military, General. I've heard it all."

"So, you're just going to sit by and let two of our crews get murdered?" John said. "Let the killers fade away until the trail is too cold to follow? That's not like you, Lynford." Using

Hardwick's first name was a big faux pas, but he didn't care. The old guy needed to know that he was angry and disappointed.

"It's not my call, John," Hardwick said. "I'm just a soldier, following orders."

"You got that right." It was all he could do to avoid using profanity. "Well, I've got news for you, *General*. The orders are wrong. Unfair. Unjust." He stood up so abruptly that his two-hundred-year-old chair tipped backward and hit the floor with a loud crack. "Unlike you, I am no longer a good soldier. I no longer follow orders. I follow my instinct. And my instinct tells me to go out and kick some butt!" He whirled around, picked up his gym bag headed for the door.

John yanked the door open and stormed past Margaret's desk without a word to her, knowing that was a sin she'd never let him forget. From the sound of Leslie's footsteps and the rustle of her dress, she was about ten paces behind. Good.

"Don't let him do anything stupid!" Hardwick called out to Leslie.

Chapter 9

Lynwood Hardwick sat still for a moment. Then he laughed, loud enough, he was sure, for Margaret to hear through the open door. No one had ever walked out on him. Not from this office. He couldn't blame Martin and Olsen. They believed that their own government lacked the backbone to track down a murdering drug lord. Until yesterday, they would have been wrong. There had been something planned, but he couldn't tell them that. The President had quashed the operation before it had even gotten started.

He glanced at the photos in the bookcase, finding comfort in the one of him in Korea. Things had been simple back then. Climb to forty thousand feet over MiG Alley, sight the enemy, and swoop down for the attack. That's not what they paid him to do now. He had been hired to advise the President and implement his policies even if he disagreed with them. By God, that's what he was going to do, even if it cost him John's respect.

Margaret had evidently worked up the courage to peek into the office. She looked at the tipped-over chair and said, "Is everything all right, General?"

Margaret. Loyal, efficient, understanding Margaret. She kept him on an even keel in stormy political weather. She was a priceless asset to have on one's side when, as he used to say in the Air Force, the shit hit the fan. Which it just had. Margaret would know this.

"No, not really," he said. He got up, walked over to the fallen chair, and set it back on its legs. "John and I just had a, ah, a spirited discussion about a certain policy decision. He disagrees with me, of course."

"I couldn't help but hear," she said. "I've never seen him so agitated. The way he stormed out of here! Do you want to talk about it?"

He smiled at her. "Thank you, Margaret, but not right now. What I need you to do, though, is get George Clark on the phone. On the secure line, please."

She walked a little closer to him and adjusted the chair to its precise location. She gave him "That Look" before leaving the room. Margaret always tried to hide it, but she got slightly miffed when something came up that was above her security clearance.

*   *   *

Hardwick picked up the handset and punched the button to activate a secure conversation. Thank God George Clark had come up through the ranks as a field operative and had no political agenda. He was mission-oriented, easy to talk to, and well on his way to becoming the most effective Deputy Director of Operations in CIA history. If anyone could handle this crisis, it would be George.

After a series of beeps and squawks while the encryption software loaded, Clark said, "Hello, Lynwood. What's wrong?"

That was George's way of chastising him for interrupting his day.

"Sorry, George. It's the Customs Service thing."

"I heard," Clark said. "The duty officer called me late last night when our operative didn't check in. It's a real goat rope out there in Arizona, with Customs Service, FBI, and us all stepping on each other's toes trying to find out what happened."

"So, this Carter fellow was your man?"

"That's right. Your file has only his code name. Carter is— or was— a retired Air Force pilot, someone we used with great success at Northern Air. His being placed at the Citation detachment seemed like a great idea. He had just sent us a report showing evidence of the first shootdown. If I had known he was in that much danger, I would have—"

"Don't beat yourself up about that," Hardwick said. He sighed. "No one could've predicted that they would be bold enough to do it again. But I'm calling about a more recent development. Have you heard about someone showing up with a piece of missing wreckage and photos of bullet holes?"

"Did I ever. That guy Briggs, the Customs Service boss, filed a report about some old fart and one of his own pilots who—"

"We ought to have that old fart working for us," Hardwick said. "He just left my office after telling me how the Citations were shot down and who did it. And he left me copies of photographic evidence."

"Huh?"

Hardwick had no time to verify the evidence. However, he trusted John's expertise. "This man, John Martin—whom I know personally, by the way, and trust—just left me a computer diskette and pictures with proof that the Citations were shot down by MiG-21s smuggled into Mexico and flown by Carlos Alvarado, a known cartel leader."

"Huh?" Clark said again. "No way."

"Everyone seems to say that when they hear the news. I'm sending you the diskette and the pictures. I want you to check them out and get back to me right away."

"Hell, there goes my day."

"There's one more thing."

It was Clark's turn to sigh. "Go ahead."

"I've— Shit, George, as of this morning, I've been ordered to suspend the surveillance out in Arizona. Forget any preparations for cross-border stuff. The President has changed his mind." He stopped just short of saying the President had chickened out. This was a recorded line.

"Let me get this straight," Clark said. "You're saying that now we don't want to know who's shooting down our Customs Service jets? Or how they're doing it? I've got five people working twenty-four-seven on this. Now, I'm supposed to ignore these shootdowns? That's a crock of—"

"It was an order, George."

Clark was silent for a long time. "Will you put that in writing?" he asked.

"Along with the diskette and photos, I'll send a signed note officially calling you off the op. There will also be a second note directing you to watch John Martin closely, starting immediately. I suspect we're going to have a problem with him."

"What kind of problem?"

"He's going to go after Carlos Alvarado. I can feel it. Martin has an old score to settle. Just a few minutes ago, he barged out of here saying he was going to kick some butt. We can't let him do that, not after the President's latest change of heart. We, that is, the White House and the CIA, would get blamed for whatever trouble Martin causes."

Clark said, "He's just a retired pilot, right? Not a trained agent? How much trouble can one man cause?"

"Don't underestimate him. He had some training in clandestine ops long ago, during the Vietnam years. You've heard of the Son Trâm Raid?"

"The POW camp in North Vietnam? He was involved in that?"

"Yep," Hardwick said. "Operation Gold Coast, I think it was called. Mind you, when I first met John, back in 1971, I didn't know the details. They were all classified, hidden even from me, his boss. All I knew is, he had a bunch of combat medals, and he was more mature, more combat-seasoned, than all the other young bucks just out of flight school, who swaggered around trying to look like trained killers. John Martin didn't have to try. He just had that *look*, you know? I got curious when I saw that Martin's first assignment had been with the 1127th Field Activities Group. Ever heard of it?"

"No," said Clark.

"Neither had I, back then. It was a human intelligence unit. Exactly what they did, no one would tell me. But you and I both know what HUMINT agencies do; they put people into enemy territory. I got a big hint when I read a couple of the citations for those medals that Martin wore on his dress uniform. The writeups were very vague about actual places or dates, which usually means the operation was secret, and the records sealed for who-knows-how-long. Martin's citations included phrases like, 'courage under fire,' 'fierce fighting skills,' and—something that should worry us— 'completed the mission against overwhelming odds.' All this happened while he was attached to a unit called the Joint Contingency Task Force."

Clark said, "Help me out, Lynwood, I've never heard of—"

"The JCTF was created to do one mission. Then it was disbanded. They—"

"Oh, I get it. They did the Son Trâm Raid, right?"

"Exactly. When I ended up as National Security Advisor, I was able to access all the Operation Gold Coast files. I should send those over to you. But let me sum up Martin's role. You probably know that, due to an intelligence failure, the Gold Coast brass didn't know the POWs had been moved out to another camp a month before. The raiders didn't find any Americans. Dammit, that must have been shitty! Fifty-four of the fifty-six raiders egressed out of there in helicopters, but two got left behind. One of them was Martin."

"He got captured?"

"No," Hardwick said. "That's where the story gets really interesting. Martin went back into a building to carry out a wounded soldier, a Sergeant Landreau. The helos were forced to leave them behind due to heavy NVA fire. Somehow, Martin got himself and the wounded guy into the jungle, evaded capture for two days, and was eventually extracted by an Air America STOL aircraft."

"That is quite a story."

"Believe it or not, there's more drama related to that extraction. The damned Air America plane, a Pilatus Porter, crashed into a mountain on the way out. Martin had to—hell, I'll just let you read that part. Bottom line is, against all odds, he survived, and so did the wounded soldier. Martin has the knack for, shall we say, unconventional action. In fact, for years I've been trying to recruit him into intelligence work, but he refuses. He lives alone on some island out in Washington state. He's intelligent, capable, and, when properly motivated, has the killer instinct."

"Do you have a file on him?"

"Yes, I'll send that too. Watch him. Discretely. Keep me informed. And don't let him do anything to embarrass us." Hardwick decided to have Clark monitor Leslie Olsen too. She was a feisty one. Another loose cannon. A female version of John Martin.

"Where is he right now?"

"I'm not sure," Hardwick said. "But he came here on a red-eye flight from Tucson. My guess is he'll return immediately, because there is a memorial service for his best friend this afternoon."

"Who's that?"

"Hank Carter."

"Shit," Clark said. "No wonder the guy is pissed. But what's Martin's big score to settle with this Alvarado guy?"

"Martin believes that five years ago, Alvarado was responsible for the death of his wife and teen-age daughter. When you add the fact that yesterday, Alvarado shot down his best friend, is that a big enough score for you?"

Clark said, "I'd better make a few calls. Get surveillance going. Then I'll get a team together to keep track of things. Please send that stuff over to the office right away."

Chapter 10

John reached the sidewalk on West Executive Avenue before he remembered his leather flying jacket. It was back at the West Wing security checkpoint. He stopped, closed his eyes, and tried to slow his breathing. This was bad. He had just insulted the President's National Security Advisor. He had stormed out of the White House, tossed his visitor's pass at the security guard, and ignored what the guard had said to him —which was probably a reminder about his jacket. Now he'd have to go back, his tail between his legs, and retrieve it.

His head throbbed; he could feel his carotid artery pulsing. "Shit," he mumbled out loud. He looked around and was relieved to find no one near him. "Shit," he said again. If he had killed Alvarado five years ago, none of this would have happened. But no, he had stopped just short of squeezing the life out of—"

"Hey, wait up! Give me a hand here."

It was Leslie, hurrying toward him, loaded down with her travel bag and his jacket.

"Forget something?" she said. When she got closer, her amused expression changed to a frown. "Are you all right? You're sweating. From the way you're standing, I'd swear you're going to karate-chop the first person who walks by."

John uncoiled his muscles and wiped his brow with the back of one hand. Sure enough, it was thick with perspiration, as if he had just stepped off a forty-five-minute session on a treadmill. "I'm okay. Here, let me take that."

She handed the jacket to him. "You're not okay. The look on your face is plain scary. Do you want to tell me about this guy Alvarado? And why you tried to kill him?"

He set his bag down on the sidewalk and put on his jacket, using the motions to stall for time. He didn't want to tell her anything. However, she had risked her job, her career as a pilot, and for what reason? To get justice for her brother's murder. She deserved an honest answer. "I'm sorry if I embarrassed you back there. But I'm so—" He struggled to find a phrase that wasn't profane. "—so angry I can't see straight. Yes, I'll tell you more, but not out here. It's kind of a long story. Let's go someplace and sit down."

"Can we make it someplace with food?" she said. "I'm starved."

John looked northeast, across Lafayette Park. The Hay-Adams Hotel was up there; he was pretty sure they still had an awesome brunch, even on Mondays. "I know just the place. It's on the other side of Lafayette Park." He saw a questioning look on Leslie's face. "Do you know DC very well?"

"Not really."

"Come on, then. We'll go through the park. You are only about a quarter mile away from one of DC's most famous hotels and restaurants. I'll tell you a little about the park on the way."

"I'd rather hear about the brunch menu," Leslie said.

"Omelets made-to-order, bacon, ham, sausage, oven-roasted potatoes, thick French toast, pastries to die for, and much more. Oh, and champagne." He led her up Executive Avenue and turned right onto Pennsylvania. It was relatively quiet on the street; anyone who had been silly enough to drive a car into downtown DC had already parked it and was at work. Most of the traffic on Pennsylvania Avenue was buses and taxis.

The low cloud deck that had greeted them at National was gone now; the sun was about forty-five degrees above the horizon but hadn't warmed up the city yet. John was happy to have his old leather flying jacket. Leslie looked a little chilled. All she had was a thin black sweater. Should he offer her his jacket? No. She'd probably make some clever remark hinting that he needed it more than she did.

About a half-block later, while they were still on the south side of Pennsylvania Avenue, he pointed out the spacious lawn and the North Portico entrance to the White House. "That big, curved drive is where all the foreign dignitaries arrive and depart. You've probably seen it a hundred times on the TV news." They crossed the avenue and entered one of Lafayette Park's two north-south walkways. Mid-morning foot traffic in the park was light.

John said, "You know who Lafayette was, right?"

"Of course. The French general who helped us out in the Revolutionary War."

"That's what most people here in the USA know. However, there's a lot more to that story. Did you know that Lafayette was made a commissioned officer at age thirteen and fought the first of his battles in America at age nineteen, by which time he was already a Major General?"

"You've got to be kidding me," Leslie said.

"Yup. His family was very aristocratic. His real name is eleven words long, only two of which are La Fayette."

"Lafayette is only one word."

"That's just how we Americans know him. I can't remember all eleven words, but the last two are 'La' and 'Fayette.'"

Their shoes crunched along the light-brown gravel path. Walking always helped him think, made him breathe evenly, which today helped him control his rage. The throbbing in his forehead had stopped, thank God. He couldn't get his mind off Alvarado. The United States government didn't seem too keen on punishing him. If they ever got around to doing anything, it would be too little, too late. So, where did that leave him? He noticed that Leslie was no longer at his side. Since he was a preoccupied fool, he hadn't noticed she had fallen behind. Constrained by the slinky, narrow black dress, she couldn't take full advantage of her long legs to match his strides. Why hadn't she asked him to slow down? Too proud, maybe.

He stopped. "Sorry," he said. "I got a little lost in thought there." When she caught up, he tried to walk at a slower pace. His legs were willing, but his brain was about to over-speed. He was angry with Hardwick, with himself for not being there when Hank called, and with Hank for allowing himself to be shot down.

"Lost in what thoughts?" Leslie asked.

John wasn't ready to talk to her about all this. He called upon his prevaricating skills. "Oh, just some info about Lafayette that most Americans don't know. Did you know that, halfway through the Revolutionary War, Lafayette returned to France and lobbied for more French support for us? He returned in 1780 and, by 1781, led French and American forces in the siege of Yorktown. That was a decisive victory for the Americans and eventually led to the British surrender. Later, Lafayette played an important role in the French Revolution."

Leslie said, "And how is it that you know so much about Lafayette?"

"Two reasons. First, being a military man, I've studied as much battle history as possible. It's the old principle of learning from other people's mistakes or their successes. Second, I had studied French in high school and college and got roped into taking more courses at the Defense Language Institute out in Monterrey. The Air Force needed people who could speak French with the proficiency of a native."

Leslie was quiet for the moment. She was probably trying to figure out why the Air Force was interested in the French language. It wouldn't take her long, once she remembered that Vietnam is a former *French* colony. They were almost at the end of the path and were in sight of the Hay-Adams main entrance. He had just a few more seconds to solve his private dilemma. He could probably find Alvarado and his MiGs, but what then? Capture him? Kill him? Both options were attractive but difficult to accomplish. According to news reports he had read, Alvarado had inherited the family drug cartel after allegedly murdering several competitors on his way to the top. He would be surrounded by a cadre of heavily armed bodyguards. How was a washed-up fighter pilot supposed to get past all that? A one-man commando raid? No, he just didn't have the resources or experience to fight Alvarado on the ground. He'd be cut down before he got within a mile of—

John stopped in his tracks, as if he had hit a brick wall. That was it! What had he just said? That he'd be a fool to fight Alvarado on the ground. So why not fight him in the *air*, where he would have the advantage of twenty years of combat experience? It didn't matter that, until yesterday, he hadn't flown in five years. He was confident he could gun Alvarado out of the sky. The old T-Bird wouldn't do the job, though. He'd need something that could go one-on-one with a MiG-21.

Someone put a hand on his shoulder.

"John!" Leslie shouted. Didn't you hear me? First you started walking faster and faster again. Then you stopped dead in your tracks. No pun intended. Seriously, that look on your face! I thought you were having a stroke."

"Not a stroke, Leslie, unless it's a stroke of luck. I'll be okay in a minute." The idea had hit him so suddenly that, although he'd never admit it to Leslie, he had gotten dizzy. His imagination had played out a full-color preview of his plan. He knew how it would begin and how it would end. He had to get back to Tucson as soon as possible. And, he had to convince Jim Whitaker to meet him there—tonight.

"What is going on with you?" Leslie asked.

They were almost at the entrance to the Hay-Adams. He hailed the first taxicab in line. "Come on," he said. "There's been a change in plans."

"What about breakfast?"

"I'm sorry. There's no time to explain. Actually—wait." This might be his chance to lose her. "You would be free to stay. Stay here, enjoy the Hay-Adams brunch. I'll pay you back for your expenses here and for the return trip. But I have to get back right now." The cabbie had the right rear door open.

"National Airport, please," John said. "An extra twenty if you can make it in fifteen minutes."

He slid onto the seat. The driver had the door halfway closed before Leslie pulled it open and jumped in. Their hips bumped together.

"Slide over, please," she said. "Make room for me."

Leslie sat silently, with her arms folded across her chest, as the cab raced through traffic and swerved onto the 14th Street Bridge.

"Leslie, I need a favor. Do you have a portable phone?"

"You mean a cellular phone?" She reached into her bag, pulled out a small black plastic instrument and handed it to him. "You've got to open that flap on the bottom, push the 'On' button and extend the antenna. Wait for it to get a signal ... oh, never mind." She took it back. "I'll set it up for you."

John looked at his watch. It was 0730 Olympia time. Whitaker was going to be pissed. The museum was closed on Mondays. This was his day to sleep in. He reached into his own bag and located his small address book. He dialed Whitaker's number, endured the expletives from the old jet mechanic, and told him about Hank's memorial service later that day. He apologized for the short notice and suffered through another litany of foul language. In the end, of course, Whitaker said he would cancel all his plans and jump on the next flight to Tucson.

"You are a good man, Whit. Let me know your flight details. I'll pick you up at the airport." Whitaker's reply was so loud that he had to hold the phone away from his ear. Unfortunately, that meant Leslie could hear the new stream of vulgar words. "Calm down," John said. "I've already thought of that. Just call my home phone and leave a message with your arrival time. And Whit—" He decided to pull a page from Hank's play book. "I really need you to be there for me."

As the taxi sped southbound on the George Washington Parkway, John decided to risk a little small talk. "You are going to get a kick out of meeting Whitaker. He's quite a character. Short, skinny little guy. Looks a lot like Sammy Davis Junior. You do know who that is, I hope."

"Yes. There was a special about him on TV about five years ago. I know I've seen him in some of those old movies, the ones with Dean Martin and Frank Sinatra. He's a singer and dancer too, right? Is he still alive?"

"As far as I know," John said. "I read something about him retiring due to medical reasons. Cancer, I'm afraid."

Leslie said, "Sorry to hear that. Well, I can't wait to meet this Whitaker fellow. I'm certain to learn some new cuss words." She gave him the briefest of smiles.

John handed the phone to her and said, "He's usually not that bad. Jim Whitaker is a retired Air Force Chief Master Sergeant. He is the world's best jet mechanic. He was my crew chief for four years. Kept that F-16 in showroom condition. In fact, he once told a general—"

"Look, John," Leslie said. "At this moment, I don't give a damn about crew chiefs, F-16s or memorial services. I just want answers. You promised me an explanation. Who is Alvarado? Did you really try to ki—"

"Not so loud," John said. He leaned closer to her and whispered, "This cab is not the right place to talk."

"Bullshit!" Leslie said in a voice loud enough to draw a glance from the cab driver.

He reached forward and closed the plexiglass privacy window separating them from the driver.

She unbuckled her seat belt, slid across the seat, and thumped her index finger on his chest. "Don't you think I have a right to know? I lost my only brother, understand? And that hurts. It hurts really, really bad." She squeezed her eyes shut. "So bad that I've run out of tears."

There was one running down her cheek, but John thought better of pointing it out to her.

"I'm *involved* in this," she said, "whether you like it or not. So, I need to know, right now, why you are so hung up on this Alvarado character and how that relates to the MiG attacks."

John took a few deep breaths, looked out the window and considered his options. On his left, the Potomac River glistened blue under full sun. The clear sky above was a few shades lighter. Oak trees bordering the George Washington Parkway had begun to leaf out and the dogwoods had already blossomed. Spring flowers bloomed and the grass on the roadside was freshly mown. A green-and-white highway sign flashed by on his right, announcing National Airport was one mile ahead.

This was about to become a test of wills. He was a split-second away from throwing out his standard angry response: *It's personal. Shut up and mind your own business.* His palms began to sweat. This woman has also lost a loved one to Alvarado, so it really was her business. He faced her and, in the process, inadvertently looked down at the generous amount of thigh she had exposed when she had slid over to confront him.

Leslie noticed and pulled the dress down.

It was a curious thing. She still looked elegant despite the confrontational set of her jaw, her rapid breathing, and the neck of her little black dress being twisted off center. Saying "shut up" to her would be like declaring war. A war he was not sure he could win. Maybe she needed to see, up close and personal, exactly why he hated Alvarado so much. She wanted answers? Okay. He'd show her rather than tell her.

The taxi had just veered right onto the airport access road and passed under the sign for departures. John opened the privacy window. "Driver? Don't stop. Take the exit back north onto the Parkway. We're going to take a little side trip."

The cabby looked at the ever-increasing digits on his fare meter and shrugged. "North on the GW Parkway and then where, bud?"

"Cross over on the Key Bridge and then go north along the C&O Canal."

Leslie opened her mouth to speak but didn't. She leaned back against the seat and closed her eyes. When she opened them again, she said, "All right. What now?"

"Sit tight for ten minutes and you'll have your answers. Don't worry. I know there's a backup flight that will work for us." He needed the ten minutes to rehearse what he was going to say to Leslie. And he wanted to use words which would have the most shock value.

*   *   *

"Keep the meter running. We won't be long," John said to the cab driver. He opened the door and stepped out. Leslie didn't move. He leaned back inside and said, "Come on, follow me." He turned and walked down a grass path between two rows of white marble headstones.

He heard Leslie climb out and close the door. He also heard the cabbie mumble, "Thank God it's broad daylight. Graveyards give me the creeps."

John was careful, but still made silent apologies to those on whose graves he might have stepped. Tulip Hill Cemetery, out here along the old C&O Canal towpath, had recovered from the cold, bleak conditions of December, when he had last visited for Nicole's birthday. If only it had snowed that day. She loved fresh snow. She used to say it transformed the world into a quiet, peaceful, happy place.

He hadn't been counting headstones but knew about how far to go. He stopped, turned left, and waited for Leslie to catch up. When she arrived, he pointed at the marker in front of him and said, "Read that. Out loud."

John watched her. She hesitated long enough to have scanned it silently, but she finally said, "Catherine Marie . . . Martin. 10th January 1976 -12th March 1990. Dearly Beloved Daughter of—" She inhaled deeply. "—John and Nicole."

"Now read the one next to it. On the right."

She looked at the larger, matching marker. "Oh, no. I'm so sorry—"

"Read it!" he said.

"Nicole Antoine Martin, 20th December 1950 – 16th May 1990. Beloved wife. Best friend. Soulmate. My—" Leslie's voice cracked. She sniffled. "I just can't, John."

He glared at her.

"My love will never die."

John ignored his blurry eyes and his own sniffles. "Listen carefully, Leslie. I don't like telling this story, so I'm going to make it short." He swept his hand over the two graves. "Carlos Alvarado is responsible for this. He supplied drugs to kids, including one especially bad batch of crack cocaine. In Tucson. Two teenagers died. One of them was my daughter Catherine. After that, my wife Nicole sank into a deep depression and died two months later. Doctors say a blood clot broke loose and gave her a fatal stroke. I say her heart was broken—" He choked up and had to whisper the rest of the words. "Broken by the loss of her only child."

He reached down and pulled a weed growing near the base of Nicole's headstone. "In my life, Leslie, the score is Alvarado three, John Martin zero. Cathy, Nicole and now Hank Carter. So, remember this. I am very sorry for your loss. But you are not the only one who's lost a loved one. And—" He had to struggle for control. "Unlike you, I'll never run out of tears." He turned and walked away. That last jibe had been a little cruel. He should apologize. But the damage had been done. He had learned long ago that words are like bullets—once you fire them, you can't pull them back.

When he got back to the cab, he said, "To the airport, please."

Chapter 11

Leslie was roused from sleep by the pilot's announcement that they were on the descent into Tucson. Arrival time would be 3:40 p.m. The weather was clear—no surprise there—with light winds and a temperature of 75 degrees. She looked out over the right wing and saw that they were going to land on Runway 29. Thanks to John's good luck, or good planning in seat selection, she was treated to a good view of the Santa Catalina mountains, twenty miles north of the city. Mount Lemmon's 9,000-plus-foot peak still had a little snow. Just north of their flight path was the Boneyard, acres and acres of mothballed military aircraft adjacent to her home base, Davis-Monthan.

Although she flew out here on an almost daily basis, she was always too busy flying her own airplane to enjoy the view. Today she had the luxury of staring down at what must be thousands of airplanes stored at AMARC, the Air Force's acronym for Aerospace Maintenance and Regeneration Center. Most pilots just called it the Boneyard, where planes went to die. Some dated back to World War II, but she could see long rows of modern fighter jets, bombers, and cargo planes. Some, she knew, would be cut up for scrap. Others would be sold to foreign countries. Some might even be called back to active service if international conditions dictated.

Her stomach growled. The first-class meal of lasagna and asparagus had been good, but not enough to satisfy her hunger.

John's promise of a sumptuous brunch at that fancy hotel in DC had really gotten her taste buds aroused. She had been *so* ready to splurge on a decadent omelet, or French toast, or bacon. Or all the above. Her belly churned again. She glanced over at John. Had he heard all that growling?

Evidently not. His eyes were still closed. His chest rose and fell with slow, even breathing. After the inflight meal, he had reclined his seat, folded his hands over his lap and closed his eyes. He hadn't moved since. His face, thank God, had lost the angry, tight-jawed look that had made her think twice about asking more questions. He looked peaceful now. It was obvious that, five years after burying his wife and child, he was still grieving. Who could blame him?

Leslie's instinct told her that John's marriage had been a good one. He seemed to be a solid man, one who loved well and mated for life. The words engraved on his late wife's tombstone verified that. After she had read those, and seen his reaction, something had triggered the urge to comfort him, to hug him, to tell him it was all right. She had held back, though, certain that touching him would be inappropriate, as if she were asking him to cheat on his wife.

Out of respect for his grief, she had bottled up all further questions about the MiGs. She had hoped to ask them during this flight, but it looked like he wouldn't wake up in time. The flight attendant came by one last time and reminded her to raise her seat back and so forth. The landing gear clunked down, and the engines revved up to approach power setting. John opened his eyes long enough to raise his seat back, coughed once and went back to sleep without so much as a glance in her direction.

John's friend Whitaker was scheduled to land half an hour after their arrival. The plan was for her to take a taxi to retrieve her Jeep. John would take Whitaker to visit his aunt, who evidently was an Alzheimer's patient in a local senior center.

She'd use that time to go home and shower. She had seen enough of Alzheimer's during her grandmother's losing struggle with that terrible disease. At 1730, they'd meet at the base chapel for Hank Carter's memorial service. God, another one. Bobby's had been only seven days ago.

Leslie leaned against the window, trying to see the Customs Service ramp at the west end of D-M. There was too much glare from the sun. Yesterday (was it only yesterday?) she had fought this same glare as she bounced along in the back seat of John's T-Bird, two thousand feet above the desert floor, on the way to Ajo. It had been uncomfortable being a passenger, along for the ride and not in control of things. What a day! She shuddered at the memory of smoking wreckage, the bullet-riddled engine cowling, and Eric Briggs's shouted orders for her to surrender her badge and weapon.

Things weren't getting any better. She still wasn't in control. John was. Back in DC, in front of that hotel, the set of his jaw and the cold look in his eyes meant he had a plan. Well, she'd just stick as close to him as possible until she found out what he was up to.

Chapter 12

John met Whitaker at baggage claim. While giving him a big hug, he whispered, "Just go along with what I say next. Trust me. I've got a good reason." He unwrapped his arms from Whitaker and faced Leslie.

"Leslie Olsen, this is Jim Whitaker, the world's best crew chief."

They shook hands.

Leslie said, "I'm sorry about your aunt. I know what it's like to have a loved one with Alzheimer's."

"Ah . . . yes. Alzheimer's is bad. But thank you for your sympathy. I'm pleased to meet you."

Good old Whit. John breathed a sigh of relief. "Well, look," he said. "You two will have a chance to talk later at the memorial service, but for now, Whit, why don't you wait here until your bag comes out. I'll walk Leslie out to the taxi stand. She needs to catch a cab over to D-M and retrieve her car. I'll meet you right back here in a couple minutes."

After Leslie's taxi had driven away, John hurried back to baggage claim. Whitaker stood next to his well-worn, Air Force-issue canvas A-3 bag. His arms were folded across his chest. He said, "My aunt? In a nursing home? Alzheimer's? You are pushing your luck, my not-so-truthful friend. What is wrong with you? Why were you in such a hurry to get rid of that woman—who is rather cute, by the way?"

"I am not trying to get rid of her," John said. "We're going to see her in an hour or so. I just need some time alone with you."

"That's very flattering, John. But, why? Something tells me I won't like the answer."

"We're going to take a little ride. I'll explain when we get there."

Where to?" Whitaker asked.

"To D-M, Davis-Monthan Air Force Base, six miles north of here. Actually, the east end of the base. Ever been to the Boneyard?"

"The what?"

John said, "Let's go. I'll fill you in on the way." He led the way to airport parking.

During the twenty-minute drive to D-M's main gate, John told Whitaker about the Boneyard but was vague on the reason for their visit. "There's an impressive variety and number of aircraft stored out there in the Boneyard, which is officially called MASDC . . . no, wait. I think they recently changed the name to AMARC. Can't remember what that stands for, but the bottom line is, it's a storage area for military airplanes.

"You gotta love those acronyms, right?"

John nodded. "You've never been here before?"

"Nope. I guess I heard about it, but I didn't really know where it was. Just someplace in the desert southwest."

"Wow," Whitaker said as they passed long rows of mothballed jet fighters. "There must be about twenty of 'em in each row. Navy F-14s, and look, there's some F-18s. Hell, they're still almost new! A-4s and—oh, now here's some Air Force fighters. F-15s! Damn!"

John took his eyes off the road for a glance at the aircraft. Sadly, some of the Eagles had been stripped of critical parts and would never fly again. Several had flaps or rudders missing. Others lacked a wheel or a main landing gear strut and leaned to one side, supported by tall concrete posts, as if they were crippled war veterans who had lost legs in combat. The row he wanted was just ahead. He slowed, pulled off onto the right shoulder and parked just a few hundred yards short of the building where he used to work.

Whitaker said, "Why are we stopping?"

John pointed to the row of jets across the road.

"Holy shit!" Whitaker jumped out of the Explorer and was halfway across the road before John got his door open.

"Vipers!" Whitaker shouted. "F-16s in the Boneyard? I had no idea."

They both stood at the chain-link fence in silence, as if they were visiting a religious shrine. Three rows of battleship-gray F-16s, noses lined up with military precision, were parked in the desert, their noses at ninety-degree angles to the asphalt road between each row. The scene brought John back to a time when he had walked the tarmac between similar rows of younger, more active F-16s, engines whining at an annoying, painful pitch during start or taxi. Unlike today's quiet scene, the view in his memory was filled with the chest-rattling boom of afterburners lighting off, sending F-16s rocketing into the sky, pushed by deafening, yellow-blue afterburner plumes. At night, it had been like watching flying blowtorches.

John used one hand to shield his eyes from the blinding late afternoon sun glare off noses and canopies covered in bright white latex preservative. Thank God none of these had yet been cannibalized. They stood proudly on their own landing gear, tires still inflated, all pieces intact. He didn't know how long the F-16s had been here. They all sat quietly now. If they had souls, though, they would be crying out for a chance to fly again, to feel the speed, to be lifted into the air by wind beneath their wings.

"Do you know anything about the history of this place?" John asked.

"Nope."

"It's been here since right after World War II. Five thousand acres of mothballed airplanes, about two thousand of them at last count. Everything from World War II transports, little Vietnam-era prop-job Cessna Bird Dogs, giant B-52 nuclear bombers, and everything in between. Some they cut up for scrap, some they cannibalize for parts, and some get sold to foreign countries. However . . ." John pointed at the rows of F-16s. "Some are very well-maintained, essentially in flyable storage."

"How come you know so much about the Boneyard?" Whitaker asked.

"See that large building at the end of the road? In my F-4 days, I used to work over there; it's the wing headquarters building. Back before my time, D-M was a big Strategic Air Command bomber base. That building was called the Mole Hole. See those things that look like tunnels leading down? That's exactly what they are. Mole holes. Entrances to underground, nuclear-blast-proof quarters for SAC B-47 and B-52 crews. There's a big concrete apron over there, nicknamed the Christmas Tree because of its shape when seen from the air, where the bombers sat alert, right here at the east end of the runway. The plan was, if the Russians attacked, the crews would run out of those tunnels, jump into their bombers, and have a very short taxi to the runway. Then they were supposed to take off, fly over the North Pole and drop nukes on the bad guys. When the bombers moved to other bases, SAC and TAC battled it out over who would rule this base, and TAC won. The Mole Hole got converted to the 355th Tactical Fighter Wing headquarters.

"Anyway, back to the Boneyard story. I used to bicycle to work out here. On the opposite side of the road from the Mole Hole, there's a big gate leading to the Boneyard and a big parking apron where they process airplanes into—and out of—storage. In the morning I would see them pull an old C-47 transport, or an A-4 jet, or whatever, out onto that apron. By noon they'd have the engines, or engine, running. A couple hours later, when I pedaled off to where the F-4s were parked and suited up to fly a mission, I'd see that same airplane take off—the one they had just pulled out of the Boneyard—on its way to delivery in some faraway place."

Whitaker said, "How do they get them up and running so fast?"

"Glad you asked that question. One day I walked over and talked to some of the mechanics about their procedures to resurrect planes from storage. I thought I might use the same techniques for storing sports cars or private airplanes. And I learned a lot."

Whitaker reached up and hooked his fingers into the fence. He leaned forward and squinted at the rows of F-16s.

John chuckled.

"What?"

"Nothing," John said. "I was just noticing how hard you're squeezing that fence. I half-expected you to climb it, vault over the three strands of barbed wire at the top and start polishing the first airplane in line."

The old mechanic whispered, as if he didn't want to wake the sleeping jets. "Man, I'd give anything to get a closer look at those aircraft."

John took a step closer to Whitaker. Should he ask him now or let him reminisce a little longer, let him relive some of his Air Force adventures? It had to be now, before this sentimental moment slipped away.

"You may get the chance." John felt his heart beating against his chest. Four, five, six heavy beats. He swallowed hard and hoped he would say the right thing. "Whit, I want you to help me steal one of these jets."

"Say what?" The fence rattled as Whitaker pulled his hands off it and spun to face him. "You want me to do *what*?"

"Well, not steal, really. I just want to borrow one for a week or two."

Whitaker's head tilted, his eyes widened, and he began panting. His expression reminded John of a dog trying to understand human speech.

"You can't be serious." Whitaker stepped closer and stared at him. He leaned to his left, then to the right and finally got right in his face, like a drill sergeant inspecting the closeness of his shave. He settled back on his heels and said, "Holy shit. You *are* serious. Damn, I don't believe it. Why steal an F-16? What the hell are you gonna do with it?"

John hesitated. How could he sum it up in one sentence? Maybe if he just started talking it would all come out okay. "An arrogant Mexican drug lord is using MiG-21s to shoot down American drug surveillance planes, right here in Arizona. And, our own government is too wimpy, or too incompetent to do anything about it, so—"

"Wait. Is that how Hank Carter died?"

"Yeah, but he's not the only one. The woman you met, Leslie? Her brother was also a Customs Service pilot. He and his crew were the first victims, a week before Hank's plane went down."

"Two shootdowns?" Whitaker said. "You're sure about this?"

"You know me, Whit. I do my homework. I've got evidence to prove it. Not only that, but it looks like the drug lord in question is Carlos Alvarado, the man whose bad cocaine killed my daughter."

"Uh, oh. I see where this is going. It's been a long time since I've heard that name. But I can still remember the newspaper headline: *Air Force Lieutenant Colonel arrested for assault on drug kingpin.* Ruined your career, just when you were on the promotion list."

"Career? Hell, that was the last thing on my mind. The man got off scot-free after killing my daughter with bad dope and killing my wife with grief!" He hadn't meant to shout, but his words echoed off the nearby F-16s.

Whitaker stepped back a little. He looked frightened, or embarrassed, or both. "I'm trying to see it your way, my friend," he said. "But stealing an airplane? There's got to be—"

"I've got to go after him. After all he's done to my family, now he's killed Hank, Leslie's brother and four others. Each Citation carries a crew of three."

"How do you know the government's not going to hunt Alvarado down?"

John said, "Leslie and I went to Washington and talked to someone pretty high up, someone I used to respect and trust. But, not after today. That person said the whole thing is being covered up. The investigation has been delayed for political reasons—national security, blah, blah, et cetera, et cetera. By the time they get off their fat asses, the trail will be too cold to find Hank's killers. So, it's got to be me. I am going to fight back the only way I know how." He jerked a thumb over his shoulder toward the F-16s. "With one of those."

Whitaker turned toward the row of sleeping warplanes. He looked up and down the road on which they had arrived. He looked over at the Mole Hole, the approach end of Runway 30 and at the gate leading to the Boneyard. "Let me get this straight. We are in the middle of a big-ass Air Force base. You want me to sneak in there, get one of those jets running after God-knows-how-many years of storage and . . . then what? What are you gonna do with it?"

"I've got a plan for that."

"Yeah, I'll bet you do. But . . . I just don't know about this. Several words come to mind. 'Impossible' is just one of them. Then there's the 'illegal' and 'jail time' words. Need I go on?"

John decided to play his trump card. "Oh, I forgot to mention one thing. We are not going to steal just any F-16. Take a look way down at the end of the third row. You might have to stand over there to see the tail number."

Whitaker moved to his right and squinted. "Still can't see it. My eyes ain't as good as yours, otherwise I'd be the effing pilot and you'd be *my* effing crew chief."

"Okay then, you'll just have to take my word for it. It's Three-Six-Eight."

"Three-Six-Eight!" My jet—uh, I mean, *our* jet? No shit? The one with my name painted on the canopy rail? Damn, John, you and me and Three-Six-Eight, we were quite a team."

Whitaker was silent for quite some time. John gave him a minute to relive the good old days, back at Nellis, where he had been the crew chief on a brand-new F-16A, tail number 79-00368, and John had been its first pilot. By some incredible coincidence and, John was proud to recall, some serious behind-the-scenes manipulations, the three of them had all been transferred down to Luke AFB near Phoenix. From there, after an unprecedented four years of being together, Three-Six-Eight had been transferred to another base, Whitaker had been reassigned to Germany, and John had stayed at Luke as an F-16 Instructor Pilot.

"But that don't change the facts of life," Whitaker said. He looked down the row of jets again. "Let's say I humor you and agree that it's possible to get Three-Six-Eight out of here. Where you gonna take it? What about fuel and hydraulic fluid and—God—hydrazine for the EPU? What about weapons? She's not good for anything without weapons."

"I've got plans for all that," John said.

"I'll bet you do. You always had a plan for everything."

This was not entirely true. He had forgotten about hydrazine, which powered one of the emergency electrical systems. Hydrazine was a toxic liquid used in rocket engines. Very dangerous and very hard to get.

The old crew chief looked down at the ground and fell silent.

John took several steps away to give Whitaker time to think.

"Hey!" Whitaker said. "What if I say no? You got a plan for that?"

The answer was no, but John didn't say so. He looked Whitaker in the eye and waited.

"I've got a museum full of airplanes that need maintenance. I can't just—"

"I've got that covered," John said. "I've already emailed Rusty Small. Remember him? Your old assistant crew chief at Nellis? He's agreed to go up to Olympia and cover for you. You yourself said he's almost as good as you are. I'll pay his expenses."

"Yeah, well, how do I explain disappearing on such short notice?"

"Tell Rowe that you've had a death in the family, and you need to stay for a week or so to tie up some loose ends. Hank was almost family to you, right? Back in the old days at least." He felt no shame in reminding Whitaker that, years ago, Hank and John had helped Whitaker through some life and career-threatening personal problems. He needed this man, needed him badly.

Whitaker walked back to the fence and stared at the F-16s. His narrow but muscular shoulders rose and fell. He mumbled something.

John hadn't heard it. "Say again?"

"I said, 'Hank helped me fix my life.' He didn't even know me that well, like you did at the time. But he had such good advice and, you know, in Hank's crazy way, he pretty much ordered me to get my shit together."

John looked out at the runway and chewed his lip. There was nothing more he could say. The decision would have to come from Whitaker's heart.

Chapter 13

Whitaker took a deep breath and said, "John, if someone didn't know you, they'd say you're crazy. They'd say there's no way you could get a jet out of there. And no way you could perform a mission with it." He waggled a finger at him. "But I know you. You really do have it all figured out, don't you?" He blinked his eyes and shook his head. "Dammit, you think I want to get dragged into this along with you? In the military, I didn't have a choice. But now? If I was smart, I'd just walk away."

Whitaker ground his shoe against the gravel and dirt. "But God help me, I can't. Some son of a bitch kills your daughter, drives your wife into fatal depression, and ruins your career. And then shoots down two Customs Service jets, kills Hank and how many others? Five? He should pay."

John expelled the breath he had been holding during Whitaker's speech. He relaxed his leg muscles; his knees had been locked as if he had been standing at attention. Whit hadn't exactly said yes, but he hadn't said no either.

With surprising quickness, Whitaker puffed up his chest, raised himself up to as tall as a five-seven man could and got his face so close that John could smell his after-shave.

"I'm not on your team yet, Lieutenant Colonel John Martin. I'm going to sit you down and make you tell me every single detail. If I like it, I'm in. If not, well . . ." Whitaker stepped back. "Details," he said. "I need details. How long have you been planning this, anyway?"

After a quick glance at his watch, John smiled at him and said, "Oh, a little less than twelve hours."

"Great," Whitaker said. "So, you're making this up as you go. That is not a good way to win my confidence, John."

"Seriously, Whit, I was walking down the sidewalk in DC when the whole plan just popped into my brain, clear as day, with every detail mapped out." He looked through the fence at the row of F-16s. Long shadows cast by their vertical tails had transformed the scene into a dizzying collage of canopies, noses, knife-edged wings and drooping horizontal stabilizers. Some were in full sun; others were partially in the shadows, the dark half almost invisible, as if it they had been cut off by a giant guillotine.

"All right," he said. "You want details? Trust me, Whit, I've done my homework on these F-16s. Three-Six-Eight and seventeen other retired A-models were sold to Pakistan. The program was called Peace Leopard, but delivery was put on hold due to politics. Something about Pakistan developing nukes. Our government didn't approve of that, so they stopped the sale. But here's the kicker. Because those eighteen airplanes are still technically 'sold,' and paid for by the Pakistanis, they must be maintained in the highest status of storage possible."

"That's crazy. We're never going to give those aircraft to Pakistan," Whitaker said.

"You and I know that because we have common sense. But remember, it's the U.S. government we are talking about here. Also, I have heard that Israel has its eyes on buying these jets. That might explain why they are maintained so well."

"How do you know all this stuff.?"

"Easy," John said. "It's all in *Aviation Week* magazine. My personal opinion is no one has a clue what to do with these F-16s. Meanwhile, they remain in 'Flyable Hold,' AMARC's term for the highest state of readiness of all the mothballed jets. Every forty-five days, each of them gets towed to the trim pad for an engine run, servicing, and a full exercise of all major systems."

"I'll be damned," Whitaker said.

"Next, they fill the fuel tanks with a preservative, a mixture of fuel and oil, and run the engine to coat all the tanks, fuel lines and bearings. Then it's drained. All we have to do is pump in some jet fuel and—"

"Hold up a minute. You haven't even told me how we're going to get in there, let alone pump fuel."

John held up a hand. "You're right. Let's drive down closer to that gate I pointed out earlier. You will see how easy it would be for me to taxi right out that gate and onto the runway. After you get Three-Six-Eight all serviced up, of course."

* * *

Fifteen minutes later, they left the parking area of the Mole Hole, which was just a hundred yards from the Boneyard's locked exit gate. John's mouth was dry, and his throat felt scratchy from all the talking. He had identified critical roads, explained how they and their equipment would get in, and the short taxi route to the runway. Whitaker had listened intently and had not asked a single question.

"Not much security out here these days, is there?" Whitaker said. "That guard shack looks abandoned." He pointed at the windowless wooden hut out on the old SAC Christmas Tree ramp area.

"Nope. No one uses this ramp anymore. The gate behind that shack leads right to the runway. The only time it's opened is when airplanes taxi in and out of the Boneyard."

"Can we drive over there and get a look at how it's locked? From here it just looks like a chain and a padlock."

"I'd rather not. Not right now, anyway," John said. "The control tower monitors what goes on out here and I'd rather not attract any attention. We'll come back with binoculars and examine it from a safe distance."

They had just passed the base hospital when John asked, "Well, now that you've seen the Boneyard and heard the plan, what do you think?"

"You really want to know? Lemme think." Whitaker rubbed his chin. "What I think is, I should take you over to the base hospital's psycho ward and check you in. But you know what, they wouldn't believe my story. I can see it now: *'Hi, ma'am. This my friend John. He's got delusions. He thinks he can steal an F-16 from the Boneyard, fly it to some secret place, arm it up, and blow away some MiGs in Mexico.'* Hell, they'd probably lock *me* up right along with you."

His old friend's lips were pursed, and his jaw was clamped down hard. John couldn't tell if that tirade had been serious or just a heavy dose of Whitaker's trademark cynicism. What was he going to do if Whitaker threatened to turn him in, to expose the plot? Kidnap him? The skinny bastard would be hell to keep tied up.

Whitaker looked out at the pink horizon and said, "What scares me is, I probably deserve a room in that psycho ward too. Why? Because, dammit, I think your plan would actually work. Given the right crew chief, of course." He looked out his window and mumbled something.

"Say again?"

Whitaker leaned his head against the headrest and gave him the briefest of smiles. "I said, 'It looks like I'm coming out of retirement.' Back on the line as Three-Six-Eight's crew chief. God help me."

John grinned and slapped Whitaker on the shoulder. "Thanks, Whit. This means a lot to me."

"Now, get me some food. I'm starved. Then we need to talk details."

"Didn't you eat on the way down here?"

"Hell, no, thanks to you," Whitaker said. "You roused me out of bed on my day off, told me to burn up the road to the airport—no time for food up there, of course—and all they had on the flight down was peanuts and pretzels. Why? Are you too cheap to buy me a meal?"

"No, no, nothing like that," John said. "It's just that the memorial service for Hank starts in about fifteen minutes. That was my excuse for getting you down here, remember?"

"Damn, okay, let's go, then. If I pass out from malnutrition, or anemia, or whatever, it'll be on you. After the funeral, I swear to God, you'd better find me some real food. No salads, no bean sprouts, none of that shit. Some meat. Fried chicken, chicken fried steak. Deep-fried shrimp would do. A big side order of French fr—"

"Yeah, yeah, yeah," John said as he pulled into the chapel's parking lot. I get the picture."

Chapter 14

Hank would have enjoyed his memorial service. It had started on time, and it had been brief. These were two of Hank's top priorities. He also would have been proud of the eulogies, especially the one delivered by his son Adam, who had flown in from South Carolina. Adam had summarized his father's younger years, his distinguished military career, and his love for flying. Eric Briggs from the Customs Service had added a few words about Hank's contributions to the drug surveillance mission. The chaplain recited a few prayers, led the mourners in a hymn, and gave his final blessing. Everyone, including a large contingent of Customs Service officers in full dark-blue dress uniforms—Leslie included—was back outside by 6:30 p.m.

Hank's family was a little under-represented at this event, but that would be rectified when his body reached the Carter family cemetery in South Carolina. His mother was here, though. The poor lady, a widow, had held it together until the casket—which had remained closed, of course—had been rolled down the center aisle. Adam had done his best to give her comfort, but John had noticed the kid was dealing with his own tears.

John needed to pay his respects to Hank's mother and son. Due to their side trip to Boneyard, he and Whit had entered the chapel at the last moment. There had been no chance to talk to Mrs. Carter or Adam beforehand. He'd approach them in a few minutes. For now, he wanted to get away from the crowd.

"Come on, Whit," he said. "Let's go over there. We'll get a better view of the flyby." He led Whitaker to the east side of the parking lot and began searching the sky. "There they are. Do you see 'em?"

Whitaker shook his head.

"Look above the right side of the Officers' Club, that building right across the street. It's a flight of four Citations." Of course, it would have to be four, but John wondered where they got the other two airplanes. As far as he knew, only two remained at Tucson. Maybe they had called in a couple from Texas. The flight, in perfect fingertip formation, was in a steep-banked, descending left turn, lining up for their run on the chapel. Their white paint, illuminated by the late afternoon sun, made them easy to see.

"Got 'em now," Whitaker said. "They're coming pretty fast. Are they supposed to be that low? Any lower and they're going to take off the steeple of this old chapel."

"You know what they're about to do, right?"

Whitaker's reply was drowned out by the wail of eight jet engines at full power. The rest of the crowd went silent and looked east at the four straight-winged Citations screaming at top speed toward the chapel. A split-second before reaching the chapel, the number three Citation pulled up and out of the formation in an elegant, steep climb. The remaining three jets continued straight ahead, still at low altitude, preserving the space left by number three.

Whitaker said, "Missing Man Formation. Pretty nice job."

"Very nice," John said. He had seen all too many of these tributes to fallen aviators. "I just never expected to see it done for Hank."

As the Citations flew away, the wild scream of their engines decreased in both pitch and volume, like a whistle-blowing locomotive passing at high speed.

John looked back at the crowd and saw Hank's mother. With one hand shielding her eyes from the sun, she was following the flight of Citations as they sped away. John wondered if she saw the irony. The empty space in that formation would soon be filled as number three rejoined the flight for landing. But the void in her heart would never be filled. Her only son was gone.

During the flyby, the six pallbearers had stood at attention next to Hank's bronze-colored casket. They picked it up, rolled it into the hearse, and shut the rear door. Five of the six, Customs Service pilots, dispersed into the crowd. They looked sharp, wearing white gloves, impeccable dark blue dress uniforms, black belts, and dark-blue, round-brimmed campaign hats—the kind worn by drill instructors. The sixth man, Adam, walked over to join his mother.

Whitaker said, "Question, John. I thought you told me Adam was following in his dad's and his grandfather's footsteps as a cadet at The Citadel. But that's an enlisted man's Air Force dress blue uniform he's wearing. And he's got staff sergeant's stripes on his sleeves."

"You got me. Maybe we'll find out more if we go over and say hello."

John inhaled the fresh air of a warm spring afternoon, but he took no pleasure in that or the developing Arizona-standard gorgeous sunset. In the west, the higher popcorn-shaped white clouds in the bright blue sky had begun to turn pink in the late afternoon sun. Hummingbirds buzzed and scolded the humans who interfered with their feeding on the chapel's nectar-rich flowers. All this was a very pleasant scene, unless you were Mrs. Carter, on your way to the airport with a casket containing the charred remains of your only son. Or Adam, who had lost his dad. Lost his role model.

Thinking about Adam triggered a flashback for John. Ten years ago, he had knocked on Hank's door at the BOQ at a remote air base in Korea where pilots served "unaccompanied" tours, meaning their families had to stay behind in the States. Phone calls and letters were the only way to stay in touch. Hank had opened the door while on the phone with his son Adam and had motioned for him to have a seat. A telephone connection to home was a rare and precious thing back then, so Hank kept talking to his son. John had listened to Hank tell Adam to buck up and be the man of the family until Hank's tour was over. It was the style and emotion of Hank's goodbye to Adam that had impressed him. Hank had said the expected words, the "I love you," phrase that most people say. But Hank had added, in a much deeper and emphatic voice, "Adam, I really mean it. I *really* love you. Deep in my heart. Always will." That was Hank. You knew it when he was serious about something.

The chaplain, Mrs. Carter and Adam were having a discussion, so John waited at a polite distance. Adam looked his way and, after a second or two to process the sight, his face brightened. He left his mother's side and hurried over to them.

Adam Carter's teenage acne was long gone. He was no longer a skinny, uncoordinated kid but a grown-up, fully developed young man in a perfectly fitted dress blue Air Force uniform with shiny buttons and badges. He moved with his father's quiet confidence. When he was about six feet away, he stopped, snapped to attention, and saluted.

John had no choice but to return the salute.

The boy—no, he was a man now—lowered his salute with a crack of his hand slapping against his pants leg. "Thanks for coming, Lieutenant Colonel Martin. I wasn't sure if you had made it. I called you but it went to voice mail."

Adam didn't need know that he had already been on his way to Tucson when his dad had died. "When I heard the news, I flew down right away. Oh, and Adam, I'm a civilian now. You don't have to salute or call me Lieutenant Colonel. You can call me John."

"No sir, no way, with all due respect. I grew up knowing you as an officer. My dad wouldn't like it if I used your first name."

John couldn't argue with that. He said, "This is Jim . . . Chief Master Sergeant Jim Whitaker, Air Force, Retired. He knew your dad back in the eighties."

Adam reached out and shook Whitaker's hand.

"You look good, Adam, "John said. "But I've got a ques—"

"Hey, that's a Four-Three-One badge!" Whitaker said. "Are you—"

"Yes," Adam said, pointing to the silver aircraft maintenance badge on his chest. "I'm a wrench-bender now, an F-16 crew chief, and I love it." He held up his hand. "I know what you're going to say, Colonel Martin. What happened to the Citadel? I wasn't ready for college, sir. I may never be."

"I'll be damned," Whitaker said. "I was a Four-Three-One my whole career. Jet mechanic—best specialty code in the whole damn Air Force. Crewed F-16s for twelve years. That's how I met John here, and your dad. Where are you stationed?"

"Shaw Air Force Base. It's close to home, which was helpful to grandma, what with grandpa being sick. Now that he's gone and—" Adam glanced at the hearse. "With dad gone too, it's even more important to be in South Carolina, close to her." He looked over his shoulder at Mrs. Carter, who was shaking hands with the chaplain. I'd better get back to my grandma. Will I see you at the wake?"

"Haven't heard about it," John said.

"The Customs Service guys set it up. An informal thing at a local bar, Rita's, which they tell me is just up the street from the main gate. Seven o'clock. Can you make it?"

"Of course." If it was for Hank, he'd be there. John looked at his watch. They had about half an hour. "First, I've got to get Whit—Chief Whitaker—something to eat."

"No need for a separate trip," Adam said. "I hear they have great food at Rita's."

"They do," said a voice from behind them. It was Leslie. She walked up to the group and said to John, "I got worried. I didn't see you and Chief Whitaker come in."

Whitaker said, "Our, ah, little side trip took a little longer than planned. We came in just as the service was beginning and had to sit in back. Uh, ma'am, is there any way I can get you to call me, 'Whit?'"

Leslie agreed.

John said, "Leslie, have you met Adam yet?"

"Oh, yes. I met him and his grandmother before the service. I just came over to pay my respects to Mrs. Carter. I understand she's not going to Rita's."

"No," Adam said. "She's going to rest up at a hotel until it's time to leave for the airport. It's one of those late-night redeye flights."

John narrowed his eyes.

Adam noticed this and said, "Don't worry. She's not going to be alone. The chaplain is sending over some ladies with cookies and tea and so forth. Keep her company for a few hours. Know what I mean?"

"So, shall we all go over and talk to Mrs. Carter?" Leslie asked.

No one seemed excited about that uncomfortable task. John rehearsed some final words of sympathy for Hank's mother. This was the part he hated. Nothing he could say would erase her pain. She wouldn't really hear him; she'd just nod politely and get teary. He would pat her gently on the back, maybe give her an awkward hug. He would silently curse life for being unfair and wish for a magic wand to wave, bringing Hank back to life.

He really wanted to tell her that he was going to find Hank's killer and bring him to justice, which, in John's mind, meant blowing him and his little MiG out of the sky. The chaplain would frown on that last description; it sounded too much like revenge—most definitely a sin.

"Let's go," he said. He walked off toward Mrs. Carter and the chaplain, who by this time were standing very close to the hearse. Hank's body was in there. He would never again trade good-natured insults with Hank, sip whiskey with him, or relive their flying experiences. All this grieving was getting to him, messing with his mind, and possibly affecting his tactical decisions. He recalled a phrase from his Air Force fighter pilot mentors: *Don't get emotional in combat. It will cloud your judgment.*

Three sets of footsteps shuffled along behind him. John didn't need to look back at their faces to see their expressions. None of them wanted to do this either, but they would.

Hank's mother had long ago lost her battle against grey hair, but she was about the same trim size that he remembered from long ago. Her posture was erect, and she wore the black dress with an easy dignity. She smiled bravely through the introductions, an awkward hug from Whitaker, a warmer one from Leslie and John's own—during which he had murmured his best several comforting words. The skin beneath her eyes was puffy and dark. Although her eyes lacked all the sparkle he had seen during previous meetings, she was surprisingly attentive for a woman who had suffered so much. Life had dealt her two cruel blows in less than a year. First, her husband, a wiry World War II/Korean War fighter pilot, had succumbed to pneumonia. Now her only son was dead.

He said, "If there's anything I can ever do . . ."

"Of course, dear. Thank you. I know you were his best friend." She attempted a smile, but it soon faded as the hearse driver started its engine. She looked at it and had to wipe away more tears. She shook her head. "You know, a mother should never have to do this for her son."

The hearse pulled away from the curb. Adam came over and took his grandmother's hand.

"We should go now, grandma."

John noticed the care with which Adam guided Mrs. Carter. The tables had been turned. She had taken care of him when he was a tiny baby. Now he was returning the favor.

She watched the hearse round the corner north of the chapel and disappear down a side street. That seemed to drive home reality to her. Hank was gone, literally gone from her life. She lost control, clutched Adam, and sobbed into his chest. She pounded ineffectively on his back with her small fists. Adam's steely blue eyes—definitely his dad's—glistened over. Rivulets of tears ran down his cheeks and fell onto Mrs. Carter's shoulders.

John swallowed hard. He lost another battle to keep his own eyes dry and turned away so the others wouldn't see. It wasn't so much for Hank. Hank was a pilot and knew all the risks. When the end had come, it had been quick. No, John decided, these tears are not for Hank but for those he had left behind. For his mother, his son, and the grandkids he would never bounce on his knee. For his faithful Black Labrador dog, who would never see his master again, and never know why.

There was no dignified way to wipe away the tears. John was about to use the back of his hand when a handkerchief appeared in his peripheral vision.

"Here," Leslie said. "It's already a little wet, but if you don't mind mixing tears . . . You don't have to turn around until you're ready."

John said, "Oh, what the hell." He faced Leslie and said, "Thank you." He dabbed his eyes with the small white handkerchief, which carried her flowery scent. He couldn't quite identify it.

"You'd better get your nose, too," she said. "Seriously, I don't mind."

He shook his head, made a half-hearted chuckle, and wiped his nose. "Does this make us blood brothers or something?" He sighed. "I mean, brother-sister? No that's not right either . . ."

"Stop," she said. "Just give me that hanky back. I'm probably going to need it. They're driving away." She held out her hand.

Mrs. Carter and Adam waved to them as they passed by in a black limo.

John put the handkerchief back in her hand just in time.

"Dammit, John, why do good people have to die?" She sobbed. Her chest heaved. She buried her face in the handkerchief.

John had a decision to make. Hold her? Don't hold her? He followed his instinct. He stepped forward and pulled her close. She cried into his chest while he squeezed her and said, "I don't know, Leslie. I truly don't know." He didn't mind that she took a long time to cry herself out. She had so many people to mourn. Her brother, Hank, and their crews.

Holding her felt good. Very good.

Chapter 15

John missed Rita's on the first try. When Whitaker stopped to catch his breath, John said, "Can you please hold your questions and let me drive?"

"I can't help it, man. Holy shit! We're going to steal an F-16. An effing F-16! Worth how much? Thirty-two million?"

"I'm not answering you until I find the place," John said. He slowed the car, made a U-turn, and headed back south on Craycroft Road. According to Leslie, Rita's was on the west side of Craycroft, just south of 29th Street, which was the next traffic light.

Whitaker grumbled, but the rapid-fire questions stopped.

"Anyway," John said, "the old A-models only cost $8.2 million."

"Oh, well then, no problem. Whitaker drew figures in his palm. "Let's see. I'll be in prison, so I'll get fired from my job at the flight museum. But my Air Force retirement pay is thirty-six grand per year. I could pay off my share of 8.2 million dollars in, what? About seven million years? Holy shit."

John tried to suppress a laugh. He failed. The poor old mechanic had said, 'holy shit' and, 'no way' at least five times since they had left the base. He did some quick mental arithmetic. The numbers were easy to work with. After 26 years of service, Whitaker was making about $3,000 per month in retired pay. "Look at it this way. In the scenario you suggest, you'd be in prison, so your lodging and meals would be paid for. Medical care too. If you split that eight-million-dollar debt with me, you could pay it off in only 114 years."

"Shit. I'm out here with a math genius who can't find his way around town. You used to live here, right? If you can't find Rita's, how you gonna find this mysterious airfield to land your —our—stolen F-16? Hey, slow down! There it is." He pointed to the Rita's sign.

Rita's street-side entrance and two large windows took up one third of a single-story white building. The other two occupants were a barber shop and a hardware store. John turned right and followed a sign to the parking lot, which was behind the bar. He opened his door and had one foot on the ground before he noticed that Whitaker wasn't moving.

"I've got some more questions," Whitaker said. "Ones you probably don't want me asking inside a crowded bar."

John pulled his leg back into the Explorer and shut the door.

"You never answered my question about the Security Police, or whoever patrols that fence. If you're wrong about their schedule, we're dead meat."

John nodded. "If I remember correctly, they drive the perimeter road every hour. We'll watch for a couple nights before we go in and confirm that. The first trip over the fence, we fuel it up and service the hydraulics. After the next patrol goes by, we go in with freshly charged batteries, peel the white latex preservative off the canopy and other surfaces, and pump up the JFS accumulators. Voilà! We're ready to go."

The leather seat squeaked as Whitaker twisted to face him. "Where the hell are we going to get F-16 batteries? Do you know how many different types and voltages—"

John shrugged. "I don't know. You're the mechanic. You'll have to find suitable substitutes."

Whitaker sighed. "You don't need me, man. You need a damn miracle. I am supposed to conjure up a crane, a welding rig, fuel tank, two types of hose of unknown damn length and something to pump fuel with. Not to mention an eighteen-wheeler truck. Oh, and I'm supposed to believe you can find 511 rounds of 20-millimeter ammo and a couple AIM-9 missiles? Good luck with that. Guess I don't have to tell you all this shit will be expensive as hell."

"Yeah, I know," John said. "Trust me. I can cover the expenses." Whitaker didn't need to know the details. The poor man would have a heart attack. Or punch him. "And I've already ordered the bullets. Missiles are kind of—no pun intended—up in the air right now, but I've got a backup plan."

"If you say so. I'm way out of my league talking about missiles and guns. But can you look me in the eye, with no bullshit, and tell me you can get them? You can arm up these jets for the mission?"

"The short answer is yes. Do you want all the details right now?"

Whitaker shook his head. "No. Later, maybe. I'll, ah, what do they call it on the TV lawyer programs? I'll stipulate that you have the money and can get weapons. Next question. How much time do we have to get all this ready?"

Thank God! Whitaker wasn't going to press him on missiles, bullets, or the money issue. None of his friends—not even Hank— knew the source, or the magnitude, of his wealth. Only two other men knew. One had died, back on that crazy day in November 1970. He closed his eyes in a futile attempt to shut out another flashback.

"Leave me behind," the wounded soldier said. He coughed up some blood. "Go. I'm gonna bleed to death anyway."

"Negative," John said. "You WILL NOT bleed out, Sergeant Landreau. That's an order. I didn't carry you all this way to have you die on me." He removed the last bandage from the pouch on

his belt. "Here. Hold this against your chest. I'll help you up. Our ride home is about to land."

Minutes later, John was airborne in the passenger seat of an Air America Pilatus Porter, looking over its long nose, which housed a powerful turboprop engine. He hoped the three-bladed prop could pull them over the tall karst ahead. Behind him was a large metal box secured to the floor with two cargo straps. Farther to the rear was Landreau, strapped to the floor in a prone position. He had lost consciousness but was still breathing. John had used a cargo strap and blanket as a tourniquet for Landreau's wound.

He looked over at the bearded pilot, who wore blue jeans, a soiled, torn t-shirt, and a combat vest that looked like NVA-issue. "Thanks," he said.

The pilot said, "I don't suppose you'd like to tell me what the fuck you've been doing up here, so far north?"

"Sorry. Unable."

The pilot grunted and concentrated on his flying. John knew better than to ask for his name, or where they were headed, so he tried to figure their direction of flight. The numbers on the crude "whiskey" compass were oscillating wildly, but if he averaged out the readings, they were headed southwest. Probably heading for the Laotian border, about seventy miles away. From there, they'd have to fly southwest to stay in Laos, then turn south to reach the nearest US base, Nakhon Phanom, just across the border, in Thailand.

John looked at the pilot again.

"Got it all figured out, kid?" the guy said.

"NKP?" John asked.

"Yup. But there's a little problem. I was in the middle of another mission when I got the call to pick you up. NKP is almost two hundred fifty miles away. About an hour and a half. The bad news? I've only got forty-five minutes of fuel left."

"John? Answer me, dammit!" Whitaker said. "How much time do we have?"

"Oh, sorry. I got distracted. Two days. No. Actually, three." John had lost track of time. "Today's Monday, right? We need to go in about midnight on Thursday. It'll be pitch dark. No moon. Perfect for getting into the Boneyard undetected. I'm giving us four hours to get the job done. By 0400 Friday, the full moon will have risen. That'll give me enough light to fly low, below radar coverage, and land without runway lights."

"Three days." Whitaker rubbed his chin. "Where are we gonna work? I need a place to work, a shop where—"

"It's all set up. I called ahead and rented a hangar at the Tucson airport. Had a real estate agent rent it in his company's name, not mine. They didn't seem to care whose name was on the lease after I promised them an immediate bank transfer for a month's rental, plus their commission. I've got a few companies in mind where you could find a fuel truck and an eighteen-wheeler. All you have to do is—"

"You over-confident sucker. Pretty sure I'd say yes, weren't you? When did you have time to do all this planning?"

"I had a couple hours to kill while waiting for the return flight from D.C. Finished up the last couple items using an inflight phone connected to the World Wide Web." He opened his door again. "We'd better get inside. Anything else?"

"You can get the web on an airliner? Damn, I need to get out more. One more thing. Okay, I've seen the layout out there at the Boneyard and, I admit, if we can get the jet started, you'd have a good chance of taking off before the cops got there. But I heard that they have a couple of air defense fighters stationed at D-M. Wouldn't they be able to scramble and chase you down?"

"They used to have F-106s on alert at Davis-Monthan. The idea was to protect our southern border from Soviet nuclear bombers. But, with the end of the Cold War, they closed that detachment. The closest air defense interceptors are at March Air Force Base, 340 miles away, in California." He pulled a folded piece of paper out of his back pocket and gave it to Whitaker. "Here's a list of what we need to get started. Names, addresses and phone numbers for the hangar, fuel truck and tractor-trailer rentals. You'll have to find the truck-mounted crane yourself. I listed a couple yards that specialize in surplus military aircraft parts. You might find the right kind of equipment at one of those places."

"What am I supposed to do? Just stroll in and say, "Hey, I'm about to steal an F-16 and I need some equipment? And what do I use for money?"

"Let's talk about that at breakfast tomorrow. We'll come up with some kind of cover story. You work for an air museum, right? That should help. Then we'll go to the bank and get you some cash." He slid out of the seat and made a note to call Tom Stevens before it got too late. He was going to take Stevens up on his offer to call anytime, twenty-four-seven, for his banking needs.

He needed to use the door for support as he pulled himself into a standing position. Was that stiffness and numbness in his back from fatigue, old age, or the bone-on-bone grinding of vertebrae—maybe a pinched nerve somewhere—that his neurosurgeon had warned him about? *"Within a year, you'll need a back brace,"* the doctor had said. *"So, take it easy. Back off on vigorous physical activity. And, of course, further flying is out of the question."*

John had disregarded that advice and convinced the air force to let him back in the cockpit. That had been almost twenty-five years ago. Still no back brace. He used frequent weight-bearing exercises and vigorous outdoor activities to bulk up the muscles in his back. These, especially the lats, would keep the pressure off those vertebrae. Rarely did he have pain. Tonight was one such occasion. He ignored it and closed the door.

"My Lord, they're already singing," Whitaker moaned as they approached the front door of Rita's. Enthusiastic, if not quite harmonious, male voices belted out an irreverent old aviator's ballad. Ironically, the melody was from the children's song, "If You're Happy and You Know It, Clap Your Hands." But this version, adapted from the military parody, was definitely not suited for kids.

Oh, there are no Customs pilots down in hell,
Oh, there are no Customs pilots down in hell,
It's full of supervisors with their heads up their posteriors,
Oh, there are no Customs pilots down in hell!

Whitaker shook his head. "You guys are weird. And besides, they slurred 'posteriors.'"

"Say again?"

"Weird!" he shouted. Then he cringed.

The language of the next verse was worse than the previous one, enough to shock even old Whitaker, who was not without sin in the vulgar words department.

Between verses of boisterous singing, Whitaker said, "I said you guys are weird. Pilots, I mean. All this singing silly songs. It's disrespectful of the dead."

"Not disrespectful," John said. "Never. Pilots don't like to think about crashes or death, but we face the possibility every day. When death comes to one of us, we joke about it and sing crazy songs to take our minds off the tragedy, to sort of thumb our noses at it. Does that make any sense?"

"No, but who said pilots had any sense?"

A white paper sign with large black letters written in felt-tip pen was taped to the front door: *SORRY. CLOSED TONIGHT FOR A PRIVATE FUNCTION.* At least they hadn't called it a party. The singing had stopped. John pushed both sides of the double doors open and stepped in.

A tall sandy-haired man intercepted them a few steps inside the door. He looked familiar but John couldn't place him. "Sorry, guys," the man said. "There's a private thing going on here tonight."

"Yeah, I know," John said. "Leslie Olsen invited us. My name's John Martin and this is Jim Whitaker. Hank Carter was my best friend. We flew fighters together, a long time ago. Jim's a retired Air Force crew chief who knows—knew—Hank pretty well."

"Ah, I see. I'm Ed Anderson, Blackhawk pilot." He pointed at the long row of tables pushed together and crowded with short-haired men, presumably all Customs Service aviators. "Leslie was there a minute ago. I'm sure she'll be back soon."

John remembered where he had seen this man before. On his first, ill-fated entry into the Customs Service building, Anderson had been one of the helicopter pilots whom Briggs had sent out to Hank's crash site.

Anderson said, "Why not come over to the table and get a beer? I'll make some introductions."

Whitaker said, "You go, John. I don't know any of those songs. Anyway, I need to hit the head and then order me some food."

"Bathrooms are down that hallway," Anderson said. "Over on the left there's some tables where they'll take your order for food. I recommend the John Wayne Burger."

John gave Whitaker his credit card and said, "Order what you want and get me a John Wayne Burger with fries. I'll join you soon."

Someone jumped up on a table and began another song.

Well," Anderson said, "No time for introductions. Sing along if you know the words. It's an old Willie Nelson and Merle Haggard song, 'Pancho and Lefty,' adapted to aviators."

John nodded his thanks to Anderson. He knew the words, all right.

Livin' in the air, we said,
Was gonna make us free and lean,
Now our skin is hard and rough,
The wings upon our chest do gleam.

Flyin' high and flyin' low,
Anywhere we're sure to go,
We don't think that we may die,
Just call it our foolish pride.

It was all wrong. Hank, with his deep baritone voice, needed to be here, not in a casket at the airport. Hank. The indestructible Hank. John sang from his heart. Hank would have done the same for him. They had changed some of the words, adapting the old song to the Customs Service mission, but John sang the Vietnam-era version. No one seemed to notice. The song ended with words John knew all too well. He could never sing this song without getting choked up. A strong baritone voice, not unlike Hank's, reverberated over all the others.

We all need your prayers, it's true,
Save some for me and you,
We will do what we have to do,
Before we all grow old.
Before . . . we . . . all . . . grow . . . old.

He turned to see whose voice that was. The baritone was Briggs. And the guy was staring right at him. Briggs stepped away from the table and walked toward him. He came to a stop a few feet away. His well-developed pecs and biceps were much more obvious now that he was dressed in a tight-fitting polo shirt and jeans.

John stood his ground and, before Briggs could say anything, fired a verbal opening shot. "Leslie Olsen invited us, Briggs. I'm here to pay my respects to Hank, not to make trouble."

Briggs stared down two nearby Customs Service pilots. They got the message and moved away. "Martin, every time I see you, I get nothing but trouble. Tonight, it's—"

"I told you why I came. And who invited me."

"Christ, Martin, let me finish my say. You and me, we've been at each other's throats from the get-go. If you want a piece of me, I'm ready. But not tonight." He turned around, went to the table, and filled two mugs with beer. He held one out and said, "Here. Take this. Tonight is for Hank Carter. As his friend, you are welcome here." Briggs held out his mug.

John clinked his mug against Briggs's and said, "Thanks."

Leslie had joined the other men at the table. John wondered if she were the only female pilot in the detachment. Adam Carter sat next to her. Everyone except Adam launched off into another irreverent song. Several of the male voices were wildly out of key, bad enough to make a dog howl. Further conversation with Briggs was impossible.

When the singing stopped, Briggs said, "I assure you, they fly much better than they sing. Come on over. Meet some of my pilots and crewmembers."

Chapter 16

John spent the next twenty minutes, during breaks between songs and toasts to Hank, meeting pilots and crewmembers from the three types of aircraft flown by the Tucson Customs Service Detachment—Blackhawks, Citations, and the smaller Cessna 172. Adam Carter was deep in conversation with one of the Citation pilots. The volume from neighboring conversations made it almost impossible to understand anything that was said. The more people drank, it seemed, the louder they talked.

"Colonel Martin," a Citation pilot said, "is it true, what Adam has been saying? About your two MiG kills on one mission?"

All conversation stopped.

"Adam says, one of the MiGs was on your wingman's ass and the wingman was Hank."

"It's John, please." He glared at Adam and sighed. "Adam can't seem to let go of the 'colonel' thing. And, he might have embellished the story a little."

"Not as much as my dad did," Adam said.

Everyone at the table laughed. Evidently these people had already been exposed to Hank's talent for exaggeration. The laughs died off quickly, as if they had all just realized that Hank Carter had told his last war story.

John dodged more questions by saying he had food waiting over at Whitaker's table. "I'll be back in a while," he said to the group. To Briggs, he said, "Thanks for the beer."

Briggs said, "You're welcome. See me before you leave. We need to talk."

John said, "Okay," and walked away.

Adam jumped up from his chair and followed him away from the group. John stopped to let him catch up. "Don't say it, Adam."

"Don't say what, sir?"

John shook his head. "Never mind."

"Sir, can we talk for a minute, in private?"

"Sure." He saw an empty table in the corner that would give them some privacy from both the crowd and Whitaker, who John noticed was very busy with a giant triple-decker burger and a large mound of French fries. A matching plate was on the opposite side of the table.

After they sat down, Adam said, "Sir, what happened to my dad?"

Why was the kid asking him rather than the Customs Service? He decided to use the party line. "They tell me it was ground impact in pursuit of a bogey, drug-runners, down near Ajo. They're talking engine failure, something about oil—"

"Excuse me, sir, but that's bullshit and you know it. My dad was better than that. The Citation couldn't kill him. No airplane could. I'm getting the run-around from the Customs Service. One minute they say it's engine failure; the next minute it's a structural problem. That's all a crock of shit. Pardon my French." Adam leaned forward and planted his long forearms on the table. His hands were curled up into tight fists. "Would you help me find out what really happened?"

There was only one possible answer. "Of course, son." He instantly regretted using that word, but Adam didn't seem to mind. John was touched by Adam's confidence in his dad's flying skills. It mirrored his own feelings. "I'll ask some questions. See what I can find out." He vowed that, someday, he'd be able to tell the young man the truth.

Adam's face brightened. "Okay. I'll give you two numbers. The first one will be my grandma's phone number in New Bern. That's in North Carolina. I'll be there for a few days after the burial tomorrow afternoon. The second one is my phone in the barracks at Shaw Air Force Base." He produced a ball point pen. "Do you have something to write on?"

John reached into his pocket for his list of Boneyard tasks and remembered he had given it to Whitaker. "Just a minute. Whitaker has a piece of paper." He stood up, walked over to Whitaker's table, and retrieved the note. Back with Adam, he put it on the table, taking care to put the Boneyard list face down.

Adam wrote his name and the two numbers on the blank side of the note. "Thank you, Colonel Martin. I'm out of here, I've got to get back to the hotel and take a shower. Our flight leaves just before midnight." He pushed back his chair, stood up and held out his hand. It was great seeing you, sir. I wish it had been for a happier occasion, though."

During the handshake, John reached out with his left hand to squeeze Adam's forearm, the way he and Hank used to do it after a successful combat mission. Adam reciprocated as if his dad had coached him to do it this way. Adam walked away.

John returned to the table where Whitaker sat finishing up his meal. He sat down and said, "This looks good. Hope it hasn't gotten too cold." Before he could pick up his John Wayne Burger, someone tapped him on the shoulder. Briggs.

Briggs said, "I hate to interrupt, but the party's about to break up and I still need to have a word with you."

"Have a seat," John said. "Have you met Jim Whitaker yet? We go way back."

"My pleasure, Mr. Whitaker. No offense, but I need to borrow Mr. Martin for a private conversation. I recommend we go out into the back parking lot. There's going to be some more loud, off-key singing. It'll be impossible to talk in here."

John followed Briggs outside. He walked about twenty feet away from the building.

"So, did you hear about the Citations getting grounded?" Briggs asked.

"Yep."

"That's a bunch of crap, you know. The Citation is a safe and reliable aircraft. Just right for the mission."

"I know," John said. "Hank told me that months ago."

"When you marched out of my office last night, where did you go?"

John replayed the unpleasant memory of knocking over Hardwick's chair in the White House and the reason for his temper tantrum. "Not your business, Briggs." The moment he said that he realized he had been outplayed.

Briggs smiled—no, it was a smirk. "How wrong you are. Six of my people are dead. Your friend is one of them. It *is* my business. So, when a stubborn guy like you says he might just go see someone in DC, an equally stubborn guy like me might get curious. I hate to use your own words against you, but you said—and I quote— 'I'd like to think we're on the same side here.'"

"You might remember, Briggs, that you rejected that notion at the time, quite emphatically."

Briggs held up his hands in mock surrender. "Okay, okay. Let's just speak theoretically for a second. Let's say I have instant access to law enforcement and NSA databases, which include airline passenger manifests. And I have reason to believe that this theoretical person might actually fly off to DC. Don't you think I could find out where you—I mean, this theoretical person—went last night? Maybe check security cameras at National Airport's taxi stand? Track down a taxi driver?"

John finally realized what Briggs had reminded him of the first time he saw him. A bulldog. Short, squat, permanent scowl on his face. Once he sinks his teeth into something, he won't let go.

"Did you learn anything in Washington?' Briggs said.

"I am not admitting that I was there. But theoretically, if I had been, and I had spoken with my very highly placed contact, I would have learned that someone even higher on the food chain has ordered a cover-up of these shootdowns."

Briggs pounded one fist into the palm of his other hand. "I knew it! Fuck it, Martin, I'm out of the loop here. Two crews dead, two aircraft destroyed, my Citations grounded. My other pilots are asking questions I can't answer. Nobody wants to talk to me about this situation—except you." He exhaled; it sounded more like a growl. He leaned in closer and stared. "You've got that look. Same as last night, in my office. Know what I mean?

"No."

"Bullshit you don't. You're going to fight this, aren't you? Leak it to the press? Find out who's responsible? Maybe more."

John debated on how to answer. Perhaps the cover-up and grounding of the Citations had been the straw that had broken Briggs's company-man, follow-all-the-orders mentality. However, it seemed unwise to say anything more to Briggs.

Briggs pulled out his wallet, extracted a business card, and wrote something on the back. "That's my home number. Call me there if you get any answers. Or need something. Off the record, of course." The corners of his lips twitched up just a little.

"You got it," John said. Briggs was full of surprises tonight. That had almost been a smile.

"One more thing," the stocky man said. "Did Olsen go with you to Washington?"

Any hesitation would shed doubt on his answer. He couldn't lie for two reasons. One, lying was bad. Two, Briggs might already know the truth. But was he bluffing about those security cameras and taxi logs? Telling the whole truth would be bad for Leslie. He said, "She asked, but I told her no way."

"Good answer," Briggs said.

They walked back inside Rita's. Briggs went off to join the dwindling crowd at the big table. John went the opposite direction to finally enjoy his burger. Whitaker was still there, but his John Wayne Burger was not. There were two empty plates on the table and a third with a single onion ring. All of these were on Whitaker's side of the table.

"The waitress wanted to pick up your plate," Whitaker said. "And, ah, I knew you were busy out there, so I . . . well, I didn't want the food to go to waste."

"It's okay. Did you get enough to eat?"

"I'm okay for now. Great burgers and fries, awesome onion rings." He pointed at the lone remaining onion ring. "I saved one for you."

John said, "You finish it." The irony sailed right over Whitaker's head.

It was gone in three bites.

"Look, my friend," Whitaker said while swallowing the last mouthful, "I need to get some sleep. In case you hadn't noticed, I am not as young as I once was. About that paper with the list of things required to, ah, 'borrow' that jet? You keep it for tonight. I'm too tuckered out to even think about it."

John put the keys to the Explorer on the table. "You think you can find the main gate again?"

"Sure."

"Okay, take the Explorer. There's a room reserved for you at the Transient Enlisted Quarters. All paid for. You can get directions at the gate. Get some sleep and we'll meet for breakfast at 0600. There's a place called Hash on Hawthorne, a breakfast place at the corner of Craycroft and Hawthorne."

"What about you?" Whitaker asked. "Where are you staying? And how are you gonna get there?"

"I'll get a room at the VOQ. I'll just walk there later. It's the first building you come to inside the main gate. Need some time to clear my head."

"Okay, fine. Now, how do I find this hash place? Wait. How are *you* getting to the restaurant?"

John said, "Hash on Hawthorne. It's only two miles north of here, right off this same street, Craycroft. Here, I'll draw you a map." He pulled the note paper out of his pocket and wrote, *Hash on Hawthorne, 0600*, but stopped before he drew the map. This paper had all the sensitive F-16 details, which Whitaker didn't want tonight. There wasn't room for a proper map anyway. "Give me a second," he said. He put the note back in his pocket, flipped over a paper place mat, and sketched a crude map. He labeled the major cross streets, added the restaurant's name and the time, and said, "Once you pass Broadway, Hawthorne is about five blocks further north. The restaurant is on the northeast corner of Craycroft and Hawthorne." He gave the place mat to Whitaker. "Oh. About me getting there? I need to hit the base gym in the morning and then I'll just jog or walk up there."

They stood up and shook hands. After Whitaker left, John went to the pay phone on the wall just inside the back door. Tom Stevens answered on the fourth ring.

"Tom, John Martin here. Sorry to bother you at home, but I need your help. I'm down in Tucson and I need access to the money in my accounts."

"Any of our branches down there can help you, John. You don't need me for that."

"I need it all in cash."

"All of it? You're talking, what? Over a quarter million dollars? That's going to raise a lot of eyebrows, require some coordination, some Federal reports. May I ask why—"

"No, you may not," John said. "Just make it happen. Please. Use the branch at 29th and Craycroft. I'll be there when they open tomorrow. And Tom? Make it all in hundreds." He hung up the phone. Stevens was a resourceful banker. The cash would be there.

On his way back down the hall, the ladies' room door swung open and nearly hit him in the face. He put up a hand to stop its momentum. Leslie peeked out from the other side.

"Oh. There you are. Sorry, I'm in a hurry to get back for last call. And maybe one more song. You should come over. I'd be willing to bet you know all the words."

She was wearing a white cotton button-down shirt with long sleeves, faded jeans and open-toed brown leather shoes. The shirt was crisp and loose-fitting, unlike the jeans, which fit her like a second skin. Outside of fashion magazines, he had never seen a woman look so elegant in such an informal outfit.

"You go ahead," he said. "I've got to pay Whitaker's food bill. It's amazing how much food that skinny little guy can put away."

After signing the credit card receipt and leaving a healthy cash tip, John decided he had had enough of this affair. His one mug of ice-cold beer had reminded him that Hank lay in a cold coffin awaiting a flight in an even colder cargo hold enroute to his final resting place. As the Customs Service crowd began another spirited song, John decided to skip the goodbyes and disappear out the back door.

Chapter 17

John had the sidewalk to himself. It was cool and dark, just right for a contemplative walk, but he couldn't concentrate. He was on the west side of Craycroft, heading south, with his back to the cars barreling down the two southbound lanes. Noise from traffic forced him to constantly look over his shoulder. Had he always been this way or was it the fighter pilot training —now instinctual—to check six o'clock? What were the odds of a car losing control, jumping the curb, and smashing him? Ten million to one?

He wasn't willing to take those odds. He decided to cross the street and walk where the threat, in this case automobiles, would be in front of him and easy to see. He looked north and waited for a break in traffic. As soon as this next car, a Jeep, passed, he could—oh, oh. It was slowing down; it was a white Jeep Cherokee driven by a red-haired woman in a white shirt.

The Jeep stopped next to him. Its passenger-side window lowered. He bent down to look inside.

"Hey," Leslie said. "There's traffic coming behind me. Let me pull off up there." She drove fifty feet ahead and pulled into the parking lot of a closed office supply store.

By the time he reached her car, she had leaned over and opened the passenger door.

"You left in a hurry," she said. "Where are you going?"

"To the base. I'm going to get a room at the Visiting Officers' Quarters."

"Walk? Nonsense. It's too late to be walking out here. I'll give you a lift."

"No, that's okay, I'd rather—"

"Don't argue," Leslie said. "I'm driving you and that's that. As Hank used to say, 'End of discussion.' Did he say that a lot to you?"

"Yes, he did. He was a strong-willed man. When he made up his mind, there was nothing you could do about it. Besides, he was always right." John was beginning to think that Leslie and Hank had been cut from the same cloth. She was decisive and strong-willed, but . . . he chuckled and said to himself, *No offense Hank, but Leslie's got you beat hands down in the looks department.*

"What?" Leslie said.

"Nothing." He got into the Jeep. "You win. Again."

During the short drive to Davis-Monthan's main gate, they passed the typical stretch of bars, used car lots, and fast-food places that catered to the military. John waited for her to question his abrupt departure from Rita's. She remained silent. The gate guard checked their I.D.s and waved them through.

"You can just drop me off in front of the VOQ office," John said.

Before he could object, she pulled into a "Reserved for V.I.P." parking space right in front of the office. She shut off the engine and said, "Why don't I go inside with you and make sure they have a room? If they don't, you'd be stuck out here without wheels." She opened her door and got out.

He had no choice but to get out and follow her to the office. The building looked just as it had years ago when he was stationed here. The exterior was painted beige now, rather than the bright white enamel of twenty years ago. He recalled that the Customs Service building was also beige, so that must be the government's current "color du jour." John wondered if they had upgraded the rooms and gotten rid of the old wagon-wheel-themed western decor.

Leslie reached the double glass doors first. She pulled one open for him and said, "After you."

"Thanks," he said. The walk from the car had put color in her cheeks and brightened her eyes. She looked fresh and energetic. He probably looked tired and wrinkled.

The desk clerk was a petite female Air Force three-striper wearing a dark blue uniform skirt and a light blue shirt with a name tag that read, "Perkins." She was apologetic but firm.

"I'm sorry, Colonel Martin. I know you made a reservation, but we just got a no-notice Inspector General team in, and they have top priority. They took every available room. We even had to bump some of our active-duty guests."

"Senior Airman Perkins, are you absolutely sure? There's nothing at all?"

"No, sir. We're completely full. Some of the inspectors had to stay downtown, and way far away too, 'cause there's a golf tournament and some other type of convention in town."

"Okay, I understand," John said. "Can you suggest a place off base that has a room?"

The young airman gave him a sympathetic smile. "I'm sorry, sir, but I've checked every place within thirty miles. I really have. And there's nothing."

"Well, okay. Thanks." He turned away from the desk. He'd have to knock on Whitaker's door over at the enlisted quarters. Those rooms were very small. He'd end up sleeping on the floor.

Leslie was already at the door and had pushed it open. "Aren't you glad I waited?" she said. "Come on. You can stay at my place."

As the door closed, John saw Senior Airman Perkins staring at them with raised eyebrows and the beginnings of a smile. Leslie must have heard his groan.

"Now what?" she said.

"Did you see the look at that girl's face when you said, 'stay with me?'"

Leslie rolled her eyes and laughed. "I didn't say, 'Stay with me.' I said, 'Stay at my place.' I have a guest bedroom, by the way. I don't see that you have any other option."

"Well, I was going to go over and bunk with Whitaker in the enlisted quarters."

"Forget it," Leslie said. "They sleep two to a room already."

He had forgotten about that. "Or maybe I'll get a taxi or rent a car and—"

"John, be reasonable. You heard what that airman said. Even if you could find a hotel, I'd have to drive you there, or drive you to the airport so you could rent a car. Either way you'd burn up valuable time. We can be at my place in fifteen minutes, get some rest, and then maybe do some talking in the morning. About MiGs and this guy Alvarado. Or did you think I had let you off the hook on that?"

He groaned again. "No, I certainly didn't think you would." That was why he had been trying to get away from her ever since they had returned from DC. The funeral had interfered, then the trip to Rita's bar, and now this. The one saving grace was that, if she was as tired as he was, she would have no energy to do any serious talking tonight. The prospect of a shower, a clean bed, and a good night's sleep sounded pretty good. "Okay. Let's go."

* * *

John wiped his boots on the straw welcome mat and walked into Leslie's townhouse. He stood in the tiled foyer while she pushed buttons on a panel just inside the door.

"Deactivating the security system," she said. "Let me turn on some lights so you can see the place."

"Nice. Very nice pueblo style architecture. That's what they call it, right?" The ceiling was framed in heavy, dark-brown wooden beams. Textured walls the color of light clay were bathed in flickering light from imitation oil lamps. Paintings of desert landscapes and Native American scenes—some original and quite good, in John's opinion—added to the southwestern ambiance. He had seen many attempts to create this theme, but few that were as successful and tasteful as this. "Did you decorate this place yourself?" he asked.

"Yes. I really love Santa Fe style. That's another name for pueblo style." She stepped down into a large sunken living room with a Saltillo tile floor, a beehive fireplace in one corner, and double French doors that led to a lighted outside patio. Green potted plants, some with colorful blossoms, were plentiful, both inside and outside the patio door.

"It was the kiva fireplace that sold me on this condo," Leslie said. She bent down and twisted a silver handle on the wall next to the fireplace. She stepped back and, a few seconds later, a whoosh of gas ignition created a fire over logs and embers that John would have sworn were real. "Pretty neat, huh? she said. "That'll keep us warm until the thermostat catches up. I turned the heater off when I left for work, and that was two days ago."

She unzipped her windbreaker and wriggled it off her shoulders. "Let me show where to put your bag." She led him down a hallway, pausing to reach into an open doorway on the left and switch on a light. "Bathroom's in there. Extra towels and washcloths in that basket. The guest bedroom is down here on the right. My room's a little further down."

She flipped on a light switch in the guest room. He stepped inside and was immediately impressed. "Again, very nice," he said. "I like how you've continued the theme in here." It was a small room with just enough space for a queen-size bed, one end table, a small desk, and a chair. Folding wooden doors, finished in a dark brown stain that matched the furniture, probably concealed a closet. The shiny tiled floor had small sand-colored rugs on each side of the bed. A large window with horizontal wooden blinds took up most of the wall opposite the foot of the bed.

"Thanks," Leslie said. "Some of the art in here is original, by Gila River tribal artists. The one over the desk, though, is just a print. The frame around that one cost much more than the picture itself."

He said, "It's still beautiful. Is that somewhere on the Gila reservation?"

"Yes. It's titled, "The Great Bend of the Gila." It shows some of the ancient hieroglyphics which still exist today, along the Gila River—not too far from where we were yesterday, or whatever day it was, in the T-33. I've lost track of time; so much has happened."

John nodded.

She said, "Well, why don't you unpack, and I'll do the same. There are hangars and empty shelves in the closet. After that I'll make us some tea and . . . are you hungry?"

"No, not really." That was a lie; he was starved. However, sitting down to a meal with Leslie would lead to her asking questions he didn't want to answer. Better to starve now and eat with Whitaker in the morning. "I'd really rather—"

"Well, I am," she said. "All I had for dinner was a handful of peanuts at Rita's. I might whip up a late-night omelet and some toast. Are you sure you don't want to join me?"

An omelet . . . one of his favorite meals. He forced himself to say, "I'm really beat, Leslie. I think I'll just unpack and take a shower."

"Suit yourself. There's terrycloth robes and slippers in the closet. Two different sizes. One of them should fit you. Join me for tea afterward." She disappeared down the hall toward her room, leaving him with no way to decline the invitation.

* * *

John pushed open the glass shower door, allowing a cloud of steam to escape, and reached for a towel. The hot water had felt so good on his back and neck that he hadn't wanted to turn it off. Now, if he could just towel off and sneak into the guest room without getting nabbed for tea-drinking, he might get some much-needed rest. His clean clothes and the robes were back in his room. All he had was the towel. Oh, well. It was only two steps across the hall to his room. He wrapped the towel around his waist, opened the door and stepped out.

"Oops!" Leslie said. "Almost got you." She was dressed in a robe and slippers, with wet hair and carrying a full laundry basket. She was also staring with unabashed curiosity at his chest and legs.

"Ah . . ." He hadn't expected her to be in the hall; she was supposed to be in the kitchen making an omelet. The knot holding the towel around him began to slip. He put a hand on his hip, over the knot, and hoped the move hadn't made him look like a nervous fool. "I left the robe in the bedroom."

She smiled. "So I see." It took her an uncomfortably long time to raise her eyes above his chest.

A tea kettle whistled. Leslie cleared her throat. "I'll just slip past while you get the robe." She turned sideways, pulled the laundry basket up against her body, and squeezed past him. "Tea will be ready shortly. Black tea or herbal?"

"Leslie, I'm really sorry, but I'd like a rain check on the tea. I'm just too tired to stay awake another minute."

She stopped, turned around and looked him in the eye. "Really? Okay then . . . sleep well. Any special time you want to wake up?"

"No, anytime is fine. Thanks for letting me stay here. I'll see you in the morning."

John closed the door behind him, walked to the window and raised the wooden shade. He found the latch and slid the window open to sample the cool, high desert air. That felt better, more like home, although nothing could compare to the sweet, fresh saltwater breeze off Puget Sound. Now, where should he hang the damp towel? A brave man would just put on a robe, step across the hall, and hang the towel in the bathroom. But he was unwilling—afraid? Yes. Afraid to risk another accidental encounter with Leslie. He opened the louvered closet door, pulled out a plastic hangar and hung the towel there.

There was one more thing to do before climbing into bed. He retrieved his watch from the bedside table and set an alarm for 0430. Leslie would be fast asleep then. It would be easy to sneak out undetected, assuming he had memorized the security code correctly. He returned the watch to the table and turned off the lamp. It was cool, dark, and quiet. Perfect sleeping weather. He climbed into bed and lay flat on his back. His head sank into a very comfortable feather pillow.

Several minutes later he was still wide awake. Was it the strange room? The fact that an attractive but dangerously curious woman was asleep right down the hall? Or was he grieving for Hank? Probably all the above. But there was one more thing. He just hadn't expected it so soon.

Pre-combat jitters. They weren't supposed to hit you until the night before a big mission. That's the way it had happened in Vietnam and the Gulf War. No matter how many missions he had flown, he always worried the night before. Would he freeze up when the missiles, flak and MiGs popped up? Let his comrades down when they really needed him? Would the "Golden B-B," the bullet or SAM or MiG that he didn't even see, kill him?

There was no mission tomorrow, Hell, he didn't even have an airplane to fly yet. Maybe it wasn't jitters. Maybe it was his conscience. Could he do it, cross over the line, become a criminal? Steal an F-16, arm it up and kill someone with it?

He wouldn't get anything done tomorrow unless he could get some sleep. He closed his eyes and forced his brain into standby. That was better. His heart rate was back to normal. Now he was able to enjoy the soft bed, the warmth of the quilt, and the fragrance of the pillow. Lavender. Leslie's scent. He had first noticed it when he had held her outside the chapel.

Chapter 18

John sat up in bed. He listened. Had it been real, or had he dreamed it?

"No! No!"

It wasn't a dream. Leslie was screaming.

"Oh, God! No, no, no!"

He swung his legs onto the floor, grabbed the towel from the closet and ran for Leslie's room. He stopped after two steps. The sobs were coming from behind him. The kitchen or the living room. John turned and ran in that direction. The kitchen was empty. He rushed toward the living room before his brain kicked in. What if there was an intruder in there with her? His only weapon was the towel wrapped around his waist. Too late now. He was going in there.

Leslie was lying on the couch. Alone, thank God. She tossed and turned under a thin blanket, whimpering. Her eyes were closed. It was a nightmare, a bad one. He considered waking her, but she stopped moving and got quiet. That didn't last long.

"No!" she shrieked. "Bobby! Bobby, Bobby, no!" She thrashed and kicked off the blanket. Her robe fell open, exposing white skin. Her eyes were still closed.

He had to wake her gently, but how? He tightened the towel around his waist and stepped down into the living room. Maybe if he turned on a light, she would wake up on her own. He reached for a table lamp next to the sofa.

Leslie screamed again. He flinched and missed the light switch. She sat up straight, opened her eyes and looked directly at him.

John knew the look. She had just seen death. Based on his experience, it could be even more shocking and terrifying in a dream than in real life. Her neck and forehead were shiny with perspiration. She was panting hard enough to hyperventilate. He had to do something.

"Leslie, it's me. John Martin. It's okay. It was just a dream." Touching her would be risky. She might not recognize him. Might consider him a threat. He kneeled and reached out anyway. It seemed like the right thing to do. He put one hand behind her head and, when she didn't resist, pulled her close. "It's all right now." He patted her back with his other hand.

"John?" She put both arms around his neck and squeezed. "It was so real. I was in the cockpit with him. With Bobby. There were explosions and fire and—" She shivered and tightened her grip on his shoulders and neck. "—there was blood everywhere."

He could feel her heartbeat. It was much too rapid. "It's over now," he said. He gently unwrapped her hands from his neck. He extracted his hands from behind her and put them on her shoulders. "You should sit up. Catch your breath." He stood up and switched on the lamp. "Why don't I get you a glass of water?"

She nodded.

"Oh . . . and, you might want to cinch up your robe."

He went to the kitchen and, rather than search through unfamiliar cupboards, picked up a glass from the counter, rinsed it out and refilled it. He noticed a silver tea kettle on the stove top. After confirming that it still held enough water, he lit the burner beneath the kettle.

When he got back to the living room, Leslie was sitting, leaning forward on the edge of a cushion, hands covering her face.

"Here you go," he said.

She looked up at him, pulled the robe tighter around her neck and took the glass. "Thanks."

He picked up the blanket and wrapped it around her shoulders.

""Thanks again." Leslie put the almost-empty glass on the table and said, "Do you want to sit down? I . . . I don't want to be alone right now."

"Sure. But I'd better put some clothes on. Will you be okay for a minute?"

"Yes."

John put on a pair of gym shorts and decided to use the robe and slippers. While looking for those, he heard the tea kettle begin to whistle. He hurried back down the hall to find Leslie standing at the kitchen counter, her back to him, putting tea bags into two mugs of boiling water.

Without turning to face him, she said, "I had to do something. Keep busy. You know what I mean?" She picked up the mugs and turned around. Her hands were shaking; she put the mugs back on the counter. "I can't handle this. I thought I was strong but this, this hurts too much. My own brother, crumpled up in a broken and burned cockpit, just like Hank was. I can't get that picture out of my mind." Her cheeks were wet with tears.

John noticed a paper napkin dispenser on the counter. He pulled a couple out and handed her one.

She wiped her eyes and cheeks. "I am so sorry. This is embarrassing. I don't mean to make you uncomfortable." She stared at him. "I know that look. You're thinking it's a woman thing, that I'm too emotional, a basket case. Well, you know what? Right about now, that's exactly how—"

"You're wrong," he said. "I don't believe that. No way I think you are weak. Not after what I've seen from you the last two days. Sure, you're hurting. You're crying. There is no dishonor in crying over the loss of a loved one."

"It's not fair," she said. "I never even said goodbye to him! He went out to fly and, the next thing I know, he's in a sealed coffin. I hate myself for getting him this job! I—" She choked on a sob. She clenched her fist and raised it. The blanket fell off her shoulders onto the floor.

John had been there. Angry at the world, at life, wanting to punch something or someone. Leslie was going to slam her fist into the wall or, worse yet into one of the glass cabinet doors.

She whirled away from him and aimed a punch at the microwave. That was going to hurt. Both Leslie *and* her microwave.

He lunged forward, got his arms around her, and stopped her punch just in time. She twisted around to face him, breathing heavily, and struggling to get free. She began to pound his chest with both hands.

"Dammit, let me go!" she shouted between sobs.

He did the opposite; he pulled her closer. "Nope. Just let it out, Leslie. All that frustration and grief. Let it out. You need this." He closed his eyes and let her cry herself out.

When she stopped, the portion of his robe where her face had been was soaked, as was the center of his bare chest. Her arms had somehow gotten inside his robe and were locked around his waist. She hadn't yet relaxed her grip.

"Maybe you need to sit down for a while," he said.

She didn't move or speak. She just held him and breathed deeply, causing certain parts of her anatomy to touch him in places he dared not look. He reached inside his robe and unlocked her fingers from around his waist. He moved her hands out from under his robe and thanked his lucky stars that he had put on those gym shorts. "Come on, let me get you back to the sofa. I'll get a warm washcloth and wipe your face." He held one of her hands and led her out of the kitchen.

When they reached the edge of the sunken living room, she said, "I'm okay now."

John took that as a sign to let go of her hand. That was a mistake. She missed the step down into the living room and fell forward. She'd crack her head on the tiled floor. There was no delicate way to catch her, so he grabbed the nearest part of her, her right arm, and pulled, which swung her around to face him. He hopped down onto the living room floor and wrapped his other arm around her back. John felt as if they were doing some type of awkward dance step as he regained his balance. Leslie's body was shaking.

Her robe was now fully open, giving him a glimpse of a silky ivory-colored bra, just barely covering her breasts and thin enough to show everything. Her torso was that of an athlete. Flat belly. Narrow waist. Low-rise bikini panties matching her bra.

Now he was the one doing the shaking. And panting from the effort of catching her. Or was it from the sight of her half-naked body? He relaxed his grip on her but did not let go.

"I'm sorry to grab you like that," he said, "but it was the only way to catch you. You'll probably have a bruise on that arm."

"That's all right." She pulled her robe together and cinched the belt. That caused her to wince. "I think I twisted my ankle."

"Hold on to my neck," he said. "I'll help you over to the sofa." He tightened his grip on her waist. "Ready?"

With his assistance, Leslie half-walked and half-hopped the remaining distance to the sofa. His right arm was around her waist; his left hand supported her elbow. He was ready to help her down onto the sofa when she swung herself around and leaned against him. Her face was close enough for him to smell her clean, makeup-free skin and freshly shampooed hair. He still had one arm around her back. She now had both arms around his neck and pulled him even closer. Their foreheads were almost touching. Things down at chest level and below were also in close contact.

"Uh, what are we doing here?" John said.

"I don't know what you're doing," Leslie said. "But I'm getting ready to kiss you and tell you thanks for being a good man. Judging by the way you're squeezing my waist, I assume you might have similar urges." She didn't give him time to answer.

Her kiss was sweet enough for him to want more. He moved his hands up to cradle her face. "Thank you," he said. He kissed her again, longer this time, half-expecting her to pull away. Her kiss had been tentative and brief, more of a thank-you than a passionate one. But his was a little more intense. She pulled him closer and returned his kiss with one of increasing enthusiasm. She snuggled up to him even closer. His brain and body were on overload. But it felt good.

"I don't believe this is happening," he said. "What *is* happening?"

Leslie put her hands on the lapels of his robe and pulled it off his shoulders, down over his back and tugged at the sleeves. It dropped to the floor. "I can see, and feel, that you are becoming somewhat aroused." She looked down at his gym shorts. "Correction. You are completely aroused." She wrapped her arms around his waist. "I want you to know the feeling is mutual." She kissed him again. Deeply.

It was impossible to keep his hands outside her robe. Before the kiss was over, it had fallen completely off, and he had explored the curves of her back, waist, and buttocks. Her heavy breathing and quiet moans during this process were quite a turn-on.

She inhaled and said, "We could psychoanalyze this all night long. Or we could just go with it."

Her hands felt good on his chest and stomach. Now they were tantalizingly close to the elastic waistband of his shorts. His hormones awakened from a long hibernation. What harm could come from letting them run wild for one night? "I vote for just going with it."

John picked her up and carried her to the large thick woven rug in front of the fireplace. He set her down gently and knelt beside her. She was elegantly beautiful. Firm in all the right places. Soft in all the right places. Lithe and supple. He was ready. Oh, was he ever ready. He straddled her and caressed her face, shoulders, breasts, and belly. Her chest rose and fell; her abs fluttered as she raised her pelvis and rubbed against him.

He bent down and kissed her. It was as if they had been lovers for years. She seemed to approve of his every move. He moved off her and put a hand on her shoulder. She anticipated his next move and rolled onto her side. This accentuated the curve of her hips and excited him even more. He reached down to unhook her bra. And hesitated.

He stretched out facing her back, putting them into the "spoon" position, and kissed her neck. "Leslie, I want you so badly it hurts. You can literally feel how much I want you. Every fiber of my body is screaming at me to make passionate love until the sun comes up."

She rolled over to face him. "But?"

She was a perceptive woman. "But I can't," he said. "One little part of my brain is telling me something is wrong here. Not with you or me, but with the circumstances of this night. Just minutes ago, you were awash with grief. Emotionally drained. Physically weakened. Perhaps even a little intoxicated. I am in no better shape, either emotionally or otherwise. I don't think either of us wants a one-night stand, as pleasant as that would be. You don't seem to be the type of woman who would be satisfied with that."

Leslie propped herself up on one elbow. She brushed shiny red strands of hair from her eyes. "So, you respect me too much to take advantage of me in this condition?"

He sighed.

She smiled and kissed him on the forehead. "That's sweet. Stupid, but sweet."

He flopped onto his back and said, "Hell, I'm not explaining it right. I'm just—"

"It's okay, John. I understand; I really do. It's quite flattering, actually. Everything you've done tonight has been flattering." She cuddled up to him and rested her right leg on his belly.

It felt so good to have her wrapped around him, to feel her breasts against his ribs, her face against his chest. "I wish we could lie here forever." He savored the weight of her leg over his stomach for several more breaths. "But we'd better get some sleep." He gently untangled himself from her limbs, stood up and offered her his hand.

She let him pull her up. They each picked up their robes.

"Separate beds, I suppose?" she said.

"That would be the safest thing."

They walked down the hall together. Leslie stopped at the entrance to his bedroom door and said, "You're a good man, John Martin. Good night."

"Good night, Leslie."

Before he could close his door, she called to him. "John?"

"Yes?" He stayed in his doorway. He didn't trust himself to get near her or her bed.

"We still need to talk. Will you be here when I wake up?"

He answered quickly. "Yes. I'll be here." He closed his door, took off his shorts and climbed into bed. He didn't often pray, but he asked God's forgiveness for that lie.

Chapter 19

"Would you like coffee while you're waiting?" the server asked. Her name tag said, "Sally."

"You bet," John said. If nothing else, he could warm his hands with it. Even with his leather flight jacket zipped up, it had been a little chilly outside Leslie's condo at 0500. He couldn't find a pay phone, so he had walked about a mile to a convenience store. Waiting twenty minutes for a taxi hadn't helped.

After filling his cup and leaving two menus, Sally, dressed in a white sweater, short red skirt, and bobby socks, walked away. Her white sneakers squeaked on the red-and-white checkered floor. At Hash on Hawthorne, everything was either red, white or chrome. Red vinyl booths, white tables—each with its own small coin-operated juke box filled with 1950's tunes—brought customers back to the "Good Old Days," when cars were big, with giant, gas-guzzling engines, and flashy tail fins. Above each booth was a picture of a 50's all-American automobile. His booth's picture was of a 1955 Chevrolet Bel Air Sport Coupe, painted in robins-egg blue and white.

He poured two spoons of sugar into his cup, stirred it, and took a sip, willing the caffeine to go straight to his brain. He needed to focus on the problems at hand—the ones on his list— rather than visions of Leslie. Leslie in her little black dress. Leslie in tight jeans. Leslie in almost nothing at all, lying on the rug in front of the fireplace. She had stirred him more than he cared to admit. Perhaps, when this was all over, he could look her up. If she would have him.

John reached into the back pocket of his jeans for the list. What he pulled out was Briggs's business card. No list. He checked all his other pockets. Still no list. He was sure he had taken it off the table last night. Had it dropped out at Rita's, or during his walk to the base? It didn't matter. He could recreate it from memory. Sally was nearby, loading up a nearby booth with plates of hot cakes, eggs, bacon, and ham. His stomach growled, scolding him for missing two meal opportunities last night. He waved Sally over and asked for a pen and paper.

Three lucky men who had just gotten their order, construction workers by the look of them, ate with gusto, clanking their silverware against porcelain dishes, talking with their mouths full. John made up his mind to order a big omelet, some buttery hash browns, and a few strips of bacon. Cholesterol and calories be damned. He could work all that off with a trip to the gym later or by pounding out a few miles of jogging.

When Sally returned with a pen and paper, she refilled his cup. He stirred in more sugar. There were a few wrinkles in his plan. They needed to be ironed out before Whitaker arrived. He leaned forward, put both elbows on the table and rested his chin in his hands. He closed his eyes and blocked the early-morning sunlight with his fingers. Maybe some new ideas would pop up while he waited for Whitaker.

Something squeaked. John opened his eyes.

Whitaker smiled at him from across the table. "Sorry, man. I tried to slide in here as quiet as I could. This plastic seat is kind of noisy."

Sally was there too, reaching for his untouched coffee cup. "This is cold by now. Why don't I get you a fresh cup?"

He looked at his wristwatch. Had he really been asleep for ten minutes? He must be getting old. He coughed to clear his throat. "Uh, sure." He pushed a menu toward Whitaker.

"Don't need it," Whitaker said. "I'll have what's on that sign by the door. The special. Make my steak rare and the eggs over easy, please. A double order of hash browns."

John ordered a Denver omelet, hash browns, bacon, and orange juice.

Whitaker leaned forward and whispered, "You spend the night here, or what? With all due respect, Colonel Martin, you look like hell."

"No, I got here about thirty minutes ago. Must've dozed off." he picked up a water glass, swished some water around in his mouth, and swallowed.

"Man, I'm hungry this morning," Whitaker said. "By the way, did you ever get anything to eat?"

"Almost."

At that, Whitaker's eyebrows raised but John wasn't in the mood to provide details. "It's a long story. Right now, I want to talk about F-16 stuff. Specifically—"

"Something I got to know, John. Got to know it right now."

John had rarely seen his friend with such a serious expression.

"What part does that girl play in all this?" Whitaker asked.

"Leslie, you mean?" John said. "None. Zero. No role at all. I feel sorry for her because she lost her brother. But she knows nothing about the Boneyard deal. Why do you ask?"

"Because that's her out there, about to come in the door."

John twisted to see the door and banged his knee on the heavy metal post that supported the table. Whitaker was right. As she pushed through the door, John was blinded by a glint of early-morning sun off the chrome door frame. When his vision cleared, he saw that Leslie's eyes were locked onto him as accurately as a laser targeting device. This could not be good news. He rubbed his knee and stood to greet her.

Whitaker also stood. "Hi, Leslie," he said. "I'm just on my way to wash my hands before breakfast." He retreated toward the back of the restaurant.

Under different circumstances, this would have been laughable. Jim Whitaker, who hadn't blinked an eye at Viet Cong rockets in '71 or flinched as Iraqi Scud missiles rained down during the Gulf War, was ducking for cover here in Tucson. The enemy? A petite, red-haired woman.

Had she followed him? Probably not. If so, she wouldn't have waited this long to confront him. So, how did she—

"Good morning," she said in a voice that warned him it would not be a good one at all. She was wearing a yellow t-shirt, jeans, white athletic shoes, and a scowl that she must have learned from Eric Briggs.

"Hi," he said. "Would you like to sit down?"

She opened the flap of a small leather purse slung over her left shoulder. She pulled out a piece of paper, unfolded it and slammed it onto the table. The noise was enough to stop conversation at the construction workers' table. Leslie glared at them. They instantly found a reason to look down and resume their meal.

She sat down on Whitaker's side of the table and said, "Does this mean what I think it does?"

John sat. He hadn't felt this uncomfortable—or guilty—since eighth grade, when he got sent to the principal's office for fighting. "What do you think it means?" he said.

She tapped each incriminating line. "Boneyard security . . . Fuel . . . F-16 batteries . . . 20-millimeter." She shoved the paper at him. "I have to admit, it's an original way of avenging Hank's death."

When he didn't reply, she shook her head and said, "Do I have to spell it out for you?"

Whitaker loomed into his peripheral vision. "Hello, young lady," he said. "Mind if I slide in beside you? I see our breakfast is here."

Sally approached with their food. She put the plates on the table in front of John and Whitaker. "What would you like, dear?" she said to Leslie.

Leslie reached out and grabbed John's plate and his glass of orange juice. She slid them over to her side of the table. She also moved his silverware and napkin. "Nothing for me," she said. "I'll just have his breakfast. It appears that he has lost his appetite."

Sally said, "Yes, ma'am," and walked away.

Whitaker covered his mouth, coughed, and lowered his head. His shoulders were shaking.

"Whit, stop it!" John said. "This is not a laughing matter."

Fork and knife already in hand, Whitaker said, "You guys go ahead and talk. Mind if I dig in?"

Before John could say anything, Whitaker was chewing a mouthful of steak and waving his fork. "Go on. Don't mind me."

Leslie sipped his orange juice. She used his napkin to dab her lips before fixing him with another laser stare. "You're going to need two, John."

"Two what?"

"Two F-16s. One for you and one for me."

Whitaker choked on a bite of eggs and rushed to cover his mouth with a napkin.

John's gut tightened in a way it hadn't since his last combat mission. Leslie's angry stare was just as intimidating as Iraqi 37-millemeter tracers. Maybe even more so. He had jinked away from the triple-A fire but the wide-eyed, red-haired woman across the table had him trapped. She hadn't even given him the chance to deny her allegation. Damn, damn, damn. So, the note had fallen out of his pocket in Leslie's guest room.

This was like a bad dream. Leslie keeps popping up where he doesn't want her. She refuses to go away. He said, "No way, Leslie. Stealing one F-16 is difficult enough. Two? That's a no-go. Anyway, it's a one-versus-one fight. Me against Alvarado."

"One-versus-one?" Leslie looked around at nearby tables, scooted forward on the seat and said, "What's wrong with you? That's not the way to fight and you know it. You, of all people! Hank told me a lot about your reputation as a fighter pilot. Mutual support was your big thing. You stuck by your wingmen and expected the same from them. That's the way to stay alive in air combat, isn't it? Not with some hare-brained, single-ship vigilante attack."

Whitaker had stopped eating. It took a major shock to make him do that. John guessed it was hearing a real, live female fighter pilot discuss fighter tactics. He and Whit had retired before the Air Force allowed women into fighter cockpits.

Leslie said, "One other thing. How do you know there's only one MiG? When I heard Hank shouting at Briggs, he said, '*They* shot him down.' Plural."

"That was probably just a figure of speech," John said. She was right, of course. He wasn't counting on just one MiG. It went against one of the basic axioms of air-to-air combat. *Always assume there's another enemy jet out there.* He'd had it drilled into him in the old days of Vietnam and had preached it relentlessly during his tenure as a fighter pilot.

"Pass the hot sauce, please."

Whittaker had recovered quickly and was almost finished with his eggs. No matter what the crisis, the man never missed a meal. When John handed him the bottle, Whitaker raised his eyebrows high enough to wrinkle his forehead. His nod was more than a thank-you. John assumed it was his silent way of saying, "She has a point there."

Leslie rubbed more condensation from her—his—juice glass. "I'm disappointed in you, John. I thought we had an unspoken agreement to go after Alvarado together."

"It's just not going to happen, Leslie."

She opened her mouth to object, but he cut her off. "Look. I'm sure your flying credentials are fine. But it's just not a good idea. It doubles the logistics I need and doubles the time I need to prepare. Most of all, I can't use you. After losing your brother, you're too emotionally involved to be my wingman. You might get us both killed."

She let go of the glass and clenched her fists so tightly that her forearms trembled. If the glass had still been in her hands, it would have shattered. She unclenched her jaw long enough to say, "Whit, would you let me out? John and I are going outside for a private talk."

The look she gave him, and the angry tone of her voice, gave John the chills.

"Yes, ma'am," Whitaker said.

She walked away.

John stood up, gave Whitaker a shrug, and walked out.

*   *   *

By the time John got outside, Leslie was already seated at one of the tables shaded by a red umbrella. No one else was out here; it wasn't warm enough yet. Her fists were clenched again. He sat down across from her.

She relaxed her hands and put them on the table, palms down. "I've got three things to say." She raised one hand and stuck out her index finger. "One, you intended to ditch me all along, didn't you?" Without waiting for an answer, she put another finger up and said, "Two, you've gone stupid or senile or something if you think you can do this with one airplane. That's tactically unsound. And three—" She put a hand with three fingers extended so close to his face that he thought she might slap him with it. "You think *I'm* too emotional? What about you? I'm the one who should be refusing to fly with you! You're the one who's been seething with anger for five years. You're the one who attacked Alvarado outside the courthouse. Yes, I know all about that. What I hadn't already learned from Hank, I got from Adam last night.

"I get why you're so angry, John. You have good reasons. But don't call me too emotional when you are about to go off the deep end and do something that most people would call crazy. All for a five-year-old case of festering revenge."

"Not revenge, Leslie. Justice."

"Yeah, right. Whatever."

He couldn't refute her logic. If he put aside his anger and emotions, if he stepped back and looked at this from a tactical perspective, he needed a wingman. Leslie had compelling reasons to fight this battle. That left only one argument against including her. How would he phrase it? "There's another reason we can't fly together," he said.

"Go ahead. I'm listening."

It took a few seconds to get the right words together. "It has to do with last night." God, this was hard. No wonder they had problems with women in combat jobs, especially ones who looked as good as Leslie. "Okay, here it is. How can I have you as a flying partner when I am still thinking of you as a bed partner?"

"Ah." She nodded. "So that's it. I wondered if you felt it too. You know what? The feeling's mutual. I've probably fantasized about it more than you have. But I can put my hormones on hold to do the mission. You? Your problem is, you're stuck back in the stone age, when women just stayed in the cave, cooked, and had babies. Grow up, John. This is the twentieth century. Women are fighter pilots now."

She sat back and folded her arms across her chest. "Let me ask you something. If I were a man, would you go with two airplanes?"

Damn. He hated it when someone's logic was better than his. "Yes, I suppose I would."

"Okay, then. Just think of me as one of the guys."

John looked away. Several cars were backed up at the stop sign on Hawthorne, waiting to turn left into busy early-morning traffic on Craycroft. He turned his head and focused on Leslie, trying to visualize her with a flying helmet, g-suit and Nomex flight suit. Leslie's F-16, a mile or two away from his airplane, flying tactical formation. He tried very hard to erase the image of her in a filmy bra and bikini panties, lying on the rug in front of her fireplace. It wasn't working for him.

"Face the facts, John. You need a wingman. I'm all you've got. Let's go kick some butt."

He considered his options. Not that he had many. What made up his mind was the thought that, if Hank had had a wingman, he wouldn't have been shot down. The wingman would have alerted him to the threat. He ran his hands over his face and through his hair. He was tired of losing to this woman. First, it was the trip to Ajo. Then Washington. Now this. He had been out-maneuvered once again. What did they call it in chess? When a player knows there's no chance to win and surrenders? Resigning. These were foreign words to him. Some pride would have to be swallowed to accomplish the mission.

"Leslie, I'll never be able to think of you as one of the guys. But from now on, you're my wingman. Let's go tell Whitaker he needs to get us two airplanes instead of one."

She beamed. He couldn't tell if she was grateful to him or just proud of herself.

Chapter 20

"Hi, guys," Whitaker said through a mouthful of pancakes. One link sausage remained on the plate.

It took John a few seconds to realize that he was eating a whole new breakfast.

Whitaker speared the last sausage with his fork and devoured it. "Wasn't sure how long you'd be, and I was still a little hungry, so—" He chewed and swallowed. "I thought you wouldn't mind if I fueled up some more."

John's stomach churned again. At this rate, he would starve to death and Whitaker would grow to three hundred pounds.

"I'd offer you some," Whitaker said. "But you're still looking kind of queasy."

Leslie smirked. Just what he needed. Another person laughing at him.

"Whit, old buddy, there's been a slight change in plans. We're going to—"

"Excuse me, Leslie," Whitaker said. "Are you gonna finish that juice? I could use something to wash this down."

She slid the glass over to him.

"This is important, Whit, so—"

Whitaker stopped him with a wave of his fork. He stopped chewing long enough to say, "I know. We're going to need another jet. No problem. I'll just double all the quantities. You'd better give me more money, though."

John said, "How'd you know that's what I'd decide?"

"You? Decide?" Whitaker polished off the orange juice, smacked his lips and pointed at Leslie. "I know my women. By the look on her face when she came in, it wasn't gonna happen any other way."

Whitaker and Leslie had a good laugh at his expense. He couldn't help it; he joined them. It might be a long time before he felt like laughing again. When they all quieted down, he said, "Whit, why don't you explain the basics while I go make a phone call." He slid out of the booth.

*   *   *

Ten minutes later, he sat back down and asked Whitaker, "Where's Leslie?"

"Rest room."

"Did you explain things to her?"

"Yeah, as much as you told me last night. She likes the idea of the eighteen-wheeler and the crane. She had some good questions, mostly about flying stuff. Like, how do we find the MiGs? How do we?"

"We're going to have a meeting tonight to go over all that. As soon as she comes back, we'll—ah, here she is." He waited until she sat down. "I was just telling Whit, there are lots and lots of details to discuss, but it's best to do that tonight. Once you hear the plan, please know that I am open to any and all suggestions. And, if what you hear tonight isn't good enough, you'll be free to walk away with no hard feelings from me. Before we go any farther, I need to ask you both two critical questions." He paused to see if he had their undivided attention.

"First, I want you to understand how dangerous this operation will be. Injury or even death is a possibility. Even if we succeed, we may get hunted down and imprisoned for a long, long time. Do you both accept this risk?"

Whitaker said, "I'm in."

Leslie said, "Yes. Me too."

"Thank you. Second, once we commit to this, we've got to disappear for about two weeks. No contact with anyone." He saw Leslie's little mobile phone attached to her purse. "Leslie, please turn that off and remove the battery. No personal phones allowed; they can be tracked. Conditions will be a little spartan. We'll live in an abandoned hangar for several days. Sleeping bags, cots, and food out of a can. Maybe no showers. Any problems with that?"

They both shook their heads.

"Okay. Leslie, I know you have more questions, but we need to get to the bank so Whit can go off on his shopping spree. After the bank, Leslie and I will go off on a separate errand. Whit, you'll have to figure out how to return the Explorer without going to the airport rental office. We need to steer clear of that in case it's under surveillance. We'll meet at the rented hangar, the address of which is on the now-famous piece of note paper. Any questions right now?"

Leslie said, "Not a question. Just a comment. You won't be sorry to have me as a wingman, John. You—"

"That reminds me," Whitaker said. "Sorry to interrupt. You keep saying wing *man*, but you're a woman. Shouldn't it be something else? What do they call a female wingman?"

That got a chuckle out of Leslie. She said, "Strangely enough, they haven't invented a new term. Crazy, isn't it? Now, to finish what I was saying, "You may not know it, John, but you are still somewhat of a living legend, even among the younger F-16 pilots. It will be an honor to fly with you."

John raised his eyebrows. "Well, that remains to be seen." He had called in a few favors during that phone call. Leslie was going to get a surprise audition. If she survived that, she was in.

Chapter 21

"Viper One, Ops check. One's 22, 25, 47."

Leslie took her eyes off John's airplane just long enough to glance down and right at the fuel gauge. The Aft/Left pointer said 2,200 pounds, the Forward/Right said 2,400 and the totalizer agreed. 4,600 pounds. Enough for one good fight. She refocused on John's airplane, 9,000 feet away, on her right. She pulled the power back a tad to maintain perfect line-abreast formation. "Viper Two's 22, 24, 46."

"Viper, this will be the butterfly setup. One's ready." John's voice was crisp and brief, like a drill sergeant. Or, more appropriately, like a good flight leader.

She swallowed, getting a second taste of the ham and cheese sandwich John had bought her enroute to Luke Air Force base. She'd need her energy later, he had said, but he wouldn't say why. When she had pressed him for details, she had almost choked on her sandwich when he explained where the "errand" was taking them.

Old habits were coming back quickly. She checked her airspeed. 450 knots, as briefed. Engine instruments? All good. Fuel? Even though she had just checked, she looked again. Still good. *G*-suit hose? Tested okay. She twisted her torso left and right, loosened up her neck, and clicked the bayonet clips on her oxygen mask one or two notches tighter. Lubricated by a thin film of perspiration, the grey rubber mask was now so tight her lips touched the internal microphone, and she could taste rubber. But at least it wouldn't droop down under high g's and pinch her nose.

"Two's ready," Leslie said. Was she, really? It had been over two years since she had been in an F-16 cockpit. She hadn't pulled more than two g's in all that time. In a few seconds, she was going to need all nine g's that the F-16 could provide. She leaned forward and felt the comforting tug of the shoulder harness straps as they extended out of the inertia reel. More than one fighter pilot had forgotten to hook those up and then needed to eject, with fatal results.

She had no reason to doubt her proficiency. They had already flown some formation, done the standard weapons checks and high-g warmup maneuvers. All that had felt good. But she needed to be better than good. She was going up against a legend. Her only consolation was that John must be equally as rusty. It had been five years since he had flown the Viper, or so he said.

"Viper One, Turn Away." His voice came through clearly. He had brought his custom-fitted helmet and mask, so there was little background noise. So had she, much to John's surprise. The poor guy had been shocked to see her own olive-drab air force helmet bag in the back seat of her Jeep. He had stared at it for a second before getting the message: She had left her condo knowing she was going to fly a second F-16. Maybe he was feeling a little inferior to the "little lady" who had out-maneuvered him back at Hash on Hawthorne. That could work to her advantage in this air battle.

She pushed on the stick to roll left, then pulled for two seconds, hoping that she had turned the required thirty degrees away from John to get some lateral separation. No way she was going to take her eyes off him to check the heading indicator. She watched his airplane go belly-up to her as he made a matching turn away. She counted silently. After ten seconds on diverging headings, they would turn back toward each other and become enemies. Leslie had flown hundreds of these butterfly BFM setups. They were part of the Air Force's building block approach to Basic Fighter Maneuvering—fancy words for dogfighting. One jet versus another.

"Viper One, Turn In. Fight's on." John called.

John's F-16 no longer looked light grey. It appeared darker, a sure sign that their separation had increased to at least four miles. And, she had to look up at him. Damn! She hadn't noticed that subtle climb of his. She had stayed level, so she was already behind the power curve. He was probably in afterburner, gaining a speed advantage as well as one of altitude. She pushed the throttle up and over the military power detent, feeling the kicks against her back as all five stages of the afterburner ignited.

Leslie rolled right and pulled hard to close the distance between them. She had to squint and blink her eyes to keep him in sight. The bastard had set this up so the sun would be in her eyes at the fight's on call. She was tempted to match his climb, but since she was already behind on power and speed, she chose a shallower climb angle to conserve energy. He pulled his nose up into an even steeper climb, right into the sun. All she could see was a black dot far above her.

She risked a glance at her Heads Up Display to check the airspeed and cursed. She had forgotten to turn down the HUD intensity. The bright green symbology would block out her ability to see him, assuming she was able to maneuver well enough to get behind him. She reached for the knob but, since this was an A-model and she was more accustomed to the C-model HUD controls, she missed it on the first try. Leslie took her eyes off John for a split-second to adjust the HUD. When she looked back, he was gone. She gritted her teeth and made the required radio call. "Two's no joy."

John didn't reply and Leslie immediately knew why. He had briefed her that this was not a training exercise. Training missions had safety rules, including a requirement to make a call when you lost sight of your adversary. This was combat. No artificial safety rules.

She was in grave danger of becoming a victim of the old fighter pilot adage, *Lose sight, lose fight*. If their aircraft had been loaded with heat-seeking missiles, she would already be dead. He could have shot her from a distance and been done with her. But John had briefed this as a guns-only engagement because he wasn't sure he could get his hands on missiles for their real mission. Today, they each had a full load of 20-millimeter bullets, 511 rounds—every fifth one a tracer—in the internally mounted six-barrel Gatling gun. At a rate of fire of 6,000 rounds per minute, that worked out to only 5.1 seconds of shooting time. Not much, but a single high explosive incendiary round in the right place could ruin her day.

Leslie had two choices. She could turn tail and run. They called that living to fight another day. But she didn't want another day; she wanted to kick his ass right now. She aimed her jet at his last known position and pulled the throttle out of AB to conserve fuel. Her instinct and experience screamed at her to use the slewable ACM function of the radar to find him, but John had briefed no radar use. All the high-tech stuff was off limits. It was her eyeballs versus his. Her skill with the stick, throttle, and gun versus his. The fighter pilot's version of a bare-knuckle fist fight.

He was out there, maneuvering—calmly, no doubt—to kill her with a lethal burst of twenty mike-mike. To survive, she'd have to fly her jet as if she *did* see him. Leslie counted to herself. *Thousand one, thousand two, thousand three . . .* Each time she reached the count of "four," she pulled hard, jinking the nose about forty-five degrees up, down, left, or right, in random order. These terribly uncomfortable, energy-wasting maneuvers would spoil any shots from her unseen adversary.

She put her left hand on the right canopy handrail and used it to pull her shoulders, neck, and head around to the right as far as they could go. She checked her six o'clock as she had been trained. Gun range first—out to about 1,500 feet, then out to 3,000 feet, high and low. Nothing. Thanks to the F-16's beautiful 360-degree bubble canopy, while twisting to the right she could see all the way around to her seven or eight o'clock position. He was not there. She looked farther out, sweeping the sky with her eyes, focusing for a few seconds at a time in all the likely locations. The sky appeared empty, but it wasn't. There was a man out there trying to shoot her down.

"Come on, girl, find him!" Leslie shouted to herself. She reversed her body to the left, grunting with the effort. She had to push off the canopy rail awkwardly with her left hand and use upper body strength to look left. Her right hand needed to stay on the stick and couldn't be used for leverage to twist her body. He had to be out there somewhere!

Leslie took a deep breath and tightened her gut muscles. She was *not* going to lose this fight. She had learned that aerial combat was, in one way, like chess. The key to winning was to anticipate your opponent's next move and counter it. But that's where the similarity ended. In chess, if you lost, you stood up, shook the winner's hand, and walked away. In a dogfight, the loser's plane caught fire or exploded, carrying the losing pilot to his or her death. The lucky ones got a chance to eject.

If she were John, what would be her next move? She tilted her head back as far as possible to search the sky directly above. If she were the attacker, that's where she would be, exploiting her advantage, sneaking into gun range unobserved. Her neck ached from the strain. She laid her helmet against the ejection seat headrest for support and pulled hard on the stick. It had only been about fifteen seconds since the fight's on call, but if John was maneuvering the way she predicted, he would be up there, high at her six o'clock, coming into gun range any second now.

There he was! Two thousand feet behind and high above her, his nose pointed down at her six o'clock. Cloud-like whorls of vapor trails streamed off his wing roots, a sure sign he was pulling *g*'s, pulling his nose up to point his gun at her. Well, as someone once said, *An enemy at your six is better than no enemy at all.*

Now that she could see him, she could defeat his attack. She lit the afterburner. He was bleeding off airspeed in a max performance turn. She was unloaded, accelerating past 225 knots. For the next few seconds, until his nose was pointed out in front of her in lead pursuit, she was safe. Leslie imagined John's right index finger poised, ready to squeeze the red trigger on the stick. He was probably gloating and thinking to himself, *Only a few more degrees of turn and I'll blow that arrogant bitch out of the sky.*

Leslie inhaled deeply. Wait for it . . . wait for it . . . now! Just as he brought his gun to bear, she rolled right, and pulled back hard on the stick, commanding a max rate turn. The bright blue sky turned dark and fuzzy. Her field of vision narrowed to a small pinhole. She immediately relaxed her pull on the stick, just a little. She had pulled too hard and too quickly, greyed herself out for a moment, and lost sight of John. A rookie mistake. The *g*-suit, now clamped down hard on her belly and legs, hadn't been able to react fast enough to prevent this.

Leslie relaxed her break turn after three seconds, knowing that her airplane had turned almost seventy degrees and spoiled John's gun shot. Her roll and break turn had put her into a nose-low attitude, which would regain some speed. She pulled the throttle out of AB to conserve fuel. If she was lucky, he would overshoot and flush out on her left side. She glanced over there. No joy. Time to jink again. She couldn't see John but, knowing him, he was saddling up into position for another gun shot. She rolled left, tightened up her muscles early this time, and pulled. Not a max rate turn. Just five g's, enough to spoil a gun shot.

Now she was pointed straight up. She pushed the throttle back into AB. Should have done that before climbing. Another mistake. She backed off on the g's and scanned behind for John's F-16. He was back there at her deep six o'clock, waiting for her next move. Which would be what? She couldn't go straight up forever, although at this weight the F-16 could theoretically accelerate going straight up. But that was at sea level. She was at about 15,000 feet. She pulled the jet onto its back, as if she were at the top of a loop, upside down, at about two hundred knots. At least that's what it felt like, judging by the lessening of slipstream noise. She didn't want to risk a look at the HUD for airspeed info.

John would expect her to continue the loop maneuver, pulling her nose down to gain speed. So, she did the unexpected. Leslie rolled wings-level, essentially turning this into an Immelmann maneuver instead of a loop. She lost sight of John but that was a risk she was willing to take. Her surprise roll-out would confuse him; maybe she'd end up above him and gain the advantage, or at least achieve a neutral position.

She was wearing herself out twisting left and right, checking for John. He hadn't been fooled. He had somehow done a barrel-roll maneuver around her tail and was back there, closing in for an easy kill. She rolled inverted and pulled—gently at first due to her low speed— until her nose was pointed straight down. A glance at the HUD told her she was at 20,000 feet. Terrain out here was about 3,000 feet. Her peacetime thinking had to change. There was no artificial "floor," no altitude to break off the engagement for safety's sake. This was a fight to the death. *Let's see if he's good enough to catch me before we both hit the ground.* She pulled the throttle out of afterburner.

Even in mil power, she'd be accelerating to almost supersonic speed by the time she got low. No way he could gun her at that speed.

She had a brief second to check inside her cockpit. Everything looked good except fuel. "Two's Joker," she called. She had another thousand pounds of fuel to burn before reaching Bingo, at which point she'd have to disengage and run for home.

No answer again. Of course. A fight to the death, remember? Running your adversary out of fuel was just as good as a gun kill.

If this were the chess match she had envisioned earlier, he might have said, "Check." Or, for a pilot of his skill, this might be "Checkmate," a position from which there is no escape. She had only two options, both of which were fatal. She could dive into the ground and die. Or she could pull up at the last second, just barely missing the terrain, at which point John would just close in for a gun kill. She'd have to make him overshoot, reverse into him, and gain the advantage. There was no way she was going to give up.

Going straight down at this speed, she'd hit the ground in about fifteen seconds. Leslie pulled the throttle to idle. She was already at corner velocity; any faster would just increase her turn radius. Might even need the speed brake to stay at 450 knots. Leslie didn't need to look back at John right now. She needed to do some quick figuring. Her quickest, tightest 9-*g* turn gave her a turn radius of 3,000 feet. Over this high desert terrain, she'd have to pull out of the dive at 6,000 feet MSL to survive. The HUD altitude tape was useless; the numbers flashed by too quickly. She looked inside at her altimeter, whose pointer was unwinding frantically, decreasing like a clock running backwards. When she saw 7,000, she closed the speed brakes, strained hard and pulled. Her field of vision narrowed under the *g*-force.

With her nose pointed up again, she backed off the *g*, cranked her upper body and head around and looked for John. Naturally, he had matched her turn. This guy was definitely not old and over the hill. He had to be in good shape to follow that high-speed dive recovery. She rolled and pulled, first to the right and, five seconds later, to the left. All that did was bleed off her speed. He followed her every move with apparent ease. She pushed forward on the stick, forcing an uncomfortable negative-*g* guns jink, a last-ditch defensive maneuver. Her feet floated up off the rudder pedals, dust and debris came off the floor, and her shoulders dug into the harness straps. Fortunately, she had strapped in tightly. The negative *g* was trying to fling her out of her seat and bash her head into the canopy.

When she recovered from the jink, she saw that John had done another lag roll, or barrel-roll, around her, preserving his speed and position. She was literally out of airspeed and ideas. His nose pulled out in lead. She tried a few more jinks but, at her low speed, they were ineffective. Red balls, 20-millimeter tracer rounds, streaked by, just in front of her nose. More red flashes, then her radome exploded, and everything went black.

"Okay, kids, your time's up. I'm putting you on freeze. Close your eyes."

That was the voice of Lieutenant Colonel Steve Grimes, a man she had met an hour ago. Leslie closed her eyes to avoid being disoriented when the motion stopped and the outside visual display, projected on a large dome, went blank. She felt the cockpit shake as if it had encountered turbulence. It sank a few feet and clunked onto a solid surface. Even though her throttle was still at mid-range, the noise stopped, and the engine gauges froze.

"You can open up now," Grimes said.

"Wait!" John said. "Steve, can we have just five more minutes? There's one more thing I really, really need to do."

There was a long pause before Grimes answered. "You're in luck, John. The next pilots aren't here yet. Close your eyes again while I put the motion back on."

"Okay. Steve, can you set us up for a BFM-1 profile? Just put us back with good fuel, a full gun, 450 knots, 10,000 feet, and Viper Two in a perch position on me."

Grimes told them to close their eyes again and, while the motion and visual system was being reset, John said, "Viper Two, when this setup begins, I want you to close in for a gun kill. Make it quick."

"Viper Two."

"You're all set. Motion and visual are back on," Grimes said.

Leslie opened her eyes to a scene above the desert with John's F-16 about a mile ahead. It took her a second or two to adjust to the renewed sense of motion and jet noise. She checked her speed. 450 knots.

"Fence check in," John called.

"Two." She confirmed the Master Arm switch was still in "Arm," checked the gun for status and flicked the button on the throttle to the "Dogfight" position.

"One's ready."

"Two's ready."

"Fight's on."

John rolled left and started a turn. She closed into gun range, expecting him to jink. But he just held the left turn, using only about four g's. Was this a trick? No, dammit, he was treating her like a rookie, giving her an easy target to shoot at.

Leslie put the pipper out in front of his nose but, just before she squeezed the trigger, he jinked left and down. She followed him and lined up for another shot. His afterburner was lit; he extended out to about three thousand feet—too far for a gun attack. She pushed her throttle into full AB and relaxed her back pressure on the stick. She let the F-16's 23,000 pounds of thrust get her close enough to gun his brains out.

Of course, he jinked again, at the last possible moment. She repositioned. He was about 45 degrees nose high, banked slightly left and—judging by the rate his nose was tracking through the sky—pulling about four gs. That was not very smart. Or was it? Damn it! He was headed into the sun. Again! By the time she got into gun range, the glare was so bad she lost sight of him. Peacetime training rules demanded that she call "No joy" and turn away from his last known position. But this was *not* peacetime. This was a two-person war.

What was his next move? He must know she'd lose sight right about now. He'd tighten up his turn while she flailed around trying to find him. That would allow him to drive away from her, get out of gun range and possibly gain the advantage. Leslie took a big chance. She pulled hard left, about six gs by the feel of it. She was betting he'd keep that left turn going. If she was wrong, she'd either cause a mid-air collision, killing them both, or allow him to fly off to the right and escape.

He showed up right where she had predicted! With sun angle no longer a factor, she got the pipper on his fuselage, right behind the cockpit, squeezed the trigger and held it down. Shit! Before the tracers reached where his jet *had* been, he had pulled up hard, in a vertical break turn. Something sparkled on his left horizontal tail and a small piece of it fell away.

Evidently, she hadn't hit anything vital. She pulled as hard as she could to match his break turn, but overshot and ended up in a vertical climb, canopy-to-canopy with John, whose jet was about two hundred feet away.

"All right, John, that's it. Knock it off," Grimes said. "Time's up."

They both acknowledged the knock it off call.

"Close your eyes," Grimes said.

The simulator's shutdown sequence repeated itself. Leslie flipped up the yellow metal unlock handle and pushed up on the toggle switch underneath. An electric motor whined loudly, and the canopy rumbled open. She unhooked the chin strap of her helmet and peeled it off her head. The grey cloth skull cap, thoroughly soaked with perspiration, stuck to her hair, which was a wet mess. She used the skull cap to wipe sweat off her face and hair.

Grimes was standing outside, smiling. He had already lowered the gangplank which connected her cockpit to the surrounding metal platform with banks of consoles and computers. He grinned at her and said, "Pretty realistic, eh?"

Leslie nodded.

"First time at the TAC ACES simulator?"

"Yes." Since John had been so secretive about her identity, introducing her only as his wingman, Viper Two, Grimes knew nothing about her experience level or service background. Leslie wondered if he thought she was a novice. She unbuckled her shoulder harness and lap belt and unhooked her *g*-suit hose.

Grimes backed up to give her enough room to climb out of the cockpit. He said, "The combination of *g*-suit inflation, inflatable bladders on the seat back and bottom, and the visual display that dims when you pull too much *g*? That all combines to make it all feel like the real thing. So real that some people get airsick in here."

She nodded.

"Look, I don't want to rush you, but we've got another mission scheduled in a couple minutes." He pointed down a short hallway. "I'll pull your VTR tape and meet you in briefing room number two in a minute. As soon as I get John out of his dome."

"Okay," she said. It was an effort to pull herself out of the cockpit. Every muscle in her upper body ached. Her legs weren't much better. She got her left leg over the canopy rail and pushed herself up, sat on the rail for a second or two, and stepped down. Once out of the cockpit, she walked up the gangplank into the control room. Thirty feet away, under an identical dome to hers, was John.

Leslie could have used a stop at the rest room to freshen up, but Grimes seemed to be in a hurry, so she headed for the briefing room and sat down. John walked in a moment later, followed closely by Grimes, who carried two cans of soda and two videotape recorder cassettes, one from each of their "aircraft." He passed out the soda, shoved one of the cassettes into a player and pushed the rewind button.

John said, "Thanks for the sodas, Steve. And thanks for the sim time. I owe you."

Grimes pulled out a chair at the head of the table, turned it around so the back was facing them and sat down, swinging one leg over the seat. His arms draped over the back of the chair. "You've got that right," he drawled. "I'm up shit's creek if anyone finds out who you really are. Look, you guys can debrief yourselves. I'm already behind schedule. But, before I go, I'd like to make two comments."

"Sure, Steve," John said. "Go ahead."

Grimes nodded. He worked his tongue around inside his cheeks for a few seconds. "John, old buddy, I have no clue why you had to run this engagement on such short notice. I know you are not going to tell me, so I'm not going to ask."

The video machine clicked. Grimes ejected the first tape, John's, and put hers in. He pressed the rewind button and the machine whirred. "All I can say is, you folks are damn lucky there was a slot available today because we are booked solid for the next two weeks. Now about the engagement. I watched the whole thing on the monitors, which give me a three-dimensional, God's eye view. I also see the view out your HUD."

He looked at her. "Viper Two, the mysterious Ms. No Real Name?"

"Sorry, sir," she said.

"Don't worry, I'm not going to ask. I've got to tell you, Viper Two, you did a fine job. You've got some excellent defensive moves. I've flown with John, and I've seen him in this TAC ACES sim beaucoup times. He's never lost. He usually gets a kill shot in less than a minute. But you managed to defeat him for two and a half minutes. You made him work for it; made him sweat, *almost* made him miss. On that second setup, you almost got him. I can honestly say that's a first. I've never seen anyone score a hit with twenty mike-mike on John." He stood up and said, "Viper Two, you did good. I'd fly with you any day." Grimes reached out a hand.

Leslie stood and shook hands. "Thank you, sir. It would be an honor to fly with you too."

After Grimes left the room, she sat down and waited. As the flight leader, it was John's prerogative to speak first. The tape machine clicked to a stop and her tape popped up. She watched John's chest rise and fall. The room was now so quiet that she could hear their breathing.

John removed the tape and studied each side of the cassette as if he were studying the facets of a diamond. He looked directly into her eyes and said, "I don't need this tape to know how you performed. Grimes is right. You fly and fight pretty damn well. As good as I've ever seen." He took a long sip of soda. "Let's go splash a little water on our faces and get back to Tucson. Any questions?"

Leslie was stunned. That was it? No tongue lashing for losing the fight? No questions about losing him in the sun and pressing in for a gun shot anyway? "Yes, actually," she said. "One question. I did a couple things that I thought were non-standard, moves that were opposite of what you might expect. But you seemed to anticipate those. How?"

"That's easy, Les—I mean, Viper Two. I've known you for three days. I've learned to expect the unexpected."

Chapter 22

"Do you mind if I recline this seat a little?" John asked.

Leslie said, "Sure, go ahead. There's a lever on the right side, way down low. It's kind of hard to find."

He pulled the lever and angled the seat back until it felt as comfortable as the thirty-degree reclined angle of the F-16's seat. He silently thanked the General Dynamics engineers who had come up with the reclined-seat idea to increase a pilot's *g* tolerance. Something to do with reducing the distance between the heart and the brain to keep the brain supplied during high *g* maneuvering. An unintended side effect had been better ergonomics. The reclined position distributed weight better than older, straight-backed ejection seats, making a nine-*g* turn in a Viper much more tolerable. That seat back angle felt so good on his back that he had adopted it for automobile travel as well.

"Back to Interstate 10, I presume?" Leslie said.

"Yes."

The traffic light turned green. Leslie turned right out of Luke AFB's main gate and headed south on Litchfield Road. After a short distance of nothing but bare, brown desert and one convenience store, the road began its series of gentle curves through the upscale neighborhood of Litchfield Park. Both sides of Litchfield Road were lined with tall palm trees and bushy Blue Palo Verdes which, oddly enough, weren't actually blue—unless you got close enough to see the blue tint in their green bark. He had once dreamed of living out here and buying Nicole one of those spacious single-story homes with exterior walls of slump block, the modern equivalent of adobe. That was back when things were going well, when he still had a family to enjoy, and a successful Air Force career path laid out for him.

Leslie didn't say very much until she merged into light traffic on eastbound I-10. She engaged cruise control and said, "I want a rematch someday. I'll kick your ass."

He looked at her and smiled. "It would be fun to let you try."

"Why didn't you let me know about the TAC ACES trip in advance? You're just lucky that I had the foresight to put my helmet bag in the Jeep. I wouldn't have wanted to do all that heavy maneuvering with an ill-fitting loaner helmet."

"Yeah, about that . . . oh, never mind. I just answered my own question."

"What?"

John said, "I was just thinking that bringing your helmet this morning was a . . . ah . . . a ballsy move. Pardon the expression." He could see her jaw tighten. She opened her mouth to speak. "Hold on, hold on," he said. "Let me finish. I was just going to say, maybe that's what I need. A wingman who's capable, one who can think ahead, and who has just the right amount of—"

"Balls," Leslie said.

"Let's just call it confidence. I'd like to leave anatomy out of this discussion. I just want the most capable wingman I can get. One with a functional, comfortable helmet."

"That reminds me, where are we going to get *g*-suits?"

"Believe it or not, they are available online," he said. "Nomex flight suits also. With next-day delivery. You'll have to give me your sizes tonight."

She was quiet for the next twenty minutes as she dealt with increasing traffic around Phoenix. He used the time to ponder the female pilot thing. In the old days, he had considered himself open-minded about it, but that had been hypothetical, way before Congress had okayed women in combat jobs. Now he was sitting next to a red-haired, hard flying, straight-shooting fighter pilot who just happened to be a gorgeous female. What was it Leslie had said? Something about putting his hormones on standby. Good luck with that.

Traffic lightened up a few miles east of Phoenix. As he had feared, Leslie bombarded him with questions.

"We've got an open road and plenty of time," she said. "Tell me everything, step-by-step. The MiGs, the Boneyard plan, the airfield, weapons and . . . everything. I heard most of it from Whitaker, but I want to hear it from you."

As he outlined his plan, she played the devil's advocate, trying to poke holes in it, and rattling off questions all the way to Tucson. He answered them all.

Just before they reached the Tucson city limits, she asked, "What will we do with the jets when we're done?"

That one caught him completely by surprise. He shrugged. "Haven't thought about that yet." What really surprised him was that she believed they might get that far. "Take the airport exit," he said.

"That's where you rented the hangar?"

"Yeah, but we're not headed there just yet." He checked the dashboard clock. "After you turn onto the airport access road —Is that Tucson Boulevard?"

She nodded.

"Head toward the terminal. You'll see two hotels on your left. Pull into the Airway Hotel. It's the smaller of the two. I've got an appointment there in a few minutes."

"For what?" Leslie said.

"To buy us an airfield."

* * *

Leslie shut off the Jeep's engine and set the parking brake. "You are full of surprises, John. Now that we're partners, I'm not sure I like that."

"Look," he said. "I set this up before you invited yourself into this adventure. So, before we go in, let me bring you up to speed." She had parked facing west. The late afternoon sun was directly in his eyes, so he pulled down the sun visor. "Last night, while I was still at Rita's, I estimated how much money I would need to do this mission. I don't have enough cash to finance this whole thing. The only way to get more cash in a hurry was to sell the T-Bird. Fortunately, I know somebody who has wanted to buy it for several years."

She snapped her fingers. "Just like that? You call somebody and he agrees to meet you at this sleazy-looking hotel and buy the T-33? For how much?"

"Yup. Like I said, he really wants it, and is willing to pay $250,000. Do you want to come in or wait out here?"

"Oh, I wouldn't miss this for the world," she said.

"Good. You can help me count the cash. I asked for it in hundreds."

"You're going to *count* a quarter of a million dollars in cash?"

"*We* are going to count it. As you said, we're partners now." He did some quick figuring. "Your half would be $125,000. 1,250 one-hundred-dollar bills. Let's see, if you can count one bill per second, or 60 per minute, that would take—give me just a sec—just over twenty minutes. With no breaks, of course." He enjoyed Leslie's look of dismay.

"I'm just kidding," he said. "I asked for signed, bank-sealed packages of $10,000 each. My banker tells me these are called 'straps,' because each package is wrapped in a narrow, mustard-colored paper band, or strap. All we have to do is riffle through each strap to verify it's not just blank paper inside and then count the total number of straps. That would be only—"

"Enough!" Leslie said. "I can do math too. Twenty-five packages. I mean straps. Is this guy really that sleazy that he would try to cheat?"

"Buck Carmody is a real slime ball. Fat, rich, and arrogant. He's a big cotton farmer and real estate developer who owns about half of southern Arizona. He is also a collector of antique airplanes, especially war birds. He's wanted to buy the T-Bird ever since he saw it at the flight museum in Olympia. I've told him three times that it's not for sale."

"So, how did you know about Dateland?"

"Dateland—well, there's a town by that name. But *this* Dateland is a defunct 320-acre date farm out in the boonies about forty miles west of Gila Bend. It was supposed to become a major tourist attraction, one of those theme parks, but the investors wisely backed out at the last minute. It's too remote out there, too far from Phoenix for easy access to a theme park. The military used to rent Dateland—not the whole 320-acres, just the airfield at the south end of the property. It's one of those triangular-shaped, World War II-era airfields and a hangar. The military uses it periodically for night special operations training."

"Hah!" Leslie said. "Now the truth comes out. How does John Martin, the man who says he was just a fighter pilot and never a covert operative, know about all this special ops stuff?"

"You asked if I had ever worked for the CIA or Northern Air. I said no. What I did for Air Force special ops is a whole 'nother story, for another time. Let's get back to—"

"Hold it," she said. "Air Force special ops? You mean like Air Commandos and all that? You bet your ass that's a story I'd like to hear, and soon. Say, right after we do this little transaction. Okay?"

"Yes, okay. Now, back to this guy Carmody. When Dateland became a practically worthless piece of real estate, Carmody bought it at auction for a hundred and fifty grand. He's getting the T-Bird, which is appraised at $350,000, for a substantial discount. I convinced him to throw in Dateland and its 320 acres of dirt as part of the deal. Let's get in there and get this over with."

"You're not too excited about giving up the T-Bird, are you?"

John didn't answer.

"Sorry, that was a silly question," she said. "One more silly question. Why not meet down at Sahuaro Aviation, where the T-33 is parked? Is he going to buy it sight unseen?"

"The short answer is yes. But, to satisfy your curiosity, I don't want to go anywhere near the T-Bird right now. Hardwick probably has it under surveillance. About Carmody, he's seen the T-Bird before and knows how well it's maintained. So, he's not worried about its condition. Anyway, I insisted that the deal be done right here. I have the registration papers in my pocket."

John got out of the Jeep, got his empty gym bag from the back seat, and waited for Leslie to lock up. They walked up a tiled entryway to the hotel's front door. A pair of automatic doors slid open.

Carmody was standing just inside. "Hello, Martin." He took a long glance at Leslie. "Why don't you and the little lady join me in my private office?" He turned and walked down the hall, past a noisy bar with saloon-style doors.

Leslie lowered her voice and said, "Ugh. Slime ball is a good description. Did you see how he leered at me? I hate him already."

"Don't do anything to screw up the deal. When we get into his office, why don't you start counting the money while I sign the papers? Oh, by the way, it would not be wise to call this hotel and bar sleazy, even though it is. Carmody owns it."

Fifteen minutes later, from her place at the end of the long conference table, Leslie said, "It's all here." She closed the lid of the brown leather briefcase.

"The case is yours to keep, sweetie," Carmody said.

John signed the last document and pushed it across the table to Carmody. "The T-Bird is yours now. Take good care of it."

Carmody didn't look at the paper. He shoved it over to his lawyer, who was also a notary public. John had already forgotten the man's name. After studying the title for the T-Bird, he said, "This is apparently genuine."

John ground his teeth. *Apparently* genuine. Typical cover-your-ass lawyer language.

The man stood up. "Let me make copies of this and the deed for Dateland. After I notarize them, the transaction will be complete."

"Dateland's yours now," Carmody said. "Take good care of it!" He threw back his head and laughed. His beer belly quivered as he guffawed. The gloating was cut short by a fit of raspy, wet, heavy-smoker's coughing. He pulled out a handkerchief and wiped his lips. "What the hell are you going to do with Dateland?"

"Hold onto it. For future development."

"Future, huh? You'd better plan on about a century." Carmody laughed again, which ended with an even longer coughing session. He pushed back his chair and struggled into a standing position. Come on, Barr, let's go." He winked and said, "Get it? Barr, a lawyer?" He coughed out another rheumy chuckle.

The lawyer's lips curled up into a "Isn't that funny?" smile, which he held until Carmody looked away. Then he rolled his eyes and frowned.

John felt sorry for him.

As Carmody walked out of the room with Barr in trail, he said, "Toodle-oo, little lady."

Leslie didn't say anything until the door closed and the clumping noise of Carmody's eel skin cowboy boots had faded. "Goodbye, shithead," she said to the inside of the door.

John had not quite erased the grin on his face before Leslie saw it.

"What's so funny?" she said.

He shrugged. "I'm glad you kept your temper under control." He patted the briefcase. "We got what we came for. Sweetie."

"Sweetie, my ass. If that jerk had called me 'little lady' or 'little woman' one more time . . ." She walked over to a countertop with a microwave, sink and mini-fridge underneath. "I've got to wash my hands. My fingertips are all grey from flipping through the money bundles."

"Wait," John said. "Help me put the money in my gym bag."

"You don't want the briefcase?"

"It might have a tracking device on it," he said.

"Wow. You are a piece of work. Paranoid."

After they had both washed their hands, John picked up his bag. He was somewhat disappointed that a quarter of a million dollars in hundreds wasn't very heavy. Maybe ten pounds. They walked out to the Jeep.

Leslie climbed into the driver's seat and said, "Where to now?"

Chapter 23

"Go east down this road," he said. "Look for Hangar 12."

They passed a somewhat dilapidated, vacant two-story office building and an equally sad-looking empty hangar with no doors and broken windows before John saw Hangar 12. It was in much better condition. "Pull up to the big doors on the west side and beep your horn three times."

"You rented this whole thing?" Leslie said. "It's big enough to hold a couple 737s."

"Got a good deal on a month's rental. The airport authority is happy to get the business. All these have been vacant since the Gates Learjet company pulled out a couple years ago." John noticed a phone booth outside the hangar. He'd have to see if that worked. It might be a good way to make anonymous calls.

Leslie beeped the horn. A smaller man-sized door opened briefly, Whitaker peeked out and gave them a thumbs up. He disappeared back inside the hangar. Chains clanked and the massive, segmented doors opened. Whitaker, dressed in an olive-drab t-shirt, camouflage pants and black combat boots, waved them in.

Leslie drove in and parked next to a baby-blue Ford F-150 pickup that looked well-used but clean. As soon as she had cleared the hangar doors, Whitaker cranked them closed.

John laughed.

"What's so funny?

John waited until the rumbling of the closing metal doors stopped and said, "Whitaker. With the money I gave him, he could have bought any kind of work boots and clothes. But what does he get? Military surplus stuff. Probably as old as he is."

"I heard that, John Martin," Whitaker said. "Don't you think I didn't. I may be old, but I ain't deaf."

Leslie smiled and said, "Hello, Whit. You've been busy. Got us a truck, I see."

"It doesn't look like much, but it's mechanically sound. Saw it in a newspaper I picked up yesterday." Whitaker handed the paper to John. "Got another one circled for you to look at later today."

"We're going to need two vehicles?" Leslie asked.

"Yes," John said. "I'll explain later. Let's see what Whit has done while we were gone." The first thing he noticed was a six-foot-long wooden workbench, complete with a full set of tools hanging from a pegboard. "You built that?"

"No, that's a prefab one from the big box store. All those tools are brand new." He glared at John. "*If* I had gotten a little advance notice, I could've shipped my own down here."

John overlooked that and said, "Nice looking forklift." It had a shiny blue body and looked brand new. "Please tell me you didn't buy that."

"Your money's safe," Whitaker said. "It's a rental, like that welding rig." He pointed at the arc welder and two small open-sided wooden crates resting on pallets. "Had to buy those, though. Pumps. One for fuel, one for hydraulic fluid." He pointed to large coils of hose. "That big, thick, heavy hose is for jet fuel and the smaller one is for hydraulics. I used the aerial photo you gave me to measure how much hose we'd need and added a little safety factor. God help us if we can't park where you planned."

"That's a good point, Whit," John said. "I've got an idea. Can you rent an extra trailer? Drive it out there early tomorrow and park it, sort of reserve our spot?"

Whitaker frowned. "Sounds like too much of a hassle to move trailers around. There's got to be a better idea. Hey! How about I just get some of those folding traffic barricades and big orange signs that say, 'Shoulder Closed.' Maybe some traffic cones."

"Great idea. Let's do it," John said. "Any luck on tractor trailers?"

"Affirmative. I'll get a look at them tomorrow. The price seems about right. But expenses are adding up. Are you sure you're prepared to finance this whole operation? Have you thought about fuel costs? Jet fuel is not cheap. And all that other—"

"Trust me, Whit," he said. "I've got it covered." He unzipped his gym bag, broke the seal on one of the traps of hundred-dollar bills, peeled off about half of them, and put that wad of cash into his pocket. The remainder he put back in the bag and handed it to Whitaker. "Here, put this in a safe place."

"What is it?"

"It's a quarter of a million dollars in cash. For your future expenses. Minus a few dollars I just took out." He didn't have the heart to tell Whitaker that the T-Bird was gone, traded for cash and a date farm. The old guy would have a heart attack. The worst part of it was that neither he nor Whitaker had a chance to say goodbye to the jet. Whitaker would have loved to touch it, tighten a few fittings, or polish it up. John doubted that the T-Bird's silver skin and long plexiglass canopy would ever shine as brightly as it had when he had taxied away from the flight museum in Olympia. Old Carmody was probably going to put it in a hanger and let it gather dust, never to fly again.

Leslie said, "That aerial photo Whit mentioned. Can I get a look at it? I still don't have a good concept of the layout."

"Sure," John said. He looked over at a card table with four metal chairs. "Whit, why don't you get that photo, and we'll sit down over there." He noticed that four cots, each with a pillow, sheets, and a green army blanket, were lined up against the wall near the table.

Whitaker laid the photo on the table. They all sat down. John put his helmet bag on the floor and so did Leslie.

"Whit, why don't you lay it all out for Leslie? By now, I'll bet you can explain it better than I."

"No shit. S'cuse my language, Leslie," Whitaker said. "John here, he just thinks up these impossible scenarios, then turns them over to me to make them happen." He rotated the photo so Leslie could see it better. "This here north-south street is Kolb Road, the eastern border of the Boneyard, at least this section of it anyway. Right across the street from the Boneyard is a residential area. As you can see in the photo, most people park their cars on the east side of the street. The west side is just a dirt shoulder, right next to the Boneyard's fence. Nobody seems to park there, but it's wide enough for a semi to fit."

"That's a row of F-16s right inside that fence," Leslie said.

Whitaker tapped his forehead with an index finger and said, "Bingo!" He pulled a pencil from his shirt pocket and circled two jets near the middle of the second row from the fence. "These are the airplanes we are going to 'borrow.'"

"Why those two?" Leslie asked.

"Well, this whole row is maintained in a higher state of readiness than all the others. I'll let John explain why."

John gave Leslie a condensed version of what he had told Whitaker about the foreign military sales program and the Peace Leopard political fiasco.

Whitaker continued. "Now, you are asking yourself, why these two, specifically? Our eagle-eyed John here noticed that this one—" He pointed at it. "This one is mine. Three-Six-Eight. Officially, F-16A serial number 79-0368. I was the crew chief on that aircraft for four years, at two different bases. And guess who the pilot was all those four years?"

Leslie looked at John and said, "No way!"

"It's true," John said. "In my idle moments, I had been tracking where Three-Six-Eight had gone after it left Luke Air Force Base. First it went to Edwards, to the USAF Test Pilot School, where it was used as a chase plane for their prototype aircraft. Then, it went to a couple different Air National Guard units before retiring to the Boneyard in 1990. Ironically enough, that's the same year I retired. That's the last I had heard of my—" He looked at Whitaker. "I mean, *our* jet until two days ago, when I learned it was part of the now-infamous Peace Leopard thing."

Whitaker said, "Enough history! Let's get back to business. We park our eighteen-wheeler next to that fence, which is not an unusual thing to see in a working-class neighborhood. We use a remote-control crane mounted in the trailer to lift ourselves over the fence, run approximately 130 feet of fuel and hydraulic hoses under the fence and service the jets. Get the hoses back out before the next security patrol passes by." He continued, outlining the plan, culminating with cutting the locks on the Boneyard exit gate and the runway entry gate.

Leslie said, "Hold on. If part of that road is dirt, aren't we going to suck rocks into the intakes and trash the engines?"

"Excellent question, Miss Leslie," Whitaker said. "Do you remember those big red metal frames that cover the intake during engine ground runs?"

"Yes, but Whit, those are just metal bars, about four inches apart, designed to keep ground crew from getting sucked into the intake during engine runs at high power settings. One of those wouldn't stop a pebble from getting sucked in."

"I'll add some small-diameter wire mesh to the frame, and we'll be good to go. Even if I can't find ready-made frames, I can fabricate them from scratch."

While Whitaker continued his explanation of how these screens would be removed before takeoff, John let his eyes wander around the hangar. The assortment of tools and equipment was impressive, considering it all had been done in one day. Whit had even bought a camp stove and a little table to put it on, over there next to the four cots.

That's when it hit him. *Four* cots? *Four* blankets and pillows? In fact, he was sitting at a card table with four chairs. Crap, crap, and double crap! He inhaled deeply and let out a long sigh. "Stop, Whit," he said. "Just stop everything for a minute."

Whitaker and Leslie stared at him.

John said, "Why are there four chairs, four cots, blankets, and pillows?"

"I was wondering how long it would take you to notice that," Whitaker said. "Look, both of you. You've heard me explain what needs to be done. Do you really think one mechanic can do it all? Build what we need, get it over the fence, get two jets serviced, two gates busted open? No offense to either of you, but you won't be much help. You're pilots, not jet mechanics. Tried to call you first, John, but you were off on your secret mission today and—being the dinosaur that you are—you don't have a mobile phone. So, I made one of those command decisions that the Air Force was always telling me to make. I found us another crew chief."

John felt his heart pounding; a vein on his temple pulsed. He wondered if the others could see that. The last thing he needed was one more person involved in all this. "And who might that be?" John couldn't imagine any of Whitaker's old cronies getting involved.

"Hank's son, Adam. He'll be here tomorrow morning at 0930." Whitaker sat back, folded his arms, and smiled at them both.

Chapter 24

As Leslie drove them away from the hangar, she said, "I am very proud of you. No cussing, no yelling, no temper tantrum."

John said, "Believe me, I considered all three of those options. I was furious. Still am. I do *not* want Hank's son exposed to danger and imprisonment. But it's too late, isn't it? Thanks to Whit, Adam already knows what we're going to do. And, being hard-headed like his dad, there's no way he's going to stay out of this."

He hated to admit it, but Whitaker was right. There was too much fabrication, too much equipment still needed, and not enough time for one mechanic to do it all—even with Leslie and John helping. The engine start and launch of the F-16s would go much faster with two crew chiefs. John chided himself for not realizing this sooner. But what could he have done about it? He didn't know any other crew chiefs well enough to ask them to commit a major crime.

"Get over it, John; it's out of your control. It's what they call a *fait accompli.* That's French for—"

"I know what that means."

Leslie said, "Let's move on to the next task, which, if I understand correctly, is to drive out to Dateland and sweep the runway. It would be nice to see the place before we have to land there in the wee hours of the morning. There are no runway lights, I presume."

"You presume correctly." John briefly entertained the idea of portable runway lights. But, if they even existed, finding them, and getting them shipped to Tucson was too much work. They had enough equipment on order already. "Don't get on I-10 right away," he said. "There are a few things we need to do first. Number one on the list is to hide your Jeep."

"What's the problem with using my Jeep?"

"I don't want to use anything registered to either of us," John said. "Hardwick is going to have us followed or try to. It's just a matter of time before they begin looking for your vehicle."

"Follow us? Me? Hardwick would do that?"

"Of course. It's what I would do if I were in his shoes. He wants to prevent me from doing something 'stupid,' remember? If he finds you, he finds me."

"All right. Then why don't I just park my car at my condo?"

"That's one of the first places they'll look for us." John pointed to the airport's long term parking sign. "How about in there? It looks like they even have covered parking."

She pushed a green button at the entrance, pulled out a parking stub and tossed it onto the center console. The gate swung up and she drove into the crowded lot. Near the end of the second row, she found a spot. "Now what? We can't rent another car."

"We're not. We're going to buy one. With cash, of course." He tapped the newspaper that Whitaker had given him. "That's how Whit got that Ford F-150 pickup you saw in the hangar. He circled a couple ads for me." John handed her the folded classified ads section. "Do you see the one with two circles drawn around it? It's a 1990 Chevy Crew Cab pickup. Loaded. 454 cubic inch V-8, four-speed stick shift, four-wheel drive. Whit says the owner's expecting us this afternoon."

Leslie shook her head. "No, that won't work. We still need ID to buy a car. If Hardwick is as smart as you say he is, he'll be checking recent sales."

John opened his door and got out. "He won't see any of our names. C'mon, let's walk over to the taxi stand in front of the passenger terminal. I'll explain more on the way."

Leslie locked the Jeep and joined him on the sidewalk leading to the terminal.

"First," John said, "I'm not at all sure that a private owner making a sale for cash will even ask for ID. The guy who sold Whit that Ford truck didn't. Just took his word for it. But if the person selling this Chevy asks, I've got a plan for that. Our first stop will be a copy shop up on Speedway Boulevard, where a little package is waiting for me with new ID for both me and Whitaker."

Leslie stopped. "New ID? What, you keep another set of ID around like some secret agent? The more I learn about you, John, the more I think you are hiding a lot from me."

He laughed. "This is the nineties, Leslie. There is this wonderful thing called the Word Wide Web. Anyone with $150 can order a fake "novelty" driver's license from thirty-three states, one of which is Arizona. It's guaranteed to pass inspection by state patrol. Next day delivery costs another thirty bucks."

"Still—" she said, pausing to let a family of four pass by. "What kind of person even knows about that sort of thing? You, however, seem to know an awful lot about, I don't know, unconventional stuff. Spy stuff. Which reminds me. I am still waiting for more info on your Air Force special ops experience."

They waited for the "Walk" sign at a crosswalk just outside the terminal. John used the time to check for surveillance and to decide how to answer Leslie's question. It might be time to tell her the whole story. She'd probably hear it soon enough from either Whitaker or Adam.

"I didn't lie to you about refusing to work for Hardwick's clandestine ops. But a long time ago, during the Vietnam War days and right after pilot training, I, ah, got recruited—it was more like ordered—into a little intelligence work. You know how the military is. Someone in PACAF headquarters checked the computer for pilots with certain language skills and aptitude test scores. My name popped up." The light changed and they walked across to the taxi stand.

"PACAF?" Leslie said. "Vietnam? You know Vietnamese?"

"No. I speak fluent French."

"What does . . . oh, I get it. Vietnam is a former French colony."

John said, "I went through several interviews, got selected for a mission, and went through a short training course. Did one mission. Then I . . . I sort of insisted that I be reassigned to fly fighters."

"What was the mission?"

"Sorry, Leslie. It's classified. I signed non-disclosure papers. They're still valid."

They waited their turn at the taxi stand behind an elderly couple, vacationers from back east by their accent and dress. A skycap helped the driver load their massive suitcases into the trunk. That taxi drove off and another pulled up.

"Where to, my friend?" the new driver asked.

"The Smuggler's Inn, corner of Speedway and Wilmot," John said. He opened the door for Leslie, who raised her eyebrows, but did not question his destination. The Smuggler's Inn was a popular hotel, restaurant, and club. It was also a block away from the copy shop where his package had been sent. He scanned the area before bending down into the cab. A green Chevy Impala was parked at the west end of the terminal. One man, dressed in a dark suit coat and tie, was behind the wheel. John got into the cab and the driver pulled away from the curb. He twisted around to look out the back window.

A younger man, also dressed in a dark suit, rushed out of the terminal, pointed in their direction, and jumped into the Impala's passenger seat. The Chevy accelerated away from the curb.

John whispered, "Shit."

"What is it?" Leslie said.

"Get close to me," he said, in as low a voice as possible. "Wrap your arms around my neck, as if we were lovers. I don't want the driver to hear me."

She turned to face him, embraced him, and rested her head on his upper chest. "How's this?"

"Wonderful." He stared at the green car while enjoying her scent, lavender again, and the feel of her being close. "We're being followed."

She moved. He held her tighter.

"No, don't look back. Hell, I should have known better. Coming back to the airport was a big mistake. They had someone waiting. Now they're behind us. Two men in a green Impala."

"Do you think they're government? Or could they be drug people? Alvarado's people?

"That's an interesting question."

They had just made a right turn onto Valencia Road. If he angled his head just right, he could see behind the taxi using the right-side mirror. The green Impala was still there, about half a mile behind them. "I don't see how Alvarado could have found out about us unless he has informers down at Ajo or at your Customs Service detachment. Or, God forbid, Alvarado has a source in Washington." He reviewed what he had seen of the men and their car. "They must be government agents. Both guys I saw were too clean-cut and too white to be druggies from Mexico. No one in the Alvarado cartel would be caught dead in a plain-Jane Chevy Impala with black steel rims and little silver hubcaps. Their taste runs to Mercedes and BMWs."

"Now what?" Leslie said. "We lose them, right?"

"Right."

"How?"

"I'm not quite sure," John said. "Any suggestions?"

"You're the one with the spy instincts and training, not me. I'd say find someplace really busy. Lose them there."

His training, such as it had been, was thirty-plus years old but she was correct. They had to find a street with lots of traffic, full of cars, buses, or trucks. Their taxi was now in the left turn lane for northbound Alvernon Way, which would take them into the city. A half-mile straight ahead was the big I-10 freeway interchange. He leaned forward and said, "Driver, we've had a change of plans. Go straight ahead and get on I-10 west."

The driver let several cars pass, cranked the steering wheel to the right and accelerated across the intersection. "That was a little short-notice, man," the cabbie said. "Now, where do you want to go?"

"Sorry," John said. "Head west on I-10."

Once the driver had merged onto the interstate, he said, "What's next?"

"Is there still a big truck stop a few miles west, just outside the city limits? The one with the restaurant? They used to have rooms for rent and showers for the truckers."

"Roy's Pit Stop. Yeah, it's still there. They still have rooms, but if you need a place to, ah, take the lady for a few hours, I can suggest—"

"Just take us to Roy's." John looked back at the on-ramp. The Impala had lost some ground, but it was still there.

The cabbie dropped them off at Roy's, which was bustling with truck traffic. John had tipped him generously. He and Leslie headed for the main entrance, which led to a restaurant and small store. Six or seven eighteen-wheelers were lined up at angles in the parking lot, some with engines still running. Passenger cars lined up for low-priced gasoline. John went to the cashier and stood while two truckers paid for their meals. He paid for a room with cash and was handed a stack of towels and two washcloths. The clerk had insisted on identification, but that had been no problem. The men in the Impala already knew who he was. He walked back to the restaurant, where Leslie sat at a window table with two glasses of iced tea.

He sat opposite her, opened a packet of sugar, and poured it into his tea. He stirred the tea and said, "Where are they now?"

"One is still in the car out there near the gas pumps. The other one, kind of young-looking, came in for a moment, saw you at the cashier and me at this table, and went back outside. He's over there, outside the entrance, studying the label on a can of motor oil."

John looked out the window. Without too much effort, he could see the front half of the Impala. One man in the car. But he couldn't turn to see the entrance without seeming suspicious, so he'd have to depend on Leslie's eyes. "The one near the front door, he's still there?"

"Yes," she said. "Now he's reading the label on a can of antifreeze. A guy in a dark suit and necktie? In the Arizona desert on a hot afternoon, studying anti-freeze at a truck stop? Why do I get the impression that these guys are—"

"Amateurs?" John said. "I hope so." The alternative was not pleasant. "Either that or they've got so much backup that they're not worried about being seen." He picked up the glass and sipped his tea. "I'm going to bet that these guys are alone, and they are rookies. So, here's what we're going to do. He outlined it for Leslie.

The room was upstairs. He led the way up a flight of narrow stairs. Once in the hallway, he could see another exit at the far end of the hall. This was a lucky break; they wouldn't have to leave through the restaurant. John opened the door to their assigned room, walked to the nightstand and turned on the radio. Spanish. He changed the station to something more believable. Leslie had done her part by turning on the shower. John apologized to the environmental gods for wasting water.

"Go," he said to Leslie. She jogged down the hall to the rear exit. He tossed the towels, washcloths, and key onto the bed, closed the door, and followed her. She had cracked the door open an inch or two.

"All clear," she said.

They came out on the shady side of the building and hurried down the stairs. There was no sign of the two men in suits. Fifty feet ahead, two trucks were pulling out of parking. One was headed for the exit to eastbound I-10. John ran to catch it. He could hear Leslie's footfalls not far behind. He hopped onto the passenger-side running board and opened the door. Leslie jumped up behind him; he pushed her through the open door. She slid across to the center of the wide bench seat before the driver, a large, bearded man, had a chance to react.

"What the hell!" the driver bellowed. He jammed on the brakes.

John was thrown forward against the open door but managed to stay on the running board. He climbed in and shut the door. The driver reached under the seat with his right arm.

Leslie grabbed the man's hand and twisted his pinkie finger to an impossible angle.

The guy howled in pain. "Shit!" He took his foot off the clutch pedal and the engine stalled, causing the vehicle to jump forward a foot or two.

"Get the gun, John."

John looked down at the floor. A large silver revolver lay just under the right side of the driver's seat. He picked it up. It was a big-bore Smith and Wesson, probably .357 Magnum. He opened the cylinder and let the six bullets fall out into his hand. He put them into his pocket.

The driver took his left hand off the steering wheel and made a fist.

"Don't do it!" Leslie shouted. She cranked the man's finger even farther back. Something in his hand popped.

"Shit, shit, shit!" he screamed. "My finger! My hand! It's broken."

"It's not broken," she said. "Yet."

John pulled out a wad of bills and waved it the driver's face. "Put your left hand back on the wheel. Please. Relax. We're not here to hurt you or rob you. We just need to get out of here in a hurry, without being seen. There's a jealous husband back there, after my butt." He pointed to Leslie. "Her husband. You understand?" He put the money in the driver's shirt pocket. "That's one thousand dollars. You get us out of here right now and the money's yours."

"And if I say no?"

John hadn't planned for that. Leslie's answer was to add the man's fourth finger to her list of what to twist.

Before she could do any more damage, John said, "No. Let him go. Really."

She did. The man rubbed his hand and, with considerable grimacing and grunting, worked his finger back and forth.

John said, "If you refuse, we'll be in deep shit. But we'll let you go, no problem." He snatched the bills out of the man's pocket. "Of course, we'll take the money with us."

The driver rubbed his hand for several more seconds. John watched the building for signs of their followers.

"Okay," the man said. "Give me the money. You guys climb up in the back of the cab."

John counted out five $100 bills and put them in the man's pocket. "Half now, half when we get to Tucson. You'll need to drop us at the corner of Speedway and Wilmot. Do you know that area?"

"Hell, no."

"Don't worry, we'll direct you. It's not that far from the interstate. Leslie, go ahead and climb up into the bunk. "I'll just crouch down here in the cab in case our friend changes his mind."

*   *   *

They stood outside the copy shop waiting for Whitaker to pick them up. John hated to drag him away from the hangar, but this was safer than ordering a taxi at 8:00 p.m. The sun had set about an hour ago and evening twilight was fading. Taxi drivers tended to remember too many details about their evening fares. John noticed that Leslie was shivering. He wondered if her windbreaker had any kind of lining.

"Do you want to go back inside?"

"No. It's not that cold. I think I'm experiencing a little post-traumatic shock from the truck stop incident. Got a little case of the shakes."

"I told you this was going to be dangerous."

"Yeah," she said. "But I wasn't counting on the excitement to begin until we actually got inside the Boneyard." She pointed down the street to the west. "Well, *Larry*, it looks like our ride is here. How'd you come up with the name Larry Brightman, anyway?"

John took out his new Arizona driver's license. "I had a friend in fourth grade named Larry Brighton. Almost used his real last name, but that might trigger red flags in some government database." He showed her the license. "Looks pretty good, don't you think?"

Whitaker pulled up at the curb. John opened the door and climbed in, leaving Leslie the more desirable outside seat in the F-150's cab.

"John, John, John," Whitaker said. "How many times am I going to have to save your ass in one day? What the fu . . . what the heck happened out there? Did you guys ever make it to Dateland?"

"No, we didn't. We'll do that early tomorrow. It's a long story, Whit. Just get us to that address on Gollob Road. Leslie can give you directions. The guy said he'd still be willing to show us the truck if we get there before 9:00 p.m."

Chapter 25

Lynwood Hardwick felt a hand on his shoulder. It was Charlotte's. The love of his life, his soul mate for the last thirty-three years. He had been dreaming about her and the sumptuous pork roast she had cooked for last night's dinner. Or, had the dinner itself been a dream? No, the aroma of pork and mashed potatoes still reached their upstairs bedroom.

"Lyn, dear, the phone. Answer the phone."

"Oh. Right." He reached for the phone. "Hardwick here."

"Lynwood, it's George Clark. We need to talk. On the secure line."

Hardwick groaned. His mouth was so dry he could hardly speak. "Okay. Give me two minutes. I'll call you back on the STU-II."

Before getting out from under the 800-thread-count cotton sheets topped with a down comforter, he propped himself up on one elbow and hugged Charlotte with the other arm. "Sorry, my love. It's George Clark. I'll have to call him back from the study."

She rolled over to face him. "What time is it?"

"Ten minutes after midnight." He leaned down to kiss her. "Try to get back to sleep. I'll be back soon." Hardwick wasn't so sure about that. Nothing good ever happened at ten minutes past midnight.

After a quick trip to the bathroom to relieve himself and swish some water around in his mouth, Hardwick sat down in his study, activated the STU-II secure phone, and tried to guess which trouble spot had flared up tonight. Korea? Chinese incursion into Philippine waters? Something in the Middle East?

"Sorry for the late-night call," Clark said. "I'll make it short. It's the Customs Service thing. At 2100 hours last night, DC time, John Martin and Leslie Olsen showed up at the Tucson Airport. Our men followed them to a truck stop just west of town. Then they disappeared."

Hardwick waited for more.

"Martin rented a room. They appeared to have entered that room, but our operatives became suspicious when they noticed the radio and shower had been on for—"

"Let me guess," Hardwick said. "Your men checked the room and found it empty."

"Yes."

"No trace of Martin? No sightings from witnesses?"

"Correct."

"Dammit, George, who did you send out there? Wasn't there any backup? Never mind." It was too late to second-guess Clark's procedures. "But hear me and hear me well. Martin is smart. He's been alerted to us now. You'll have to dig deep— really deep— to find him."

"We're searching anything and everything connected to Martin and Olsen. When we get something, I'll call you—wait a minute. Something new just came in. I'm going to put you on hold, okay?"

Charlotte walked in with a steaming cup of coffee and set it on a coaster on his desk. He put a hand over the phone's mouthpiece and said, "Thank you. I'm on hold here." He took a sip. "Mmm. Perfect."

"I know you, Lynwood. And I know your job. You won't be back to bed anytime soon. You will need this coffee." She turned to leave the study.

"Wait," he said. "What I said. I wasn't referring to the coffee, but to you. You are perfect. You are just right for me. I love you."

"Great line, Lyn. It's BS, but a great line, nevertheless. "I love you too." She smiled and walked away.

"Lynwood, you still there? I lost you for a moment."

"Yes, George. That was Charlotte. She brought me coffee, but she's gone now. You're free to talk."

"You know Martin, right? So, I am going to lay out some information for you. With your permission, I'll put you on speaker phone. I've got two of my best analysts here in the office. Albin and Budd. I think you know them. Maybe you can help us make some sense out of this, give us some leads to follow."

"Go ahead. The sooner the better. Martin's got a head start on us."

"Okay, I'll turn it over to Albin."

"Hello, General Hardwick," Albin said. "First the good news. Martin used his credit card a lot on Sunday and Monday. He left a pretty good trail for us."

Hardwick said, "Of course. He didn't know anything was wrong then."

"There are some interesting purchases here. He bought jet fuel at three different airports on Sunday. Olympia, Washington, Elko Nevada and Ajo, Arizona.

"Jet fuel?" Hardwick said. "Does Martin own an airplane?"

"Yes. He doesn't even own a car but there is an airplane registered in his name, a T-33, which is a type not familiar to me, but I looked it up. It's a—"

"I know what it is," Hardwick said. "Where is it right now?"

Budd said, "It's parked at Tucson International Airport, and it's under surveillance, of course."

"We did some checking with the FAA," Clark said. "Martin departed Olympia, headed for Tucson, about four hours before the second shootdown. So, who, or what, made him fly there?"

"Don't waste your time trying to figure that out," Hardwick said. "Martin already told me he got a call from Carter on Sunday and that Carter mentioned 'Blue Bandits,' which is the fighter pilot code word for MiG-21s. You've seen the pictures of wreckage that Martin gave me? Hell, Martin is light-years ahead of all of us on solving this. He's found more clues to the shootdowns in one day than you guys have in a week. The problem is—" He hesitated. "George, are Albin and Budd read in on the, ah—"

"If you mean, do they know that the U.S. government is officially not investigating the shootdowns, yes, they are aware."

Hardwick said, "Hold on a second. Don't be jealous, but my wife just brought in a refill for my coffee." He mouthed a thank-you to Charlotte and blew her a kiss. "Okay, we're clear again. Look, people, my written assessment of John Martin clearly states that he intends to attack Alvarado. I just don't know how. Is there anything, anything at all, in his recent travels or purchases that will tell us what he's planning?"

"Martin's credit card purchases are interesting," Albin said. "On Monday, he bought a round-trip ticket from Seattle to Tucson for a James Whitaker. Whitaker, it turns out, is an aviation mechanic at the Olympia Flight Museum. That's the place where Martin's T-33 resides. Whitaker is a retired Air Force Chief Master Sergeant, with extensive jet fighter maintenance experience. He arrived in Tucson as scheduled at 1610 on Monday, spent Monday night in a room at Davis-Monthan Air Force Base paid for by John Martin, but has since disappeared."

"Lynwood, does the name Whitaker mean anything to you?" Clark asked.

"No."

"Let me throw out one theory," Clark said. "Could this T-33 be used as a weapon? Lynwood, you're the fighter pilot. Could it?"

"It's remotely possible, but very unlikely. It is an unarmed trainer from the 1950's. Martin would be hopelessly outclassed if he went up against a MiG-21 with a T-Bird. He would want a—oh, shit. Do you have a printout of Whitaker's service record? What airplanes did he work on? Where was he based?"

"Hold on," Clark said. "Budd, do you have that info?"

Hardwick's heart pounded. It wasn't the caffeine. Now he knew what Martin was planning and he had to stop it.

"Here it is," Budd said. "Whitaker worked on many jets, but his last eleven years were spent as an F-16 mechanic and—"

"Shit!" Hardwick said.

"He was an F-16 crew chief, then a maintenance superintendent. Multiple overseas deployments. He was at Nellis Air Force Base from 1985 until 1988, then Luke Air Force Base for two years, then . . . I suppose I should compare that with Martin's—"

"Don't bother," Hardwick said. He knew Martin's record by heart. He even remembered a conversation during which Martin bragged about having flown the same F-16 tail number, with the same crew chief, for four years at two different bases. "Let me guess, Martin and Whitaker were both assigned to Nellis and Luke at the same times."

"Just a moment," Budd said. "Yes, that's correct. But how does that help us?"

"Gentlemen, John Martin is planning to steal an F-16. He is going to use it to do exactly what our President does not want us to do. As he told me on Monday, Martin is going to go out there and 'kick some butt,' which in his military mind means, he is going to find and destroy the MiGs. Our job is to stop him."

"Do we want to get the Pentagon involved?" Clark asked.

"Yes. Might as well go right to the top. Let me get the White House operator on the line." He tapped the Flash button on the STU-II. When the operator came on, he said, "National Security Advisor Lynwood Hardwick here. I need you to ring up the Chairman of the Joint Chiefs of Staff and get him on this conference call. Yes, I am aware of the time of night. This is a national emergency."

After a brief delay while the Chairman was awakened and activated his secure telephone, Hardwick said, "General Stanford, it's Lynwood Hardwick. I apologize for the late hour, but I've got a bit of a crisis here. It involves a credible threat to Air Force F-16s, especially those in the southwest United States. There will be a full explanation in the White House situation room later this morning, but for now, I respectfully suggest that you order an immediate increase in flight line security for all F-16 bases west of the Mississippi—active duty, Guard and Reserves. No, it's not terrorists. A renegade ex-Air Force pilot is going to try to steal one."

Chapter 26

John gave up trying to find a comfortable position on the hard canvas army cot. There was no way he could get back to sleep. His back was killing him, and Whitaker's snoring echoed off the hangar's metal roof. He got off the cot and stretched. These accommodations were a severe step down from the pillow-top mattress and fine sheets in Leslie's guest room. The light pink sky outside the hangar's skylight windows told him that sunrise was only a few minutes away.

His mind was on all the loose ends, some of which had popped into his head just last night. He'd use the next half hour or so to make a new list. Whit would have to rent a fuel truck with enough capacity for at least 14,000 pounds of Jet-A and drive it to Dateland. That was a little over 2,000 gallons. Did they make trucks that big? Had Whit figured out how to get liquid oxygen? Aircraft batteries? He trusted Whitaker to solve these and other technical issues. Whitaker, in turn, had trusted him to handle one mission-critical task. It had been one of Whitaker's first questions the other day, when they stood outside the Boneyard's fence. Where would they get air-to-air missiles, bullets for the guns, and bombs? An F-16 without weapons was a cute little jet, but a harmless one.

As Whitaker had put it, the whole weapons thing was "above his pay grade." He had accepted John's plan on faith, trusted that the ordnance would be there. It would. The ammo was the first thing John had ordered, during that redeye flight from DC to Tucson. He'd have to double the order and hope it all would arrive in time. Live bombs were out of the question—impossible for a civilian to get. But inert, concrete-filled 500-pounders, training ordnance, were easy to buy. Leslie, the last-minute addition to this adventure, would have to be briefed on all this. Perhaps on the way to Dateland.

Another essential part of his battle plan was something neither Whitaker nor Leslie knew about yet. Destroying the MiGs while they were on the ground was too much of a challenge, required a long fight deep into Mexico, and had no guarantee of success. They would have to lure them into the air and kill them face-to-face, cockpit-to-cockpit. To do that, they'd need some help from either ground-based or airborne early warning radar. He needed to contact Sam Paxton and convince her to help. Without Sam's help, they would have little hope of finding the MiGs.

He shivered. Dressed as he was in gym shorts, t-shirt, and socks, it was easy to get chilled. Rather than get dressed, he decided to take a shower. When Whitaker had showed them around the hangar, he had been very proud to point out the shower stall in the small bathroom and the fact that he had lit the pilot light for the gas water heater. He had also stacked four towels and washcloths on a wooden chair.

John stepped into his boots, aware of the odd combination of gym shorts and work boots, but he was unwilling to walk on the dusty concrete floor in his socks. After lacing them just enough to avoid tripping on the loose ends, he walked past the still-snoring Whitaker and the empty cot reserved for Adam. Some distance away, a blue tarp hung with rope gave Leslie some privacy. When he got close to the hangar's bathroom door, he realized he was not the only one awake. The shower was running. Leslie was evidently an early riser.

He made his way back to the "kitchen," which consisted of two tables made from ¾-inch plywood and sawhorses. On one table was a camp stove and some cookware. The second held grocery bags of food, a stack of paper plates, cups, and disposable cutlery. Next to that table was a large ice chest. The "dining room" was the card table and folding chairs. He found the percolator-style pot and some ground coffee. When the pot was filled with water and on the burner, he walked over to his cot and picked up his clothes. The t-shirt could stay on for today. He slipped off the gym shorts and reached for his underwear. He had gotten one foot inside the briefs when he heard footsteps behind him.

"We have to stop meeting this way," Leslie whispered. "I'll look the other way while you finish."

John looked over his shoulder. "Good morning," he said. He did some embarrassing and inelegant hopping around while trying to pull up the briefs and step into his jeans. "Can you watch the coffee while I go brush my teeth?" He gave up on the shower idea. Maybe later.

By the time he returned from the bathroom, Whitaker was standing at the stove scrambling some eggs with one hand and sipping coffee with the other. Sausage sizzled in a second pan. Leslie had put the coffee pot on a square piece of one-by-six-inch pine board and sat at the table with both hands wrapped around a mug of coffee. On a second piece of scrap lumber, pressed into service as an improvised cutting board, was a long kitchen knife, an apple, an orange, and a banana. Three place settings were laid out, including glasses of orange juice.

"Well, isn't this cozy?" he said. "Whit, you may have missed your calling. Maybe you should open a diner. No, never mind. You'd eat up all the profits. Literally."

"What's wrong, John? Get up on the wrong side of bed, or what?"

John held up his hands in surrender. "My apologies. I shouldn't insult my host, the innkeeper at Whitaker's Hangar of Horrors. Take these cots, for example. Or torture devices.

I'm not sure what they are. I don't suppose you considered something as practical as an air mattress?"

"All right, you two," Leslie said. "Knock it off. We've got a lot of talking, planning, and work to do."

John made peace with Whitaker and praised both his cooking and the amount of equipment he had amassed in such a short time. "Oh, and by the way, you were right about our needing a second crew chief. I apologize for getting angry with you."

"Yeah, okay," Whitaker said. "I could tell. You had that look, like you wanted to ream me a new . . . ah . . . a new one, but you didn't say one word. When you go silent, I know you're really pissed."

When the meal was finished, the table cleaned off, and more coffee brewed, John asked them to sit down. He said, "We are already behind schedule because of yesterday's little adventure with the men in suits. But, before we get into details on the F-16s, I'd like to make one thing clear. Some very smart people in three-letter government agencies are looking for us. We must become invisible. That means no contact with anyone back home. No personal mobile phones. Leslie's is already disabled, right?"

She nodded.

"Whit, you don't have one of those, do you?"

Whitaker said, "Me? Are you joking? No."

"No personal email. Don't use your credit card. Don't use your real name for *anything*. In fact—hold on." John stood up, walked over to his cot, and picked up the FEDEX envelope from last night. He pulled out Whitaker's fake ID and returned to the table. "Whit, here's a new commercial driver's license for you, complete with hazmat and fuel tanker endorsements. And a credit card in your new name. It's got a $4,000 limit, so use cash wherever you can. You are now Curtis Kinney."

"Where did you get that picture of me?" Whitaker asked.

"From the flight museum web site; the staff directory."

"Hell, John, aren't you being a little paranoid? They don't even know I'm here."

"Don't bet on it. On Monday, I used my credit card to buy your airline ticket. I used that same card to pay for your room at the TEQ. By now, they have probably pulled up your service records. Hardwick will be quick to figure out the F-16 angle. But he probably thinks we're going to try for jets at an active Air Force base. It's very unlikely that he will expect us to steal airplanes from the Boneyard."

John stopped to think about the last time he had used his personal credit card. It was about 2100 Monday, when he paid for the food at Rita's. None of which he got to eat. He glared at Whitaker.

"What?"

"Nothing," John said. "I was just trying to remember when I last used my credit card. I think we've all been 'off the grid,' as they say, since Monday night. Let's keep it that way. Whit, you'll have to tell Adam when he comes in. If he's got a mobile phone, make him promise to disable it and do all that other no-contact stuff I just told you about."

"You got it."

Leslie reached out for the coffee pot, refilled her cup, and offered some to John.

"Thanks," he said. After one sip, he thought of another problem. At all costs, they had to stay away from the airport. But Adam was flying in this morning. There was no way to get in touch with him now; he was already on the way.

"You've gone quiet," Leslie said. "That's not a good thing."

"Sorry. Just thought of another glitch. Adam is arriving this morning, and. he's expecting us to meet him at the airport. How do we get him here without showing our faces, or one of our vehicles, at the airport?"

It was Whitaker who had the best solution. He would hire a messenger service to meet Adam's flight. The instructions would be to take a taxi to Hash on Hawthorne. Whitaker would pick him up there.

"Sounds good," John said. "No, wait. Hash on Hawthorne won't work. Leslie still had her phone turned on then; Hardwick could find out and have the place watched." He saw the looks he was getting. "Okay, so I *am* a little paranoid. I'm just trying to cover our tracks. It must be someplace new. He looked at Leslie. "Is Hi Corbett Field still there? In Randolph Park?"

"Yes," she said. "It's now the home of the Tucson Toros, a minor league baseball team."

John said, "Whit, please make a note of that. Hi Corbett Field, main entrance. Randolph Park. That's where you'll meet Adam. So that's all settled."

"Except, I think we need a backup plan," Whitaker said.

"Okay, how about this?" Leslie said. "Call the airline, get them to pass that same message to Adam upon arrival. Also, include in both messages that, if there is no contact at the Hi Corbett Field, he should call his grandmother for instructions. If things go sideways at the airport, we could call Adam's grandma. You have her number, right?"

John wanted to laugh but thought better of it for two reasons. First, he couldn't think of a better plan. Second, he didn't want to insult Leslie or stifle her thinking; she was beginning to think like a covert operative. Still, he couldn't help but smile at the thought of a grandmother being a critical player in their project. "Sounds good. But . . .Whit, tell the airline, no messages over the airport PA system. I don't want Adam's last name broadcast all over. If whoever is watching the airport has half a brain, they might relate that to one of the shoot-down victims."

Whitaker said, "And how do I convince the airline to not use the PA?"

John closed his eyes and thought of the famous line of poetry about a tangled web and deceiving people. He tried, and failed, to remember who wrote that. This whole going off the grid thing was using up all his brain power.

"I've got it!" Leslie said. "Just tell them that he's deaf. Not only will that prevent a PA announcement, but it will also motivate them to help this 'hearing challenged' passenger."

John breathed a sigh of relief at getting Adam's arrival straightened out. "Now, let's move on to today's agenda. Leslie and I need to drive out to Dateland, leaving Whit to—"

"Wait a second," Leslie said. "How are we going to communicate?"

He had a plan for that, sort of. "We need to buy some untraceable mobile phones, but I don't know much about them. Leslie, where could we get some phones just like yours?"

She said, "My phone is a Motorola MicroTac. Very small but very pricey and, as far as I know, only available by special order. I'd recommend the Motorola Flare. It's not a flip phone, not as cute as the MicroTac, but very functional. The Flare is about the size of my hand and about an inch thick. It's available at electronics stores for around three hundred dollars." She closed her eyes and was still for two or three seconds. "I bought one for Bobby at Christmas time last year." She sighed, reached for a paper napkin, and wiped a single tear from her left eye.

"We should start with two each," John said. "After you use it once, you smash it, throw it away, and go to the next one. Let's buy only two at a time, using a different store for each purchase. Whit, since you and I have the fake IDs, that'll have to be us. I'll buy some for Leslie and me when we depart for Dateland. When you pick up Adam, get your phones while you're out."

"Now that I think about it, we're going to need some access to the World Wide Web, but I shouldn't use my own laptop or my—"

"They're calling it the Internet these days, John," Leslie said. "But you'll need a phone line for dial-up access. Is there a phone in here?"

"Yes, ma'am," Whitaker said. "Look over on the workbench. It works; I checked the dial tone. It's got about a twenty-foot cord."

"There's no way anyone can trace that phone to us," John said. "Like the hangar rental, the phone is listed under the real estate company's name. Perhaps, though, as my new co-conspirator Whit says, we should have a backup plan for communication. I think I've got an answer for that, but I need to check something outside first." He stood up. "Be right back."

John went outside to the phone booth he had noticed earlier. He pushed the folding doors open, stepped in, and picked up the phone. After hearing an encouraging dial tone, he dialed toll-free directory assistance. An automated voice answered; he hung up. Good. The phone worked. He memorized the number and stepped out of the booth. Morning twilight had given way to a full-blown desert sunrise, but his view of it was blocked by the tall hangar.

He walked over to the northeast corner of the building and watched for a minute or two as the orange sun peeked over rising terrain to the southeast. When John came back inside, bright rays of early-morning sunlight poked into the hangar's dusty interior as if they were laser beams. He sat back down and said, "The pay phone outside works." He had them both write down the number and described how, if they lost contact with each other, whoever was in the hangar would monitor the pay phone at fifteen minutes and forty-five minutes past the hour.

"Any questions?" he asked.

Leslie said, "A while ago, you were saying something about not using your laptop. Then I interrupted you with a question about the phone line."

"Yeah, okay, the laptop. I can think of at least one reason why we need World Wide—ah, Internet— access here. We need to check the weather. I suspect that other reasons will come up, so I need to buy another laptop."

"You think the government can track your laptop?" Whitaker said.

"Maybe not the laptop itself, but my Prodigy account." He noticed Whitaker's confused look. Leslie was rolling her eyes.

"You use Prodigy?" she said. "That is *so* outdated. There are much better web browsers—"

"Whoa, whoa," Whitaker said. "Can somebody translate all this into plain English?"

John took a minute to explain how his IBM ThinkPad 700T laptop's internal modem connected to an online search engine —in his case, Prodigy—using a telephone line. He further explained that he'd need a new ThinkPad and a new Prodigy account under his fake name. Hardwick would be monitoring everything—phone, email, Internet provider and bank accounts.

"I should be able to pick up a new laptop at the same electronics store that sells the phones. It won't be cheap, but it's the safe way to go. Let's move on. Whit, do you have that list handy?"

Whitaker pulled a piece of paper out of his pocket, unfolded it, and flattened it out on the table.

John pulled it over to his side of the table and scanned it. Some items had already been checked off, but a great many remained. "Be honest with me," he said to Whitaker. "This is a shitload of stuff to do before tomorrow night at midnight. Even with Adam's help, can you do it all?"

"Hell, John, half of this stuff is already done. I just haven't checked it off yet. I've got all the materials here to fabricate what we need inside that trailer. Some things I can't do alone. It'll take all four of us to manhandle, uh . . ." He glanced at Leslie. ". . . to *handle* that big crane into place, 'cause one of us will have to man—shit, I mean to *operate*—the forklift. "Ma'am, I'm sorry, I am just not ready for this 'women in combat' thing."

Leslie laughed. "Get used to it, Whit."

Whitaker said, "Well, the good news is, this shopping list you gave me? All but one item will be delivered today."

Leslie picked up the list and read it out loud. "Flight suits, g-suits . . . hey, how'd you get my size?"

John said, "I forgot to ask you, so I took an educated guess."

"You guessed well." She looked at Whitaker. "All these things with check marks, they're on the way? Nomex gloves, parachute harnesses, vests, survival radios, portable HF radio? You can get all that?"

"It's hard to believe, but all that stuff is available online from aviation and military surplus web sites," Whitaker said. "I ordered it all from a computer at the local public library."

Leslie said, "By the way, John . . . or Whit . . . why in God's name do we need a High Frequency radio? The F-16s, at least the ones we are going to fly, don't have HF."

Whitaker pointed to him. The old mechanic could fix most things on an F-16, but he wasn't that good with airborne radios. John said, "The portable HF is not for us in the F-16s. It's the best way for AWACS to contact us in the hangar down at Dateland. UHF and VHF/FM have limited range for air-to-ground communication over long distances. But HF is perfect for that."

She moved her finger down the list. Her eyes got very wide. "Whoa, whoa, whoa!" she said. "Are you telling me that you can just order up some 20-millimeter ammo, four AIM-9s, and four five-hundred-pound bombs as easily as I might order a new pair of shoes?"

Whitaker said, "John should take the credit for that. I don't know how or where he found out about this, but there is some guy on the Internet that sells actual AIM-9 missiles, just without the rocket motors and warheads. They're inert. You can get the "P" or the newer "L" version. The web site says, 'For display purposes only.' Four of 'em are being FedExed out here as we speak."

John knew Leslie would have something to say about that. He didn't have to wait long.

"A question for our fearless leader here," she said. "What good will an effing inert, 'for display only,' missile do for us?"

"Exactly that, Leslie. It will *display* that we have missiles. If Alvarado sees that our jets have missiles, he will maneuver differently. If we get into missile range, he may do a break turn, which will allow one of us to close in to gun range."

"Hmm," she said. "Good point. But it's even more unbelievable that you can buy 20-millimeter ammo. The government won't allow that, will it?"

"That one was a little harder to arrange," Whitaker said. "And—I hate to say it—that's the reason why we can't be ready tomorrow night. John wanted a full load of ammo, 511 rounds for each jet. But the 20-millimeter rounds themselves won't be here until Friday by noon. So, John, I think we need to postpone our visit to the Boneyard by one day. I'm pretty sure you don't want to go out there without bullets in the gun."

"You're damn right," John said. There was no other choice. It was risky, though. Every hour of delay gave Hardwick more time to find them. He said, "We can postpone by one day. I've already checked on moonrise for backup days. On Friday, the timing will have to slip by about 40 minutes, as moonrise is later Saturday, but it should still work. To sum it all up then, we go into the Boneyard Friday night, take off from D-M at moonrise on Saturday, land at Dateland about an hour later. Ah! It was Sir Walter Scott!"

"Say what?" Whitaker said.

"Sorry, I just remembered. That's the name of the guy who, in 1808, wrote the famous phrase, *Oh, what a tangled web we weave, when first we practice to deceive.* Wish I could remember the name of the poem. 'Marmot?' No. Ah! It was 'Marmion.'"

Leslie and Whitaker looked at him as if he were crazy. He said, "Because that's what we're doing, right? We are getting more and more tangled up in plans. The project keeps snowballing. What's the score now? Two pickup trucks, two semis, a forklift, a power cart, literally a ton of bombs, four missiles, about a thousand rounds of twenty mike-mike? I get the feeling this will never end!"

"Oh, that reminds me," Whitaker said. "About the ammo. All I could get was TPT. You said that was acceptable, right John?"

"For God's sake, John!" Leslie shouted. "Those are inert target practice rounds! What are you thinking?"

"Take it easy, Leslie. It's all we could get. The live high explosive stuff requires an FFL, a Federal Firearms License. At least they're tracers, so you can see your bullet stream. I've seen the damage 20-millimeter TPT can do to a truck. At Luke, one of our guys accidentally strafed a Fish and Wildlife Service truck out on the tactical range. Fortunately, the driver was out of the vehicle, trying to orient himself. He had taken a wrong turn and strayed onto the gunnery range. To the pilot, it looked like one of the targets. No one was injured but the truck was destroyed. Those rounds weigh about half a pound and travel at or above the speed of sound. I think a few hits from TPT will bring down a MiG."

"I still can't wrap my head around the fact that a regular person can buy 20-millimeter, even TPT," Leslie said. "How is that possible?"

John said, "That's kind of a long story. How about if I explain it during our drive over to Dateland? We need to get going." He turned to Whitaker and said, "Is there anything else giving you a problem, Whit?"

"Only one thing. When Adam comes in, I think we need to send him down to Dateland to join you. I can get by alone until you guys come back, especially now that we've got an extra day."

"Why send Adam to Dateland?" Leslie asked. "John and I can handle sweeping the runway."

Whitaker said, "That truck you're driving? The big Chevy 454? You're gonna have to leave it at Dateland. You'll need it to tow the airplanes into the hangar, to get them out of sight right away. Adam and I won't be there until well after you have landed. Adam will be your ride back here. Also, he can help with the sweeping."

John closed his eyes and rubbed his face with both hands. It was embarrassing that he had overlooked the need for a tow vehicle. He was supposed to be the leader, the mastermind, the one who thought of everything. What else had he forgotten?

Chapter 27

John pushed the shopping cart with two of everything they needed to clean the runways at Dateland. They put leaf blowers, brooms, string trimmers and the gas can into the pickup bed. Leslie put four small boxes, each containing a Motorola Flare mobile phone, on the passenger side floor.

"Here, catch." John tossed the truck keys to Leslie. "Why don't you drive us to Dateland? I need a little time to think."

Leslie caught the keys, walked around to the driver's side door, and opened it.

He got in on the passenger side and said, "I'm going to call Whit on that pay phone outside the hanger, give him the numbers of these mobile phones." He looked at the dashboard clock. 9:15 a.m. "Never mind. Whit's already on the way to pick up Adam."

"Good," Leslie said as she maneuvered back onto I-10 from the mega-store's parking lot. "You can use this time to tell me about the miracle of how a private citizen can buy ammo for an F-16."

"Okay. I know what you're thinking. There is no way our government would allow a civilian to buy ammo for a jet fighter. You are correct. But, when I did a web search for twenty mike-mike ammo, I learned that there are companies out there that actually sell that stuff. Some of the 'good old boys' have devised a way to make a rifle out of a single M-61 barrel, the same one that is bolted together to make the six-barreled guns in all our modern fighters. It's perfectly legal, and, if they shoot bullets with inert warheads, that seems to be a right protected by the 2nd Amendment."

'What do they need a 20-millimeter weapon for?" Leslie asked.

"No idea," he said. "But I've seen videos of guys sighting down a long barrel—a 20-millimeter, military grade barrel—on a firing range, shooting at who knows what, preparing for who knows what? Some kind of doomsday scenario, maybe. Certainly not deer hunting. Of course, most of that is with inert rounds. Believe it or not, if you have an FFL, you can even buy HEI rounds."

"That makes no sense whatsoever, "Leslie said.

"I agree. Anyway, there are dealers out there, civilians, who are selling 20-millimeter ammo with inert bullets, mostly for people who use it in these single-shot, home-made weapons. They are perfectly willing to sell us 1,022 rounds of TPT, no questions asked."

"Dare I ask how much this costs?"

John said, "I think Whit said it's $11.00 per round, plus surcharges for shipping hazardous materials."

"I'm not a math wizard," Leslie said, "but if I just move the decimal point three spaces to the right, I get $11,000. Isn't that a little pricey?"

"Think of it as one bullet, at a cost of $11.00, going through the heart of the man who killed your brother. Is it worth it?"

"Well, when you put it that way . . . But what I mean is, this whole project, the purchase of Dateland, the rented hangar, all that equipment, jet fuel, et cetera. You don't seem to blink an eye at the cost. How can you afford that? Or is that too personal a question?"

"Yes, it is," he said.

Neither of them had much more to say until they approached the interchange where I-8 split off from I-10.

"Interstate 8, right?"

John nodded.

Once established on I-8, Leslie pointed at the sign showing distance remaining to Gila Bend and said, "We're going to need gas at Gila Bend. This thing is a gas hog."

"That's good," John said. "I need to stop soon anyway to make a call, preferably at a pay phone." He checked his watch and estimated their arrival time in Gila Bend. The last time he had spoken to Sam, she had mentioned that Wednesdays and Thursdays were her days off. But that was a long time ago. He'd be lucky to catch her at home.

Leslie said, "Would you like to share a little about this phone call?"

There wasn't any reason to keep Sam's involvement a secret. "It's someone who can help us find the MiGs. I'm surprised you haven't brought up that question yet."

"Well, I figured we'd just do sort of an armed recce around La Coruba until we find them. There can't be too many jet-capable runways down there. Drop bombs and strafe the hell out of them."

That had been his initial plan. If he had to, he'd do it that way. But there were flaws, the most obvious of which was, they would be invading Mexico.

He said, "What if we could catch the MiGs in the air, in U.S. airspace?"

"That would be even better, but how would we know . . . oh, wait. Are you telling me that you've found a way to know when the MiGs are airborne?"

"Maybe. I've got a contact at AWACS, Sam Paxton. She's a GCI controller who worked with me in the Pacific. Korea, Philippines and so forth. We sort of bonded after I visited her remote radar site—you know, interface between pilots and GCI controllers—and I reciprocated by getting her a back-seat orientation flight in a B-model."

"Sam's a she?"

"Yeah. It's short for Samantha."

Leslie looked at him with narrowed eyes. "And just where was this remote radar site in the Philippines?"

"Ah . . . it was on a hill overlooking the South China Sea about seventy miles north of Manila. I think it was called Wallace Air Station; it was used to monitor Chinese activity out near the Spratly Islands. Territorial disputes out there still exist to this day. But I read that we've turned Wallace over to the Philippine Air Force. That's too bad. It sits out on a beautiful little peninsula called Poro Point. Do you know it?"

"No. I never made it to the Pacific. I was in Spain in my F-16 days."

"Poro Point also has a very high-end, lush, ocean-front resort. One of those tropical places where you can swim up to the bar and order a drink."

"And your stay there was all business, of course."

"Yup, it was all about coordination for an upcoming training exercise."

"Then how come you know so much about this glamorous resort? It sounds like you and Sam might have done some of that 'interfacing' while swimming up to the bar."

"No, no, no," he said. "Well, yes about swimming up to the bar. But it wasn't what you think. Although—" He exaggerated his sigh just to get a rise out of Leslie. "She did look pretty good in a biki—"

"Stop. Stop! Too much information! Get back to *our* mission."

"Right." Had he just seen a little envy, or jealousy, from the woman who said she could put her hormones on standby? "Back to what Sam can do for us. First, she is an excellent radar controller; she can identify targets and run an intercept better than anyone I know. Second, Sam is now a supervisor and Stan-Eval on the AWACS planes. She can pick and choose which flights she goes on to do her evaluations or training. As

I'm sure you know, there's always one AWACS bird monitoring our southwestern border. So, the trick is to get her up there, with a way to communicate with us, on a day when the MiGs might launch."

"You didn't think this through very well, John. Alvarado has already won the battle. The Citations are grounded, remember? Why would Alvarado bother to launch his MiGs?"

"What if the Citations started to fly again, and word of that were leaked to the news media?"

"In your dreams," Leslie said. "Never going to happen. At least not anytime soon. You should've realized that."

John asked, "Do you play chess?"

"What? Not often. Not very well."

"There's a principle in chess . . . well, never mind. It's the wrong analogy. What I'm trying to say is, you have committed a dangerous error of judgment. You have underestimated me."

"Are you are telling me that you've found a way to get the Citations airborne?"

"Not me, Leslie. Briggs. That night at Rita's? He opened up to me, got almost friendly, and gave me his business card with his private number. Told me he knew I was up to something and hinted he was in favor of, well, whatever I was planning. I was supposed to call him if I ever needed anything. So, I did."

John gave her a condensed version of last night's phone call with Briggs. While shivering in the phone booth outside the hangar, he had convinced Briggs to somehow get a Citation airborne once a day, beginning on Friday, and fly it near the border at a predetermined time. "Which reminds me, I've got to update him on our one-day delay. We don't want the Citation flights to begin until . . . crap!"

"What?"

"I'm just not thinking straight these days." He looked at her and said something that hurt his pride. "I need some help, Leslie. Help me think this through."

"Sure," she said. "Tell me what's wrong."

"Briggs has agreed to fly a Citation as a decoy to lure Alvarado into the air, beginning on Friday. Even under our original timetable, that would not have worked. I am such a dumb shit. I forgot to give us a whole day to get the jets ready. So, under the new plan, the ammo arrives Friday about noon. Late Friday night, we go into the Boneyard. We take off from D-M at 0430 Saturday. And—this is the part I overlooked—we must use Saturday to prep the jets for our mission, load ammo and missiles. The earliest we can launch our attack on the MiGs is Sunday. Do you agree?"

Leslie was quiet for several seconds. She said, "Yes, that makes sense. I can see the problem. You don't want the Citation to be out there without us to protect it."

"Correct. I'll phone him with these changes ASAP. Briggs said he'd drop a hint to the local media about all this, make it sound like a big deal, when in reality it's only a few maintenance test flights. He said it would be no problem getting that approved. Briggs suspects that there's an information leak somewhere up or down the chain of command in Customs Service, or FAA, or maybe local air traffic control. Some way that Alvarado gets notified of the Customs Service flying schedule."

"What if he double-crosses us? Turns us in?" Leslie said.

"These shootdowns have shaken Briggs to the core. I think he's ready to go rogue, or at least help me do that. I've only interacted with Briggs a couple times, but I see him as a man of his word. He wants to help us fight back against whomever shot down his crews. What do you think?"

"I agree," Leslie said. "By the way, you said, 'help *me* go rogue.' Does he know I'm with you?"

John chuckled. "He asked, 'Is Olsen with you?' I said, 'I haven't seen her since yesterday.' Which was true."

Leslie frowned.

"I know. It was prevaricating. But it was the truth. It was after midnight and you were asleep behind that tarp, out of sight, so I really hadn't seen you yet."

"Bullshit," she said. "Briggs knows I'm here."

"I agree. But I'm not going to be the one to tell him that."

Leslie pulled into a truck stop on the outskirts of Gila Bend. It was almost a carbon copy of the one where they had eluded the two agents in suits. John surveyed the parking lot and saw no threats. He handed Leslie his—or rather, Larry's—credit card. "Why don't you fill us up and I'll make my call to Sam?" He walked off to the phone booth.

Unfortunately, Sam wasn't home. He left a message. "Sam, it's John Martin. I've got a big problem and I need your help. Call this number." He gave her his mobile phone number. "But do it from a pay phone. Keep this to yourself. And thanks." He pushed the accordion doors of the phone booth open and walked back to the gas pumps.

Leslie had the truck's hood open and the dipstick in her hand. She saw him and said, "Needs a quart of oil."

John went into the store and bought two quarts of oil, a can opener, and a small plastic funnel. When he handed Leslie one quart, the opener, and the funnel, he said, "I got an extra quart for later, just in case."

Leslie pulled a paper towel from a dispenser next to the gas pump and used it to protect her hand as she unscrewed the greasy oil cap. She poured in about half the can, waited several seconds, and rechecked the quantity. "It's going to need the whole quart," she said. She emptied the can and tossed it into the trash. She got down on her hands and knees to examine the lower end of the engine. "No drips, so it's probably not a leaky gasket. This old V-8 is just worn out inside."

Before John could compliment her on her automotive know-how, his phone rang. Caller ID said, *Oklahoma Call*. Tinker Air Force Base, home of Sam's AWACS unit, was in Oklahoma. He hopped into the passenger seat and closed the door. Leslie climbed into the driver's side. He gave her the "cut" signal. He didn't want her to drive them further out into rural southern Arizona and lose the mobile phone connection. He pushed the button to put the call on speaker phone.

"Hello?" he said.

"John, is that you?"

"Yes. Thanks for calling back so quickly. Look, Sam, I don't have much time, so I will be very direct and very honest. Do you trust me?"

"Of course, You saved my life."

Leslie's eyes widened.

Sam said, "I told you, if you ever needed anything, anything at all, just let me know."

This was a moment when John had to be truthful, convincing, and brief. "Sam, if I had a valid reason—one that affects national security—to get you on the schedule for southern Arizona AWACS surveillance, beginning this Sunday, for about four days straight, could you do it?"

Sam did not reply immediately. John gave her a few seconds.

"Yes," she said. "As Stan-Eval, I can do no-notice check rides on the controllers assigned to those flights."

"Could you arrange some time to operate the radar scope by yourself? With no one looking over your shoulder?"

"Holy shit, John, what is going on? Does this have anything to do with . . . ah, is this a secure line?"

"About as secure as I can get. This is an anonymous mobile phone; I'll use it just this once."

"Okay, then," Sam said. "Rumor has it that someone, someone very highly placed in Washington, has ordered a coverup. They've seized AWACS radar data from two recent missions and made the crews—"

"Was one of those missions last Sunday, late afternoon?"

"Yes. The other one was—"

"About one week prior, right?" John asked. When Sam said yes, that answered one of his burning questions. Why hadn't the all-seeing, all-knowing AWACS picked up the MiGs as they headed north and entered US airspace? The answer: AWACS *had* seen, and recorded, all that. But someone had covered it up. Even Hardwick didn't seem to know.

"Sam, by now you have guessed that what I need is, shall we say, way off the books. You don't have to get involved. But I have to know. Are you still willing to help?"

"Yes."

Her answer came so quickly that Leslie's eyes got even wider.

John said, "Would you have access to UHF and VHF/FM radios where you could talk to me if I were airborne in a . . . if I were airborne? And, how about an HF freq to talk to someone I trust, on the ground, in southern Arizona?"

Another long pause.

"Yes, to both questions." Sam said.

Leslie whispered, "A woman of few words."

John nodded. "Thank you, Sam. You won't regret this. Now, give me an email address where I can send more details."

After John had copied Sam's email address and said goodbye, he said to Leslie, "Those are the last two pieces of the puzzle to fall into place. We can lure Alvarado and his MiGs into the sky and Sam can help us find them. The rest will be up to us." He buckled his seat belt. "Let's go. It's another forty miles to Dateland."

Chapter 28

"You want Exit 67," John said. "About five miles ahead."

"Okay," Leslie said. "So, how did you save her life?"

"Huh?"

"Sam. I heard her say you saved her life."

"Oh, that. Hah. It wasn't only her life I was trying to save. It was mine too. Remember that orientation flight I told you about, where Sam was along for an F-16 back seat ride? This was down at Clark Air Base in the Philippines during a Cope Thunder exercise. It's the PACAF version of Red Flag. I was flying down in the weeds below radar coverage, going pretty fast, ready to pop up and drop some live bombs. To make a long story short, I had a bird strike, a massive compressor stall, jettisoned the bombs and fuel tanks, and headed for Clark's SFO pattern. Engine wasn't producing much thrust. Then it over-temped and I had to shut it down, glide in for a base leg flameout approach. Made it okay, though."

"That was her first flight in a fighter?"

"Yup,' he said. "And she tells me, the last." He looked ahead and saw the Dateland hangar. "Hey, look at two o'clock, about a mile north of the highway. See that wooden hangar? That's our airfield. Dateland. You can't see the runways yet, but they're on the other side of the hangar."

They had to drive a short distance past the airfield to exit the interstate.

He said, "Turn right at the stop sign and then an immediate right onto the frontage road."

Leslie stared at the road sign as she made the second turn. "What a strange name for a street. How do you even pronounce that? Cee-ell-ell Cananea?"

"It's not so strange, given that 'Cll' is an abbreviation for 'Calle,' which in Spanish means street or road. Cananea is the name of a city in Mexico where there is—or was—a big copper mine. In the early 1900s, it made the news due to some labor disputes that were rather brutally suppressed. Incidentally, the Cananea mine was owned by an American named William Greene who, back in the early 1900's, lived down near Nogales. Even more of a coincidence is the brutal suppression was led by a Mexican army colonel named Emilio Kosterlitsky."

"And why is that fact a coincidence?"

"Oh," John said. "I forgot to explain. Tonight, we're having dinner at a restaurant owned by Emilio Kosterlitsky's great grandson, Emilio the Third."

Leslie said, "Something tells me that's not a coincidence. There must be more to the story." She slowed the pickup. "Is this the gate?"

"No, that's a little-used gate on the southwest corner of the field. Go about another thousand feet down this road, near the hangar and all those old foundations. That's the main gate. And the only one I have a key for. Yes, there's more to the Kosterlitsky story, but let's save that for the dinner table."

"When did you learn so much about this area?" Leslie asked. She stopped the truck just short of the gate.

"That's kind of a long story. Why don't I tell you all about it while we clean the runway?"

"Nice try, John. We're going to use leaf blowers, string trimmers, and noise-canceling earmuffs at opposite ends of a 6,000-foot runway. You're doing it again."

"What?"

"Prevaricating," she said.

How right she was. "Sorry," he said. "I can tell you a lot about the history of this area, but . . . remember that non-disclosure agreement I signed long ago? It includes what went on inside that gate."

"Oh, come off it," she said. "We are about to steal two F-16s and, against the wishes of our own government, shoot down a MiG or two. You're trusting me to keep *that* a secret, but you won't tell me about some clandestine boondoggle that happened, what, a quarter-century ago?"

John gritted his teeth. He opened the door and got out of the truck. It was all he could do to resist slamming the door. He marched over to the gate, unlocked it, and waved Leslie through. After relocking the gate, he got back into the truck. He pointed to the hangar and, without looking at Leslie, said, "Go."

The truck didn't move. Leslie said, "Whitaker is right. When you get pissed off, you get quiet."

John closed eyes and took a few breaths. "In my younger days, when someone said something offensive, I might have grabbed them by the shirt, pulled them close to me, and yelled at them. Or, I might have put a fist through a wall or a window. Or their face."

Leslie said, "What did I say that was so bad?"

"That 'clandestine boondoggle,' as you called it? People died. Lots of people." Only one American, though, and that would haunt him forever. "Someone I didn't even know died trying to save my ass. His family still doesn't know where, how, or why their loved one died. And you think *you* deserve to—" He forced himself to stop before he said something he'd regret.

"I'm sorry, John. I didn't—"

"Just drive."

Leslie nodded and put the truck in gear. She drove them up to a dilapidated World War II-era wooden hangar.

"See that road on the right side?" he said. "Take that. It leads to the north side of the hangar, the ramp, and the runways."

When they drove onto the concrete, Leslie whistled. "This ramp is huge!" she said. "But where are the runways? Oh, I suppose that's one just north of the ramp. But it's in extremely bad shape. Lots of weeds and bushes—even some flowers—are growing out of the asphalt. Those yellow ones look like marigolds. Out here in the desert? I wonder what those silver-white ones are." She reached down to shut off the truck.

"Hold on," he said. "You want to drive over to the west, right in front of the hangar." Before she put the truck in gear, he put his hand on her arm. "Wait. I've got something to say." But, how would he say it? He hated apologizing.

"You may be right," John said. "Maybe you deserve to know more about my past." What was still classified, and what wasn't? He'd throw her a few morsels of information and let her do her own research. "I'm going to say these five words once and then we're going to move on. Operation Gold Coast. Son Trâm. That last word is spelled capital T-r-a-m. If you can find anything in the public domain about those, more power to you. As of now, the subject is closed, okay? We've got our own mission to concentrate on."

"Okay," Leslie said. She drove several hundred feet across the ramp, stopped in front of the hangar, and shut off the truck.

They got out of the pickup and stood looking north.

John said, "By the way, yes, those are Desert Marigolds, native to this area. The silver flowers you asked about? They're desert lilies. And all those ground-hugging weeds are spurge and knotweed. Can we move on to more important matters?"

"Well," she said. "Who would have guessed that we were such experts on desert plants, native and otherwise. Here's a test, Mister Plant Expert. See those two trees out there? Out in that brown sand just north of the ramp. Do you know what those are?"

"Yes."

She waited.

He smiled. "What, you think I don't know? Want to bet on it? Whoever loses gets to clean two-thirds of the runway, not half."

"No thanks," she said. "I've already underestimated you once."

"Elephant trees. There used to be more. And some palo verdes." He looked over the ramp and the taxiway leading to Runway 01. "It's so flat out here it's hard to see much, but cleaning this up is going to be a big job. You're right; this ramp is big. It's 2,000 feet long and 300 feet wide, parallel to the runway you see—06/24. That one's not used any more. At the east end of that is the approach end of Runway 34. It's in about the same shape as 06/24. Don't try to taxi on either of those. The one we're going to use is over there." He pointed to the southwest. "On the far-left side of the ramp, you can see the taxiway that leads to the approach end of 01/19, the longest, and best-maintained, of the three runways. It's 6,600 feet long and 200 feet wide. All three runways connect to form a triangle, like so many of the old Army Air Corps fields.

"We need to weed whack, sweep and/or blow off debris between here and there, as well as the entire length of runway 01/19. To save time, why don't you drive me up to the north end of 01, come back here, and work your way toward me?"

"Sounds like a plan," she said, "But can we get a look inside the hangar first?"

*   *   *

Three hours later, John sat on the open tailgate of the Ford pickup with Leslie and Adam, who had arrived just as they were finishing up. He pulled two bottles of water from the ice chest in the pickup bed, handed them to Leslie and Adam, and reached back for one more. He twisted the cap off his bottle and said, "Cheers." They tapped their plastic bottles together.

Leslie said, "To a clean runway, a hangar with electricity, and a tow bar."

"Hear, hear," John said. "Thank you, Adam, for the tow bar." It was Adam who had thought of the latest flaw in their plan. This was one more example of his little mistakes that could ruin the mission. First, he hadn't realized that they would need a vehicle to tow the jets. He and Leslie wouldn't be able to push two eight-ton F-16s around with their bare hands as if they were little Cessna 152s. Whitaker had saved the day on that one, but even he had forgotten that a tow vehicle is useless without a tow *bar*, to connect the aircraft to the tow vehicle. Adam and Whit had fabricated one in a hurry. Adam had brought the two-piece assembly down and bolted it together while they had finished the runway cleanup.

As embarrassing as this was, John was thankful that he had smart people on his team. It was going to take all their skills and brain power to get the job done. "Well, my friends, let's get out of here. There's a lot to do back in Tucson."

Adam drove, with Leslie in the center and John on the right side of the single bench seat. Once they were eastbound on Interstate 8, John pointed out the hills southeast of Dateland. "Leslie, those hills top out at about 1,100 feet MSL, about 800 feet above Dateland's field elevation. We shouldn't get anywhere near them, but just be aware of them on the way in, when it's dark."

"Thanks," she said.

Unlike the big Chevy that they had left in the hangar, the Ford pickup ran smoothly at highway speeds. Adam cruised at or slightly above the speed limit which, in these rural areas, was 75 mph. Once John was sure that Adam was not too fatigued to drive safely, he relaxed and enjoyed the view of Sonoran Desert. It was so much different than the tall trees and lush dark green vegetation of his Puget Sound home. But the desert had its own beauty, its own best seasons. Spring was one of them. And one of the best times of day to enjoy the desert colors was now, when they were highlighted by late afternoon sun. All this reminded him of the days when this desert, and the sky above it, had been his home.

It was spring of 1972. He had just married Nicole when he got orders to ship out to Vietnam, this time as an F-4 pilot, not a special ops person. They had driven out into the desert south of Tucson to view a meteor shower. They found a dark side road, walked into the high desert, spread out a blanket, and laid on their backs. He had serenaded her with two verses from a popular Eagles' song, *"Peaceful, Easy Feeling."* She had smiled when he sang, *"I want to sleep with you in the desert tonight, with a billion stars all around."* And so, they had . . .

"John?"

He opened his eyes.

Leslie said, "Sorry, were you asleep?"

"I refuse to answer that on the grounds it may—"

"Okay, okay, I said I'm sorry! Are you awake and alert? Because I am going to be asking you some very serious questions here."

John rubbed his eyes, sat upright, and looked outside. A road sign announced the junction with I-10 was thirty miles ahead, which meant they had already passed Gila Bend. He had dozed for about forty miles. They would be back in Tucson in an hour and twenty minutes. He opened his water bottle and took a long drink. "Go ahead."

Leslie said to Adam, "Sorry if this gets a little technical and flying-related, but I've got some burning questions and serious concerns about out little, ah, project. I am trying very hard to visualize this scenario. First, and most unbelievable, we steal two F-16s from the Boneyard. We somehow get them out to Dateland, hide them in the hangar and load them up with fake AIM-9s and live twenty mike-mike ammo. Oh, not to mention four *inert* 500-pound bombs, sitting over in a corner as a backup plan. We sit out there, on alert, until your sexy friend Sam calls us on HF with a launch order. We take off. How do we find—"

"How do you know that Sam is sexy?" John asked.

"I heard her voice. She is sexy. Also, there was that comment you made about how she looked in a bikini."

John was a little embarrassed to talk about this with Adam present, but he said, "Does it matter? If you must know, nothing happened between us. That was years ago. Now she is a USAF Major, well-respected in the AWACS community. You should be happy that she is willing to help us. Don't lose sight of the goal, Leslie. We are going to wipe Alvarado and his MiGs off the face of the earth."

"Okay, I get all that. But here's the question. Will Sam be able to give us vectors to the MiGs?"

"Yes," he said. "She'll stay with us until the merge. I'm not sure how long she can stay after that. This whole thing will happen very quickly. If the MiGs launch, Sam will see 'em on radar as they track north from La Coruba. She'll let us know via a coded HF message to our radio in the hangar, manned by Adam or Whit. We launch our F-16s, which will be cocked, on alert status. Once we're airborne, Sam communicates with us on UHF as primary and VHF/FM secondary. If you've never seen what AWACS can do, it's impressive. She will see their airspeed, altitude, and track. She will know their type of aircraft."

He hesitated for a moment. Should he have even mentioned that last part? Was it still classified? Hell, she probably knew more about it than he did. The technology came out during her time in the F-16, not his.

"Without revealing anything that's still classified," he said, "are you familiar with the term, Non-Cooperative Target Recognition?"

"NCTR?" she said. "Of course, we had that, and more, on the C-models I flew. But I thought the A-model radar, APG-66, isn't it? That doesn't do NCTR."

"Correct," John said. "The ones we are going to borrow don't have it. But, as you probably already know, AWACS has NCTR and many more high-tech bells and whistles. So, Sam will be able to ID them as MiG-21s. Once we get within twenty miles of the MiGs, we should have them on radar. If our radars are inop, Sam will vector us in. Failing all that, we will know where they're going in relation to a pre-designated bullseye. We will use what Hank called the Mark One, Mod—"

"Mark One, Mod 0 human eyeball," Leslie said with a smile. "He said that to me a gazillion times."

John clenched his jaw so tight it hurt his teeth. "Man, how I miss that guy." He looked away, out into the desert. "Trust me. We will find those MiGs, Leslie. Once we find them, we will kill them."

Chapter 29

It was 5:30 p.m. when Adam drove them up to the hangar in Tucson. He beeped the horn but, judging by the shriek of a metal grinder from inside, Whitaker wasn't going to hear that. John got out and tried the door. It was locked. When the noise inside stopped, he pounded on the metal door. "Whit! It's us," he shouted. "Open up."

Something clattered onto the floor. Several seconds later, John heard footsteps approaching the door.

Whitaker opened it and said, "Thank God you're back. I'm starving. If I recall correctly, you promised to take us all out to dinner tonight. Lemme get the big door open so you can drive in."

John stood aside as the big hangar doors opened wide enough to admit the Ford pickup. He walked in behind it and saw two large semi-tractor trailers and an aircraft fueling truck parked parallel to one another. A shiny blue forklift sat beside them.

Adam shut off the Ford's engine. He and Leslie got out and stared at the assembled vehicles. Whitaker walked back near the hangar wall and pushed the button to close the hangar doors.

Leslie said, "Whit, how did you get all this in here so fast? We've only been gone for, what? Eight or nine hours?"

"Cash talks," Whitaker said. "I got lucky and found both tractor-trailers at the same lot. That shiny red Mack tractor cab is only a year old and has a sleeper that looks more comfortable, and more spacious, than most of the TEQ rooms I've stayed in. The white cab, also obviously a Mack—you can't miss the seven-inch tall letters on the grill—is not a sleeper, so that's the one going to the Boneyard."

Adam led them over to the large trucks and trailers, one of which had a faded green logo painted on the side and the words, *Old Pueblo Moving and Storage*. The other trailer was plain white. He said, "How long are the trailers?"

"Twenty-eight feet long and 110 inches high inside," Whitaker said. "Plenty big enough for—"

Someone pounded on the man door. Whitaker said, "That'll be our fuel bladders. Everything else we need, except the ammo, is already here." He pointed to a stack of wooden crates, cardboard boxes, and other soft packages near the opposite end of the hangar. "I'll tell the delivery guy to leave them outside." He jogged off.

Adam said, "I should have been here to help him with all this."

"Don't worry," John said. "You'll get your chance. I have a feeling we'll all be pitching in to help. At least now we have more time." When Whitaker returned, he told him about the latest changes to their agenda.

"That's great!" Whitaker said. "Now I don't have to feel guilty about taking some well-deserved time off tonight, sipping margaritas, and eating Mexican food at Cocina Kosterlitsky, that place you recommended. I, ah, took the liberty of making us a reservation for 6:30."

John had a long list of questions about the trucks, the equipment, and Whit's plan to use it all, but he didn't see any problem discussing those over margaritas.

* * *

John led the way across 1st Avenue and, when the traffic light changed, across University Boulevard. He stopped at the tall, white-washed stucco archway with open wrought-iron gates. At the center of the arch was a matte-black, laser-cut metal plate bearing the words, *Cocina Kosterlitsky*. He gestured to the courtyard inside with an open hand. "After you, madam. And gentlemen."

Leslie pointed at the archway. "That name doesn't sound very Mexican. Are you going to explain that?"

"Oh yes." he said. "But it's a very long story, one better told over our first round of margaritas."

Leslie and the others filed past him into Cocina Kosterlitsky's courtyard, which hadn't changed since his last visit, about ten years ago. Just inside the gate was a courtyard paved with dark brown Saltillo tile. Scattered around the perimeter were hand-carved oak benches, lush green succulents, and bright red flowers embedded in equally bright, hand-painted ceramic pots.

Adam said, "Nice fountain. I'd love to sit out here and just listen to the water."

John resisted offering details about the imported Cantera stone, found only in Mexico and South America, from which the fountain had been made. He needed to move everyone inside, get them started on dinner, and bombard Whitaker with questions.

They were met at the front desk by a petite young woman with jet-black hair, a bright smile and a tulip pinned over her left ear. She wore a traditional Mexican outfit, a white blouse with flowery trim around the neck, and a long, ankle-length dark blue skirt with horizontal rows of embroidered flowers on the lower half.

"Welcome to Cocina Kosterlitsky. I'm Verónica. Do you have a reservation?"

John gave her his name.

She consulted the guest list, put a check mark next to his name, and said, "Right this way, please."

She led them to a booth at the far end of a spacious dining room. Thick, hand-hewn oak beams supported the high, whitewashed stucco ceiling. The walls, also stucco, were a subdued yellow with irregularities consistent with the Old Spanish Colonial style—paint applied with rags rather than brushes. Wooden-legged tables were covered in bright multi-colored tile. Cabinets were either tiled or painted in the full spectrum of primary colors.

"Will this be okay?" Verónica asked.

John said, "It's perfect. Thank you." They were far from the nearest occupied tables, which would allow for a nice private conversation. John decided to do the gentlemanly thing and pulled out a chair for Leslie. Whit and Adam took the two chairs on the opposite side.

Adam turned his head and kept his eyes on Verónica as she walked away.

Whitaker poked him in the ribs. "C'mon man. How about you study the menu and not the young lady?"

A young man dressed in white pants, matching loose white shirt, and a red bandana around his neck approached and said, "Hello. I'm Benjamin. I'll be your server tonight." He set down two plates of tortilla chips and a two bowls of salsa. "May I start you out with some drinks?"

They all wanted margaritas, although Adam requested a non-alcoholic one.

"I'm not much for alcoholic beverages," he said after Benjamin had left. "Besides, someone's got to be the designated driver."

Conversation stopped while they studied the menu. Adam asked some questions about Mexican food, which Leslie answered.

She closed her menu and looked at the cover. "That reminds me. John, I know the drinks aren't here yet, but you promised to explain this name, Cocina Kosterlitsky."

"Okay. The owner of this place is Emilio Kosterlitsky the Third, whom I met long ago, when we were both in our twenties. I was a first lieutenant, and he was a busboy here. Now, he owns the place. I wish you could meet him, but he's out of town, visiting relatives in—believe it or not— the family's hometown of Kosterlitsky, Mexico.

"Oh, come on," Leslie said. "You're telling me there's a town in Mexico with that name?"

"Look it up. It's a small town about fifty miles south of Tucson, just a few miles south of the border. Emilio the Third is the great grandson of a Russian naval officer, Emil Kosterlitsky, who emigrated to Mexico under somewhat mysterious circumstances, and changed his name to Emilio. The story goes—well, wait." He flipped the menu over to the back. "You can read the whole story here. But the bottom line is, the original Emilio, the Russian guy, was a soldier of fortune, a fierce fighter, a crack shot, and yet a cultured man who spoke seven languages. All these qualifications, and his knowledge of the US-Mexico borderlands, came to the attention of J. Edgar Hoover, who recruited him as a special agent for the FBI."

John had to pause while a strolling Mariachi band stopped to play a love song at a nearby table. The four men wore colorful embroidered charro suits, sombreros, and brightly polished, high-heeled leather boots.

Whitaker leaned forward and said, "My God, that's a whopping big guitar!"

When the band moved on, Leslie said, "That's not a traditional guitar. It's a guitarrón, which is more like a bass violin—with a much deeper tone than a guitar—and held against the chest. The other one, to the left of the guitarrón, is a vihuela. Only five strings and a higher pitch than a regular guitar."

"As much as I enjoy learning about all this musical culture stuff," Whitaker said, "right now I'm obsessing on one thing. John, you got my curiosity up about this guy Koster-whatever and the FBI. Continue, please, but make it brief, which I know is a major challenge for you." He grinned and paused for effect. "I see the waiter coming with our drinks, and we'd better get ready to order. I'm starving."

John gave them the highlights, spiced with sensational but true facts: Kosterlitsky's swashbuckling, authentic cavalry charges as a Mexican soldier, his time spent in U.S. camps for political prisoners, his undercover operations, and the town in Mexico bearing his name. He didn't think Whit and Adam needed to know about Kosterlitsky's involvement in the Cananea massacre and the coincidence of Calle Cananea being the street leading to Dateland.

Whitaker said, "Whew! So, that was the *short* version?"

"There's one thing you haven't explained," Leslie said. "What is *your* connection to this place, John? I told you before, I know there's a story here somewhere."

Could he answer that before the drinks arrived? No. He said, "Hold on for a minute. Here comes Benjamin."

The young man returned with their drinks and took their dinner orders.

Before John took his first sip, he said, "In the 1960s and 70s, when the Vietnam War was in full swing, a lot of special operations units were stationed around here, or had temporary duty here, at Fort Huachuca, D-M, and Yuma."

"Ah, one question," Adam said. "Why here? This is all desert. Vietnam was mostly jungle, right?"

"Right. But the major attraction was, and still is, the vast amount of military restricted airspace and gunnery ranges in Arizona. After initial training here, we—I mean, those forces—got more training in actual jungle terrain." John looked around the dining room. "Cocina Kosterlitsky was a favorite watering hole for military special ops, probably because of old Emil's legend as an undercover operative. This is where I was recruited into my very brief career in air force special ops. For Adam's benefit, that was right before I got into the F-4 and met your dad."

Adam said, "I might know more than you think, sir. My dad talked about you a lot."

John laughed. "I'm sure he did. Some of what he said might even be true."

Chapter 30

More tortilla chips were eaten, mostly by Whitaker, margaritas were sipped, and salt licked off the rims of glasses. John said, "It's time to change the subject, though. Whit, congratulations. You've done a fantastic job ordering all that stuff and getting it delivered in a hurry. And the trucks? Unbelievable."

Adam said, "May I ask a dumb question? I'm the new guy here, so I wasn't in on all the planning. Why two trucks?"

"Whit, you've been handling all that while we've been sweeping a runway. Why don't you explain?"

Whitaker waved a tortilla chip in the air as if it were a baton and he was the conductor of a symphony orchestra. "Okay, I'll lay it out for you. And just to be fair—" He nodded at John. "I did not dream this up myself. John gave me the basic plan and I just tweaked it a little." After dipping the chip in salsa, munching, and swallowing it, he said, "Adam, I am going to give you a crash course on what the Boneyard is and how they store the jets . . ."

A minute or two later, Whitaker had consumed six more chips with salsa, described the upgraded conditions under which the Peace Leopard jets were stored, and sketched out their location on a napkin. He said, "Leslie, can you pass me that other bowl of chips? I forgot to ask for a refill." He raised his large, bowl-shaped Margarita glass and said, "Who wants to make a toast? I can never do it right."

John picked up his glass. "To the food supply chain. May it not break under the pressure of feeding Jim Whitaker."

"Damn," Whitaker said. "That's not exactly what I was expecting. Can I get a do-over? Something more along the lines of, 'Jim Whitaker is a brilliant mechanic, one who—'"

"Whit, just keep going with your, ah, 'crash course,'" John said. "Which, by the way, is a very poor choice of words."

Whitaker grunted. "Okay. Where was I? Oh, yeah. So, the planes are out there right near this north-south fence. On the other side of the fence—" He tapped his finger on the napkin. "—is Kolb Road, a residential area. We park the white tractor-trailer there. Someone else drives the Ford pickup and parks nearby. That's our getaway vehicle. For me and Adam, I mean. We'll abandon the tractor-trailer."

"You're going to leave it there?" Leslie said. "What a waste!"

John said, "A waste, yes, but a necessary one. Whit and I both agree that, after we taxi out and take off, all hell will break loose at the Boneyard and D-M. Law enforcement, including helicopters, will be out looking for anything suspicious. An eighteen-wheeler pulling away from the Boneyard fence at 0430 would attract too much attention." He guessed what Leslie would say next. "Yes, I know that the Feds will probably find and seize that tractor-trailer. We can't avoid leaving footprints and fingerprints behind. Who cares? Once Hardwick finds out, he'll know it was us."

"That trailer will be loaded up with all the stuff we need to service up the jets," Whitaker said. "Those fuel bladders you saw? Four of 'em hold 500 gallons each and the fifth holds 250. That's enough to fill two F-16s with full internal fuel. There will be plenty of room left over in the trailer for everything else we need."

He went on to describe in detail all the other supplies, pumps, hoses, and hydraulic fluid needed. Fuel, air, and hydraulic lines would be routed under the fence, but larger objects, including the four of them, would be lowered over the fence on a small but sturdy telescopic crane mounted inside the trailer and controlled by a handheld keypad.

John was happy to sit back and let Adam ask the technical questions. Would the trailer accommodate all that weight? Whitaker pulled a piece of paper from his back pocket and showed everyone his calculations.

"Everything we want to put in there, including 14,000 pounds of jet fuel, will total under 25,000 pounds. The trailer is rated for 40,000. No problem."

"What about batteries?" Adam asked. "Where did you find F-16 aircraft batteries? You either need those or an external power cart to start the jets."

"I found a suitable substitute," Whitaker said. "Same specs, aircraft quality, and just a little smaller in size, so I know they'll fit. Got two of 'em in the hangar right now, plus a 28-volt charger."

For every question that Adam asked, Whitaker had an answer. Until Adam asked about hydrazine.

Whitaker said, "John said he'd come up with a solution for that one."

With three sets of eyes on him, John gave the only answer he could. "We're just going to go without it. Hydrazine is a highly controlled toxic substance. It's too difficult to obtain on the civilian market. Even if we could buy it, we'd need specialized protective gear and storage tanks."

Adam said, "But, isn't the EPU your backup source of electrics? What if the engine-mounted generator fails? I've heard the jet will go out of control without electrical power."

John gave Adam a brief refresher on the F-16's quadruple-redundant electrical system. The Emergency Power Unit was third on the list of systems that keep the jet flying. "If the generator fails, but the engine is running above a certain rpm, the EPU is powered by engine bleed air. It's only at low rpm, say in the case of engine failure, that the hydrazine kicks in. Even if the EPU fails, the aircraft battery keeps the flight controls going. And, if for some reason the generator, EPU, and battery all fail, I still have the FLCS batteries to get me safely home."

Their server reappeared and asked if they needed more drinks. No one was ready for that, but Leslie asked for more chips and salsa.

After Benjamin had deposited two new bowls of chips and salsa on the table, Whitaker leaned forward and said through a mouthful of chips, "Okay, I figure it will take us two or three trips over the fence, between security patrols, to get the jets ready. Shortly before moonrise—0430 on Saturday, right?"

John nodded.

"We'll be ready to launch just before moonrise. Prior to engine start, Adam, 'cause he's younger than I am, will jog out to the Boneyard gate, cut the lock, and open the gate. He will then jog a couple hundred feet more, out onto the Christmas Tree ramp, and do the same for the gate to the runway. Meanwhile, we start up the jets. You guys taxi about a hundred feet onto the paved taxiway road. Adam returns and helps me remove the home-made intake screens that prevent you from sucking up rocks and dirt. You guys taxi out and take off. Adam and I run back to the fence and disappear. Piece of cake." He sat back and exhaled heavily.

Benjamin arrived with a large aluminum tray balanced on one hand. Without consulting any notes, he gave each of them the correct plate, took their order for another round of drinks and departed.

Conversation again came to a halt while they enjoyed their dinners. John shared an order of fajitas with Adam. Leslie looked happy with her Ensalada Tucson, which had a romaine lettuce salad tossed with ranch dressing, black beans, tomatoes, queso and—in John's opinion—a very small piece of grilled chicken on top. Whitaker, of course, had the largest plate at the table and got busy with a "Chimichanga del Mondo" which, as the name implied, had everything in the world in it. It was half the size of a football. Dessert was out of the question; they were all too full. John ordered after-dinner coffee. Leslie had some herbal tea. Adam and Whitaker switched to ice water.

Adam said, "I've got a good handle on Friday night's trip into the Boneyard. And, having been out there at Dateland, I know Colonel Martin and Leslie can put the jets to bed out there. But I've got some questions about all that stuff in the Tucson hangar. How and when are we going to get that, and the fuel truck, over to Dateland?"

"I'm glad you asked that," Whitaker said. "Because I got one more little wrinkle to iron out. Adam, you'll get your questions answered. But first . . . dammit, John, you've got me thinking like a master criminal here. The current plan is for Adam and me to drive the empty fuel truck and the tractor trailer full of equipment out to Dateland on Saturday morning, after the, ahem, theft. The tractor trailer is no problem. You see hundreds of 'em on the Interstate. But the fuel truck? When we stop at that dinky little airport at Gila Bend, several hours after the theft, buy 5,000 gallons of Jet-A fuel and head off west on Interstate 8, that, my friends, is a big, big red flag."

Leslie said, "You are so right. Believe me, our government has ways of tracking jet fuel purchases. So, we've got to fill that truck before Friday night."

"Do we still drive it down to Dateland on Saturday?" Adam asked.

"Give me a second to think about this," John said. He took a sip of coffee and mulled over the options. After a second sip, he said, "It's too big a risk to take. That truck should not be on the Interstate on Saturday. It needs to be safely in the hangar at Dateland before we steal the jets. Does everyone agree?"

All three nodded their heads.

"That means somebody will have to fill it tomorrow, preferably at the Tucson airport where it won't stand out, and then drive it down to Dateland."

"But" Leslie said, "only Adam and Whit have the proper licenses for the fuel truck. They need to be here, working on the trailer. And, whoever goes, how will he get back?"

Benjamin came by to inquire about refills, but everyone declined. John asked for the check and finished his coffee. He glanced at Leslie's teacup and saw that it was empty. "Let's go," he said. "I think I've got a solution to the fuel truck-slash-driver problem." He put enough cash onto the table to cover the bill and a generous tip.

Once they had squeezed themselves back into the pickup, Whitaker suggested they do a drive-by of the street where they planned to enter the Boneyard. On the way, John said he needed to make two phone calls. The first was to directory assistance for Yuma. He dialed the number for Apex Taxi service and spoke for a minute or two. Apex was happy to accept the job but needed a credit card deposit, so John read them "Larry's" credit card number. He disconnected.

"Well, that's my second burner phone," he said. "I guess I'll have to get a couple more, maybe tonight. You guys heard my end of the conversation, so you can probably figure out the plan. Tomorrow, Adam drives the fuel truck to Dateland, locks it up in the hangar, and walks to the gas station and tourist area, about two miles from the runway. The taxi will pick him up there. He pays the driver the balance in cash and the taxi takes him to Smuggler's Inn here in Tucson, where we pick him up."

Whitaker said, "Meanwhile, you two pilots will become my helpers getting stuff loaded in that trailer. Shit! Wait, there's another glitch."

Leslie groaned.

Something hadn't sounded right in Whitaker's fuel truck plans. Of course! "It's the fuel bladders, right?" John said.

"Yeah. They need to be filled, which means using our fuel truck for that. Adam can't just drive off to Dateland first thing in the morning. He'll need to be at the fuel barn, early tomorrow, load up with enough fuel for the bladders, and deliver that to the Tucson hangar. Then he'll go back, top off the truck, and head for Dateland."

Leslie gave Adam verbal directions to the stretch of Kolb Road they had identified. He pulled off onto the shoulder.

"Uh, one stupid question," Adam said. "How do we know this spot will be vacant on Friday night?"

"Got it covered," Whitaker said. "Back at the hangar, I've got some rented sawhorses and a couple of those orange fold-up signs that say, 'No parking,' and 'Underground utility work.' We'll put those out tomorrow."

They sat in the truck staring at F-16s just inside the fence. The sun had set an hour ago but there was still enough twilight in the west to make out the jets and the service roads leading to their planned exit route.

Adam commented on all the other types of aircraft nearby. "I wish we could just pick up a jet with a crane and load it onto a flatbed truck. That'd be so much easier than the current plan."

"Hmm . . ." John said.

"Don't give the man any more ideas!" Whitaker said. "Anyway, an F-16 is too big for that scenario." He chuckled. "I'd like to see it, though. Driving down the street with a thirty-two-foot-wide Viper jet on my trailer!"

"Yeah," Adam said. "I guess that might attract a little unwanted attention. Well, what's next?"

"To the hangar, Adam. Let's all get some rest." John hoped that, among all the supplies Whitaker had stacked against the wall, there would be some air mattresses.

Chapter 31

John should have known better. He had looked forward to sleeping in, but that would be impossible now, after the earth-shaking rumble of the hangar doors and the revving of the fuel truck's diesel engine. He sat up, swung his feet onto the floor, and watched the fuel truck back out of the hangar. Whitaker was standing at the exit with the door controller in his hand. As soon as Adam was clear, the doors clanked closed just as noisily as when they had opened.

The sun was already up and jet noise from early-morning departures sealed the deal; there was no way he could get back to sleep. Whitaker wouldn't allow that anyway; he was already standing at their makeshift kitchen table, staring at him.

Whitaker grinned and rubbed his hands together. "I've been waiting a long time for this moment. Today, I get to order you around for a change! It's 0530. Let's get crackin'. You and Leslie are now my apprentice mechanics and fabricators. First order of business is those fuel—"

"No, *boss*," Leslie said. "The first order of business is breakfast, and I believe it's my turn to cook."

John hadn't heard her approach. She was already fully dressed in loose-fitting jeans, a t-shirt and her recently delivered black leather flight boots.

He said, "Give me a minute to freshen up and I'll help."

By 7:00 a.m. Leslie had produced a hearty breakfast of pancakes and sausage for the four of them, the fuel bladders were full in Trailer One, and Adam had departed to refill the truck and drive it to Dateland. He and Leslie went to work on Whitaker's agenda for preparing the equipment and loading the trailers.

They worked hard until 3:00 p.m. Whitaker looked at the trailers, slapped John on the back and said, "It's been a good day so far. You and Leslie might have a bright future as mechanics. Where'd she go, anyway?"

"Shower."

"Right. Well, it's time for me to pick up Adam; he's due at Smuggler's Inn at 1530."

John waved to him as he drove the Ford pickup out of the hangar. Before he closed the doors, he looked to the north, over the sprawling suburbs of Tucson, and saw thunderheads gathering near the top of Mount Lemmon. That reminded him to check the latest weather forecast for tomorrow night and Saturday morning. Low clouds in southern Arizona were rare but, if they showed up Saturday, it would ruin their plans. He pushed the button to close the doors and walked back to the table, where his laptop was already open. He bent down, minimized the page on the screen, which was a digital file of the F-16A Dash One, and searched for a weather forecast.

Leslie walked out of the hangar's bathroom with a towel wrapped around her hair and wearing a clean pair of denim jeans, a pink long-sleeved shirt, and sneakers. She said, "Where's he going?"

"To pick up Adam. He'll be at Smuggler's Inn in thirty minutes."

She looked at her wristwatch and said, "Everything must have gone smoothly down in Dateland. Adam's right on schedule." She pointed at the laptop. "What are you looking at?"

"Weather forecast. It's all good for tomorrow night and Saturday. Clear skies and calm winds all over southern Arizona."

He stretched out his arms and twisted his torso. When he arched his back, he flinched.

"Something wrong?" she asked.

"Nothing a hot shower won't fix. Assuming, of course, that you left me any hot water. We did a lot of heavy lifting today. Even with a hydraulic lift and weapons racks, muscling all those heavy hoses, bombs and other stuff into the trailers was quite a workout."

Sure, his lats ached, but the burning pain in his lower back wasn't due to overworked muscles. Once in a great while, his old spinal injury—or injuries, plural—acted up. X-rays after the Son Trâm raid had shown compression fractures of two vertebrae in his lower back. He had refused surgical treatment and made sure the X-rays got lost. They would have ended his flying career before he had a chance to strap on an F-4.

If he wasn't careful, he'd slip back into 1970 and start asking himself the same old questions. Did the crash of the Pilatus break his back? Or was it carrying Landreau out of the wreckage? How about dragging the dead pilot's body out? He allowed himself a brief smile. It could have been the strain of those three heavy rucksacks. Money, they say, is the root of all evil.

"You're smiling," Leslie said. "Or you were. Are you off in another world again?"

"No, no. Just thinking about that hot shower waiting for me." That was at least partially true. "I've earned it, wouldn't you say?"

Leslie said, "You bet. For a couple of dumb pilots, I think we did a pretty good job, especially cutting out that section of the trailer's roof and fabricating a sliding door up there. Although, I guess neither of us could have done it without Whit's supervision. That guy has a lot of energy for an old fart."

John laughed. "Don't let him hear you say that. But he is amazing. After, let's see . . ." He added up the hours since their

0530 wakeup. "After nine-plus hours of heavy work by the three of us, he's still going strong. I don't know about you, but I'm tired."

"Yeah, me too. This morning at breakfast, I was actually going to suggest we find a gym to work out, but I think I've had my exercise for the day."

John asked her about her routine for keeping in shape and discovered it was remarkably like his. Cardio three times per week—for him it was kayaking or a stationary bike; for her it was a treadmill or jogging. On the other days, they both did some form of resistance or strength training using either machines or free weights. Coincidentally, they both used Sunday as a day off from heavy exercise. "We might want to find a gym tomorrow, early in the day," he said. "Just to burn off some nervous energy." He grabbed a towel, a washcloth, and some clean clothes and headed off to the shower.

When he returned, Leslie was sitting with her elbows on the table and her chin resting on her hands. Her eyes were closed. He didn't want to disturb her, so he wandered over to the trailers and admired their work. Trailer One, as Whitaker had named it, would be going to the Boneyard fence tomorrow night. It had required extensive and exhausting modifications to its interior and roof. Whitaker had vetoed John's first plan to strap down all five fuel bladders in the front of the trailer. That would have put too much weight at the front. They had strapped two of the 500-gallon bladders plus the 250-gallon one into the front.

In the center of the trailer was their *piece de resistance,* a telescoping metal crane designed to raise up through the opening they had cut in the roof. The opening was sealed by a sliding frame, complete with nylon rollers, which Whitaker had designed and built. Leslie and John had installed it. The crane was anchored to the floor by twelve half-inch stainless-steel bolts. After drilling holes for those, he had crouched under the trailer, at great expense to his sore back, and tightened the lock nuts while Leslie held the top end with a wrench. According to Whitaker, the crane, operated by a handheld remote, could lift all their bulkier and heavier equipment over the three strands of barbed wire at the top of the fence. Only the fuel, air, and oil hoses would need to be routed under it.

The remaining two 500-gallon bladders had been secured over the rear wheels, leaving just enough room at the back for the smaller items—a hydraulic servicing cart, aircraft batteries, LOX tanks, a large coil of fuel hose, and a toolbox. All these items were secured with cargo straps.

A horn beeped three times. Whitaker and Adam were back. Leslie got to the door before he did. The hangar doors opened, and Whitaker drove the pickup in and parked next to the white Mack tractor, which was attached to Trailer One.

Adam got out of the truck and said, "Everything's ready down there. Here's the keys." He tossed the keys to Dateland's main gate and hangar to John. "Now, show me what you guys have done."

Leslie volunteered to give Adam a tour inside Trailer One. They climbed up and disappeared into the center of the trailer. John heard the "sunroof," as Whitaker called it, slide open and the whir of the crane's electric motor. He heard Adam's exclamation: "Wow! That is really cool!"

Whitaker hadn't climbed up into the trailer. This fact, by itself, was not cause for alarm. After all, he had worked on it all morning. However, John was concerned that he had walked away and was now between the two trailers, near the cabs, bent over as if he were in pain.

John went down the narrow space, intentionally scuffing his boots on the floor to announce his approach. "Whit," he said. "What's wrong? Are you hurt?"

Whitaker straightened up and shook his head. "No, not hurt. But . . ."

John gave him some time.

"I don't know, man. I just don't know if I can go through with this."

"Why not?"

"It's that kid." Whitaker pointed at Trailer One. "He's not like us. We are a couple over-the-hill guys who don't have much to lose. But Adam? He's got his whole life ahead of him. Except that I just recruited him to break about a hundred Federal laws and risk prison time. That makes me feel like shit."

"I hear you," John said. He felt the same about Leslie. The main difference was Leslie had forced herself into this operation, while Whitaker had actively recruited Adam. What could he say to make the man feel any better? He considered a gentle approach but discarded it. "There is nothing I can say to make you feel better. Do you want to know why?"

"Gee, thanks, that was a great help. But go ahead. Tell me why."

"Two things," John said. "First, I need to know. Do you believe, *really believe,* in our mission?"

"Yes."

"Okay, then. Welcome to the club—the exclusive club of combat leaders. Because that's what you and I are. We are going into combat against an evil man and his MiGs. But we can't go it alone. I wish we could, but we need help. In my case, to win this battle I need a wingman. If something happens to Leslie out there, it will hurt me for the rest of my life. But I'm going to use every ounce of my fighter pilot experience to make sure we survive this mission.

"Likewise, the burden of recruiting Adam rests squarely on your shoulders. He's your 'wingman' now. Protect him. Do the mission but do it in such a way that you both survive and stay out of jail."

Whitaker stood still. His chest rose and fell twice. "You said there were two things, two reasons that you couldn't make me feel better. So far, I still feel like shit. Gimme your second reason."

"That's a no-brainer," John said. "Listen to those two." He pointed at Trailer Two. Leslie and Adam had moved there and were trading excited words about the equipment and how it would be used. "Get real, Whit. There's no way in hell you are going to get Adam off this job. He has inherited a very large dose of his father's stubbornness."

That brought a brief smile to Whitaker's face. "All right, John, you sly devil. Your underwhelming motivational speech has cured me. Let's go check those tie-downs in Trailer Two. Out of my way!"

John backed up to let him pass but Whitaker stopped, turned, and gave him a tight hug.

"Thanks, John. I really mean it."

"You're welcome."

"Oh, one more thing. I will poison your coffee if you ever tell anyone about this conversation."

John had all he could do to keep up with the small man as he strode off to Trailer Two. When they reached the trailer, the lift gate was in the raised position. Leslie and Adam were already inside. Whitaker lowered the lift, waved him onto it and they both rode up.

"Why is there an empty space at the rear, where we're standing?" Adam asked.

Whitaker said, "That, my boy, is where the pallet of ammo goes when it gets delivered tomorrow. Then you and I are going to load 1022 rounds of twenty mike-mike into the Universal Ammunition Loading System using that silver thing with rollers, which I believe is called a replenisher tray. That's a lot of loading and cranking with a giant speed handle, so we may need help from John and Leslie. The good news is, once the UALS is loaded, it makes loading bullets into the jets very easy. Except, we have to do it manually, using that same speed handle."

"Dare I ask where you got this UALS from?" Adam said.

"I just called up the manufacturer," Whitaker said. "I told them I was representing an air museum—that's believable right?"

John and Leslie nodded.

"And I told 'em we needed an operational one for display purposes. They didn't seem to care much. They just wanted my money—well, not *my* money, but you know what I mean. Ordered it Tuesday night and it was delivered yesterday, along with the special speed handle to hand-crank the bullets into the jet."

Adam admitted that, although he had seen the UALS in use by weapons specialists, he had never understood how it worked. John felt the same. It was a big thing, a heavy flat trailer about five feet long and over three feet wide, with eighteen-inch tires. On the flat bed was the replenisher tray and a snake-like pile of flexible metal cage into which the rounds would be loaded. Once the cage was loaded and connected the drum in the F-16s gun bay, ammunition could be hand-cranked into the jet. The UALS weighed almost a ton even when empty. Thank God for the forklift; without that, they couldn't have gotten it into Trailer Two. That reminded him of a question.

He said, "Will our forklift handle the weight of this thing after it's loaded with 1,022 rounds?"

"Just barely," Whitaker said. "That little blue forklift is rated for one and a half tons. The UALS, with ammo, will weigh 2,600 pounds." He moved forward and bent down to check the tie-downs on the rack of four AIM-9 missiles. "This is all good." He continued to the next section, near the center of the trailer. He checked all the smaller equipment—the battery charger, a second hydraulic servicing cart to replace the one they'd leave at the Boneyard, a toolbox, and a cardboard box of cleaning materials.

John noticed a bottle of Armor All, a can of car wax, and a small bottle of white paint in the box with rags and other cleaners. That was a classic Jim Whitaker touch. "Whit, do you want to tell the Armor All story or shall I?"

"Go ahead, John. You're much better at bullsh—at exaggerating—than I am."

"Okay, Adam, picture this. And it's no bull; I was there. Nellis Air Force Base. A big weapons competition, a Turkey Shoot for all 12th Air Force fighters. It all begins with an inspection by a two-star general, who walks down the line of jets. When he gets to Three-Six-Eight he stops, looks at Whit and me. We're standing at attention. He looks at the tires. They are shiny black. Whit has sprayed them with Armor All. He has painted the raised letters on the tires white. The general climbs up the ladder, which, by the way, is slick with Armor All, and looks down into the cockpit. Every switch in that cockpit, every panel, shined brighter than the day it came off the assembly line. Thanks to Armor All, of course. The general climbs back down and walks around the jet, stops at the intake, bends down, and looks in. Runs his bare hand over the highly polished white paint. Looks at his hand, which has not even a speck of dust on it.

"'Sergeant,' the general barks, 'Come over here.'

"Whit hustles over, comes to attention and snaps a perfect salute. 'Yes, sir!' he says.

"The general looks at his name tag and says, 'Sergeant Whitaker, this is the cleanest and shiniest intake I have ever seen. It is so clean I could eat my lunch off it.'

"Whit salutes again and says, 'With all due respect, general, I would not let you eat your lunch off my intake.' The general laughed and moved on. But Whit won the prize for the cleanest

F-16—in fact, Three-Six-Eight was judged the best-maintained jet among all the participating squadrons."

Adam slapped Whitaker on the shoulder and said, "Good for you. Especially the part about telling off the general."

Whitaker said, "What John is too modest to say is, he and his wingman went on to win the Turkey Shoot in both categories, air-to-air and air-to-ground."

"And what Whit is too modest to say is, based on that general's recommendation, Whit was invited to be a crew chief for the Thunderbirds. Which he turned down to stay with Three-Six-Eight when we deployed to Saudi."

"Enough stories," Whitaker said. "Adam, why don't you check our Mk-82s. Let me know if those crates they're in are strapped down good enough. Then this baby will be ready to roll. All we have to do is add our cots and food and so forth."

After Adam reported all the equipment was secure and ready to travel to Dateland, John announced that he'd buy them all a well-deserved dinner. They decided on a Thai restaurant on the far west side of town, one where Leslie was unlikely to meet any of her Customs Service colleagues. There was nothing left to discuss. All the necessary plans had been made; all contingencies covered. Sure.

Chapter 32

"My goodness, you're up early," Leslie said.

John got up from his chair at the table, where he had been reading a digital copy of the F-16A flight manual and refilled his coffee cup. "Want a cup?" he asked. She nodded.

"I woke up at about 0430, quite by accident," he said. "Decided to go outside to watch the moon rise. To get an idea of what it will be like tonight—or rather tomorrow morning, Saturday. Couldn't get back to sleep, so I've been brushing up on the Dash One."

"I should look at that too," she said. "I haven't flown an A-model since RTU. All my time since then has been in the C-model. Or you could just fill me in on the important stuff."

He pushed the laptop over to her side of the table. "Why don't you browse through this first and then we'll sit down and talk about the major differences. After we have a bite to eat."

"Eat?" Whitaker said from his cot. "Did someone mention food? I smell coffee! John, I think it's your turn to make breakfast. I like my eggs over easy and my bacon nice and crisp."

The rattle of cups, saucers and dishes roused Adam. Thirty minutes later, they had finished off breakfast and another pot of coffee.

Whitaker said, "Well, this is the big day. Adam, you and me need to get right to work. We've got to fabricate that piggyback frame so the forklift can be carried on the back of the trailer. Got to get that done before noon, when the ammo is scheduled to arrive."

"Will you need our help?" Leslie said.

"For the ammo loading, sure. But for the piggyback frame? Not really. It's a two-person job. Hah! See that, Leslie? I said, 'two-person,' not 'two-man.'"

"There is hope for you, Whit," Leslie said.

John said, "It's still early. If you don't need us for a couple hours, Leslie and I need to run a couple errands."

"We do?" she said.

"Yes. A trip to the gym. It was you who suggested it yesterday. I, for one, need to burn off some nervous energy, get my heart rate up, take my mind off what we're about to do." He looked at Adam and Whitaker. "Is there anything you guys need while we're out?"

Adam shook his head. Whitaker asked him to fill up the pickup's gas tank.

Leslie suggested the University of Arizona's gym, which had a daily rate for non-students. She was confident that none of her Customs Service friends worked out there since they had free access to Davis-Monthan's base gym. After a ninety-minute session of combined weight training and cardio workout, John enjoyed a long shower—another fringe benefit of going to the gym.

When he met Leslie in the lobby, she said, "Sorry if I made you wait. I just couldn't resist standing under that shower for an insanely long time. Is there even a shower at Dateland?"

"I think I saw one in the bathroom," he said. "Not sure about hot water, though. Don't worry. Whitaker bought one of those camp-style solar things that heats a small bag of water."

"Ugh."

On the way back, John mentioned he needed to stop at a print shop. He pulled a flash drive out of his pocket and said, "In addition to the Dash One, I downloaded a copy of the inflight checklist. I need to print two copies on card stock, punch holes in them and buy some of those little metal rings to hold it all together. I don't know about you, but I'd hate to miss something critical by trying to do it all from memory."

They were back at the hangar by 11:00 a.m. While waiting for the ammunition delivery, John suggested to Leslie that they discuss some technical details. He gave her thirty minutes to refresh herself on the F-16A Dash One. While she did that, he watched Whitaker and Adam attach the piggyback frame, freshly painted in flat black quick-dry paint, to the rear of Trailer Two. Using its quick-release pins, they removed it and set it aside.

"Why not leave it on?" John asked.

"Can't use the trailer's lift gate with the piggyback frame attached. And, when the ammo gets here, we'll sure as hell need the lift gate to get it up into the trailer. Once that's done, the piggyback goes back on, at which time we drive the forklift onto the piggyback. By late this afternoon, this baby will be ready to roll."

"Lunch time!" Whitaker said. "I got us some awesome cold cuts, sliced cheese, onions and all the fixings."

When the table had been cleared, Whitaker and Adam returned to Trailer Two to set up the UALS and its replenisher tray. John invited Leslie back to the table to discuss any significant differences between the A-model and the C-model. She had handled the A-model simulator quite well, so her stick-and-rudder skills were not in question. His main concern was to educate her on the use of the F-16A's radar, which was relatively primitive compared with later versions of the F-16. Once that was done, it was time to talk tactics.

"I've got one question before we get into the tactics part," Leslie said. "It's about the Inertial Navigation Set." These jets have been moved around a lot since the INS was last aligned. Won't that make it impossible to get a good alignment?"

He educated her on the rarely used Best Available True Heading alignment procedure. The BATH alignment was crude compared with a normal full INS spin-up, but it would get them airborne with a useable INS for attitude reference and ball-park navigation. It depended on a good measurement of the true heading of the parked jets, which they would have to type in manually. John showed her the 1:50,000 map and aerial photo from which he had derived that figure.

"I think it's accurate to within a degree or so. Good enough to get us to Dateland." He paused. Leslie seemed comfortable with the procedure. "Let's move on to the meat of the mission: the tactics. Leslie, you are an experienced fighter pilot, so I don't want to insult you by being too basic. When we attack these MiGs, I will call the play and I will expect you to know what to do. Do I need to go over the flight leader-wingman contract?"

"No, I'm a believer in that," Leslie said. "I was a flight leader too. But I can also be the world's best wingman. I've even read your Playbook, including the preface, where you stress the importance of mutual support."

"What?"

"You didn't know? They published your Playbook article in the Fighter Weapons Review years ago. It was touted as the ultimate in 'KISS Principle' fighter tactics. Keep It Simple, Stupid. Very effective. Simple but effective."

Those four words, *Keep It Simple, Stupid,* were a good summary of his life. Maybe he should have them inscribed on his tombstone. Or something like: *John Martin, 1950-whatever. Simple but Effective.* He said, "You'll have to tell me more about that later." He flipped open a spiral notebook and picked up a pencil. "For now, let's just review a few formations and attack plans."

John spent very little time sketching out a single air-to-ground scenario, or "play." It was extremely unlikely they would fly down there to bomb and strafe Alvarado's airfield. But, if they did, at least they knew the tactics. He wanted to move on to the air-to air scenario, but Leslie held up a hand.

She said, "That tactic you just described. It assumes our respective flight paths must be deconflicted by time—twenty seconds—to allow for the frag pattern of live bombs. But we're delivering inerts. There's no frag pattern on an inert. Do you want to make any changes?"

She was a good thinker. He respected her for that. But there were two things wrong with her logic.

"That is a very good point," he said. "However, let me offer two reasons why we should stay with this plan. First, if our inert bombs hit MiGs loaded with fuel and weapons, there will be explosions and frag danger. Do you agree?"

"Yes, I see your point."

"Second, it's just too much work, too complicated, to invent a new tactic for this special situation. Let's stick to things we know will work."

"You got it," Leslie said. "The KISS principle again."

He smiled and nodded. "Now the critical part," he said. "Air-to-air tactics." He leaned forward and looked into her eyes. "You may think you're well trained, but I can tell you from personal experience, when the bullets and missiles start flying, you might forget everything you've—"

"John," she said.

"What?"

"Are you saying all this because I'm a woman? Because you want to protect me?"

"Give me a break! You are *not* a woman! I mean, you are, of course." He omitted any adjectives to describe how nice of a woman she was. "But in my mind, right now you are just another F-16 pilot. Viper Two, my wingman. My mission is to attack and destroy the MiGs and bring you safely back home. I gave this same damn speech hundreds of times to male wingmen. You would be well off to listen to it as a wingman and not a woman."

"Okay, I get it," she said. "Sorry."

John rubbed his forehead, took a deep breath, and tried to concentrate on the mission, not the woman-wingman conundrum. He flipped to a new page and picked up the pencil.

"If you've read the Playbook, you've seen these before. Just remember, they were written before the F-16 carried beyond-visual-range missiles and they are very basic. As you say, the KISS principle."

Leslie said, "I especially loved the 'NOB' intercept technique. 'N' for 'Nose.' Target on the nose until 20 miles. 'O' for 'Offset; offset at 20 miles. 'B' for 'Bring 'em to the nose at 8 miles.'"

"Thank you," he said. "The radar cues in the F-16 HUD, especially the Target Locator Line, make intercepts so simple. You wouldn't believe all the complicated intercept geometry we had to learn in the older fighters like the F-4."

John chose his next words carefully. He didn't want to sound arrogant, overconfident, or like someone who has underestimated his enemy. "While we should be prepared for anything, I believe we are going to be fighting a MiG-21, or maybe two, armed with guns only. If they had missiles, they would have used them on one of the two shootdowns. With that assumption, we just need one or two intercept tactics to get us into gun range. We'll use the sweep and the visual bracket."

He diagrammed the sweep first, showing both F-16s off-setting to the west of the MiGs, which he presumed would be northbound. He outlined his opinion of the strengths and weaknesses of this tactic. "It's simple for the wingman, who just has to stick with the leader, fly a 'loose-deuce,' or fighting wing, position and watch what happens. The disadvantage, in my mind, is that both F-16s are on the same side of the bogeys and are easier to be seen, thus losing the element of surprise."

John sketched out the next option, a visual bracket attack. At twenty miles, they would split off to opposite sides of the bogeys and essentially run their own intercepts on each MiG, while keeping each other in sight. In a perfect world, they would sneak up on the enemy undetected and kill them one by one. If both MiGs could be lured into attacking one of them, the other F-16 could enter the fight unobserved and kill one of the MiGs. Then it would become a race to see which of them would get the privilege of shooting down the second MiG.

He tore off the page he had used to diagram the tactics. "Oh, yeah. One more thing: Joker and Bingo fuel. If we engage the MiGs in US airspace, Joker is 3.5 and Bingo is 2.5. If we have to go all the way down to La Coruba, fuel will be very tight. It'll be one pass, then haul ass. Let's use 4.0 and 3.5 for that scenario."

Leslie nodded.

"Questions? Suggestions?" John asked.

"The tactics part is all good. My only question is, since one of your MiG kills was with a gun, how close do I need to be before opening fire?"

"Excellent question. In true Weapons School fashion, I will say, 'It depends.' Not too far out; that's a low probability of kill. Not inside 500 feet with high closure; you might frag yourself. I would recommend opening fire at 700 feet. But you're going to be too busy to look at all that fancy range info on the HUD. So, I'll draw you a picture of what the MiG should look like in your HUD at a 700-foot range." On a fresh page, he drew a circle. "Let's say this is your LCOS reticle, which by the way, is a fixed 50-mil diameter if you have a radar lock." Inside the circle, he sketched in the fuselage and wings of a MiG-21. "Please tell me that looks like a Fishbed."

"Not bad," she said.

"So, the key is, the MiG's wingspan should cover about two-thirds of the LCOS reticle if you're at 700 feet. Saddle up for a gun shot, get a tracking solution, and squeeze the trigger when the sight picture looks just like this."

"Can I have that page?"

He tore it off and gave it to her along with the tactics page. "One more thing. That picture assumes a radar lock. What if you don't have a lock?"

She didn't hesitate. "I'll have my wingspan knob on the HUD preset for twenty-three feet, the MiG-21 wingspan, and the manual range knob set for 700 feet, which is counterclockwise from the detent."

"Good girl! Oops, I mean, good *wingman*."

"If I wasn't on the other side of this table, I'd punch you on the shoulder. Hard." Leslie scooped up the diagrams, folded them and put them into the back pocket of her jeans. She stood up and stretched. "Listen," she said.

John heard a diesel engine and the screech of air brakes outside the hangar door. "Whit! I think our ammo is here."

Whitaker went out to accept the delivery. Adam readied the forklift but waited until the truck had left before opening the main hangar door.

"It's all here," Whitaker said, tapping the invoice. Two pallets. Eleven boxes of ninety rounds each and one with thirty-two. Adam, let's get this stuff inside."

They worked in pairs to load rounds into the UALS. By 1:30 p.m., the job was done. The blue forklift had been attached to the piggyback frame and raised into the traveling position. John's shoulder and forearm muscles burned from the effort of cranking bullets into the machine. He needed another shower.

Leslie looked at her hands. "Ugh. I've got to go wash up; might as well shower too. Everything from the waist up hurts. With twenty-twenty hindsight—no pun intended—it was probably not such a good idea to go to the gym today."

While she was gone, John sat with Adam and Whitaker and shared a paper plate of potato chips and some bottled water. Adam kept looking over his shoulder at the fully loaded tractor-trailers.

"I can't believe we did it. And it's not even two o'clock yet. What do we do now?"

John said, "I hate to say it, but I think we should all try to get some sleep. Then, have a light—"

"Yeah, right," Whitaker said. "Sleep in the middle of the day? Like that's really going to happen. Don't know about you guys, but I got so many butterflies in my stomach, I'm about to lift off."

John said, "I'm nervous just like everyone else. But we've all been up since about 0600. If we don't get some rest now, by the time we get to the Boneyard we will have been awake for eighteen hours. Overtired. Prone to making mistakes. That won't do."

"What won't do?" Leslie said. She still wore this morning's jeans but above those, she now had added a University of Arizona sweatshirt.

John explained the dilemma. They all needed rest but were too pumped up to sleep.

Leslie said, "Okay then, how about this idea? I will whip us up some omelets, some bacon, and brew some nice herbal tea. Call it a brunch. By the time we're finished, it will be almost 1500. All that good food will make us lethargic and promote a good nap."

"Food! I like the way you think, woman!" Whitaker said. "I'll help."

* * *

Every time John changed his position, the cot's wood frame squeaked and creaked. He had started out on his back, rolled over onto his left side for a few minutes, then tried laying on his right side. Now he was on his back again, wide awake, staring at the hangar's ceiling. It was so quiet that he could hear his own heartbeat. This was worse than his first few experiences with pre-combat anxiety. Back in the Vietnam era, unseen war planners had chosen his targets, told the crews what weapons to load on his Phantom, and given the order to launch. He wondered if those anonymous staff officers in Hawaii had lost any sleep after they ordered jets into Route Pack Six, deep inside North Vietnam.

Now he was doing the planning and issuing the orders. Whitaker had pronounced all the equipment ready to go, but what about the four people involved? Were they ready? Was *he*—John Martin, over-the-hill fighter pilot—ready? Would his plan work?

Any thoughts of getting to sleep were erased by the whining of a large four-engine jet taxiing out for takeoff. It was probably one of those late-night cargo jets, maybe a 747, loaded with packages for next-day delivery. When the jumbo jet revved up for takeoff, the hangar doors rattled. John remembered Hank telling him that just one of those 747 engines had more thrust than an F-16 in full afterburner.

He got off the cot as quietly as possible, got dressed, and grabbed his leather jacket. Maybe a walk outside would be good for him, clear his mind enough to allow a little sleep. Whitaker and Adam still slept soundly; perhaps both were used to jet noise at night. Leslie had taken advantage of the bed in the sleeper section of Tractor-Trailer Two and apparently had slept through the 747's takeoff.

He managed to open the door without making too much noise. Once outside, he turned left and walked along the hangar's west side. Just before turning the corner onto the south side, which faced the runway, he heard the man-door open behind him. But it wasn't a man. It was Leslie.

She looked to her right and then to her left and saw him. When she got closer, he saw that she had been wise enough to wear a windbreaker.

"I guess you couldn't sleep either," she said.

He resumed walking with Leslie at his side. "Did the jet noise wake you?"

"No, I was already wide awake. Never got to sleep. Too much on my mind."

"Same here," he said.

Their boots thumped in unison against the concrete and crunched against occasional small pebbles. Neither of them spoke until they stopped midway along the south side of the hangar to watch another cargo jet take off. They both plugged their ears until the 747 was airborne and climbing out to the west.

John said, "While you were lying up in that luxurious bed, unable to sleep, did you come up with any flaws in our plan?"

"No. I tried to think of every way something could go wrong. You seem to have it all covered. That decoy move out to the east is a great idea. And I feel good about the comm plan between us, Sam, and Briggs. Whit and Adam seem pretty sure about the Boneyard stuff." She stopped and asked him, "What about you? Any last minute changes?"

"Not a change, really," he said. "But there's one contingency we haven't discussed. The single-ship option. What if only one jet gets airborne? If it's you, do you feel comfortable doing the mission without me?"

"That would be a real shame, but yes, I'd do it. If there's more than one MiG, I guess I'd have to make my first shot count. A three-second burst would use up more than half my ammo."

John was impressed. Not many F-16 pilots had ever considered how quickly the bullets spewed out when you squeezed the trigger. He said, "When and how did you arrive at that figure?"

"Oh, years ago, back in my early air-to-air training. I mean, it's easy math. The gun fires 6,000 rounds per minute, or 100 rounds per second. So, I've got about five seconds of gun use. And, in a combat situation, I am probably going to be a little jittery. I have to strike a balance between trying to conserve bullets and throwing enough of them out there for a high probability of kill. How long of a burst do you recommend?"

"That's another one of those 'It depends' questions," he said. "Is it a fleeting opportunity? A snapshot? Or do you have a stable, tracking, LCOS solution? In the scenario you suggest, where you are one F-16 versus two MiGs—and you've got to kill them both—I wouldn't even recommend a snapshot. Go in for a tracking gun kill and squeeze the trigger for two seconds max. You're going to lose some rounds when you let go of the trigger; the ammo feeder takes a split second to wind down. Imagine squeezing the trigger and counting 'one thousand one, one thousand two.' Let go of the trigger after you've counted to two."

They walked the rest of the way in silence. When they arrived at the door, John said, "Are you going to be able to sleep now?"

Leslie shrugged. "I don't know. But I sure am going to try."

He sighed. "Me too. Good night."

John undressed, got back onto his cot, and took a deep breath. He closed his eyes. The walk and the talk with Leslie had uncluttered his mind and allowed him to think of home. The salt water, the cool, humid air, and the tall trees. Peace and quiet. Kayaking with his loyal and water-loving German Shepherd, Rex . . .

He was paddling across Drayton Passage. Rex was in the boat, alerting to harbor seals swimming nearby. But something was wrong. Each time his paddle touched the water it triggered an annoying electronic beep rather than the usual splash.

John sat up. It took him a second to orient himself. He wasn't in his kayak but on a cot in a hangar. The alarm! He pushed the button on his wristwatch to silence it. When he did so, the backlight showed him it was 2300.

Time to go.

Chapter 33

"Are you *sure*?" John asked.

"I'm tellin' you, man, the other night Adam and I watched this fence for a total of five hours," Whitaker said. "Security drives by at about 15 minutes past the hour, every other hour. Not once per hour, like you thought. They come by, on that dirt perimeter road just inside the fence, on the even hours: 0015, 0215, 0415, et cetera."

Whitaker stopped Tractor-Trailer One just short of their intended parking spot on Kolb Road. John hopped out to move the fake road work signs that had guaranteed the spot would be vacant. He waved at Adam and Leslie, who passed by in the Ford pickup. They turned left onto East Lilac Place, went to the end of the cul-de-sac, swung around, and parked facing west about a half-block from the Boneyard fence. Within a minute, all four of them were inside the trailer.

"We've got about ten minutes before the next patrol." John said. "Time to camo up."

Rather than use a greasy camo stick to paint their faces, Whitaker had bought them all lightweight camouflage balaclava facemasks. By 0010, they were ready to go. Adam and Whitaker wore black work pants, shirts, and boots. Leslie had a black Nomex flight suit and black boots. Each of them had a headlamp with three settings: red light, dim white, and bright white.

John had been unwilling to part with the dark brown work boots he had worn during the T-Bird's flight down to Tucson, but the rest of his outfit was as black as the others'. He turned off the trailer's interior lights. It was as if everyone had disappeared. "The camo looks good," he whispered. "Everybody keep your lights off except Whit."

Whitaker used his red low-light feature to find his way to the fisheye peephole he had installed on the right rear wall of the trailer. Once there, he turned off the headlamp.

They all waited, motionless, in total darkness, until the sound of a vehicle rolling down a dirt road broke the silence.

"It's them," Whitaker said. "Give them time to get around the corner and drive off to the west." The vehicle noise receded and then faded away to nothing. "John, I say we're clear. Good to go."

John inhaled and said, "Let's do it!"

Adam positioned a ladder under the sliding roof, climbed up, and opened it, revealing a perfectly clear desert sky filled with twinkling stars. He climbed back down, buckled a tool belt around his waist, and picked up a larger canvas bag of other tools. With the wireless remote in one hand, Whitaker climbed the ladder and raised the crane into position. Adam stepped onto the wooden foot plate and said, "I'm ready."

His first job would be to erect a black cloth frame which would hide the raised crane from anyone passing by in the neighborhood. Then he'd be lifted over the fence and down into the Boneyard, where he would open all the aircraft servicing panels.

The crane's motor had been wrapped in insulation for noise reduction, but John still winced as the motor raised Adam up. In here, it sounded loud. He hoped no one was out on the street for a midnight walk with their dog.

John and Leslie were the next to go over the fence. Leslie carried a razor knife, a soft plastic putty knife, and a large pair of pliers. John carried duplicates of these and a small wooden ladder to get them up onto the wings and fuselages of their respective jets. They had planned on thirty minutes to remove all the white vinyl latex preservative that covered the canopies and other critical surfaces. After that, they would help Adam and Whit with moving equipment, servicing the jets, and removing any safety covers from the pitot-static and angle-of-attack sensors.

Adam, having finished opening all the necessary panels on both airplanes, returned to the fence to help Whitaker unload and install the aircraft batteries. He pulled out the hose for hydraulic servicing and Whitaker dragged it to the airplanes.

John finished his job before Leslie and hopped down from Three-Six-Eight. Whitaker motioned John over to the right main landing gear.

"We got a little problem," Whitaker said. He pointed at the right main tire.

It was flat.

"Might just be a slow leak. We've got a compressor to pump it up," Whitaker said. "But I can't count on that. Don't want you to land with a flat tire and break my airplane. My plan is to borrow a good tire from the next plane over. I checked its tires; they're both good."

John said, "We've got about thirty minutes left before the next security patrol. Is that enough time?"

"No. Don't want to risk it. Have to do it after 0220."

Adam and Leslie joined them. Both said, "Uh, oh," when they saw the flat tire.

"Oh, shit," John said. "We don't even have a jack!"

"Calm yourself, Mister Pilot," Whitaker said. "Your resourceful maintenance supervisor here has remembered that the white tractor has a jack capable of lifting a fully loaded trailer." He pointed at Adam. "Between us two ace mechanics, we'll figure out a way to make that work on an F-16. Adam, is your jet ready?"

"Yep. All it needs is to top off tire inflation and load the fuel. Well, pump up the JFS too, but we don't want to do that until right before start."

"Let's close up all these panels and get the equipment back into the trailer," Whitaker said. We need to be back in there by 0205."

They were all back in the trailer by 0200, seated on the floor, balaclavas removed, munching on granola bars, fruit, and drinking bottled water. Adam had examined the truck's jack and come up with a plan to hook it to Three-Six-Eight's main landing gear. Whitaker had endorsed the plan. The four of them sat on the trailer's floor, two on each side, and worked out a plan to replace the bad tire and still be ready for launch at 0430. Leslie and John would feed both the air and fuel hoses under the fence and pull them up to the aircraft. That was about all Whitaker would allow them to do; he didn't trust them to pump the fuel or service the tires.

"Let us crew chiefs handle that part," he said. "The super-quiet, low-flow pump we're using will take a lot of, ah, special skills, which—no offense—you guys don't have. Also, it will take a lot of time, about twenty minutes per jet. Adam, we need to have the fueling complete by 0345 to give us time to pull those hoses back out and get them out of sight. Then, at 0420 or whenever the security truck gets clear, you need to sprint over and cut the locks on both gates."

"Yeah," Adam said. "I'm going to be doing a lot of sprinting. Out to the gates, then back to help you remove the FOD screens. Then we'll both be running like hell to get out of there." He looked at Whitaker and smiled. "I'll try not to get too far ahead of my, er, more mature fellow wrench-bender here."

"You, my man, may be surprised how fast these little, short legs can carry me when I am properly motivated. We'll see who has to wait for who. But . . . all this talk of running is making me tired," Whitaker said. "Adam, can you be the lookout for the security patrol?" He slumped down a little lower against the trailer wall and closed his eyes.

John wondered how the guy could just close his eyes and take a nap. Was he putting on an act or was he immune to stress? Leslie and Adam both looked at him and shrugged their shoulders. According to his watch, they had about fifteen minutes before their next—and final—trip over the fence.

"Adam," John said, "before you go over there, I've got something for you." He reached into the upper pocket of his flight suit, extracted Hank's Juvat Nickel, and put it in Adam's hand. "I know it's too dark to see what this is. Take good care of it. It was your dad's. He'd want you to have it."

* * *

At precisely 0425, John switched the battery on, pushed the switch to lower his canopy and grimaced when the whine of its electric motor broke the pre-dawn silence. Like the good wingman she was, Leslie lowered hers. Thanks to Whitaker and Adam, their jets were fully fueled and ready for start. Adam was out there cutting the locks and opening the gates. Whitaker stood between their two jets. The canopy closed and its locks clunked into place. He gave Leslie the visual signal for engine start.

He lifted the JFS switch out of its detent, pulled it aft to "Start 2," and was rewarded with a huffing sound, followed by the successful windup of the small jet fuel starter's engine. From Leslie's aircraft, he heard similar sounds. When engine rpm reached twenty percent, he lifted the throttle over the cutoff detent and pushed it forward into idle. Three-Six-Eight's engine rumbled, engine temperature and rpm needles rose, and the engine coughed out a large plume of white smoke. John had expected that and had warned the others; it was residual oil from storage, cooked off by the start process. It was dead calm outside, and cool, so the ten-foot diameter smoke cloud stayed close to the ground. This was a blessing. The last thing they needed was the tower controller to notice the smoke and call in the fire department.

Once the engine reached idle, John had to resist rushing the after-start checks. The hydraulics needed about ten seconds to flow through the lines. Lubricant in the generator's constant speed drive could benefit from the same. At least that's the habit John had acquired years ago for jets in cold weather; it might be the same for a mothballed jet, so he counted to ten before moving the stick or initiating any of the flight control self-tests. There were twenty-two steps in the after-start checklist, all of which—back in the day—John could do from memory. Today, however, he followed the checklist.

He twisted around in the seat to see the ailerons, rudder, and horizontal tail move when he cycled the stick left, right, forward, and aft. Whitaker gave him hand signals to confirm proper movement, although he was difficult to see in the near-total darkness. John acknowledged with a thumbs-up. This was somewhat of an unnecessary step. Thanks to the F-16's 360-degree bubble canopy, and with the proper amount of twisting his torso, he could see everything from the cockpit. In fact, he could twist far enough left to see even the right-side rudder and speed brake deflection. A side benefit of this twisting was that it loosened up his back for checking six later. After all these years, John had never told Whitaker he didn't need those signals. He respected Whitaker's dedication for doing things by the book.

John had hacked the cockpit clock at engine start. It now said one minute, thirty seconds. The BATH and Stored Heading alignment was complete. He moved the INS switch to "NAV" and looked over at Leslie. She gave him a thumbs-up.

He put his left hand on the throttle and took a deep breath. Once he pushed that throttle forward, there was no turning back. A small voice in his subconscious was asking, *Are you sure you can do this?* He answered that question out loud. "Hell, yes!" He signaled to Whitaker that he was holding the brakes. Whitaker disappeared under the airplane. When he jogged back out, the old guy gave him a chocks-out signal, saluted, and pointed to the runway. John returned the salute and pushed the throttle up.

He taxied onto the paved service road between the rows of jets and continued far enough to allow Leslie some spacing. He turned thirty degrees right and stopped; now his exhaust wouldn't kick up FOD into Leslie's engine. Adam was there, giving him the crossed arms, "hold the brakes" visual signal. John mimicked that. Adam approached from the side, under the wing, to unhook the FOD screen. He reappeared on the opposite side, tossed the screen away, and pointed toward the runway. He snapped to attention and saluted. John gave him a heartfelt salute in return, waited about five seconds to ensure that Leslie's intake cover had been removed, and continued taxi to the runway.

Although it was tempting to taxi fast, he kept it slow until he was through the first gate, across the Christmas Tree ramp, and past the second gate. He checked the roads, ramp area and runway for signs of any security vehicles and saw none. No flashing red lights racing toward them to spoil their morning. They still had the element of surprise. John stopped on the center of his side of Runway 30. Five seconds later, Leslie pulled up into position. He gave her the runup signal and moved his throttle up to 80 percent. Leslie's nose dipped under the force of her engine's acceleration. John glanced down at the engine instruments, released brakes, and pushed the throttle to the mil power stop.

At 122 knots, he raised the nose, lifted off, and retracted the landing gear. On a cool morning, with a clean F-16, acceleration was impressive. As he passed the base operations area, he noticed several blue vehicles with lights and flashers speeding toward the runway. They weren't going to get there in time to stop Leslie. The tower was probably calling them on Guard to abort or identify themselves, but they wouldn't hear that. He had briefed Leslie to turn off that channel. They didn't need any distractions.

As he passed over the departure end of the runway, he started a gentle climbing left turn. At 350 knots he pulled the throttle back about an inch to give Leslie a power advantage for her rejoin. After turning on all his exterior lights, he realized he had forgotten to turn on the radar. No big deal—yet. He switched it on while visually scanning his intended direction of flight, which would take them over the approach path for Tucson International. There was no traffic, even down low in Tucson's landing pattern.

He lost sight of Leslie's airplane for several seconds due to the brightly lit background of Tucson's city lights. When she got a little higher, above the lights, he saw her closing in for a rejoin. He turned off his strobe when she slid into route formation. She maintained a distance of about two wingspans—sixty feet—from him. That was close enough to maintain position when he maneuvered, but far enough out to check things in her own cockpit. John maintained a legal VFR 7,500-foot altitude, a speed of 350 knots and flew southeast toward the dark, rising terrain. Right now, someone in D-M tower would be on the hot line, frantically asking Tucson Approach Control to track them. At least, that's what he wanted them to do.

Chapter 34

John turned a few degrees left to aim them at the south side of the Rincon Mountains. With the moon's elevation now about ten degrees above the horizon, he could see the 8,472-foot Rincon Peak clearly. He keyed the mic and said, "Viper One, go Winchester." Leslie acknowledged. Would anyone at D-M tower know what that meant? John doubted it, but he was certain that the tower's audio tapes would be reviewed in detail by Lynwood Hardwick, who would know. Back in Lynwood's day as a fighter pilot, Winchester was fighter pilot shorthand for UHF frequency 303.0. John didn't want to make Hardwick's job too easy; he had to make it look like they were flying off to the east, trying to get below radar coverage, and changing to a private, unmonitored radio frequency.

With less than a minute remaining at this relatively safe altitude, John got right to work typing seven sets of coordinates into the navigation computer. He got those loaded just in time for them to pass by the mountain. At this altitude, they would disappear from approach control's radar scope, masked by the mountain. He pulled the power back slightly, began a shallow descent, and kept his groundspeed at 360 knots.

Leslie had the difficult job of maintaining formation at low altitude, in the dark, with rising terrain looming ahead. That required a lot of trust. John reached into his g-suit pocket and pulled out a 1:500,000-scale Tactical Pilotage Chart, folded accordion-style, with their route already drawn out and minimum safe altitudes noted. He unfolded it to the first page and shoved it under the elastic strap on his plastic kneeboard.

John started a right turn to fly southeast down the San Pedro River valley. After checking to see if Leslie was matching his turn—she was—he made sure they flew right over the little town of Benson. Perhaps someone would hear them, see them, and report it. Five minutes later, he began a gentle climb to 9,500 feet. At that altitude, they would show up as unknown fast-moving targets on at least three different air traffic control radars: Albuquerque Center, Tucson Approach, and Fort Huachuca. After a minute at altitude, with an ops check complete—she had 5,800 pounds; he had 6,000—he slowly pulled his throttle back to idle and then pushed it forward an inch.

At 6,000 feet, he leveled off, let the airspeed bleed off to 200 knots and said, "Viper, landing gear down . . . now . . . speed brakes . . . now." If anyone searching for them heard that, they'd assume the F-16s were landing. He turned the cockpit lights rheostat down to reduce glare off the canopy and focused outside. There was a north-south asphalt road, a ranch house with a lit parking lot which he presumed was the Thompson Ranch. The INS bearing pointer and range showed the airfield, oddly named "Thompson International" on his chart, about four miles ahead and twenty degrees to the left. That checked with his earlier map study.

Thompson International was an unlit, 3,600-foot-long, 60-foot-wide dirt strip. It was totally unsuitable for the F-16, but John hoped their not-so-stealthy route to get here might draw Hardwick's people out for a visit. He had no doubt that Hardwick would take this personally and pull out all the stops to find him. It would be great if they wasted valuable time investigating Thompson Ranch, only five miles north of the Mexican border and 205 miles from where they'd really be—Dateland.

John descended to 5,300 feet, which was about a thousand feet above the runway. He turned east, as if he were lining up to land. He had no intention of even trying to see the dirt strip. He just wanted all this to *look* like they had landed here. Once the INS bearing pointer swung around to point behind him, John mentally switched to the second phase of their plan. He turned his cockpit lights up to an uncomfortably bright level so Leslie could see his visual signals. He added power, signaled for speed brakes closed, then landing gear up. From now on they would be running silent unless a radio call was absolutely necessary. Leslie, whom he had prebriefed on all this, followed all his commands flawlessly.

He turned southwest and accelerated to 360 knots, much slower than he'd prefer in a real combat situation, but adequate for what they were doing. The goal now was to stay as low as possible without flying into the ground. He pumped the stick gently, fore and aft. This porpoising motion was Leslie's prebriefed signal to back off and slide behind him into a one-mile radar trail position. This was the safest way for them both to survive flying low over unfamiliar terrain. John didn't like it very much. True flight leaders always wanted their wingmen in sight. He took his right hand off the stick, reached for the exterior lights master switch, and located it by feel. After a quick glance at the console to confirm he had the right switch, he turned it off and put his hand back on the stick. He was now running totally dark and was confident that Leslie was also.

Without looking down at the panel, John flipped the INS thumbwheel to the next waypoint, a ridge just south of Miller Peak. He turned to the preplanned heading and checked that with the inertial system's bearing pointer. Everything looked good. They passed south of and well below the 9,400-plus-foot height of the peak. He felt good about the plan. Stay low, hide behind the mountains, and zigzag across the desert down near the border until it was time to turn north for Dateland. They were transiting either closed military operating areas or wildlife sanctuaries, both of which had almost zero human residents. Chances of being seen by anyone on the ground or encountering another airplane were almost zero.

After passing turnpoint Four, with a long 115-mile leg to fly on the same heading, John let himself relax and enjoy the view. The moon lit up the desert almost as if it were daylight. The taller Sahuaro cacti cast long shadows on the hills. His airplane was running well, and his fuel state was good. Leslie must be the same or she would have said something. Dateland was only 120 miles—

"Viper Two, contact. 30 right, 25 miles, high."

Well, that just blew his theory of being out here alone. He saw them on his radar screen. "Viper One, contact." It was a flight of two fast-movers. Could these be air defense fighters scrambled to track them down? He and Leslie had been airborne for thirty-three minutes. If they were F-15 Eagles from March, they would have needed a high-speed dash to get here this quickly, which meant they would soon be low on fuel. He did some quick mental arithmetic.

"Viper flight, check 30 left. Push it up to 450."

"Two."

He hoped Leslie would recognize this as a "Beam" maneuver intended to minimize the chance of detection or, if the Eagles already had a lock, this might break it. It wouldn't be wise to climb, but now that they were off course, he didn't want to plow into a hill he didn't see. Thank God—again—for the full moon. He looked instinctively at the panel where the Threat Warning System screen was or should have been. There was just an empty hole in the panel. The display and its software had been removed due to its classified nature. He had no way of knowing if the bogeys had locked onto them.

Now the bogeys were at the far-right side of his radar scope. "Viper One, check 20 right."

"Two."

John went back to basics. Look out the window. Fifty degrees right, very high. Yes!

"Viper One, tally two, right two o'clock. High."

"Two, no joy."

He didn't fault Leslie for not seeing them. She had her hands full staying in trail and avoiding the terrain.

Christ, if they were Eagles, they were clueless. They still had their lights and strobes on! That told him they were racing at top speed toward the decoy airfield and had not seen them at all. They disappeared to the east. He checked the bearing and distance to the next checkpoint.

"Viper, check twenty left. Bogeys no factor. Slowing to 360."

"Two."

Ninety miles to Dateland. They were going to make it.

*   *   *

Fifteen minutes later, John, with Leslie still in radar trail, lined up on a left downwind leg for Dateland's Runway 19. Leslie would get a good look at the field thanks to illumination provided by the full moon. He switched to a new, pre-briefed, private FM frequency and said, "Viper One, check."

"Two."

He turned a very conservative five-mile base leg and said, "Viper One, base, gear down, full stop." As stupid as that sounded—no one would hear it except Leslie— he had a reason. After all the excitement, he didn't want her to forget to lower her landing gear. Just before he touched down, he heard her say, "Viper Two, base, gear down, full stop."

John had told Leslie to use her landing light if she really needed it. He found he *really* needed it, just for a few seconds, right before touchdown. It was not his best landing but at least he didn't bounce. He taxied to the ramp on the north side of the hangar, shut the engine down and raised his canopy. Leslie taxied up beside him and shut down. He left the parking brake set, which was not recommended after landing due to the possibility of overheating the brake discs. He unstrapped, unhooked his comm cord and g-suit hose, and perched on the left canopy rail. There was no dignified way to climb down from a clean F-16, one without external wing tanks. John let himself hang from the left canopy rail, with his midriff over the strake and his boots about two feet from the ground. He let go and gravity did the rest. Leslie used the same technique but made it look much more graceful.

She walked up to him, grinning, and gave him a high five. "Holy shit, John, we did it!"

"Yes, we did," He couldn't quite believe it. But here they were. He said, "I'll be right back. Got to get us some chocks."

When he returned from the hangar, he handed one set to Leslie and used the other to chock Three-Six-Eight. When she came over to him, she said, "Uh, is there a ladder inside, or something to get us back into the cockpits to release the parking brake?"

"Maybe," he said. "But it would be quicker if I just boost you up onto the wing and you release the brakes on both jets." They did her jet first, then his. She slid off Three-Six-Eight's wing onto the ramp without any help from him.

Half an hour later, they had towed both jets into the hangar, re-chocked them and settled into two of the four lawn chairs delivered by Adam on Thursday. John identified another minor, but annoying, flaw in their plan. They hadn't pre-positioned any food or water. They'd have to wait until Whitaker and Adam arrived for refreshments. Except . . . John stood up, walked over to Three-Six-Eight's missile rail, where he had hung his *g*-suit. He retrieved his water bottle from the lower pocket and called to Leslie, "Got any water left in yours?"

"All of it. I was a little too busy to drink any on the way here."

He went to Three-Four-Nine's wingtip, pulled the air-force-issue, olive drab plastic water bottle out of her *g*-suit, and gave it to her. It was molded into a curve to better fit the leg pocket of the *g*-suit and resembled one of those silver metal hip flasks from which old timers sipped booze. This caused a brief flashback to his Vietnam F-4 days before these bottles were available. Most people had just used baby bottles, which were not an item commonly found in a combat zone. The wiser pilots packed a couple before they left the States.

John sat back down, uncapped his bottle, and said, "I propose a toast." He waited until she had unscrewed her cap.

"To Three-Six-Eight and Three-Four-Nine. Welcome back to active duty!"

Chapter 35

"General Hardwick, sorry to interrupt, but it's George Clark. He says it's an emergency and to use the secure line."

"Thank you, Margaret. Tell him I need two minutes." Hardwick hung up his telephone and said to the South Korean ambassador, "I apologize for the interruption. Mister Ambassador, I assure you that our commitment to the defense of South Korea is as strong as ever. You have my word of honor that the upcoming sale of air defense missiles to the Republic of Korea is on track, on schedule. And I am looking forward to my visit to your country. I hope to see you there next month." He stood up, walked around his desk, intending to offer a handshake, but hesitated. Was shaking hands okay in Korean culture?

Ambassador Jay Lin Lee stood.

Hardwick gave a slight bow and said, "It's been a great honor to have you in my office."

Lee bowed. "The honor is all mine." He stuck out his hand.

After a sincere and firm handshake, they said their goodbyes.

As soon as the ambassador was out of the room, Hardwick closed his door, returned to his desk, and activated the secure link to the CIA. Which crisis had reached the boiling point today? Why did these things always happen on weekends? He and Charlotte had tickets to a Saturday matinée performance at the Kennedy Center. He held the receiver away from his ear while the encryption system crackled and squealed.

"They did it, Lynwood," Clark said.

"Did what?"

"Your guy, John Martin, and that woman, Olsen. About an hour ago, they stole a couple F-16s."

"You're telling me that, despite heightened alert status and tight security at every F-16 base west of the Mississippi, they still managed to fly off with two of our latest jet fighters?"

Clark said, "The jets they stole came from something called the Boneyard, which I am not too—"

"I know what it is, George. Hell." It was the one place that he hadn't covered with extra security. He hated to admit it, but he had been outplayed by John Martin. That insubordinate bastard was going to spend the rest of his days in a federal prison. "Please tell me someone tracked them."

"I'm sending some stuff over to you right now. It's a little technical for me, but the gist of it is, radar tracked them flying east, then they disappeared off the scope."

"Fuck."

"But there's more," Clark said. "Two fast-moving targets were picked up a few minutes later, heading south toward the Mexican border, where—"

"Damn, damn, damn! Sorry, go on."

"If I read this correctly, they slowed down, descended, and landed at a remote desert airfield just north of the U.S-Mexico border. Air defense fighters were scrambled from March Air Force Base but got there too late. They didn't see a thing. If there's a runway out there, it must be very well-camouflaged. I hope it's okay with you, but I authorized one of our covert "go" teams to fly out there in a Blackhawk. Their ETA is in . . . let me check . . . one hour."

"Good work, George." Hardwick realized he had some work to do. He'd have to make some sort of retroactive orders that would make George's search legal, perhaps get Air Force OSI and the FBI involved, since the CIA wasn't really supposed to be snooping around inside our own borders.

"Lynwood, are you still there?"

"Oh, sorry, George. I was just trying to think this all through." He had a hundred questions. How did they do it? Did anyone at the airfield see anything? Who the hell was in charge of the Boneyard, anyway? He seemed to remember it was run by a separate Air Force unit and not under the command of the fighter wing at Davis-Monthan Air Force Base. Who was on the scene right now, collecting evidence? Probably the Air Force OSI. Did Martin steal weapons too? And . . . hell, it was just too much to digest sitting at this desk.

"George, I'm going out there, right now, this morning, as soon as I can get a jet warmed up out at Andrews. Pick a good man—or woman—from your team and have them meet me at Andrews in one hour. There will be FBI and AFOSI with me too. We'll use Davis-Monthan's fighter wing command post as our headquarters. Let me know by satellite phone as soon as your team reaches that runway."

"You want to get that deeply involved?"

"Damn right. In addition to the obvious national security risk, this is a personal fight now. Me versus John Martin."

Hardwick ended the call and buzzed Margaret on the intercom. He gave her the easy job—calling the 89th out at Andrews and arranging a no-notice flight out to Davis-Monthan. The next two tasks were his responsibility. He dialed his home number.

"Charlotte, something big has come up. I am very sorry, but I can't make it to the Kennedy Center today. Why don't you invite Terry? I'm going straight from here out to . . . out of town for several days. Can't say much more than that, except, I love you and I will miss you."

He hung up and, for the hundredth time, promised himself to retire after this crisis was settled. He didn't need this kind of stress. Charlotte didn't need this kind of a husband. Would the whole country fall apart if he quit? His ego told him yes, but his intellect said the opposite. He knew several people who could take over and do a great job.

He had one more call to make. When he picked up the phone, he had to laugh at his priorities. Charlotte came first. Next, he'd have to find a polite way to tell the President that some shit was about to hit the fan.

Chapter 36

By 7:00 a.m., John had explored every inch of interior space in the hangar at Dateland. He had located the main water valve and turned it on, so the bathroom now had running water. He had also turned on power to the hot water heater. Leslie would be pleased; there was a shower stall. She wouldn't have to use the solar camp shower that Whitaker had purchased. He ambled back to their sitting area, where Leslie was busy doing calisthenics.

"Just . . . burning . . . off . . . some nervous energy," she said while doing sit-ups.

John sat down and tried not to stare. She looked good even in the loose-fitting black flight suit. He wished that they had brought reclining loungers rather than flimsy, straight backed aluminum folding chairs. It might be nice to lay down for a while, close his eyes, and relax. Who was he kidding? He couldn't shut off the adrenalin and anxiety; there was no way he could sleep. Whitaker and Adam would be here in about an hour, at which time they would have a quick camp-style meal and go to work preparing the jets for the mission.

Leslie picked up her water bottle and shook it. "Empty. Does the bathroom have water yet?"

"Yes, but you'd better let it run for a couple minutes before filling that bottle. The water came out brown when I was in there a couple minutes ago."

"Yuck. I can wait for bottled water from Trailer Two." She sat down next to him. After half a minute of silence, she said, "I've got a question for you. Why did you choose a time of 1430 for the Citation to enter its orbit?"

"Sun angle. I figured the MiGs would launch and arrive at bullseye about 1500. At that time, the azimuth of the sun will be 245 degrees and its elevation will be 48 degrees above the horizon. In other words, right in the eyes of the MiGs when we are converting to their six o'clock."

"Wow, you have really thought this out."

"It's rare that we get to pick and choose the time to enter a fight, but for this one we get to stack the deck in our favor."

"If the MiGs take the bait. What if they don't?"

"We'll give them two or three days," he said. "After that, we'll load up the Mark-82s and destroy Alvarado's hangar roof, then strafe it. We're bound to hit something important, maybe even start a fire, even with inert MK-82s."

Leslie asked more questions about the communications plan, which John answered to her satisfaction. He was pleased to learn from Leslie that the Citation had HF capability in addition to UHF and VHF. If necessary, Briggs could communicate with Sam on any of these three radio frequencies.

"By the way," Leslie said. "Do either Whitaker or Adam know how to operate that backpack-mounted HF unit?"

"Not yet."

"Do you?"

"Yes. I had occasion to use one of those in my, ah, early Air Force days," John said. "I'll get Adam and Whitaker all checked out on that later today."

All this talk about radios highlighted another issue that worried John. The entire plan depended on Sam's identification and tracking of the MiGs. Briggs couldn't do that, since he was going to be out there without his crew of sensor operators, ostensibly on a maintenance test flight. His instructions were to run north to safety when the bogeys were twenty miles south of bullseye.

"A penny for your thoughts," Leslie said. "I don't like that look on your face."

"Yeah. If I could see myself, I wouldn't like it either. It's nothing about our attack plan, though. I'm just wondering if Sam's part in all this is too hard to cover up. In a perfect world, Sam's plan might work. She's going to be the only one on the radar scope for that twenty-minute period. She knows how to pull the circuit breaker for both the radar and radio recording system. AWACS will not be able to track our engagement or our flight back to Dateland.

"But, if our flight attracts attention from any other source, of which there are many, the first question Hardwick will ask is, 'What did AWACS see?' It will look very, very suspicious if AWACS has an equipment failure at the exact time we engage the MiGs."

"So," Leslie said. "Do you have a plan that would protect Sam?"

"No, not really." He closed his eyes and tried to recall the conversation during which he had recruited Sam. Had he stated the risk to her adequately? "Have you heard of that term, 'plausible deniability'? That's all she has going for her. My hope is that no one digs that deep into the AWACS failure."

"But if they do? She's letting it all hang out for us," Leslie said. "I'd like to meet her someday."

John tried to visualize a scenario in which all five people involved—six if you counted Briggs—came out of this without getting arrested. Maybe they'd all agree to meet at Rita's, once a year, on the anniversary of Alvarado's shootdown. But that was very, very premature, and extremely unlikely. Not just the party at Rita's but the idea that they could escape capture. He had already resigned himself to spending a considerable number of years behind bars.

"Hey, hello?" Leslie said. "You're off in left field again."

"Sorry."

She said, "What you said a couple minutes ago about our flight being detected by other sources? That's a real threat. We got lucky last night. Well, not lucky, really, but by using good tactics. We flew extremely low, at night. Our next mission will be in the daylight and most likely up at medium altitude. I can think of five different ways we could be detected. Albuquerque Center, Tucson Approach, and three Aerostat balloons with radars that cover the whole southern border in this area."

"You are correct about us being up at medium altitude," John said. "But we'll start out low, pop up just in time to get an altitude advantage on the MiGs, and then dive back down to the deck when it's over. One way or another, it will all be over in a minute or two. I don't think the government can react fast enough to interfere with us. Once we get low, Albuquerque Center and Approach will be clueless. And those Aerostats? I've already given that some thought. There's three of them in our area, right? One south of Fort Huachuca, one near Yuma, and another over in Deming, New Mexico."

She nodded.

"What altitude are they tethered at?"

"10,000 feet."

"Okay, I admit, they might see us. But consider this. It's a line-of-sight thing. When we egress, at high speed and extremely low altitude, terrain-masking behind mountains as high as 9,000 feet, I think even the Aerostats will have a hard time tracking us."

Leslie agreed. She wandered over to look at the airplanes. John spent the next twenty minutes doing his own abbreviated workout, which included pushups, sit-ups, and pull-ups using a metal bar wedged between two of the hangar's trusses. Halfway through his post-workout stretches, he heard a diesel engine. After confirming that it was indeed Tractor-Trailer

Two, Leslie went outside to greet the crew chiefs while John cranked open the door using the manual chain and pulley system. Unlike the Tucson hangar, this one didn't have a fancy electric motor for the big door.

Adam drove the big rig into the hangar, parked it next to the fuel truck and hopped down. Whitaker made a beeline to Three-Six-Eight without even saying hello. Adam was a little more polite.

"Nice to see you guys," he said. "Excuse me while I go check out my jet." He hurried off to inspect Three-Four-Nine.

John looked at Leslie and shrugged. "Did you notice that Three-Four-Nine is now 'his' jet, even though you're the one who flew it down here?"

"That's okay with me," she said. "It's the sign of a good crew chief."

Whitaker returned from his inspection and said, "Congratulations, John. You too, Leslie. It looks like you managed to get these airplanes on the ground and into the hangar without dinging them up."

John decided to take the high road rather than trade insults, even good-natured ones, with Whitaker. "The real thanks go to you and Adam. Without you, we would've never gotten the jets started, let alone off the ground."

Whitaker gave a slight bow before he turned away and said to Adam, "Help me get the forklift off. We need to get inside that trailer ASAP."

When the two mechanics had gotten far enough away, Leslie whispered, "Wow, he's all business today, isn't he?"

"Don't be too sure," John said. "I predict that the first thing he'll bring out is—"

"Breakfast is on the way!" Whitaker shouted. He pushed the lever for the hydraulic lift, lowering himself, the camp stove, and the ice chest to the floor. He sent the lift back up for

Adam, who was ready with the table, chairs and a box of plates and utensils.

"I wanted to stop for fast food," Whitaker said. "But the kid said that was a bad idea, being as how we were pulling a trailer filled with all kinds of illegal, or at least very questionable, shi—ah—stuff. By the way, John, you will be pleased to know that the highway patrol truck inspection stations were still closed when we passed by. Okay then! Who wants to do the ham and eggs? I'll do the toast and coffee."

They all pitched in and enjoyed a hearty breakfast with coffee and orange juice. By the time Leslie and John had cleaned up the pans and utensils, Adam had the fuel hose pulled out and hooked up to Three-Six-Eight.

Whitaker motioned John over and said, "It's not the best idea to refuel inside, but I'm pretty sure you don't want to pull these jets out where they might be seen on satellite photo. What we got to do is, open both the front and back hangar doors. That'll give us a lot of ventilation. Also, can somebody make sure the camp stove is off? No need to tempt fate with flame and jet fuel fumes and all."

John agreed and went to open the south side doors while Leslie checked the stove and cranked open the north doors. When both F-16s were fully fueled, John closed the southern doors and walked back to where the other three stood. He noticed that Whitaker was rocking back and forth on his feet. His eyes were darting back and forth between the jets and the trailer. Anyone who didn't know him would think he was high on some type of drug. Whitaker probably was intoxicated, but this was a legal high. He was in his element, preparing aircraft for combat. John let the old guy order them around like they were recruits in basic training.

They had the ammo loaded into both F-16s, two AIM-9s mounted on each aircraft's wingtips and the hydraulics serviced before lunch. By 3:00 p.m., tires had been checked and the aircraft batteries put on a trickle-charger. They took a short break, complete with snacks and apple juice—Whitaker's favorite beverage besides coffee. Adam and Whitaker then went off with the box of plexiglass cleaner, Armor All, auto wax and white paint. John heard them issuing challenges to each other over whose jet was going to be the shiniest.

"Don't ask *me* to be the judge," Leslie said.

John said, "Not me either. If they ask, I'm just going to say it's a tie." He pushed back his chair and stood up. "I'm going to get the HF radio out of the trailer. I need to check out those two frequencies we chose to see if they're good. HF freqs are sensitive to daytime atmospheric conditions."

"Is Sam available for a radio check?"

"No, but I have a plan for that. I just need someone about 250 miles from here, which is the same distance between us and the AWACS orbit. I looked up a ham radio operator in Deming, New Mexico, who—"

"John, just go do it. Spare me all the details!"

After powering up the radio, he called Adam and Whitaker over and gave them a tutorial on the PRC-104 portable HF set. A helpful amateur radio operator in Deming confirmed that their primary and secondary HF frequencies were useable at this time of day. John asked both crew chiefs to transmit and receive short messages.

"Adam, it looks like you feel pretty comfortable with this," he said. "So why don't you plan on being the radio operator?" Adam nodded his agreement. "Let's go over to the table where I can lay out a chart. There are a few terms that Adam needs to know. Whit, you might as well listen in, and would you get Leslie to come over?

When they all got seated, John decided against the aeronautical chart; it would take up too much space on the table. He opened his notebook, found the page with a similar but much smaller diagram, and turned it around so the others could see. This one represented his second effort at sketching the "God's Eye," view of the intercept and the important ground references that Sam would be using. He had discarded the first draft; it had too many erasures and side notes that would just confuse everyone.

"Whit and Adam, there's one good reason why you guys need to hear this. In a normal air-to-air scenario, we'd just go out there and enter an orbit, waiting for any bad guys to show up. We can't afford to do that." He looked at the crew chiefs. "Any idea why we can't?"

"Can't afford to waste fuel, and you can't just go hit a tanker to refuel in mid-air," Adam said.

"True," John said. "But there's another reason. Once we climb, we'll be seen by air traffic control radar. I'd be willing to bet that my old boss Hardwick has people watching anything that moves in the southern Arizona skies. So, this whole intercept, shootdown and return-to-base must happen in twenty minutes or less, before anyone can react. We need to be back in this hangar ASAP. If we can do that, I think we can defeat the surveillance.

"Now, how does that relate to this diagram?" He tapped the page's upper left corner. "This little circle is us, our hangar, Viper Ops." He moved his finger over and slightly down. The second circle is a ground reference which we're calling "Bullseye." That's a commonly used term for AWACS and fighter pilots, a location marked on everyone's maps or radar scopes. It's a dry lake. In fact, it is the same dry lake that Hank was looking at the day he died."

"Is that just a coincidence?" Leslie asked.

John looked directly into her eyes. "No, it is not."

"Whoa, say no more," she said. "I'm getting the thousand-yard stare here."

"You guys have already lost me," Adam said. "What's a thousand-yard stare?"

Leslie said, "It's the look you get from someone who has seen combat deaths; someone who has dealt out some death of his own. John wants Alvarado to die at the same spot where Hank did. My brother Scott crashed only a few miles from Bullseye. So—I'm just guessing here—I smell revenge in the air."

John tapped the diagram again. "Back to this little paper. Down in the lower right corner, that third circle is Alvarado's ranch, home of the MiGs and cleverly nicknamed, 'Ranch.' The thick cross-hatched line is the Mexico-U.S. border. Notice how the line between Ranch and Bullseye is about twice as long as the one between Viper Ops and Bullseye." He looked at Whitaker and Adam. They were lost. He had overwhelmed them with details before he had even gotten to the point.

Whitaker leaned forward and looked at the diagram. "Got it. It says here Ranch is 125 miles from Bullseye. Viper Ops is only 70. So what?"

"Glad you asked," John said. "Here's the point. Sam—oh, wait. Whit doesn't know about Sam yet." He explained his connection to Sam and what she was going to do for them. "Sam will see the MiGs almost as soon as they're airborne. She'll give us a call on HF, but we can't launch then. It would be too early. We need to give the MiGs a little time to travel north, until they reach a point where their ETA to Bullseye equals ours." He decided to spare them the excruciating details of intercept geometry, positioning for optimum sun angle, and altitude splits. "Sam will give us updates on their position but will not give us the "Scramble" order until the MiGs are 83 miles south of Bullseye. So, Adam, when you start hearing reports from Sam on the MiGs, don't get too excited until she gives the Scramble order."

"John," Whitaker said.

"What?"

"You could have saved that big lecture on geometry, or whatever it is. Those last two sentences? That kind of says it all."

"Okay. Point taken." John flipped the notebook closed. "School is over for the day."

Whitaker said, "Should we fire these jets up now, get 'em set up for alert?"

"That's a good question," John said. He evaluated the risk versus reward of starting up the aircraft more than eighteen hours prior to the first alert time. Would the jet noise make someone curious? Would they even be able to identify the source of the noise if they were miles away and couldn't see into the hangar? If they waited until tomorrow, there would be less exposure. But what if they found a maintenance problem?

"I think we should crank them up tonight, after dark, run them just long enough to set up for alert. If anything's going to malfunction, I'd like to find out about it today. Then, tomorrow about noon, we do it again, just for safety's sake. What do you think?"

"Sounds like a good idea," Whitaker said. Adam and I will rearrange these vehicles and move the airplanes a little so the exhaust will go out the open doors."

*   *   *

By 9:00 p.m. that night, John had exhausted all forms of distraction. Both F-16s had started flawlessly and were ready for launch. After a dinner of tuna salad sandwiches, potato chips, and chocolate pudding for dessert, Leslie had suggested a Tic-Tac-Toe tournament. Adam had won that one. John had won the Hangman competition. Whitaker had yearned for a deck of cards, saying that he could have easily taken all their money in seven-card stud. It was too risky to go outside. Although unlikely, it was not impossible that Hardwick would be monitoring satellite images of all jet-capable runways, even at night. Multiple walks around the hangar's inside perimeter had not helped. He did not look forward to lying on his cot, staring at the ceiling of yet another hangar, unable to sleep. He went into the bathroom to brush his teeth and change into shorts.

When he returned to their small "living room," with table, chairs, and ice chest, he noticed Leslie sitting at the table and looking at the laptop screen.

She looked up when he approached. "Just studying up a little more. Thinking about some contingencies. Did you know that even with generator failure, the gun will fire?"

He sat down and said, "True, the jet is still pretty good without a generator as long the EPU is powering the essential buses. However, don't forget that we don't have hydrazine, so you'd have to keep rpm at 75 percent or higher so engine bleed air could run the EPU. Oh, and by the way, your radar won't work. The question is, would I want you as a wingman if your generator fails?" He stopped to consider the value of a generator-out wingman in combat.

She straightened up in her chair, stared at him, and said, "Why—"

"Hold on a second, before you go on a rampage. The answer is yes. To get Alvarado, I'd risk it. I'd need the mutual support. And your gun, of course."

She was silent for a long time. "Well, remember what you just said, John Martin, in case it's *your* jet that has the generator failure."

"Think positive, Leslie. Two of us. We roll in on the MiGs unseen. We splash them both. We make an uneventful landing back at Dateland. Everything works according to plan." He stood up. "I'm going to try to get some sleep."

She looked up at him, opened her mouth, then closed it. She said, "Good night, John."

What had she wanted to say? Perhaps something about the chances of their plan actually working. He fell asleep trying to remember who first said, *No plan survives first contact with the enemy.*

Chapter 37

The Pilatus Porter's right wing clipped a tree. John's view of the mountain tilted, spun around and his head hit the door frame. When he came to, he was hanging upside down in his seat. He pulled the quick release on his lap belt and shoulder harness and fell out of the seat onto the top of the cockpit. His first thought was for Sergeant Landreau, but the Air America pilot was closer. And covered in blood.

"Sorry, kid," the pilot said. He tried to reach into his pocket but winced. "Open my shirt pocket. Take the key. It's for that box. Open it." The man wheezed and said, "It's Yamashita's gold. The Tiger of Malaya, from WWII. No one else knows. It's yours now, I guess."

"Shut up." John said. "I'm going to get you out of here."

"Don't bother," the pilot said. "Let my family know. My name's—"

He had died there, unnamed, no identification, on a mission that his own government would never acknowledge. John had whispered to unhearing ears, "I'll find your family and tell your story."

Sergeant Landreau had survived the crash but was still comatose. John used his survival radio to call in the Jolly Green, then got Landreau out of the wreckage. He went back for the pilot's body. Two hours later, the three of them, and three rucksacks full of Yamashita's gold bars, were hoisted into the helicopter. Yamashita's gold. Holy shit.

That had been his voice, but another familiar one came through loud and clear.

John opened his eyes. He was in a large room with a tall ceiling and a row of windows up high. There wasn't much light outside; it must be either evening or morning twilight. It troubled him that he didn't know which it was. Leslie was next to his bed, looking down at him.

"John? Are you awake? You were thrashing around and mumbling."

"I am now," he said. "Give me just a second to—"

"It's happening again. You're a million miles away. Just like in DC," she said. "And you're covered in sweat. Are you . . . well, that's a dumb question. It's plain to see you are rattled about something."

John wiped his face and neck, then dried his hand on the blanket. His heart rate had slowed but was still pounding much faster than normal. He moved his head to look up at Leslie. That just made him dizzy. When his vision cleared, he saw the trusses and tall roof of an aircraft hangar. Oh, yeah. The rented hangar in Tucson. Getting ready for the theft. No, that wasn't right. This was the Dateland hangar, with their two stolen F-16s sitting thirty feet from his cot. Shit. His head was spinning. He hadn't even known where he was! He propped himself up on his elbows and said, "Let me go splash a little water on my face. I just need a few—"

"So," she said. "That's how you got your wealth? Gold? In Vietnam. From Yamashita. He was a World War II Japanese general, right? You called him the Tiger of Malaya."

Had he mumbled all that? "It was a dream, Leslie. Not real."

"Bullshit," she said. "It was not a dream. It was a *flashback*. To a real-life experience. Look at me, John. Tell me that's not true."

Her eyes bore into his. He felt hopelessly outclassed, even though this was a one-on-one confrontation. She was stripping off layers of his psyche as easily as she would peel the skin of a tangerine.

"It might help to talk about it," Leslie said.

"I have my doubts," he said. "But, as usual, I do not seem to have a choice."

Ten minutes later, she knew the whole story.

"Did the special forces guy, Sergeant . . ."

"Landreau."

"Did he survive?"

"Yes, he got medevacked out to Udorn Air Base. I checked on him later. He made it."

"The Air America pilot," she said. "Did you ever get his name?"

"I used my Operation Gold Coast credentials to get a ride over to the Air America hangar at NKP. That's Nakhon Phanom, a Thai air base very close to the Laotian border. It housed lots of USAF air-rescue and air commando units back in the day, along with some hush-hush, CIA-sponsored Air America aircraft.

"When I walked into that hangar, I must have looked like a ghost, or a demon, or something, still covered in mud, camo on my face, bloodstains on my jungle fatigues. Oh, and with two loaded CAR-15s still slung over my shoulder. They blew me off. Didn't even admit they had lost a plane. Couldn't blame them, under the circumstances. It wasn't until years later that I found out his name from a private source."

"And the CIA, or military, or whoever, just let you walk away with twelve bars of solid gold?

"Hell, no. They never knew I had it. I told them it was equipment from a classified mission, which had to stay with me until I returned stateside."

"Come on," Leslie said. "Someone must have known that the pilot's first mission had been to get that gold."

"I'm not so sure. I was waiting for someone to ask. They never did. Leslie, you can't imagine how confused things were in Southeast Asia back then. The closer you got to the front-line units, the crazier it got. Airplanes of all types, and helicopters—well, technically, a helicopter *is* an aircraft—littered the tarmac of every base from Hickam in Honolulu to NKP, where I ended up, and everywhere in between. CONEX containers, those big metal ones you see on tractor trailers or stacked on cargo ships, were piled up everywhere, filled with who-knows-what. You've heard the stories, right? Containers of fancy office furniture and couches airdropped to soldiers dug into foxholes on a hillside. Meanwhile, the food and bullets they really needed got delivered to the REMFs in Saigon or Bangkok."

"REMFs?" Leslie said.

"You never heard that one? It stands for Rear Echelon Mother—ah, you can guess the rest. Someone living well back from the action, who gets a hot meal in the mess hall, a hot shower every day, and a comfy bed to sleep in every night.

"So, if you can visualize that kind of chaos, you might understand how three rucksacks with twelve gold bars could get 'lost' in the fog of war. My theory is, they didn't want to admit to the operation. Also, it's possible that the side trip to pick up that gold was an off-the-books thing. It was not uncommon for those Air America boys to find some, ah, extra fringe benefits while they were out on a mission. Wine, women, and—in this case—maybe a big metal locker of gold bars left behind by Yamashita when Japan lost the war."

Leslie said, "I knew about Japanese troops literally raping and pillaging in China, the Philippines, and Singapore. But Vietnam?"

John shrugged. "Why not? Japan occupied that too. When I read up on Yamashita, he was the general in charge of that whole area. In 1945, he reportedly hid artifacts, artwork, jewels and up to 4,000 tons of gold in caves in northern Vietnam. By that time in the war, the Allies ruled the seas, and it was too dangerous to ship it back to Japan. Yamashita either got orders to hide the stuff or decided to do it on his own. He never got the chance to retrieve it. MacArthur put him on trial for war crimes and had him hanged."

"Weren't those rucksacks a little heavy?" Leslie asked.

"Damn right. That's why I needed three. I emptied gear out of Landreau's ruck, mine, and one NVA pack I found in the wreckage of the Pilatus. In my exhausted state, each one felt like it weighed a thousand pounds. Weeks later, I looked it up. Each of those bars weighs 27.4 pounds, so each ruck weighed just over a hundred pounds."

Leslie's eyes narrowed. "Wait," she said. "You said each bar *weighs* 27.4 pounds. As in, the present tense. You still have them? Where are they? What are they worth?"

He sat up and swung his legs onto the floor. "I'll answer those questions in a minute. But right now, I need to use the bathroom so badly that my thumbs hurt. Be right back."

When he returned, he felt better. At least he knew it was just before dawn on Sunday. At 1400 today, they would be ready for launch. Leslie was seated at the table. He sat down across from her. With a little luck, he could finish this conversation before Adam or Whitaker woke up.

"I'll answer your third question first. I haven't checked lately, but, as of December 1994, those twelve bars, weighing a total of 4,800 ounces, are worth almost two million dollars. That's almost a thousand percent more than they were worth back in 1970. As to where they are, that's really none of your business. But, since you asked, they are held in the vaults of two Swiss banks."

"You haven't sold any of them?" she asked.

"Well, here's the thing. I don't really own them anymore."

"Say what?"

"Remember Sergeant Landreau? He recovered from his wounds but was medically retired and became an accountant. Together, we formed a non-profit corporation called the Gold Coast Group. I'm the CEO; he's the CFO. The Swiss bank accounts are in the corporation's name. Gold Coast Group provides scholarships for the kids, and now grandkids, of Operation Gold Coast veterans. We also provide financial assistance to any Gold Coast spouses who need it. Including Roger Younger's wife. Roger was the pilot of that Pilatus Porter."

"Wow," Leslie said. "That's . . ." She reached out and touched his hand. "That's wonderful. Touching." She let go of his hand. "But weren't you tempted to keep just *one* of those gold bars?"

"Nope. I don't care if I never see another gold bar. As you have seen, I get occasional nightmares about the whole Gold Coast experience."

She reached out her hand again.

"Don't feel sorry for me," John said. "The corporation pays me a very substantial salary. Landreau turned out to have a great aptitude for arranging loans using the gold as collateral. Then he turns around and makes investments that make us even more money. I don't understand it all, but he says that the investments alone will support the corporation. According to Mike—that's Landreau's first name—we'll never have to sell any of that gold."

"You should write all this down. It would make a good story," Leslie said.

"Nope. There might be hell to pay if someone finds out how I got that gold. But, hey, if you're interested, I should tell you something. Those twelve bars? They were only about one-quarter of the gold that was in that metal box. It's probably still there."

"Want to go find it someday?" Leslie said. "I presume you have the coordinates."

"Yes, I have the coordinates, but no, I don't want to look for it. The crash site is in the high terrain of northern Laos. Not the friendliest place to be, even today." John noticed that the sun was about to rise. "What time is it?"

"Time for breakfast!" came a loud voice from Whitaker's cot. "What are you two doin' over there, whispering? Shake a leg! What's on the menu? I'm hungry!"

Whitaker's unexpected, ebullient shouts brought John's heart rate back up into the danger zone. He'd almost prefer another Vietnam-era nightmare. He said, "Whit, I hate to tell you this, but it's your turn to cook."

Chapter 38

After John had dressed and freshened up in the bathroom, he joined Adam and Leslie at the table, which was now set for breakfast. Whitaker was standing, whipping up something in a bowl.

"Pancakes again?" John said.

"You just wait," Whitaker said. "Wait 'till you taste these. Now, get out of my way, I got work to do." He concentrated on the bowl. "You might be right, John. Maybe I need a second career as a chef. Chef? Crew chief? They sound kind of the same, don't they? I kind of like cooking up stuff, especially for breakfast. Would you finance me if I opened a restaurant? What should I call it? Whit's Waffle House? No, I think the 'Waffle House' name is taken. How about Jim's Joint? Huh? Whatcha think?"

"I think you should forget the 'Jim's Joint' idea," John said. "Up in Olympia, people would think you're serving pancakes laced with marijuana. Whatever you call it, don't count on me for financing. Most of my savings has gone into our little project here."

"That's right, I forgot. After this adventure, you'll be as broke as I am. You might have to sell the T-Bird to stay afloat."

It was dirty pool for Whitaker to harass him before he had his first cup of coffee, especially after last night's dreams. John picked up the coffee pot, poured some, and stirred in a spoonful of sugar. He debated how to respond. Leslie was staring at him. When Whitaker wasn't looking, he gave her a brief shake of his head. This was no time to tell Whitaker that his prized T-33 had already been sold. John chose to distract Whitaker with a little friendly but sarcastic bantering.

"You might have to wait a while to open that restaurant. In my opinion, you should name it Parolee's Pancakes. Because, as you predicted the other day, you're probably going to be in jail for the next umpteen years. With me as your cell mate." He watched Whitaker grimace at that vision.

"I might as well ask for the electric chair," Whitaker said. "That would be preferable to being your roommate in prison."

"Okay. Okay, enough of this dark humor," Leslie said. "But I do have a suggestion for naming Whit's restaurant. How about Crew Chief's Café?"

Whitaker closed his eyes, opened them, and smiled. "I think I like that!" He turned his attention to the stove top and busied himself with flipping pancakes. When he had eight ready, he put two on each of four plates, added some sausage and a sliced orange as garnish. Adam handed out the plates. Before he sat down, Whitaker poured more batter onto the griddle. John was glad he did; his lemon-chiffon pancakes were deliciously fluffy and light.

After breakfast, Adam said he'd like to go outside for a walk. John told him that would be a bad idea. There were a lot of smart people trying to track them down. He was sure that Hardwick would have enlisted the help of NSA, FBI, Air Force, and local law enforcement. Someone would be studying satellite photos of every jet-capable runway in this region. The local sheriff would have received a bulletin to be on the lookout for anything suspicious around any airport.

"As unlikely as it seems," he told Adam, "if one of us is seen out here, at a location that's supposed to be vacant, it might arouse suspicion and ruin our plan. Try doing what I did yesterday. Walk laps around the inside of the building. Do some pushups."

After a painful two hours of doing nothing, it was time to fire up the jets and repeat yesterday's preparation for alert. Whitaker suggested they do this one aircraft at a time to minimize the exhaust blast which, even at idle, acted like a giant leaf blower in the dusty hangar. That procedure went off without a hitch.

By 1400, everything had been checked, rechecked, and triple checked. John and Leslie were back in their flight suits, g-suits, and survival vests with loaded .38 caliber revolvers. At 1415, with John standing nearby to render help if needed, Adam turned on the HF radio and established contact with Sam in the AWACS. John had given them call signs. Sam was "Wallace." The Dateland site was "Viper Ops." Once airborne, John and Leslie would be "Viper One" and "Viper Two." The Citation was "Rita." Everyone knew the reference point, the dry lake, was "Bullseye."

At 1430, John climbed the ladder and strapped into Three-Six-Eight. Leslie, already strapped in, gave him a thumbs-up. Whitaker opened the hangar's north door, revealing another bright, almost cloudless southern Arizona day, then returned to his position just left of Three-Six-Eight's nose. It was so quiet he could hear the truck traffic on Interstate 8, more than a mile away. The only other sound was Adam's radio checks with Sam; these were scheduled every ten minutes.

John had sat many hours of alert in both the F-4 and the F-16. Usually, it had been in a relatively comfortable alert facility with warm beds and hot food, but sometimes it had been like this. Cockpit alert, which afforded the quickest response time. It was also the most stressful. He felt all dressed up for a party but had nowhere to go—yet.

By 1600, it was obvious that the MiGs weren't going to launch. As agreed in advance, at that time Sam made a "Stand

Down" call, which Adam acknowledged. John unstrapped, climbed down, and watched as Whitaker installed various safety covers and closed the canopy. Adam did the same for Three-Four-Nine.

The four of them gathered near the open hangar door, savoring the fresh air and the view. John noticed the three glum faces and said, "It's like fishing. You don't always get a bite the first time you throw your line into the water. We'll be ready again, this same time tomorrow."

"Great," Whitaker said. "I've got another twenty-three hours to kill. Wish I would have brought a couple books. Anybody got an idea of how to make the time go by faster? Outside of eating, of course, heh, heh."

* * *

Whitaker and Adam opened the north hanger doors for their second day on alert.

"It's time to suit up," John said.

Leslie said, "It's my mother's birthday. This year it's on a Monday, the same as when she was born. That's why Monday is her favorite day of the week."

"I'm sorry you can't call or email her," John said.

"She'll be worried. Especially after Scott's death, I think she needs me more than ever." Leslie stood up and said, "Let's do this."

They zipped up their *g*-suits and vests and walked to their respective airplanes. John had confidence in Adam's radio skills, so he climbed up the ladder and strapped in. Whitaker handed the ladder to Adam, who took it to Three-Four-Nine. Leslie went up the ladder and hooked up her harness.

At 1430, John rechecked that all the switches in his cockpit were set for an alert launch. He had nothing more to do but listen to Adam's voice on the HF speaker.

"Wallace, this is Viper Ops, checking in. Ready."

"Viper Ops, Wallace, roger."

John leaned his head back against the ejection seat and closed his eyes. He kept it there for a few minutes and then passed the time by doing stretching exercises, rocking back and forth in the seat to keep circulation going.

"Viper Ops, Wallace. Two bogeys, Ranch 330, 10, low."

"Roger." Adam said. He looked up at John and called out, "Did you guys hear that?"

John said, "Yes." He hacked his cockpit clock.

At two minutes, eighteen seconds, John heard the radio crackle with Sam's voice.

"Viper Ops, Wallace. Two bogeys, Ranch 330, 26, medium."

The bogeys were headed north and climbing. If they had covered sixteen miles in two minutes, they were obviously fast movers.

"Bogeys Bullseye 150, 85, medium. Scramble!"

John zeroed out and restarted his clock. By the time Adam had turned to give the start signal, John had already grabbed his helmet off the canopy rail, put it on and closed the canopy. As soon as the canopy locked into place, he signaled Leslie to start her engine. He started his engine, ran through the brief scramble after-start checklist and, after warning Whitaker, did his normal twisting to see that the flight controls moved properly. Whitaker gave him a thumbs-up. John looked down at the left console. The FCNP INS status said "30." The NAV READY light was flashing. He rotated the Function Knob to NAV. Good to go in less than two minutes. Beautiful.

Leslie was ready. John gave Whitaker a "Remove Chocks" signal, waited for him to do that, and returned his salute. He pushed power up just enough to get the jet moving, then went back to idle to minimize the exhaust blast on Leslie's airplane and Adam.

Once outside on the ramp, he accelerated to taxi speed. Something bothered him. Had Sam said, "bandits" or "bogeys?" He was pretty sure she said bogeys. Why hadn't her magic radar stuff identified the bogeys as MiG-21s? She must be confident of their type, or she wouldn't have launched them. It was too late for second-guessing. He was at the approach end of Runway 01.

The windsock hung straight down, which was a little unusual for a desert afternoon, but lucky for them. This runway would get them airborne in the least time and their takeoff direction would keep them away from the populated area to the southwest. He was on the runway, with Leslie in position at his side, within thirty seconds. He pushed hard on the brake pedals, gave the runup signal, and checked his gauges. All good. No red warning lights or yellow cautions. He released the brakes and pushed the throttle up to mil power.

Once airborne, John raised the gear, delayed several seconds, and started a right turn. Leslie joined to tactical formation, line abreast, about 9,000 feet away, on his right. His old habits returned quickly. He rechecked his lap belt. It was tight enough to hold him during heavy maneuvering but not so tight that he couldn't twist around and check six. He tightened the chin strap on his helmet and pushed the bayonet clips on his oxygen mask a few clicks in so the mask would not slide down his face during high-*g* turns.

He keyed the microphone and said, "Viper One, check."

"Two."

"G-warm-up. In-place ninety right, now." He did a five-*g*, ninety-degree right turn and watched Leslie do the same. He felt his *g*-suit inflate and tighten around his lower abdomen and legs. Three seconds later, he turned back to original course, also using five *g*s.

"Viper, ops check. One's 29, 33, 68."

"Two's 29, 33, 67."

John accelerated to 450 knots, the best combat climb speed for a clean jet, but kept them at very low altitude until they were forty miles northwest of Bullseye. They had crossed over Interstate 8 and were now inside the expansive, mostly unpopulated military training area that covered most of southern Arizona. Since it was a Monday, they might accidently encounter some Air Force, Navy, or Marine jets out here, but for now his radar scope was clean. He pushed the throttle to the mil stop, pulled it back a tad, and began a climb.

Albuquerque Center, Luke Approach, and those Customs Service balloon radars would pick them up soon. Someone would make a report and Hardwick would know about it immediately. They had to get the job done quickly and hustle back to Dateland. It was time to arm up the gun and shut off the exterior lights.

"Viper One, Fence In."

"Two."

Passing 20,000 feet, John used his left index finger to pull the mic switch on the throttle. "Wallace, Viper One on uniform."

"Viper One, Wallace. Your bogies are now Bullseye 150 . . . ah, standby."

John kept the climb going into the mid-30,000-foot range until Leslie called and said, "Viper One, you're marking."

"Viper One copies." He pushed the nose over, descended about a thousand feet, and checked his six. No contrail.

"Viper One, Wallace. Two Blue Bandits, I say again, *Blue Bandits,* Bullseye 150, 55, medium." That was the call he had been waiting for. Alvarado's MiG-21s had been positively identified and were about to cross into U.S. airspace. He couldn't remember Sam's voice ever sounding this excited. But those had been peacetime training missions. This was for real.

Chapter 39

At combat speed, Three-Six-Eight's nose bobbled a little, reacting to the slightest twitch of his hand on the stick. Its engine no longer purred at the lower, peacetime rpms of a cross-country flight from Point A to Point B. The Pratt and Whitney engine roared. No, it was more than a roar; it was a scream. He could feel its power vibrating against his back and thighs. Slipstream noise, the whistling of airflow over his canopy and fuselage, was loud enough to hurt his ears. John imagined that, if this jet had a soul, it knew that it was on an important mission—like a racehorse galloping down the home stretch to win the sweepstakes. The western sky was clear, with the sun at precisely the elevation and azimuth that he had predicted.

Enough, dammit! Back to business. That was the problem with flying fighters. Awesome, often indescribably beautiful sky, clouds, and terrain flashed by, but fighter pilots strapped into their killing machines couldn't take the time to savor the view.

John laughed into his oxygen mask. He had always joked that his brain had only three channels, and, being a male, one of those was always preoccupied with sex. One of the remaining channels was focused on the mission: Kill the MiGs. The other channel *should* be checking Leslie's six, keeping her alive. He did that, of course. But he allowed himself five seconds—during which he would travel just under one mile—to savor the view from 30,000 feet.

This was not the TAC ACES simulator, with its artificial sky, horizon, and computer-generated terrain. This was the real world, with Arizona's clear, bright blue sky above and various shades of brown desert below. From this altitude, the hills and mountains appeared as dark gray blobs. Small white cumulonimbus clouds had popped up over some of the peaks, as if they were airbursts of anti-aircraft artillery. Between some of the ridge lines were thin black ribbons of thirty-foot-wide highways. Ripples in the terrain led to green bands of vegetation, and even some trees, along dry stream beds.

John shook his head. It was time to ignore the glamorous pleasures of flying a jet fighter six miles above the desert. He needed to get down to business. He aimed for a point slightly north of Bullseye and check-turned to a heading of 150, which would put them on a reciprocal course to the MiGs. He adjusted his radar search but didn't expect the MiGs to show up on his scope until they were thirty miles apart, which would be in another twenty seconds. He already showed one radar return on his scope, a single contact five miles north of Bullseye, but that was probably Briggs. He didn't want to waste valuable time confirming that with Sam. She would issue the order for Briggs to retreat to the north when the MiGs were—

"Rita, Wallace, Bugout 360."

He wouldn't hear Brigg's reply since he was talking to Sam on another frequency. But that call meant the MiGs were thirty miles south of Bullseye.

"Viper One, check twenty left."

"Two."

Even without radar contact with the MiGs, John wanted to build some lateral offset to facilitate his attack. Leslie might be wondering why he had offset to the east and not west, which would have given him a sun advantage. If things went according to his plan, she would soon find out.

"Viper One, Wallace. Bandits Bullseye 150, 20, medium."

John's scope was blank. "Viper One, clean." He looked out at Leslie. She had adjusted to his check turn and was back in line abreast formation, about 3,000 high. Perfect. He checked her six and his. Neither of them was showing contrails.

If he couldn't get radar contact with the MiGs in the next thirty seconds, he'd have to depend on Sam's vectors. Finally, two small white squares showed up on his radar scope. He gave the antenna one more sweep to confirm it, then locked up the leader.

"Viper One, sorted, eastern, Bullseye 150, 15, 10,000."

"Viper Two, clean."

On any other day, he would have stayed in the search mode so the MiGs wouldn't get a warning of his lock-on from their Sirena-3 radar warning receivers. Today, he *wanted* them to see a spike from his radar on their RWRs. Three seconds later, he got his wish. His HUD display showed the MiGs had turned toward him. Either they had locked him up with their own radars or just turned toward the RWR spike. John used two or three valuable seconds to visualize this from a "God's-eye" view. He was twenty miles from the bandits, who had turned "hot" into him. He couldn't wait for Leslie to get a radar lock. He needed to call a play ASAP.

John squeezed the microphone button and told Leslie, "Viper Two, Bracket Right. Push it up."

"Viper Two."

He had let his speed bleed off a little. They needed to enter this fight at 450 knots, the upper end of the F-16's "sweet spot" for energy maneuverability. He watched Leslie bank right and pull off to the west, opening a space between them which would almost guarantee that the MiGs wouldn't see them both. John reviewed what he had seen of the MiG formation before he locked the leader. The wingman had been on the leader's left side, forty-five degrees back, and a half-mile away, presumably in fighting wing position.

"Viper One, Wallace. Bandits Bullseye 150, 10, medium."

"Viper One." John felt like a juggler with three balls in the air. One was maneuvering his own airplane for a kill. The second was checking Leslie's six and keeping her informed. The third was communicating with Sam. It was time to reduce the number of balls.

"Wallace, Viper One, Judy."

"Wallace."

Sam would still be there, ready to give vectors if needed. But she would know from his Judy call that he had a good radar lock and didn't need any more help from AWACS.

John knew where the MiGs *should* be but didn't waste time trying to find them visually. They were so damn small. He yanked the airplane farther to the left to get more offset. He needed something simple, like the NOB technique. He was still locked onto the lead MiG, which he firmly hoped was being flown by Alvarado.

"Viper Two, contact!" Less than a second later, she added, "Viper Two, sorted, western."

By eight miles range to his target, John had the proper amount of offset and altitude advantage. A glance out at Leslie showed her lateral offset on the wingman was a little tight, but she had extra vertical turning room. He rolled the airplane 135 degrees to the right and pulled back on the stick until he felt about four *g*'s. His view of the outside world tilted. Clouds and blue sky above the horizon rotated over his left shoulder and, to the right and below, his field of vision was filled with desert. Anyone who was not a fighter pilot would become disoriented about now and, perhaps, get a little queasy as their world—and their stomach—had literally turned upside-down. John was pleased that it felt normal to him. It felt good. He was rolling in to attack the enemy.

He pulled on the stick gently, with just enough pressure to turn his jet smoothly, without creating any white clouds of vortices that would give him away. He followed the target locator line in his HUD until it became a green target box with a little black dot in it. At four miles range, the black dot assumed the shape of a MiG-21. A second MiG was off to the west, in fighting wing position.

This was the exact sight picture that he had seen weeks ago, back in DC's Lafayette Park. He knew then, as he did now, how this would end. This MiG was going to die.

He took a deep breath and said, "Viper One, tally two."

"Viper Two, tally two."

The MiGs were headed directly toward him, almost on a collision course. John turned even further left to get some turning room of his own and checked Leslie's position. She appeared to be diving, accelerating, and closing in on the number two MiG, which was still in fighting wing position on his leader. He doubted if either MiG had seen Leslie yet. She was about to enter this fight unobserved, diving down from out of the sun.

The MiGs kept angling toward him. John was going to pass the lead MiG canopy-to-canopy, less than 500 feet apart, with the MiGs heading northeast and him heading southwest. He had less than a second to think of his next move, but it was a no-brainer. First, deny the MiGs a head-on gun shot. Next, lure them into a right turn, which would ensure a shot for Leslie. The lead MiG flashed by in a right bank, close enough that John could see the pilot's white helmet and dark green visor. The MiG was painted in dark green and brown camouflage paint and had a large red "55" painted on the nose. That was probably left over from its previous owner, the Albanian air force.

He turned left, *away* from the MiGs, in a loose, 4-*g* climbing turn, hoping the MiGs would take the bait. John lost sight of them for several seconds, but he knew right where to look. Sure enough, back in his eight o'clock position, he saw that the lead MiG had cranked his jet into a hard right turn to get inside John's turning circle. John wondered if the MiG pilot—God, how he hoped this was Alvarado—was suspicious about his lazy, low-*g* turn. The lead MiG was pointed right at him and doing his best to slide in closer for a gun shot. Unfortunately, the pilot had lost all interest in checking his wingman's six. Well, unfortunate, that is, for the wingman. Very fortunate for Leslie.

"Viper Two, engaged, western."

Dammit, she was going to get the first kill. "Viper Two, press."

John raised his nose and increased his left bank so he could watch the whole thing. This would also get him some vertical turning room for whatever happened next with his own MiG, which was not yet a threat. He had drawn this same scenario on a white board—or a chalk board back in the old days—a hundred times before, in Air Force briefing rooms all over the world. The good guys were always drawn in blue; the bad guys were always red, perhaps because of the Cold War era fixation on the red flag of most Communist countries. As if he were still swiping the blue pen across the board, Leslie's F-16 streaked across the center of the imaginary turning circle which represented the MiG's flight path.

A brief cloud of vortices rolled off the Leslie's wing roots. She was turning hard, pulling lead, saddling up for a gun shot on MiG number two. The poor guy was flying perfect fighting wing position, which would be great if this were an air show. But he was doing nothing else to contribute to the fight. Notably, he wasn't checking his own six.

John allowed himself a moment—more like a split-second—to ruminate on the MiG wingman's good flying. As if that were an effective combat tactic. In the words of Major Mick Mannock, World War I's second-leading British ace with 61 kills: *"Good flying never killed an enemy yet."*

Smoke spewed from Leslie's gun port and quickly disappeared with the slipstream. Pieces of metal flew off the cockpit area and dorsal fin of the MiG. Her aim was very good. The backbone of the MiG exploded in a ball of fire. The nose spiraled off in one direction and the tail fluttered down like a falling leaf. He didn't see a parachute.

"Splash one Blue Bandit!" Leslie shouted.

John wondered if she would come to regret that enthusiastic radio call. He had made a similarly jubilant call after his first kill. Later, after the victory roll, the triumphant landing, subsequent pats on the back from fellow pilots, and champagne, he had wondered about the man he had killed. Did he have a wife, kids, or parents who would mourn his death? Tonight, after hours of lying awake in bed, the excitement would wear off. Leslie would ask herself those questions. By morning, if his experience was any guide, she would be a different person. He watched her fly away from the fireball and separate to the north.

"Viper Two, Blind. No Joy." Predictably, she had lost sight of John and the other MiG. There was no shame in that; she had needed to focus on the gunsight.

John pushed his nose down, unloaded to almost zero g and said, "Viper Two, pitch back left. Fight is one mile east of you, angels fifteen." The unload maneuver had opened some distance from "his" MiG—hell, he was just going to call him Alvarado—which would allow a few seconds for Leslie to regain situational awareness.

Leslie called, "Viper One, press."

John smiled. Leslie, like Sam, was a woman of few words. In air combat, that was a valuable skill. Many lesser-skilled fighter pilots would have added the redundant words, "Tally" and "Visual," but that was all included in the word, "Press."

He said, "Viper One, engaged." It was his turn now. He didn't need to waste words on which MiG he was fighting; there was only one left. The question was, how could he kill this guy quickly? Although it seemed like an hour since they had launched—he was all too familiar with the temporal distortion experienced in combat—according to his cockpit clock, it had been only twelve minutes, thirty-four seconds since they had taken off from Dateland. Air Traffic Control, having been put on alert by Hardwick, would have seen them as they climbed, less than three minutes ago. Air defense fighters would soon launch from March AFB, eager to redeem themselves for missing the stolen F-16s on Saturday. He needed a quick kill.

John took a good look at Alvarado, who had gained a position of advantage and was about 4,000 feet behind him and 30 degrees off his tail. That was about to change. He lit the AB, set his helmet back against the headrest, rolled left, and tightened up his gut muscles. He pulled what felt like nine gs for about four seconds. After slacking off to seven gs, he raised the nose into an energy-conserving upward spiral. He kept his speed at 330 knots, the speed at which an F-16 could make its quickest tightest, energy-conserving turn.

The MiG couldn't match this. Alvarado would either overshoot or zoom into the vertical to maintain his three-nine advantage. John had a plan for either contingency. Alvarado chose to pull up into a steep climb. The MiG was superior to the F-16 at extremely slow speeds and Alvarado obviously knew that. What Alvarado hadn't planned for was, what if John refused to follow him up? What if John just kept up his high-energy, climbing spiral and let Alvarado zoom up until he was out of airspeed?

Alvarado's nose was too high.

"Thank you!" John said to himself. The chess game was over. Alvarado was out of airspeed and ideas. Even the venerable MiG-21 could not sustain that climb indefinitely. John maintained his 330-knot spiral and was pleased to see the MiG skid to one side, flop over on its back and stall. It didn't enter a spin, though. Alvarado somehow got the nose pointed down. John watched as the MiG fell right through the center of his 7-g turning circle. He took a second to look around for Leslie. She was high and to his right. Her six was clear.

If Alvarado were smart, he'd just accelerate going straight down and run away. But the fool kept turning at low speed, perhaps to deny him a missile shot. Thank God for the fake AIM-9s. Or maybe he just didn't know any better. John lowered his nose and closed in for the kill. He pulled the throttle out of AB; he had too much energy. When he got closer, he sacrificed some of that airspeed during a hard turn to get his nose out into lead. Alvarado jinked hard left. John followed easily. He tried to get into Alvarado's mind. Would he reverse to the right? Or would he push his stick forward and bunt over with negative g?

John gambled on a right jink and began his own roll an instant before Alvarado did the same thing. The MiG's nose appeared at the bottom of his HUD and tracked up towards his pipper. He didn't bother trying to lock on with the radar. He made a small adjustment to match Alvarado's turn rate. When the MiG's wingspan filled the reticle, John let the LCOS pipper settle on the MiG's backbone and kept it there. He squeezed the trigger for three seconds. Tracers arced out toward the MiG. Puffs of smoke erupted from hits on the MiG's right wing and tail section. A few small pieces of metal flew off the tail. John pulled off to the MiG's left side to avoid any more debris. A metal panel about the size of a cookie sheet peeled off from the MiG's upper right wing, loomed large enough to make John duck, and disappeared over his right shoulder. Black smoke billowed from the tailpipe. But the MiG was still flying. Damn. Leslie had killed her MiG with one shot. How was he ever going to live this down?

John repositioned for a second shot. The MiG's nose was now almost vertical. Before he could get a stabilized tracking shot, something exploded on the fuselage, and he had to jink away to miss a large piece of the MiG. Then a second explosion. It was the ejection seat! Alvarado had punched out of the crippled jet. The first explosion, the first piece that had sailed by, must have been the canopy jettisoning.

He pulled off to the right and watched the MiG wobble, slow to zero airspeed and flop over onto its back into an inverted spin.

He keyed his mic. "Splash one Blue Bandit." It was a silly radio call, for an audience of one, who already knew the score. He looked to the northwest, saw the parachute, and flew toward it. He still had bullets in the gun. He circled the pilot in the parachute harness but was too far away to see his face. Yes, or no? Shoot him while he was defenseless in the parachute? No. It would not be honorable.

Alvarado was a lucky man. He had punched out over a stretch of north-south two-lane asphalt highway. There were no cars in sight; it was a local road, probably used by local ranchers. The drug dealer might have to walk, but if he hurried, he could be back across the border in one day. He'd live to fight another day. That was unacceptable. John took a closer look at the road. It was wide enough and straight enough.

"Viper One, ops check. One's 37."

"Viper Two, Joker."

It was the same old problem. Leslie. He had to get rid of her to implement this new plan. He'd order her to fly back to Dateland. No, forget that. She wouldn't leave, not Leslie. He wouldn't if the roles were reversed. "Viper Two, do you have a tally on the parachute?"

"Affirmative."

There was no way to say this with tactical brevity. "Viper Two, I want you to slow to max endurance airspeed and orbit this area. If you reach bingo fuel, I want you to RTB, with or without me. Acknowledge."

"Viper Two."

He descended toward the highway using idle and speed brakes.

"Ah, Viper One, say your intentions."

He ignored her. She'd understand soon enough.

Chapter 40

Lynwood Hardwick stood up and addressed his team. "Guys, it's time for a break. It's almost 3:00 o'clock. We've been cooped up in here for the last two days. I'm going outside for some fresh air. Anyone want to join me?"

The Air Force OSI guy, "Mister" Brent Richardson, put down his pencil and said, "Yes, sir."

OSI agents never revealed their military rank, probably to increase their status with whomever they were investigating, but Hardwick had checked. He was a Captain with a good record as an investigator.

"Me too, sir," said Claudia Yellin. "Just let me finish this last page. Only two more airfields to mark—negative, of course. No F-16 sightings anywhere so far." She had come highly recommended by George Clark, who had said if he couldn't be there personally, Yellin was his top choice. She had experience in aerial reconnaissance and satellite imagery. A former army intelligence officer, she was now a CIA GS-13 and, according to Clark, one of his best and most trustworthy analysts.

The trustworthy part was important since she—or anyone from the CIA—really shouldn't be here at all. This was a domestic issue. They were hunting John Martin, now labeled a domestic terrorist, as Pompolatis, the FBI man, had been quick to point out.

On Saturday, when they had all met on the rainy tarmac out at Andrews, Hardwick's first look at FBI Special Agent Fred

Pompolatis had been a real turn-off. Sure, everyone had a right to look a little disheveled after being roused from home on a Saturday morning and rushed off to Andrews. But this man gave new meaning to the word "rumpled." He was overweight, puffy-faced, and bald. His belly strained the buttons of his wrinkled shirt, visible inside an equally wrinkled suit coat and raincoat that had seen better days. He was short and evidently couldn't find pants that fit his ample waistline without being too long. His pants cuffs had dragged on the wet concrete.

Hardwick had waited for Agent Pompolatis to reveal some hint of investigative brilliance during the four-hour flight out to Davis-Monthan. He had hoped that this man was a rotund version of the fictional, always-rumpled master TV detective, Columbo. Unfortunately, Pompolatis's first words had been, "I ain't sure why I'm here. The FBI don't investigate domestic terrorists. It's against the rules."

That had prompted Hardwick to take the agent aside—not easy to do in the small cabin of the Gulfstream— and reason with him. Motivate him without alienating him. It was either that or fire him and send him back to D.C., but that was not his style of leadership. After two minutes of whispered conversation, he got Pompolatis to promise that, from now on, he would be the poster boy for inter-agency cooperation.

"Pompolatis, what about you? A little fresh air?"

"Ah, sure, why not? I'm not getting anywhere trying to trace Martin's bank and credit card history. Finally got a warrant to search his house up in Washington State, but agents aren't there yet. Something about a ferry boat schedule." He put down his crossword puzzle and stood up.

Hardwick led the way out of their brightly lit borrowed office, which on a normal day was the command post's conference room, into the semi-darkness of the work floor. They were on a narrow, raised walkway about six feet above the main area. Rows of workstations, each with its own monitor or screen and a metal telephone console filled with buttons, occupied the lower level. Half of them were empty, leaving Hardwick to wonder what type of crisis would be needed to fill the place up. He remembered that this was originally a SAC Nuclear Alert facility, where they had to keep tabs on B-47s and B-52s loaded with enough firepower to destroy the world seven times over. Back in those days, he could imagine all these chairs being occupied.

Lieutenant Colonel Fischer, the Chief of Command Post, came up the five steps from the lower level. "Headed out, sir?"

"Yes. All of us need to get outside and stretch our legs, get the juices flowing, so to speak. There's nothing new, I take it?"

"No sir, nothing at all. The 355th is doing night training tonight, so no one's airborne right now. Well, there is one Customs Service jet airborne, but we don't monitor them. We just get a printout from the control tower."

"A Citation?"

"Yes, sir. I was told it's just a maintenance check flight. They haven't flown in about a week. Since that last crash."

Hardwick thanked Fischer and made a mental note to find out who had authorized the Customs Service to fly that test flight. He continued out the door and into an elevator, which took them up to the first floor, but they were still twenty feet underground. Yellin went up the sloped tunnel ahead of him and struggled with the double doors at the top. She held one side open. When they were all out, she let go of the door and it wheezed shut, pulled inwards by double hydraulic cylinders.

"Those doors are something," she said.

"Yes," Hardwick said. "An airtight seal. Thick enough to withstand a nuclear blast. Relics from the Cold War." He walked down the sloping walkway to the parking lot, which was part of the original concrete Christmas Tree ramp for bombers. He stopped a few feet to the east, on the ramp. The other three stopped, Yellin on his left and the other two on his right.

Richardson said, "General, if I read the report correctly, this is the exact spot where the theft occurred. That gate over there—" He pointed to the north. "That's where the F-16s taxied out. They taxied across this concrete ramp here, right out in front of us, and out this other gate on the right. Right onto the runway."

"A ballsy move," Yellin said, which earned her glances from Pompolatis and Richardson. "But smart. Totally unexpected."

"Don't rub it in, Ms. Yellin," Hardwick said.

She grimaced. "Oops. Sorry, General. I didn't mean to—"

"Don't worry. I'm not offended. Frankly, I am a little embarrassed, professionally, and personally. You see, I used to be John Martin's commander. He was a good man back then."

"I have a question," Yellin said. "The briefing book says this guy Martin is a former Air Force Lieutenant Colonel. Has a good combat record. Seemed to be headed for a long and successful Air Force career, until he got a bug up his ass about Alvarado. Don't get me wrong, I get his motivation. But he's just a pilot, right? Not some criminal mastermind. How did he figure this out? I mean, stealing two jets that are out here in mothballs? That's crazy."

Pompolatis said, "You got that right. He must have a screw loose somewhere to believe he can hunt down a drug lord who flies MiGs."

Hardwick was impressed with Yellin and Richardson. They had read their briefing books. But they had overlooked one thing. He walked toward the Boneyard fence to get a closer look at the row of F-16s there—the ones John Martin *didn't* steal. His footsteps made crunching noises on the concrete.

"Ms. Yellin, about your comment that Martin is 'just a pilot,' there's something—"

"Oops again," Yellin said. "My foot-in-mouth disease is acting up today. You used to be a—"

"Forget it. Take another look at Martin's military record. Well, hell, you're all too young to know this, so I might as well just tell you. His first assignment was to the 1127th Field Activities Group. You won't find many details on that unit because it's all need-to-know information, even now, twenty-five years later. Before Martin was a pilot, he was a covert operative. A damn good one." Hardwick swept his hand around from the north, through south, and out to the west, at which time the sun, about forty degrees high, blinded him. He shielded his eyes with his palm. "This whole thing has been a signature John Martin op."

"General! General Hardwick, sir!"

They all turned to see an airman in camouflage fatigues running toward them. She stopped, bent over to catch her breath, and said, "Colonel Fischer says to come back inside. Hurry."

Hardwick was panting when he got back into the "Pit," as the lower section of the command post was called. His eyes weren't yet fully adjusted to the darkness. He located Fischer and said, "What do you have?"

"Unidentified aircraft just crossed the southern border. I've alerted NORAD and they've scrambled some F-15s from March. Uh, stand by one second." Fischer turned around, leaned down, and said something to an airman seated at one of the consoles. "He'll get Albuquerque Center and Luke Approach on the speaker so you can hear everything." He pointed to another airman at a large map covered with plexiglass. "That guy will plot all the reports on the map, give you a visual of what's happening."

"Okay . . . good," Hardwick said. He realized he was screwed. He was in the wrong place! He was spoiled by all the high-tech screens and data links in the White House Situation Room. He needed to see this in real time, but the command post did not have radar screens. "Colonel, I need to be somewhere where I can see this on a radar scope. ASAP. What do you suggest?"

"Well, the control tower has a scope and screen that shows everything approach and center sees."

"How fast can you—"

"Two more bogeys!" The words blasted out from the console speaker. "Ten miles northwest of Ajo. Fast movers. Skin paint only. What the hell! Nobody out there is using IFF!"

Hardwick finished his question. "How quickly could you get me over there? To the tower."

"Ten minutes to drive over, another minute or so in the elevator."

Hardwick shut his eyes, got a mental picture of what was happening out there, and confirmed his earlier thought. He was royally screwed. The southern bogeys were probably MiGs. The northern group would be the F-16s, Martin and Olsen. By the time he got up in the tower, this battle would be over. "Colonel Fischer, can I talk on that thing?" He didn't wait for an answer. He tapped the airman on the shoulder and said, "Son, I need your chair."

The airman looked at Fischer, who nodded. When the young man got up, Hardwick read his name tag. Sullivan.

He sat down and raised the handset from its cradle. It was the old military style with a button in the center. He squeezed the button.

"This is Lynwood Hardwick, the President's National Security Advisor. Who's this?"

"Byron Youngblood, Senior Controller, Albuquerque Center. Who did you say you—"

"We don't have time to screw around. Tell me what you see on your radar."

After a three-second delay, Youngblood said, "Two flights of two. No squawks, just raw radar returns. They've merged. Now it's one big stationary blob."

Hardwick turned to Fischer, who was now standing next to him. "Where are the F-15s?"

Fischer looked at the wall clock. "They launched only two minutes ago. They'll be on station in twenty-five minutes."

Hardwick sighed. This was his fault too. He should have moved the F-15s closer. "Youngblood, give me a location for this 'blob,' as you call it."

"Roger. From the Gila Bend VORTAC, they are on the 155-degree radial for 45 miles."

"Copy." He released the talk button and said to Fischer, "Get a chopper headed to that location with armed Security Police. Have the SPs bring an extra rifle and body armor. Richardson, you're taking a little trip into the desert on that chopper. Report back by radio."

"Yes, sir!"

The console lit up with other phone calls. Hardwick motioned Airman Sullivan over. "Handle those from another console. Let me or Colonel Fischer know if it's anything critical."

He squeezed the radio talk button. "Albuquerque, Hardwick here. Update, please."

"It's very strange," Youngblood said. "Returns are fading in and out. They've moved southeast a little. Hold on . . . now I'm down to one return which appears to be orbiting. Flying around in a circle."

"Roger."

Someone tapped on his shoulder. He swiveled his chair around so quickly that Airman Sullivan jumped back as if he had been shocked. "What is it, Sullivan?"

"Sir, there's a phone call that you need to hear. It's from National Park Service, down near the Mexican Border. Something about a plane crash. It's Line 6." Sullivan pointed to the console. "Just push that button, there."

He told Youngblood to stay on the line and said, "Thanks, Sullivan." Before the young man disappeared, Hardwick said, "You're doing a great job, son. Keep it up."

"Thank you, sir."

He pushed the button and said, "Hardwick here."

"This is Officer Sanchez, at the Organ Pipe Cactus National Monument Visitor Center. One of our officers out on the Ajo-Tucson Highway called in a report of an explosion and fire. On his way to investigate that, he saw a plane, well, in his words, 'fall out of the sky and crash into the desert' about three miles southeast of the first fire."

Hardwick picked up a pencil. "When and where?" He jotted down time—just three minutes ago—and the coordinates, which Sanchez gave him in UTM format. Hell, army grunts and hikers used UTMs, but they made no sense to a pilot. "Sanchez, could you convert that to lat/long? On second thought, forget it."

It was going to be a bitch converting them to latitude and longitude. He wouldn't wait. He was willing to bet his career that those UTM's would be very close to the Gila Bend radial and distance mentioned by Youngblood.

Sanchez said, "One more thing, sir. The officer said both locations now have large plumes of black smoke. He's on his way to investigate with an ETA of twenty minutes."

"Thank you, Officer Sanchez. Keep us informed. Oh, and tell your officer that he might be seeing an Air Force chopper soon."

He punched off the telephone and selected the radio. "Youngblood, this is Hardwick. Any news?"

"Negative. Still a single contact, orbiting, same location."

"Colonel Fischer, how far out are the F-15s? Never mind. I already know the answer. Too far. Have NORAD send them to the Gila Bend 155 for 45. I need their ETA to that point."

The fucker had done it. Martin and his sidekick Olsen had splashed two MiGs. He called Yellin and Pompolatis into their private room and told them to sit. He picked up a black marker, found Gila Bend on the chart laid out on the table, and put a big "X" at the Gila Bend 155 radial for 45 nautical miles.

He said, "Our two stolen F-16s are out there right now. F-15 fighter-interceptors may find them, but I doubt it. Where will the F-16s land? Before we leave here today, I want the answer to that question."

"I heard all that radio chatter about bogeys and unknowns," Pompolatis said. "And then a comment about only one radar return. How can you be so sure that the MiGs didn't win? Maybe the F-16s got—"

"Trust me. I know John Martin. There are two MiGs in smoking holes out in that desert."

Chapter 41

John kept the idle descent going until it looked like he was about a thousand feet above the terrain. Alvarado was still descending in his parachute and facing north, into the wind. Good. He could maneuver unseen by Alvarado. John check-turned away from the road, slowed to 200 knots, and lowered the landing gear. With his left thumb, he pulled the speed brake switch aft for long enough to extend them fully, then released it. The speed brakes would automatically return to the correct position for landing—forty-three degrees. He checked his fuel and computed his landing airspeed.

After one look up at Leslie—she was orbiting at about 5,000 feet AGL—he turned base and checked the landing gear. Three green lights. The gear was down and locked. One more look north and south. No automobile traffic. He turned final, chose his aim point, and put the HUD flight path marker on the center of the road.

After touchdown in blessedly calm air, John lowered the nose and used the rudder to maintain his alignment on the road's center stripe. He was easy on the brakes, came to a stop on an almost-level stretch of highway, and shut the jet down. There was a very slight uphill incline, but it was enough that the aircraft might roll away while he was gone. He was tempted to set the brakes but discarded that idea. This was literally the worst place to have a brake overheat, a melted fuse plug, and subsequent flat tire. The solution? It had to be quick.

He unstrapped, removed his helmet, and unhooked his g-suit hose. He stood up in the seat, climbed out onto the left strake, hung there for a second, and dropped to the ground. It didn't take him long to find three rocks of sufficient size to use as wheel chocks. He put one behind each main tire and the third in front of the left main.

John walked north along the road to finish what he came for. He assumed that Alvarado would walk south. Should he hide somewhere and ambush him? There was no time for that; he had to get the job done and get airborne as soon as possible. He unsnapped the holster, pulled out his .38 and kept walking. It didn't take long.

The bastard had tied his parachute to a low branch of a palo verde tree and was sitting in the shade, looking like he didn't have a care in the world. Shit. He must have a mobile phone and has just called someone for a ride. If his ride came from the south, his return path to Three-Six-Eight might be blocked. He would have to finish this quickly.

John made no attempt at stealth. He just walked in a straight line toward Alvarado's shelter. When he got within a hundred feet, Alvarado crawled out, stood up, and looked at him. John kept walking. He stopped with fifty feet of distance between them.

"It *is* you! Martin, the crazy American officer!" Alvarado turned sideways and pointed up at the area where Leslie was orbiting. John resisted the temptation to look. He kept his eyes on Alvarado.

"I am confused, my gringo friend." He pointed in the general direction of Leslie's jet noise. That F-16 shot me down. And yet, here you are, dressed in flight gear. Ah, now I see—"

"Yes, you idiot, there are two of us." Now it was John's turn to point at the sky. "That one killed your wingman." He watched Alvarado's face. "You didn't even know he was gone, did you?"

The man was silent.

"I am the one who shot you down." John walked five steps closer. "And now I'm here to finish the job."

"What, no court of law?" Alvarado laughed. "How did that work for you last time?" He laughed again. "Anyway, you don't have the balls."

Something large flashed by several hundred yards away on John's right. It was Leslie's F-16, about 500 feet above the desert, heading south. An instant later, the sound wave of a low flying, high speed jet hit them. Both he and Alvarado instinctively ducked.

When Alvarado straightened up, he had a small semi-automatic pistol in his right hand. John pulled his trigger twice, then dived to the right just as two puffs of smoke emerged from Alvarado's gun. On the way down, he grunted as something sharp and painful impacted his left thigh. Alvarado twisted left and fell to the ground.

John remained prone and rolled several feet right toward a large patch of prickly pear cactus. This wouldn't stop any bullets but would hide him while he assessed the damage to his leg. It hurt like hell, but he could work through that. Would it support him, though? He got into a crouched position without too much pain and looked around the left side of the cactus. Alvarado was back on his feet and running east, uphill, toward a clump of scrawny mesquite trees. His right hand, still holding the automatic, was pressed against his bloody left shoulder.

Once Alvarado reached the relative safety of the bushes, he yelled, "Martin, you will die here! I saw where I hit you. The upper leg. Maybe in your, how do call it? Femoral artery. A lucky shot, I admit. But you will bleed out in a few minutes."

John slid his hand down inside the *g*-suit to the site of his pain. It wasn't wet. He brought his hand out and looked. No blood. He looked closer at the bullet hole and saw what had saved him. Alvarado's bullet had chewed up the *g*-suit and then hit the survival knife in its pocket on the g-suit's left leg. That's where the bullet had stopped. He'd have a bad bruise, but that was all. He stood up and walked a few steps. It hurt like hell to walk normally, but he didn't want Alvarado to see him limping.

"I'm coming for you Alvarado. Come out and fight, or run, I don't give a shit. Either way, I'll shoot you down like the rabid dog you are."

John felt very far out of his comfort zone. It had been almost twenty-five years—at Son Trâm—since he'd aimed a sidearm at another man. Later, he had killed men from the cockpit of a supersonic jet fighter, when the odds were heavily in his favor and without seeing their faces. This was different. This was close-up and personal. He had four bullets left to finish this fight, to achieve his goal, which Three-Six-Eight's 20-millimeter cannon hadn't quite accomplished. His Smith and Wesson .38 had a longer range than Alvarado's little handgun and he needed to exploit that advantage. They were about fifty feet apart, with Alvarado on the east side of a small arroyo. John walked up to the west edge, closing the distance another few feet.

Alvarado emerged from behind the mesquite and walked toward him.

John locked his eyes on Alvarado's, assumed a shooter's stance and lined up his sights on the center of mass.

He could hear Leslie's jet orbiting to the south. No, that increasing crescendo of engine noise wasn't from orbiting. It was a howling F-16 engine at full power. She was approaching them at high speed. He couldn't take his eyes off Alvarado. Would he surrender?

Alvarado grinned and raised his gun hand.

John fired twice.

Alvarado disappeared in a red mist, which was instantly obscured by a huge cloud of dust. The "BRRRP" of a 20-millimeter gatling gun rattled his ears. One second later, Leslie's jet flashed by, so low that she kicked up whorls of dust. She had been within a tenth of a second from ground impact, but now, at least, she was climbing out to the north.

John ran forward and saw gouges in the desert from Leslie's bullets. Alvarado had been standing right there. Ten feet north of that, he saw enough pieces of Alvarado to know that this guy wasn't going home today. Or ever.

Mission accomplished. He holstered his weapon, turned around and ran south toward Three-Six-Eight. He had to stop after five steps. His left leg wouldn't take it. He settled on a fast walk. On the way, he could hear Leslie's aircraft but didn't want to waste valuable time looking for her. How much time had this consumed? Maybe ten minutes since the last fuel check. Leslie might be at or past bingo fuel by now, but there she was, up there orbiting.

He reached his jet and searched nearby for something to use as a ladder— a fence post, a road sign, anything. There was nothing. He limped over to the left main tire, pulled out the rock and tossed it aside. This would be something new; he hoped he had the strength. John reached up and grabbed the AIM-9 missile with both hands, just aft of the forward fins. He crouched down, launched himself upward, and swung his right leg up and over the center of the missile and onto the wingtip, as if he were mounting a horse. It was painful and it took two tries, but he got up onto the left wing and, from there, it was just a few seconds more to get back into the cockpit.

John strapped in, got all the switches set for start, and pulled the JFS switch to Start 2. He was rewarded with the familiar huffing and puffing, then whining, of a successful JFS start. Ninety seconds later, he was at 125 knots on a slightly curving southern Arizona highway. He pulled back on the stick, the nose gear lifted off, and he was airborne.

John had no idea where Leslie was, but he knew she would be out there, ready to join up. "Viper One's blind. One's Joker."

"Viper Two's at your right five o'clock, two miles."

"Viper One, visual. Check forty-five right." He turned east and climbed. Another decoy move for Hardwick's benefit. After he saw that Leslie had made the turn, he said, "Viper One, fuel check. One's 14, 19, 33."

"Two's, ah, 12, 16, 28."

Leslie would be okay on fuel; they were only fifteen minutes —1,500 pounds of fuel—from Dateland. She'd be wondering why he was headed east, though.

He said, "Headed east about ten miles. Decoy move."

"Viper Two."

What was going to be his reference for ten miles? He had no clue. He was still climbing, now passing about 8,000 feet AGL. This was probably high enough and far enough.

"Viper Two, go fighting wing."

"Two."

When she had closed in to fighting wing position, forty-five degrees back and still on his right side, he said, "Taking it down. Heading west." He rolled his jet upside down and pulled into a Split-S. He leveled off at about 300 feet above the desert. He porpoised his airplane and saw Leslie move out to line-abreast tactical formation.

When the terrain was not a threat, he glanced down at the left console and put his index finger on the INS thumbwheel. With his eyes focused back outside, he flicked the thumbwheel one click aft and looked in the HUD to confirm his selection. He needed a small course correction.

"Viper One, check twenty right."

"Two."

From now on, they would stay very low, hide behind the mountains, and zigzag across the desert floor on their way back to Dateland. He had a map in his lower *g*-suit pocket but didn't pull it out. He had it memorized. Five short legs, four turns designed to keep them hidden behind high terrain and away from the prying eyes of ground-based radars and possible F-15 interceptors. Even at the relatively slow groundspeed of 420 knots, they'd be back at Dateland in thirteen minutes.

Chapter 42

Fifteen seconds later, it was time to turn. He dipped his left wing to signal a turn. Leslie turned left. When she had turned almost forty-five degrees, he rolled right. She rolled out, completing her part of the delayed forty-five left tactical turn. It was easy to lead a flight when you had a good wingman, and Leslie was one of the best. They had about two minutes until the next turn. Nothing was on his radar scope. His search area was surface to 30,000 feet; hers was 27,000 to 50,000. He visually checked her six, her nine, and her twelve. Clear.

Leslie was five hundred pounds lower on fuel than he was, but she would be all right—if the rest of their flight was uneventful. John flicked the INS wheel to Destination 3. His INS was a little off, probably thanks to his rushing the alignment back on that road, but his Mark I, Mod 0 eyeballs—thank you, Hank—told him he was on course. Updating the INS at the next checkpoint was possible, but unnecessary.

It wasn't until they had run across the desert, flying a few hundred feet off the ground, hiding behind the mountains, that he got the shakes. He had been too busy being the perfect flight leader, unflappable, displaying the all-knowing and all-seeing situational awareness of a great fighter pilot. Now, with a few minutes of time on this heading, his brain had the free time to digest what he—they—had just done.

They had just shot down two MiGs, in peacetime, with no orders from "above" to do so. Alvarado and his unfortunate wingman were dead. This was not a bad thing. But that last kill had not been clean. Not as simple as a heat-seeking missile up someone's tailpipe, or 20-millimeter HEI rounds punching holes in an adversary's fuselage, followed by a satisfying explosion and fireball. Pistol shots at close range, where he could see his adversary's face—that had been unexpected. The image of Alvarado's body parts scattered over a ten-foot, fan-shaped area? Red meat, splattered on the desert? That was a little too up close and personal for his taste. He would have nightmares about that. Had he fired first? Was Alvarado already dead when Leslie's twenty mike-mike pulverized him? Did it really matter who had killed him? He needed to settle down, take a drink of water, but that would have to wait until—"

"Viper Two, contact, thirty right, twenty miles, high. Correction. Now forty right, eastbound."

Those bogeys would soon fly off her scope. He needed more information. "Viper One, no contact. Check thirty right."

"Two. Viper Two's Bingo."

Great. A threat was out there, and his wingman had no fuel to spare. John turned thirty degrees right, tilted his radar antenna up, but saw no returns. He looked outside, back at the radar scope, and outside again. "Viper One, tally two, two-ship, one o'clock, forty right, very high, heading southeast. Marking." At this range, they were just two fast-moving little black dots, but he was willing to bet these were air defense fighters launched from March.

"Viper Two, tally two."

John watched the black dots and contrails continue east. Their direction and altitude had not changed. Wherever they were going, they were not a threat. The bogeys were now too far east to catch them. John exhaled heavily and felt his heart rate decrease.

"Viper One, check forty left. Bogeys no factor."

"Two."

Five minutes later, when Interstate 8 and the Dateland hangar came into view, he looked at his fuel gauge. If he had 2,600 pounds, Leslie would have about 2,100. That was plenty for what he had in mind. He check-turned them a little to the right so they'd cross the Interstate at a point free of traffic. No need to scare the motorists with high-speed, low-flying jets. A mile north of the highway, he abandoned all further attempts at radio silence. Would climbing up to traffic pattern altitude give them away to the authorities? Maybe. He didn't care. A tradition had to be upheld.

"Viper Two," he said. "Go to one-mile trail."

"Two."

That's all she needed to know. She'd soon figure out what he had in mind.

"Viper Ops, Viper One."

"Roger. Go ahead." It was Adam's voice.

"You two had better get outside. There's something you need to see."

John lined up with Dateland's Runway 19, stayed at about 500 feet, and slowed to 350 knots. When he reached midfield, he raised Three-Six-Eight's nose slightly and did a victory roll. He returned to wings level momentarily before pitching out to the left. Halfway through his climbing turn to downwind, he looked back and saw Leslie's victory roll.

After an uneventful landing rollout, they taxied in and shut down on the ramp just north of the hangar. He and Leslie remained in the cockpits while Whit and Adam towed both jets back into the hangar. John unstrapped, disconnected his oxygen and *g*-suit hoses, and removed his helmet. The ladder clunked against the left canopy rail. Whitaker climbed up to greet him. John put his helmet into the helmet bag and his small plastic knee board into one of its side pockets. Takeoff had been at 1447. It was now 1534. After eight days of crisis, complex preparation, and unexpected complications, the whole flight had lasted only forty-seven minutes. Longer than he had planned, but still acceptable.

When Whitaker took his helmet bag, John said, "We did it, Whit. Two MiGs destroyed."

Whitaker nodded and backed down the ladder. When John tried to push himself up and out of the cockpit, his left leg gave him trouble. He used his right leg and both arms to boost himself up and over to the canopy rail, where he sat, unsure if he could turn around and go down the ladder normally. "Whit, you'd better put that helmet bag down and spot me. I've got a little problem with my leg." He shuffled himself around and descended the ladder slowly, with minimum use of the bad leg.

"What happened?" Whitaker asked.

"Got shot. But the bullet—"

"Shot?" Whitaker pushed him aside and scrambled up the ladder. "Where did it hit? I don't see any damage." He jumped onto the ejection seat and looked up at the canopy, then out to the front, over the right side of the nose and the right wing. He turned around and inspected the left side of Three-Six-Eight.

"Whit. Come on down. Your jet didn't get hit. Just me, during a little scuffle on the ground."

"Say what? On the ground?"

"It's a long story," John said. "I'd rather only tell it once, so let's go sit down." He watched Leslie hang from Three-Four-Nine's canopy rail, drop down to the ramp, and head straight for him.

"Saw you favoring your right leg. What's wrong?" she said.

He pointed at the torn *g*-suit. "Alvarado got off a lucky shot before you, ah, before—"

Something popped. John flinched and looked to his left. It was Adam, holding a frothing bottle of champagne in one hand and a stack of plastic cups in the other.

Chapter 43

Whitaker said, "You got some bad timing, young man. Hold off on that bubbly stuff. John here has been shot. Probably needs some medical attention." He took a closer look at the torn *g*-suit. "Get that thing off and let's have a look."

"Not yet, Whit. Adam, pass out those cups and pour." When they all had a full cup, John raised his into the air. "To all of us. All six of us."

"Six?' Leslie said.

"Two darn good pilots. Two outstanding crew chiefs. And two great airplanes." He pointed his raised cup at the two F-16s.

The three others said, "Hear, hear!"

They emptied their cups.

Whitaker said, "John, come with me." He led him over to his cot. "Let's get that *g* -suit off. The flight suit too. You got a pair of shorts here someplace?" He turned to Leslie and said, "Young lady, hide your eyes."

John unzipped the legs of the *g*-suit first and then the waist. He showed Whitaker the gouged and bent survival knife that had deflected the bullet and prevented a more serious wound. After tossing the punctured *g* -suit onto the cot, he unzipped his flight suit, let it fall to the floor and stepped out of it.

"That's a mighty nasty big bruise you got there. Are you sure something ain't broken? You need an X-ray or something?"

"It's right over my femur, which is a pretty thick bone. I don't think I'd be walking if it were broken. Let's see how I feel in the morning. Now, give me those shorts."

Leslie and Adam joined them. Whitaker insisted that he sit down. All three of them crowded around him to examine the multicolored bruise that covered half of his upper left leg. He considered telling them that Whitaker had been more concerned about Three-Six Eight's health than his own wound. Maybe another time.

Adam and Whit bombarded them with questions about the air battle. Leslie described the intercept and gave John credit for setting up her unobserved entry. "I got in close," she said. "Then I forced myself to get even closer before I fired. You know, after I fired, I was so busy trying to avoid debris that I didn't really see the rounds hit. When I looked over at the MiG, it had already broken into two flaming pieces." She shuddered. "There was no chute."

Leslie told the story of John's engagement from her point of view. "Initially the lead MiG had gotten behind John's three-nine line." She stopped when she noticed Adam's lost look. "By that I mean, the MiG had gained a slight advantage. But I think John had to hold back because he was providing support for me. It didn't take long before John had turned the tables. He let that MiG run himself out of airspeed and ideas, then saddled up for a guns kill. I didn't see the MiG pilot eject, but several seconds later I saw the 'chute.

"When I saw John descend toward that road, I thought he was going to strafe the MiG pilot. But when I saw his landing gear come down, I knew right away what he was doing. My first thought—no offense John—was, 'You are a stupid shit.' But, as it happened . . . well, maybe John should tell the rest of the story."

John didn't really want to relive the ground encounter with Alvarado, but they had to know. When he got to the graphic part, he let Leslie take over.

"At first, I was just flying by to see what was happening. But I saw John go down and that made me very, very mad. I cranked the jet around and rolled in on Alvarado. Finished the job that we came out there for."

"I'll say you did," John said.

"By the way, John," she said, "You will be pleased to know that I aimed a little to the right to make sure I didn't hit you. I also got way too close before I fired. I was lucky that I didn't FOD my own engine with ricochets."

They all sat silently for a moment. John saw Whitaker and Adam close their eyes, as if they were trying to visualize the sounds, sights, and the emotions of that encounter. Adam excused himself and returned a moment later with a second bottle of chilled champagne.

"Great planning, Adam," Leslie said. "How did you know one bottle wouldn't be enough?"

"Just a lucky guess." He peeled the foil wrapper off the second bottle and twisted off the wire. "This is one occasion when I don't mind a little alcohol."

Whitaker said, "Point that thing away from the jets, young man, before you pop that cork."

"Yes, Chief." Adam said. After two or three twists, the cork popped, flew off toward the north hangar door, and bounced on the concrete. He filled their glasses, then walked off to pick up the cork.

"That Adam's a good man," Whitaker said. "He doesn't want to FOD an engine with a stupid champagne cork." He put down plates of ham sandwiches, chips, and apple slices. "John, now that we've heard the whole story of the air battle, the incredibly stupid move you made to land on that road—holy shit, what were you thinking? And, since we've all seen your bruise and determined that you will survive, would you please put on some long pants? There is a lady present. Gym shorts are not appropriate."

John stood up, grabbed his jeans from his cot and headed off toward the bathroom.

"Don't worry," Leslie said. "This is not the first time I've seen his legs."

John stopped and glared at Leslie.

"Oops," Leslie said.

Adam said, "Huh?"

Whitaker put his fingers in his ears and said, "Too much information! Somebody change the subject."

John stared at the two crew chiefs. "It's not what you think," he said.

"We are *not* involved," Leslie said. "Well, I mean, of course we *are* involved. As in, involved in this project. But not romantically involved."

John kept walking toward the bathroom, but that didn't prevent him from hearing what Leslie said next.

She whispered to Adam and Whitaker, "Not that that would be a bad thing . . ."

It took him just a few seconds to put on the jeans. However, it took most of a minute to work up the courage to push open the door and walk back out there. How could he face Adam and Whitaker now that they suspected Leslie was more than a good wingman to him? Shit, shit, shit.

Fortunately, the two crew chiefs were absent. They had walked over to their respective jets and were studiously wiping down hydraulic struts, opening panels, and doing their best to not make eye contact with him.

John reached for his champagne glass.

Leslie put a hand on his wrist and stopped him. "I'm sorry if I embarrassed you."

John looked directly into her eyes. She met his gaze. He closed his eyes, shook his head, and laughed. Slowly at first, then his chest heaved with ill-concealed mirth. Tears rolled down his cheeks.

"What?" Leslie said. She let go of his hand and started to laugh. The more he laughed, the more she joined in. "What? What? Tell me!"

He forced himself to stop and breathe. Was this a reaction to the stress of combat, or the irony of an old fart learning to deal with a female wingman? After another bout of mirth, he said, "I'm sorry." He picked up his glass and took a sip, which turned into a big gulp. "Why did I have to be born into this generation? Why couldn't I have been a World War II fighter pilot? With only a *man*—" He dissolved onto more laughter and had to pick up a napkin to wipe his eyes. "—only a man as my wingman."

"Bullshit, John. If you had been flying fighters in World War II, I would've been the female pilot who picked up your P-47 or P-51, or whatever, from the factory, flew it up into Newfoundland and across the Atlantic to deliver it to you in England. I would have known more about that plane than you did. I would have had more flight hours than you."

"Okay, then," he said. "I change my request back to 1918. World War I. I'm in France. I fly my SPAD through hordes of Fokker Triplanes, shooting down several in one day. I land back on my grass strip and drink brandy with my fellow *men*. I fall into my bed at night thinking about my next sortie, with my fellow *male* pilots. Not like today."

"What's not like today?"

"When I fall into my cot tonight, I might be thinking about how nice it would be to fall into a bed with my wingman. I don't know how to deal—"

"I thought we already covered this," Leslie said. "Let me explain again. You are handicapped. Your veins are filled with testosterone. I have a healthy female sex drive, but I am also genetically predisposed to use female logic. We females do the mission without regard to the anatomical makeup of the person in the other cockpit. By the way, dammit, why do they call it the *cock*pit?"

He shrugged. Leslie giggled, which set off another round of laughter so severe that he had to put down his champagne to avoid spilling it. Leslie joined in.

She looked at the row of cots and said, "The question—or questions, really—are, is the mission complete yet? Is it time to let hormones and testosterone take over? Here? In this hangar?"

She had two good points. First, they were in a hangar with two guys and no privacy. Second, there was more to do. The mission was not yet complete.

He said, "I am encouraged by your admission that hormones and testosterone are in play here. However, as a reasonable man, a term which may seem oxymoronic to you—" He paused for effect, prepared to join her in more giggles.

She sighed.

"I acknowledge that the mission is not yet complete," he said. He looked over at the two jets.

Leslie saw where he was looking. She was silent for a while. "You are wondering what to do with these jets."

"Yes. And that is a decision that involves you, me, and those two guys." He pointed to the two crew chiefs. "Let's go over there and join them."

John stopped in front of Three-Six-Eight's pitot boom and looked aft. This was his favorite view of the F-16—the "Little Grey Jet," as described in the parody sung by F-16 pilots all over the world, using the Beach Boys tune, "Little Deuce Coupe."

Well, I'm not braggin' boys, so don't put me down,

But I fly the neatest little jet around.
She's only single engine, and she's got one chair
But she'll gun a fuckin' MiG right out of the air.

She's my Little Grey Jet,
You all know what I fly.

Three-Six-Eight's pitot boom, the tip of the spear, poked out of the radome at about chin-level for a man of his height. The narrow radome seamlessly blended into the rest of the fuselage. Several feet aft of and below the radome was the engine intake, a reminder that this was a war machine. Shaped like a confident smile or sneer, it hinted at great power hidden within.

A clear plexiglass bubble canopy poked out of the fuselage at a spot directly above the intake. Behind the cockpit, a blended-body strake widened out and, seemingly without effort, merged into the short wings. The left and right horizontal tails, so critical to the F-16's maneuverability, completed the picture.

"She looks great, Whit," John said.

"Just like the old days."

"Yeah." John wished for the old days when things were simple. Back then, someone else gave to the orders to attack. Someone else sacrificed their soul in the interest of "the mission." He looked around, desperate to find a distraction, something that could erase the fact that he had organized the execution of two people. He pointed at Three-Four-Nine. "Look over there. Adam is wiping that jet down as if it were a racehorse that had just won the Kentucky Derby."

"Well, it did, kind of. Right?" Whitaker said. "Shot down a MiG-21. Also strafed poor Mister Alvarado into kingdom come. Does that bother you, John?"

"Does what bother me?"

"That Leslie might have been the one to waste Alvarado, not you."

"The mission was, as you so aptly put it, to waste Alvarado. Leslie and I, as a flight of two, accomplished that mission. That's all that counts."

Whitaker said, "Come on. I know you. You're gonna go to your grave believing it was a bullet from your little peashooter .38 that killed him."

"Don't tell Leslie that. Look, can we talk about something else?"

*   *   *

Ten minutes later, John had them all seated around the table. He had outlined all the options. "There are risks attached to all three," he said. "Option One: Walk away right now. Leave the jets here. If we run away from here tonight, leaving everything behind, someone will eventually find this hangar and Hardwick will link it to us, at least to Leslie and me. They might never know about Adam's involvement, but Whit is vulnerable too. They probably know I bought a ticket for Whit to come to Tucson. Option Two shouldn't even be an option. We can't fly these jets to some secret, private airport and hide them forever. We do not *have* a secret, private airport, nor can we fly them there without being seen. What would we do with the jets anyway? Sit and admire them while they deteriorate in some old barn?"

John let that sink in. He had already decided which option he'd prefer. But he wasn't out here by himself. He had a wingman and two crew chiefs to take care of. Their votes mattered. That gave him an idea. What he should do is—

"Tell me more about Option Three," Adam said.

John leaned forward, put his forearms down on the table and linked his hands together. "Option Three. We fly the jets back to D-M. They go back into the Boneyard. Leslie and I get arrested. As for Whit and Adam, their chances are the same as in option one. But—" He focused on Adam first, then Whit. "Let there be no mistake. I know Hardwick. He's smart, and he's got all the resources of the Federal government on his side. He'll probably find you, arrest you, and you will do time in prison."

He let the others absorb that information and watched as each of them turned to look at the two F-16s. John looked too. He knew what the jets would say if they had a voice.

"I tell you what," he said. "Let's put it to a vote." John reached out for his notepad, opened it, and tore off a blank page. He folded it twice, tore it into four pieces and slid one piece over to each person.

"Write down your choice," he said. "Option One or Option Three."

"What if there's a tie?" Whitaker said.

"We'll flip a coin," John said. He hoped someone had a coin. "Whit, give me that pencil."

He tossed the pencil onto the table. Each person marked a ballot and, without John prompting them, folded it into a small square. He collected the papers and shuffled them around a little so no one would know whose was whose. He opened the first one, looked at it and flipped it over. After opening the rest, he said, "It's unanimous. These jets—" His vison got a little blurry; he had to stop for a moment, swallow, stall for time. He squeezed his eyes shut. Shit. They were going to see their fearless leader with tears in his eyes. His voice broke as he said, "These jets are going back to the Boneyard."

"Oh, thank God!" Leslie said.

"Super!" said Adam.

"It's the right thing to do, people," Whitaker said.

"Okay," John said. He wiped his eyes with the back of his hand. "Here's how it will happen. We launch before sunrise. As soon as we are airborne, Adam and Whit drive away." He turned to Whitaker. "Don't go back to Tucson. Drive to San Diego. Fly back home from there."

"And what will you guys be doing with *our* airplanes?" Whitaker said.

"We'll just fly them over to Davis-Monthan. Give them back to the Boneyard."

"And go to jail," Whitaker said. "For a long, long time."

"Yes." He looked across the table at Leslie. "Are you prepared for that?"

"Yes," she said.

Adam said, "I have a question. Why take off so early?"

"Call me suspicious, or paranoid, or whatever," John said. "I'm frankly surprised that Hardwick's people haven't found us already. But if they finally get the bright idea to check out Dateland, or get some report of unusual activity out here, I would expect a raid just before dawn tomorrow."

Everyone was silent for a while, as if they had just realized the consequences of their actions.

Leslie picked up the half-full bottle of champagne. "Refills, anyone?"

Chapter 44

"All right, folks," Lynwood Hardwick said. "Sorry for the delay, but we needed to wait for Mister Richardson to return from the crash site. By the way, Richardson, over on that side table is a box lunch for you; you're welcome to eat while we talk."

"Thank you, sir, but I'll wait."

Hardwick said, "First, let's get some introductions out of the way. There are three people attending by conference call." He looked at his notes. "Mister Brian Youngblood from Albuquerque Center. Next is Lt. Colonel Phil Benson, Commander of the 22nd Fighter Squadron, California Air National Guard, based at March Air Force Base. Last, but not least, is Captain Ken Fenwick, also from the 22nd. He was the flight lead of Magic 91 flight, scrambled earlier today in response to our little, ah, incident." For the benefit of those on the telephone, he introduced the three members of his team and added which agencies they represented. "Also here is Lt. Colonel Fischer, D-M's chief of command post."

"Now let's get down to business. I'm not one to sugar-coat things, so let me be very clear. The goal of this meeting is to find a murderer. Two murderers, actually. And to find the murder weapons, which in this case are two stolen F-16s. We are going to sit here, review the facts, and figure out a plan. I am open to all ideas you might have." He left out the fact that this whole fiasco could easily blow up into a major international incident. Yellin had raised her hand. "Yes?"

"General, may I suggest you review the classification of this briefing?"

"Good idea. Why don't you do it?"

Yellin said, "This briefing is classified Secret, NOFORN, SCI. The "SCI" stands for Sensitive Compartmentalized Information.' Basically, what this means is—"

"It means your government will cut off your balls if you ever go public with any of this," Hardwick said. "No offense meant, Ms. Yellin."

"Couldn't have said it better myself," she said.

"Okay," Hardwick said. "Ms. Yellin, whose handwriting is infinitely better than mine, has written a timeline on this white board. Let's review that and see if anything jumps out at us as a clue. God knows we need one. For the benefit of the three people on speakerphone, I'm going to read it out loud." He stood up and walked to the board mounted on the wall.

Yellin had been concise. She had written only six lines.

"'*Saturday, 22 April, 0417: Theft of two F-16s.*' Below that is a long row of question marks, because we lost radar contact with those jets and don't know where the hell they landed. The next line down says, '*Monday, 24 April, 1455: Four unknown targets appear on ABQ Center radar; they merge.*' Below that, it says, '*Monday, 1501: Park ranger reports smoke, fire and two crash sites.*' Then we have, '*Monday, 1505: Two unknown targets egress to the east.*' Finally, on the last line, '*1507: Radar contact lost.*' Those are all the facts we can gather from air traffic control and the eyewitness. Mister Youngblood, do these times and events correspond with your records?"

There was a momentary delay and the sound of papers being shuffled. "Yes, those times check," Youngblood said.

Hardwick returned to his chair at the head of the table. He said, "Mister Richardson, now would be a good time to hear a report on your visit to the crash sites."

Richardson stood and walked over to the map pinned to a cork board on the wall. He picked up a wooden pointer and put the tip on an area that had been circled in red by Yellin. "By now, I guess everyone knows the location of these sites. Exact coordinates will be in my written report. When I arrived at the northernmost one, the first one reported by the park ranger, the fire had burned itself out. Most of the smoke was gone. I am not a trained aircraft accident investigator, but my impression is, this airplane exploded in mid-air and broke into two sections, which landed about a hundred meters apart. The front half was crumpled and badly burned. One of the larger pieces was the ejection seat, which was still in the cockpit with the . . . ah . . . the charred remains of the pilot still strapped in the seat. There was apparently no attempt to eject. Agent Pompolatis tells me that a forensics team is en route from FBI Headquarters to make a thorough examination. Oh. I forgot to say, based on a large section of the tail that apparently broke off before impact and was relatively intact, I positively identified this aircraft as a MiG-21.

"After leaving part of the team to secure the first crash site, the helo took me three miles south, where I found the wreckage of a second MiG-21, still smoking badly—thick black stuff—but with no visible flames. This one had seemed to hit while fluttering down at low speed, like a falling leaf . . . I don't know what they would call that in pilot language."

"Maybe in a flat spin," Hardwick said.

"We kept our distance from the wreckage, due to the possibility of ammunition cooking off under all that heat. However, I could clearly see that the canopy was missing, and the ejection seat was gone. That led to a foot search of the nearby area, which didn't turn up anything. I returned to the helicopter, we took off, searched some more, and found a parachute and a body about a half-mile south of the second crash site. That's where things got a little weird . . . and even more gruesome."

Richardson paused and took a deep breath. "I'm not sure I can adequately describe the scene. You'll have to see the crime scene photos yourself. Basically, this body, presumably the MiG pilot, had been cut into several pieces by large caliber bullets. I have to tell you; it was gross. Nearby soil and brush had gouges that could only have been made by high velocity, heavy-weapons-style rounds."

"How do you know it was the MiG pilot?" Pompolatis asked.

"We don't know for sure, but evidence suggests that. We found a flight helmet and a parachute harness commonly used by MiG pilots. A Soviet-made parachute was tied to a bush, presumably to form a sun shelter. But here's where it gets a little weird. Not far from the . . . body parts . . . was a small semi-automatic pistol and two shell casings. We'll wait for forensics to confirm this, but I believe the gun had been recently fired."

"At whom?" Hardwick said.

"Good question, sir," Richardson said. "We found a second set of footprints about forty feet from the MiG pilot's, ah, body parts. Again, forensics will confirm this, but my initial guess is these prints are from a different person."

Hardwick had a moment of sensory overload. He glanced up at the first and last entries written on the board. Their entire body of knowledge about today's events covered only one twelve-minute period. MiGs streak up from south of the border. They are intercepted and shot down by two unknown radar blips, presumably the F-16s, which disappear. Now, there's evidence suggesting someone else was on the ground near the pilot of the second MiG. "Were either of these MiGs two-seaters?"

Richardson said, "No, sir, they were both single-seaters."

"Does anyone have a theory about who this mystery person could be?"

No one spoke.

Pompolatis shifted in his seat and said, "Were there any vehicles nearby?"

"Negative," Richardson said.

"Any sign of tracks leading away from this crime scene?"

"Yes, the mystery man's footprints angled southwest until I lost them on a paved road. I assume this person continued south on that road. Exactly how far south we won't know until we get a report from the Pima County sheriff's office, who called in one of their professional trackers."

"That brings up another question," Hardwick said, looking at Richardson. "Do I need to worry about any jurisdictional disputes?"

"No, sir, the deputy I spoke to seemed quite happy to accept my statement that this is a military matter and a national security issue. His department will render any assistance we need, but he's okay with the Air Force and FBI taking control."

Hardwick said, "One last question. Did you find any identification on either of the dead MiG pilots?"

"No, sir. The first body was burned almost beyond recognition. However, about the second one? I saw his face, which was one of the few intact parts. I got pictures, which Agent Pompolatis will forward to NCIC—that's the FBI's National Crime Information Center in case you didn't know. NCIC might be able to ID the second man.

Hardwick reached into his briefcase and pulled out a manila folder. He opened it, extracted an eight-by-ten glossy photo, and slid it across the table to Richardson. "Is this the guy?"

Richardson examined the photo. Almost immediately, he said, "Yes, sir. That's him. Same distinctive mustache. Same receding hairline. Same eyes."

Hardwick said, "Lady and gentlemen, the man in that picture, the one that was chewed to pieces by what I predict were twenty-millimeter bullets fired by an F-16, was Carlos Alvarado." He realized that the three people on speakerphone and Lt. Col Fischer had no clue who Alvarado was or why he would be flying a MiG in Arizona. They would also be unaware of John Martin's motive for shooting him down. How much help could they be if they didn't know the whole story? He'd have to trust them.

"My team already knows this story, but the three on speakerphone don't. Neither does Lt. Colonel Fischer. So, you four, listen up—and remember what Ms. Yellin said about how highly classified this is." He gave them the whole history, beginning with the Citation crashes, Martin's history with Alvarado and his research that linked Alvarado to the shootdowns. "Martin and his partner, Leslie Olsen—the sister of one of the first victims—have somehow managed to steal two F-16s right out from under our noses and gone off on a vendetta against Alvarado."

"Quite a successful one, it seems," said Yellin.

"I have a question, sir."

It was the F-15 flight lead, Captain Fenwick. His voice echoed and sounded tinny through the speakerphone.

Fenwick said, "Does Albuquerque Center have a record of—maybe a radar track—of the F-16s before they merged with the MiGs? If so, we could project that back, sort of get an idea where they came from."

"Yes, I've got that here," Youngblood said. "Since these were all raw skin paints with no IFF, I can't say for sure. But, assuming the MiGs came from the south and the F-16s from the north, we got a few sweeps of the antenna on that northern group. They were heading almost due south—a magnetic track of 150."

Hardwick knew they had already checked all the jet-capable runways in the direction that Fenwick had suggested, but he didn't want to discourage the young man, who probably felt some guilt about not getting there in time to help. He said, "Thank you, Captain. We have checked some, but not all, of the likely airfields in that quadrant. Why don't you pull out some charts of your own and take a look for yourself? Put yourself in the shoes of the thief who, by the way, we know to be an experienced fighter pilot. Work with Ms. Yellin. If you identify any we have not checked, let us know."

"Yes, sir."

Lt. Colonel Benson said, "Sir, what about AWACS? I was under the impression that they always have one aircraft monitoring the southwest border. But Captain Fenwick tells me they reported Gadget Bent when he checked in. How long was that in effect?"

Hardwick nodded, not that Benson could see that. "Yes, I asked about AWACS right away. I believe it was Colonel Fischer who told me they were Gadget Bent." He noticed that Yellin, Richardson and Pompolatis were giving him blank stares. "For those that don't know, 'Gadget Bent' is a code word for radar inoperative. Colonel Fischer, do you have a record of when that outage occurred?"

Fischer opened a notebook and flipped through several pages. "Here it is. AWACS radar was out of service from—hold on . . . they've got it in Zulu time." Several seconds later, he said, "They were offline from 1445 to 1520 local time. Something about an equipment overheat light."

"That's quite a coincidence," Richardson said.

Hardwick said, "Mister Richardson, why don't you dig a little deeper into the AWACS outage? Make that a priority right after you get us copies of those pictures from the crash site."

Hardwick leaned back in his chair and sighed. "I know what you're all thinking. Martin has done us a favor. He has eliminated someone who sends drugs up here to corrupt the minds and bodies of our citizens. He is, or was, an arrogant criminal who was bold enough to shoot down two Customs Service surveillance jets." He watched the faces of those in the room. No one nodded agreement, but he knew that, in their hearts, they were rooting for Martin. The three on the conference call probably felt the same. Hell, part of him agreed with them.

"But that's not the way our country is supposed to work," he said. "No one should take the law into their own hands and execute someone. We have these things called laws, a concept called due process, and the right to a trial by jury. Finally, dammit, we can't let a private citizen go around stealing F-16s and using them for his own private vendetta, however noble that may seem. That is why we are going to hunt down John Martin."

Chapter 45

Whitaker unhooked the tow bar and gave Adam a thumbs-up gesture. Adam drove away with the Chevy pickup and tow bar to pull Leslie's jet out of the hangar. "You want to do a walk-around?"

"Maybe next time," John said.

Whitaker frowned. "Very funny." He walked a few steps away from Three-Six-Eight's nose and looked east. He sighed. "Always did like desert sunrises,"

John joined him and stood on his right. A band of clouds on the eastern horizon had gone from purple to pink and would soon be red. What was that old mariner's phrase? *Red sky in morning, sailor take warning.* That seemed appropriate for the day's events.

"Whit," he said. When the old guy turned to face him, John stepped forward and gave him a tight hug, which he held for a long time. He said, "Thank you, my friend. Thank you for everything." He released him, gave him a manly slap on the back, and said, "Don't forget what I said. You and Adam get out of here ASAP after we get airborne."

Whitaker looked away at the developing sunrise. "I'm trusting you to take good care of my jet."

John nodded. "You know I will."

They both patted the nose on their way back to the ladder. John climbed up, sat down in the seat, and strapped in. When Leslie was ready and her eyes were on him, he lowered the canopy, twirled his finger in the air, and started the jet up. Everything went smoothly during the start and after-start checks. Leslie gave him a thumbs-up. On his signal, Whitaker pulled the chocks, came to attention, and gave him the crispest salute he had ever seen. John returned it with equal gusto.

After a brief taxi to Runway 01, he was airborne, with Leslie out on his right in tactical formation. His plan was to stay low until about fifty miles southeast of Davis-Monthan. That might prevent, or at least delay, any intercept by air defense fighters. He didn't want any unwanted guests interrupting his final flight.

"Viper One," Leslie called. "Take a look on the Interstate, nine o'clock, about two miles."

John looked. Five or six vehicles, all with light bars flashing, were racing west. The first two vehicles in the caravan were highway patrol cars; the rest were vans or pickup trucks in Air Force blue. He clicked his mic twice. There was no need to say more. An early takeoff had proven to be a very wise, or lucky, decision. If Whitaker had followed orders, he and Adam would be long gone before those guys arrived at Dateland.

* * *

John kept them at low altitude and on a course that would avoid the site of yesterday's encounter with the MiGs. This would also keep them clear of the manned gunnery ranges used by fighters from Luke or Davis-Monthan. Near the town of Sells, twenty miles north of the Mexican border, he turned east. The sun had just popped up above the distant clouds; its glare made it painful to look in that direction. He aimed well south of Kitt Peak, the big observatory on the north end of the Baboquivari Mountains and chose an east-west valley to follow up the west slope of those mountains. Since they were already in a climb, he decided to risk going higher. Tucson was less than ten minutes away. They had a little time to play.

The thought of playtime in the sky brought back a memory, a not so pleasant one, but one related to today's mission—returning the jets. Putting them back to sleep. Years ago, he had done the same with Ned, an old mixed-breed family dog. Ned was old, sick, and in obvious pain. The decent thing to do for Ned was to euthanize him. On the way to the vet's office, he had detoured to one of Ned's favorite city parks for one last walk. Although almost blind, Ned knew his way along the manicured paths, sniffed his favorite bushes and rolled in the cool grass. John sat beside him. They stayed for a long while. John knew this was Ned's final opportunity to be free and alive. It was almost as if the dog knew it too. Once inside the vet's office, he gave Ned a pat on the nose and rubbed his back while the injection was given. The dog hadn't understood what was going to happen. John had held him until it was over and found no shame in shedding tears.

It would be the same with Three-Six-Eight. He would fondly pat its grey nose, run his hand over the strake, back toward the gun port, out onto the wing root. And then walk away. Three-Six-Eight would not understand it was going to be towed off to a slow death in the dusty Boneyard. There was one difference between Ned and Three-Six-Eight. This jet was not sick. Racing along at 420 knots above the Sonoran Desert, this machine was very much alive and healthy. He would give Three-Six-Eight and its partner, Three-Four-Nine, a few more minutes of freedom and life. A final chance to play in the park. But someone else had to vote on this decision.

He rocked his wings and started a gentle climbing right turn. Leslie began her rejoin to fingertip formation, closed in nicely, increased her bank angle to slow the closure rate, and slid into perfect position, three feet off his right wing. She hadn't even needed the speed brakes to slow her closure. After making the hand signal for a fuel check and getting a satisfactory reading from Leslie, John decided to give up on visual signals for a moment. This might betray their presence to anyone listening, but there was no way to signal his next question.

"Want to play a little?" he said.

Leslie didn't answer. She looked out to the northeast, over the mountains, in the direction of Davis-Monthan. After a brief glance inside her cockpit, she looked at him and gave him an unmistakably enthusiastic and yet somewhat solemn head nod and a thumbs-up. John assumed she knew what was waiting for them on the other side of the mountains. Like him, she didn't want this flight to end. Right now, they were climbing into a clear morning sky, soaring above the desert, looking down on mountain peaks. Their jets were vital and alive. Why not exercise them a little?

John pushed the power up to mil, pulled it back an inch, and continued climbing. He searched the sky for other aircraft and saw none. His radar screen was clean. The higher he climbed, the more of Arizona and Mexico he could see. Jagged mountain peaks which had seemed so imposing at lower altitudes now appeared as little dark bumps on a lighter brown desert floor. The sky was bright blue and, except for the eastern horizon, clear of clouds. Those would form later, about mid-day, as the atmosphere warmed. He leveled off at 10,000 feet, accelerated to 450 knots, and tightened the throttle friction to maintain a setting just below mil power. He wouldn't need to touch it again until the maneuver was complete.

He chose a ground reference, lined up on it and lowered the nose slightly to maintain speed. The jet felt ready, with just the right amount of slipstream noise, just the right amount of vibration, as if Three-Six-Eight were straining at its leash, ready to run. John pulled the nose up to the horizon, noted the altitude and airspeed, and began a loop. Using outside visual references to keep the wings level, he raised the nose at a rate of about eight degrees per second. His *g*-suit inflated reassuringly to minimize the four *g*s generated by the climb—except for the upper left leg, where Alvarado's bullet had torn the suit's inner bladder. That hole made an embarrassing flapping noise, not unlike that of a whoopee cushion.

The earth tilted away and disappeared under his feet. Soon the wingtips pointed straight up, perpendicular to the horizon. John looked over at Leslie, who was in perfect position, apparently glued in place, three feet off his right wingtip. As the laws of physics had their effect, airspeed dropped off during the first half of the loop. John relaxed back pressure on the stick, which slowed the rate at which the nose tracked through the sky. He knew that pulling too hard would result in an egg-shaped loop rather than a perfect circle. When the airplane was upside-down, with much less slipstream noise due to the low speed, everything got remarkably quiet. With no bogeys to chase down or shoot, he had a rare chance to enjoy flying for flying's sake, to savor the peaceful, easy feeling of being at the top of a loop at 200 knots. It was as if time and motion were suspended. Although inverted, he was kept in the seat by a small amount of centrifugal force. *G*-force was minimized by the low speed and reduced turn rate. The airplane seemed to fly itself through this phase of the loop, allowing him to enjoy the view.

John tilted his head back to look out the "top" of the canopy, which was now facing the earth, not the sky. There was no need to crank his neck back at a severe angle as he had in the F-4. The F-16's reclined seat made it easy. As the nose began to fall, he checked his altitude. He had gained about 10,000 feet, which was adequate to safely finish the loop. Many a pilot, including one entire aerobatic team with his good friend as Number Three, had been killed because they continued a loop with insufficient altitude to pull out before hitting the ground. Once the nose is committed down on the back side of a loop, there is no turning back. You either complete the loop, hit the ground trying or eject at high speed. His friend, regrettably, had chosen the second option.

Gentle back pressure on the stick kept the nose moving down into the vertical position. Noise and vibration increased until, without looking at the airspeed indicator, he knew it was time to pull harder on the stick. The view of the sky was gone, replaced by the brown desert floor. Mountains, desert scrub brush and dirt roads grew in size and detail. John blended in more stick pressure until, again without consulting any cockpit gauge, he felt the familiar four-*g* squeeze around his belly and legs. Blue sky re-entered his peripheral vision at the top of his helmet, a horizon came into view and, in a few more seconds, he was back to level flight. He allowed himself a quick check of the instruments and found he was at 10,000 feet, right where he had started, and at 445 knots, only five knots different than his original speed. Not bad.

These parameters were also the start point for his next maneuver. He signaled Leslie over to his left wing just to challenge her more. When she was in position, and airspeed was back to 450, he picked out a small cloud just above the horizon and began a barrel roll. He lowered the nose, pulled off to the right about forty-five degrees, and, using that cloud as the center of his roll, pulled up into a gentle left bank. At ninety degrees of bank, he was one-quarter of the way around the imaginary horizontal "barrel." What a pretty picture! Leslie in perfect fingertip position on his left wing. She, of course was looking to her right, at him, unable to see the ground below. But he had a fantastic view of her airplane, its left wing pointed straight down at the Sonoran Desert fifteen thousand feet below.

Maintaining his offset from the cloud, he backed off the stick pressure as his speed slowed. When he was upside down, enjoying the same low-speed tranquility as he had at the top of the loop, he looked over at Leslie again. She was a smooth flyer. Right in position. No bobbling of her nose.

A few seconds later he was again at ninety degrees of left bank, on the way down the opposite side of the barrel. Speed increased, as did the roar of the slipstream, not unlike that of a waterfall. Leslie was above him now, presumably enjoying the view. Finally, he arrived at his original altitude, wings level, at 450 knots. If he had done this correctly, he had just described a helical spiral, as if his airplane had been flying along the shape of a giant, stretched-out coil spring.

Now it was time for Leslie to have some fun. He gave her a visual signal to assume the lead. She acknowledged that. He slid back into the wingman's position and waited. His job was simple now. All he had to do was keep the three visual references lined up and make smooth but timely throttle movements to stay in position. It didn't matter if she were flying straight up, straight down, or turning. Wherever she went, he would go. That's where the element of trust came in. He knew enough about Leslie's flying skills to trust her with his life. He wasn't worried. He could—and would—stay with her through anything. That was the mission of any good wingman.

She warmed up with another loop. At the top of the maneuver, he checked his speed and altitude with a brief glance at the HUD. This was not a sign of mistrust; it was what any good wingman would do. No, that wasn't quite correct. The "good" wingman followed his leader. The *great* wingman had enough situational awareness to monitor all parameters for everyone's safety. John hadn't flown formation in more than five years, so he was having trouble monitoring enough things to qualify for the "great" category. As they used to say in his F-4 days, *Just keep the wingtip in the star,* a reference to the Phantom's visual cues for perfect fingertip formation. F-16 references were different, but the concept was the same: whatever the dive, bank, or speed your leader flies, you match it.

Leslie led him through a barrel roll—evidently, she thought those were fun too—and an Immelmann. She gave him a fuel check, lowered her nose, and accelerated to 300 knots. Then she signaled for him to resume the lead.

It was time to point towards D-M and land. John's intellect told him this flight had to end. His heart wanted to fly on forever, but fuel and common sense dictated otherwise. He had his own feelings about which type of formation they should use at D-M, but he wanted it to be a unanimous decision. He pressed the mic button and said, "Do we return in fingertip or tactical?"

She answered, "Are we fighter pilots or airshow weenies?"

John nodded. He wiggled the rudder pedals. She pulled away into route position. Then he porpoised his airplane, which was her signal to go tactical. She spread out to 9,000 feet line-abreast formation on his right side. Since they were headed south, he signaled a 90-left tactical turn to get them headed toward D-M. His job was to roll right, check her six, then turn back left. But he never got past the "check her six" part.

Two F-15s were out there, high and fast, at their six, closing on them.

Chapter 46

"Viper Two, break right. Two bogeys, six o'clock, three miles, high." John kept up his right turn, pulling his nose around to face the Eagles.

Five seconds later she said, "Viper Two, tally two."

Her words came out clipped, almost grunted. She must have strained hard during the 5-*g* turn and cranking her head around to find the bogeys.

Well, well. Hardwick must have gotten smart and moved the F-15s closer. To get here this quickly, they must have been on alert at Luke or Davis-Monthan. He didn't have a plan for this and didn't have much time to develop one. They were almost merged with the F-15s. Leslie would be expecting some guidance. Running was out of the question, as was fighting them. He had no quarrel with the Eagles. That left only one thing: a peace offering.

John started a gentle climbing turn to the left, pulled the throttle to idle, and rocked Leslie into fingertip position. When the airspeed bled off to 300, he leveled off and added power to maintain that speed. He rolled out of the turn when he was pointed in the general direction of Davis-Monthan. "Viper Two, this is the plan. After you join up, we're going to lower the gear. Show them we're not hostile."

"Two."

His brain worked better when he had a plan. Evidently the F-15s hadn't planned for their targets to slow down, because they both overshot badly and flushed out in front of them by about a mile. John ignored them for a moment. When Leslie was in position, he reduced power, climbed some more to slow down and, when airspeed hit 200 knots, signaled Leslie for gear down and speed brakes. Step One of his plan was complete. They had "surrendered" to the Eagles.

Step Two was to establish radio communication. He tapped the side of his helmet and gave Leslie the visual signals for 243.0. He could have just said, "Go to Guard," but visual signals seemed more appropriate, more old-school.

"Viper One, check."

"Two."

"F-15s thirty southwest of Tucson, this is Viper One on Guard."

"Ah, Viper One, go ahead. Are you the F-16s out here, with the gear down?"

"Affirmative." John watched as one of the F-15s passed overhead and assumed a trail position, presumably to shoot them if they misbehaved. The other Eagle, who was probably the flight lead, with its giant speed brake fully extended—it was about three times the size of an ironing board—joined up on his right wing, about a hundred feet away. The speed brake retracted.

"Viper One, this is Magic 61. Proceed to Davis-Monthan immediately. My orders are to shoot if you do not comply. Confirm weapons safe."

John resisted the temptation to say that D-M was where they were headed until they had been rudely interrupted. "Viper One, weapons safe."

"Viper Two, weapons safe."

"Magic, Viper One. I have a request." John outlined his plan to return the jets, fighter-pilot style, in tactical formation.

There was a long pause.

"Okay, Viper One, press on. We'll be in trail. We'll be making a full stop behind you. If you do anything other than fly down initial, pitch out, and land, we *will* shoot."

"Viper One copies."

John gave Leslie the appropriate signals for gear up and speed brakes closed. He directed her to a combat-spread tactical formation, lowered his nose and accelerated to 300 knots. He flew east to avoid Tucson International's traffic pattern. The F-15s were about a mile behind, also in tactical formation. He allowed himself one look back at the pristine, mostly uninhabited desert floor, its Sahuaro cacti, and the sparse green clusters of drought-resistant trees. He would never again enjoy the thrill of flying low, dodging hills at jet fighter speeds—480 knots, which was about 810 feet per second. Nor would he savor what he was doing right now: descending from high altitude under a perfect blue sky, the engine rumbling in idle, his jet's nose pointing toward home like a horse headed for the barn. John drank in all these sights and sounds with special reverence. If Hardwick had anything to say about it, he'd be locked up until he was too old to walk, let alone fly a jet fighter.

From Dateland to Tucson, and south to the Mexican border, so much had happened down there—on the ground and in the air—during the last two weeks. Eight human lives lost, six friendlies and two bad guys. Two MiGs blasted into small pieces. It all seemed like a dream, most of which was a nightmare. Hank's charred body. Government lies and coverups. The sight of Alvarado cut into pieces by twenty mike-mike ammo. On the happy side, there was the support of his crusty old crew chief, Whitaker, and Hank's son Adam. Those memories would last forever, as would his conflicted thoughts about Leslie. She flies a great jet. And she looks so good in a little black dress. How desirable she had looked that night, when he had laid her down on the rug in front of her fireplace! That seemed like so long ago.

John forced himself back to the unpleasant reality of returning these jets. As if to underscore the gloomy days to come, John had to maneuver around a dark grey cloud over Keystone Peak, just southwest of Tucson. Small, wispy tentacles of virga hung below the two-mile-wide cloud; if the mountain's vegetation was lucky, some of that moisture would reach the ground. Once past Keystone, he was back in bright morning sunlight, but his mood was still dark. He looked ahead at two ugly open-pit mines and Tucson's urban sprawl to the north. These did nothing to improve his outlook. What was going to happen to him and Leslie? Would Whit and Adam get away clean? He willed himself to put these worries on standby and get back to leading this flight.

"Viper and Eagle flights, go 297.2." They acknowledged. When he checked in, Tucson Approach Control told them D-M's active runway was 30. That was a little unusual; winds were usually out of the east in the early morning. Approach asked him if he was familiar with Golf Course, a ground reference point for entering the traffic pattern. He said yes. Evidently, that hadn't changed in twenty years.

He flew from Golf Course to the extended centerline of Runway 30 and changed over to tower frequency.

"Davis-Monthan tower, Viper One, flight of two, and Magic 61, flight of two, five-mile initial, full stop."

"Uh, Viper One, tower. Say your type aircraft."

"F-16s. We're the ones from the Boneyard. We're bringing them home." John assumed everyone would know what he meant by that.

"Ah, stand by one."

John pressed in toward the runway and descended to 4,200 feet, D-M's overhead pattern altitude. Several seconds later, a different, deeper voice said, amid a lot of background noise from alarms and telephone ringers, "Viper One, D-M tower. Command Post requests that you hold at Golf Course for five minutes, over."

It was too late for that. Couldn't they see that he was already way past Golf Course? Maybe it was the early-morning sun angle. "Tower, Viper One, unable. Viper One is min fuel." A small white lie. Well, they could just add that to his list of offenses.

"Ah, roger. Stand by."

John chuckled to himself as he remembered the words to an old Korean War-era fighter pilot song, *Itazuke Tower,* which told the story of a P-51 in trouble, needing to land, but the tower was on a coffee break and would not approve the landing. The pilot ended the song from Fighter Pilot Heaven, having never gotten permission to land. John was not going to follow that script.

At that moment, by coincidence, he was flying over the Boneyard and could see the row of F-16s from which they had borrowed Three-Six-Eight and Three-Four-Nine. The sun was high enough now to reflect off the bright white protective sealant on their canopies and radomes. It was almost as if they were smiling up at their fellow jets, saying, "Way to go! You showed them what we can do!"

"Viper One, say intentions."

By this time, John had flown over the approach end of the runway and was halfway through his break to downwind. Leslie and the F-15s would follow him within seconds. Did the tower guy not understand the situation? They were going to land with or without permission. He tightened up his mask, which had gotten slick with perspiration and slipped lower on his face during the two-*g* break turn. When he rolled out on downwind, he said, "Tower, Viper One . . . ah, and Magic 61 will need dearming for AIM-9s and guns." It would be too hard to explain that their missiles were fakes. Might as well let them think they're real.

"Viper One, tower, I say again, you are not—"

"Viper One—John? This is Hardwick. After you dearm, taxi to the transient ramp and shut down."

"Roger." So, Hardwick was there in person. This was going to be interesting. He lowered the landing gear, popped open the speed brakes and said, "Viper One, base, gear down." With additional emphasis he added, "Full stop." How correct that term was. No low approaches, no more touch-and-go landings for him, ever again. He was pleased that, when Leslie made her call, she mimicked the pause before she said, "Full Stop."

Chapter 47

With its nose proudly in the air, Three-Six-Eight sailed over the approach end of the runway and touched down smoothly at the 500-foot marker. John held the nose up for aerodynamic braking and lowered it to the runway as speed and lift decreased. Now he was just a high-speed tricycle rolling toward the end of D-M's 13,643-foot-long runway. In fact, he'd have to add power to get there, but that was the price to be paid for landing like a fighter pilot, at the 500-foot point on every landing, no matter how long the runway was.

During rollout, he had time to reflect on all the things that had gone right or wrong since Hank's "Blue Bandits" telephone message. Six Customs Service crewmembers had died along with their aircraft. Two bad guys and their MiGs had been destroyed. Was that a fair trade? Would the families of the victims ever know the truth? These were questions he was not qualified to answer. All John knew was this: Hank's killers had paid the ultimate price. Hank would have done the same for him.

"Viper One, tower. Contact Ground on 275.8. Dearming crew is waiting. Follow-Me vehicle is en route. Plan to park in front of Base Ops. Break. Magic 61, taxi to dearming and hold there."

John made a right turn to exit the active runway, followed the yellow painted lines to the dearming area, and stopped. Leslie pulled up beside him. A two-man crew wearing large "Mickey Mouse" ear protectors approached. He gave them the closed-fist visual signal confirming he was holding the brakes. One man holding a pair of chocks ducked under the jet. He came back into view and signaled the chocks were in. John released the brakes. The second man put safety pins in the gun and missile rails. After signaling for John to hold the brakes again, they pulled the chocks. The procedure was repeated on Leslie's jet. The two dearming guys scurried away. Their eyes were focused on something happening behind the aircraft.

Leslie twisted around to look over her tail and pointed in that direction. John looked back and saw a reception committee, with a blue Follow-Me truck in the lead, racing down the parallel taxiway toward them. What got John's attention was the two security police, one male and one female, leaning out of the pickup bed. They were dressed in full battle garb—helmets and flak vests—with M-16s already aimed at his cockpit. Even more impressive was the second vehicle, a Humvee with a 7.62 mm machine gun mounted on the roof and manned by a very eager-looking Security Policeman. A belt of ammo snaked out of the cab into the gun. John could see four other armed SPs inside the Humvee.

He waited while the heavily armed Humvee stopped behind them and the Follow-Me truck swung around in front, with two SPs now hunkered down behind the tailgate. Behind them, mounted on the forward edge of the pickup bed, was the rear-facing, white-painted vertical wooden sign with "Follow Me" painted in large black letters. Below that were two red arrows and lights, one pointing left and one pointing right. A flashing yellow light sat on top of the sign.

The female SP, whose M-16 was aimed at him, seemed to be staring down one of the six barrels of his gatling gun. Perhaps she was comparing her 5.56 mm bullets with the F-16's 20 mm shells and worrying about her disadvantage in firepower. He admired her bravery; she might not know that his gun was dearmed. Without taking her eyes or her aim off him, she backed up to the rear window of the pickup, banged on it with one hand and gave the "let's get moving" signal.

The blue Follow-Me truck pulled away slowly. John pushed the throttle up enough to get moving and then pulled it back to avoid jet-blasting those in the Humvee, Leslie's jet or the F-15s. Even inside the cockpit, with his custom-fit helmet designed to filter noise, he could hear the engine change pitch as rpm increased or decreased. With these old Pratt and Whitney engines, throttle movements, especially at or near idle, caused a unique momentary whine as the variable exhaust nozzle changed position. The sound reminded him of the pneumatic air wrenches used at tire repair shops. He steered to the center of the right side of the taxiway and headed southeast; Leslie would offset on the left side and stay 150 feet behind. It was going to be a long, one-mile-plus taxi to Base Ops. The sun glare blocked his view to the south, but there wasn't much out there anyway. Nothing but bare desert, a few outhouse-sized buildings housing navigational aids and, of course, the runway on which he had just landed. He looked left, at the main part of the base, where the aircraft parking areas, buildings and hangars were located.

The Customs Service Ramp and operations building was at this end of the ramp; it was easy to identify. Two Citations, two Blackhawks and one little Cessna 172, all painted in Customs Service dark blue and white, glinted in the sun outside a big hangar. This was the ramp from which Leslie's brother, and Hank, and their crews, had taxied out for their final flights. He saw the building where he had met Briggs and Leslie on that afternoon, nine days ago, when this adventure had begun. He noticed some movement up ahead. There was something going on next to the taxiway. The Follow-Me vehicle came to a halt, leaving John no choice but to stop. Ten seconds later, the truck pulled away, giving John a better view of what had made it stop. Several hundred yards ahead, a long row of people stood uncomfortably close to the taxiway. This was unheard of at any airfield and even more strange for a limited-access military base.

John added power and resumed his taxi. As he got closer to the row of people, he saw they were *Customs Service* men and women, about twenty of them, in full dress blue uniforms with matching blue campaign hats, gold badges, and shiny black leather Sam Browne belts with sidearms. They were lined up in a perfect row, standing at parade rest. One man stood front and center. It was Briggs. He saw Briggs turn his head to one side and bark out a command. They all came to attention. Briggs gave another command. Twenty right arms—twenty-one counting Briggs—snapped up in a precisely timed salute and held it. John turned his head to face them and returned their salute. When he passed Briggs, he saw the man raise his left hand and give him a thumbs-up. He returned the gesture. They would, of course, hold that salute until Leslie taxied past.

He was flattered, emotional, and yet a little angry, not at the reception but at the person who had arranged it without telling him. It was not a simple thing to get a bunch of Customs Service officers into formal dress and out on the ramp at a precise time. How had Leslie done it? Maybe she had made a quick call to Briggs on another frequency at some point during this morning's flight. Well, he shouldn't complain. It was a thank-you he would never forget.

John taxied past rows of A-10 Warthogs, too many to count, lined up on the same concrete on which had taxied his F-4 back in the day. The big oak tree still stood outside his old squadron building, providing shade for a new generation of fighter pilots. As he passed the last A-10s, he saw the large "Welcome to Davis-Monthan AFB" sign outside Base Ops. The Follow-Me truck turned left off the parallel taxiway, swung around almost 180 degrees, and came to a stop pointing southeast. Before John made the sweeping turn to line up for parking, he noticed a group of people standing outside the Base Ops doorway. Some had uniforms, some wore civilian clothes. One man was taller and more solidly built than all the others—Hardwick.

He swung Three-Six-Eight around and followed the Transient Alert ground crewman's signal to stop. Leslie pulled in beside him. After chocks and gear pins were installed, the ground crew gave him the "cut" signal. John gave Leslie a preparatory signal, tilted his head back and nodded forward. He lifted the throttle up and over the idle detent and shut the airplane down. He unlocked the canopy and gave Leslie another signal. Two electric motors buzzed as the canopies opened simultaneously. The pitch of their engines dropped off from the eardrum-rattling, high-pitched screech of idle power to a gentler and lower frequency whine of decreasing amplitude. When he shut off the battery switch, whirring gyros and other cockpit electronic gear wound down with a sound like a table saw shutting off.

No other aircraft had engines running, which was unusual for a busy fighter base. John assumed they had halted normal operations for their arrival. He unsnapped his chin strap and pulled off his helmet and skull cap. There were more items to disconnect, but he delayed that. He just sat there and enjoyed this rare opportunity to hear and feel all the sounds of his jet shutting down.

An airman approached on his left and hooked a ladder to the canopy rail. He said, "Need any help, sir?"

"No, thanks." It was time to face the music. He released his shoulder harness and lap belt. He unplugged various cords and hoses, finishing with the CRU-60 oxygen connector, which—based on a habit formed long ago—he returned to its storage clip on the right cockpit sidewall. If not stowed properly, and the next occupant lowered or raised the ejection seat, the CRU-60 could get trapped between the ejection seat and the inside edge of the right console.

Did he really care about the next occupant of Three-Six-Eight or possible damage the CRU-60 could do? Of course. He had promised Whitaker to take care of his—Whitaker's—jet. Besides it was procedure, an old habit. *Good habit patterns. That's what keeps fighter pilots alive.* Those were words he had instilled in Hank and others. If only he had added, *Always have a wingman*, his friend would still be alive.

He turned off the few remaining switches and put his helmet into its protective nylon bag. It was a custom-fitted, lightweight, high visibility model that he had paid for out of his own pocket. Would he ever get it back? If so, what would he do with it? He no longer owned a jet and, by the time he got out of jail, he'd be too old to fly. After one last look around the cockpit, he swung his legs up onto the canopy rail in the approved way, without stepping on the seat cushion. He pushed himself up onto the canopy rail, picked up his helmet bag, and backed down the ladder. His boots made five metallic clunks on the ladder's steps before he reached the tarmac. He felt a little less alive without a stick in his right hand, throttle in his left, and his feet on the rudder pedals.

That thought made him chuckle, but it was a half-hearted one. Why now? Why get all emotional about flying and "his" airplane? In the past, flying the F-16 had been all business. He had respected the jet, learned how to care for it and use it effectively, just as an infantry soldier cares for his rifle. Both are weapons, killing machines. Not something to fall in love with. Well, this was a hell of a time in his life to fall in love with flying.

Three-Six-Eight's turbine blades had not quite stopped spinning. As they cooled and shrunk a bit, they clacked and rattled against the hub from their position deep inside the grinning, shiny white intake. By the time he had unzipped his *g*-suit, unbuckled his harness, unzipped his survival vest, and hung all of them over the left AIM-9, engine rotation had stopped. Leslie was still in her cockpit. The two crew chiefs got very interested when she removed her helmet, shook out her long red hair and backed down the ladder. John also heard a few murmurs and sharp intakes of breath from the crowd of people waiting outside Base Ops. She followed his lead, hung up her equipment on Three-Four-Nine's left wingtip and walked over to him.

Before she arrived, he took off his flying gloves, stuffed them into a *g*-suit pocket, and looked over his airplane. He ran his bare hand along the leading edge of airplane's left wing, along the strake, across the ladder, and then along the long nose. As he had envisioned just before he had started that first loop today, he patted Three-Six-Eight's nose and said, "Goodbye, old friend."

Three individuals from the crowd stepped forward—Hardwick, a woman in civilian clothes, and a short bald guy in a rumpled grey suit. The grey suit guy hurried ahead, which was not easy for him since Hardwick and the female, both of whom were much taller, took longer strides. John decided he must be the head man from whichever law enforcement agency had been elected to arrest them. The man was walking so fast, and so awkwardly—with feet splayed out like a duck's—that the heels of his shiny black shoes scraped on the concrete. His unbuttoned suit coat trailed out behind him, revealing a paunch, a silver badge, and a holstered semiautomatic pistol. His bald head was covered in sweat.

John turned to Leslie and said, "Watch out. This guy doesn't look like he's done much field work lately. Don't make him nervous."

When Grey Suit Guy got within twenty feet, he put his right hand on the butt of his weapon, stopped, wheezed a little, and puffed up his chest. "John Martin? Leslie Olsen? Special Agent Pompolatis, FBI. You're under arrest! Get on the ground, face down. Spread your arms and legs!"

John said, "No."

Leslie gave him a questioning look.

Pompolatis pulled out his gun and aimed it at him. The barrel was wavering. "What?" he said. "What do you mean, 'No'?"

John had already nicknamed this man Agent Pompous, but thought better of using it, at least until the gun was put away. He raised his hands. Leslie did the same.

"Agent . . . *Special* Agent Pompolatis, we are unarmed. We are surrendering to you voluntarily. Handcuff us if you want, but we are not—"

"Get down on the fucking ground or I'll—"

"Pompolatis, holster your weapon!" Hardwick's voice boomed. "That's an order!"

Hardwick and the female had stopped a few feet behind Agent Pompous. That was probably a wise decision since, with that gun in his hand, Pompous was literally a loose cannon.

"They've got their hands up, for God's sake," Hardwick said. "If you must, just cuff 'em.

Pompous's chest was heaving. If he passed out, he'd inadvertently squeeze off a round. John moved ever so slightly to the left, away from Leslie, and was pleased to see that Pompous didn't track him with his gun. If it went off now, no one would get hurt, but a ricochet might hit Three-Six-Eight. What would Whitaker have to say about that?

Agent Pompous sighed, holstered his weapon, and looked at the single set of handcuffs on his belt. John took this as one more piece of evidence that Pompous didn't perform well in the field, under stress. How long had he known there were two suspects?

Pompous looked over his shoulder at Hardwick and the woman. "Um . . . Ms. Yellin, I don't suppose you have a pair of cuffs on you?"

"No," she said. "At—ah—at the agency, we don't carry them."

"All right," Pompous said. He stared at John. "Stay where you are." He walked up to Leslie. "Lower your arms. Hold out your left wrist." He slapped one end of the handcuffs on her left wrist and repeated the process on John's right wrist. He stepped back, rattled off a long list of Federal charges against them—including First Degree Murder—and read them their rights. "Now, you two." He pointed at Base Ops. "We are going to walk over to that building, where a car is waiting. You will be taken downtown for questioning and booking. I will be right behind you, so don't—"

"I know, I know," John said. "Don't try any funny business."

Leslie raised her left hand a little, which dragged his hand up, and looked down at the handcuffs. "Cute," she said, and winked at him. She began walking. When they marched past Hardwick, the general set his jaw and shook his head. John wasn't sure if that meant he was disgusted at John, Leslie, or Agent Pompous. Probably all of them.

When they reached the sidewalk outside Base Ops, Hardwick said, "Agent Pompolatis, may I have a word with you, in private?"

"Stop here," Pompolatis said to them. "Sir, I'm not leaving my prisoners until they are in cells downtown. Can we just talk here?"

"Look," Hardwick said. "I acknowledge that you have jurisdiction here. But I hope you can appreciate that there are high-level national security issues involved. These two have critical and time-sensitive facts that I need. So, I am asking you to let me interview them, alone, before you take them downtown."

Pompous shook his head. "No way, sir. After they are booked, you can—"

"Pompolatis, I don't have time to fuck around with you. You can agree to let me interview Martin and Olsen or I can call the President, who will call the Attorney General, who will in turn call the FBI, et cetera, et cetera. Shit will roll downhill, and you will be at the bottom of that hill, up to your asshole in it. Now, which way do you want it?"

Pompous wisely chose the path of least resistance and agreed to let Hardwick borrow his prisoners.

Hardwick said, "Thank you. Now, get those cuffs off."

When they were uncuffed, Hardwick glared at them with a look so hot it could have melted steel. "You two. Come with me."

Chapter 48

Hardwick marched them into Base Ops, past empty flight planning tables and the weather forecaster, and out the street-side door without saying a word to the wide-eyed staff. The woman, Yellin, was beside Hardwick. John was pretty sure she was CIA; no one else in government referred to themselves as "the agency." FBI Agent Pompous and another man in civilian clothes brought up the rear. Two black SUVs were parked at the curb.

Hardwick opened the front passenger door and said, "Ms. Yellin, you drive. Back to the command post. Martin and Olsen, get in the back."

Under Agent Pompous's watchful eye, John opened the back door for Leslie. She pulled herself up and into the back seat and slid over to the left. He followed and closed the door. The FBI man hurried back to the second vehicle; the other plain clothes guy was already behind the wheel of that one. Who would he be? His hair was cut short. He walked with a military bearing. A military man in civilian clothes. Office of Special Investigations, maybe? OSI agents wore civilian clothes. That made sense. One of OSI's missions was to investigate theft of Air Force property and boy, had there ever been a theft! When everyone was buckled in, Yellin started the engine and drove off to the southeast.

John pushed the button to lower his window. He saw Yellin's eyes looking at him in the rear-view mirror. "Don't worry," he said. "I'm not going to jump out. Just need a little fresh air." Her eyes went back on the road ahead. Leslie ran her window halfway down. The breeze felt good; outside temperature, he guessed, was in the low sixties. By the end of the day, it would be about eighty degrees, but by then he and Leslie would be breathing stale air in jail cells.

Yellin drove them southeast east along Phoenix Street, paralleling the flight line, stopped at Yuma Street, and made the slight right turn onto Yuma. The early morning sun glare bothered her. John watched her struggle with the sun visor, but the azimuth of the sun was just far enough left to shine in no matter where she positioned it.

"John!' Leslie said. "Do you see where we're going?"

"Yes." It was very surreal. Rincon Peak, their first checkpoint after the theft, was clearly visible in the distance, silhouetted against a clear blue desert sky. Its east slope was still in the shade. They passed the spot along the Boneyard's fence where John had recruited Whitaker. On their left, the gate through which Three-Six-Eight and Three-Four-Nine had escaped to fly again was closed and locked with a shiny new chain and a large bronze padlock. The SUV's tires crunched on the loose stones of the concrete apron in front of the command post. Yellin parked no more than a hundred yards from the second gate that Adam had opened early Saturday morning. The other vehicle, carrying Agent Pompous and the OSI guy, pulled in beside them.

It made sense for Hardwick to use this building. The command post was the most secure place on the base. He had probably worked out of here while trying to track them down. The privacy of the command post was a perfect place for Hardwick to interrogate them. John felt a twinge of sympathy for the man. There was no doubt Hardwick was a man who put his country first. When you added up the pluses and minuses of his long career in government service, he still came up a net winner to most people, but this business of covering up two shootdowns? John could not tolerate that.

With Hardwick leading the way and Yellin and the others behind them, he and Leslie walked up to the old blast doors, down the tunnel and into the elevator. After it clunked to a stop, Hardwick strode out, pushed a buzzer on the wall, and stood in front of the one-way glass. The door clicked and Hardwick pulled it open. Inside, John noticed that things hadn't changed much since he his last visit, almost a decade ago.

Hardwick said to the five of them, "Wait here." He descended several steps into the command post's lower floor and spoke with a lieutenant colonel. That officer turned, looked at them and nodded. Several airmen stared at him and Leslie. Probably more at Leslie than him. Had they been briefed on who these mysterious figures in black flight suits were?

Hardwick came back up to the narrow catwalk, pointed to Yellin and the other two men, and said, "I need a few minutes alone with these two. You three can wait in Colonel Fischer's office, over there." He pointed toward a doorway about twenty feet away. Pompous opened his mouth to complain but said nothing. The three of them squeezed past Hardwick and filed off toward the office.

Hardwick nodded his head toward a nearby set of double doors. "In there." He pushed both doors open and said, "Sit." He glared at them as they walked past.

John stepped into the room. It was a conference room with a large, narrow table and eight chairs, three on each side and one at each end. Aeronautical charts were spread out on the table. Notepads, pencils, and photos shared the remaining space with food wrappers and half-empty coffee cups. He and Leslie chose two chairs on the least-cluttered side of the table, facing a large white board mounted on the wall. Written there was an interesting synopsis of recent events and hand-drawn diagrams noting the crash sites of both MiGs and the flight path of their F-16s. The line for the F-16s ran east and ended with a big question mark—the point at which they had disappeared from radar.

Hardwick closed the doors, walked to the opposite side of the table, and stood with his back to the whiteboard. He leaned forward and put both hands on the table. "John, you are an insubordinate, arrogant son of a bitch. But I already knew that. This time, though, you have really gone off the rails. You are a danger to yourself and others. You have murdered two people using stolen United States aircraft. You have embarrassed the United States of America which, in case you hadn't noticed, I love very much."

He straightened up, folded his arms in front of him and looked at Leslie. "Ms. Olsen, I am saddened to say that everything I just said to John applies to you. You obviously are not capable of following instructions. Do you remember the last words I spoke to you?"

Leslie inhaled and said, "Yes, sir. You said, 'Don't let him do anything stupid.' But—"

"Forget it," Hardwick said. "I know what you're going to say. In your mind, what you did was not stupid. That is pure bullshit. You murdered two people, for God's sake!" He pointed at the door and said, "There's more than one person out there who wants you both in prison for the rest of your life or even sent to the gas chamber. Three different state and Federal agencies are arguing over who will prosecute you. Arizona still has the death penalty, by the way."

John had to suppress a smile. As inappropriate and irresponsible as it was, he couldn't help thinking this death penalty news would be a comfort to Whitaker if they really did end up in a cell together.

Hardwick closed his eyes. When he opened them, he bent down and said, "You two have become my enemy and—" He focused on Leslie. "As John will tell you, that is not a good place to be. I take my oath of office very seriously. I swore to protect the United States against all enemies, foreign *and* domestic."

John waited for it; he knew what Hardwick's next sentence would be.

"Martin, what do you have to say for yourself?"

"I make no excuses for our actions, sir." In John's military days, that sort of reply always caught senior officers by surprise. "But I do have one question. May I ask it?"

Hardwick said, "Go ahead."

This was a long shot, but John had noticed one little chink in Hardwick's armor. "You just said there were people out there who want us imprisoned, or worse. But, what about you? What do *you* think should happen to us?"

Hardwick said, "I—" He stopped, pulled out a chair and sat down. He put both elbows on the table, rubbed his eyes and face and lowered his hands to the table.

John noticed that Hardwick's fists weren't clenched. His palms were flat on the table. He took this to be a good sign.

"Martin, let me add one thing to my list of your annoying flaws. You are too fucking perceptive. Was it something in my eyes? The short answer to your question is, I do not know what the hell to do with you, but now someone else is involved. Did you know—of course you don't—that the President has gotten wind of these shootdowns? I had to brief him on the stolen F-16s. Do you know what he said? He said, 'How the, expletive deleted, did you allow this to happen?' He meant me, as if I had personally fueled up your jets, opened the gates for you and turned you loose on those MiGs. Shit."

Hardwick leaned back in his chair and surveyed the table, the room, and both their faces. "Okay," he said. "Technically, you are still both commissioned officers in the Air Force and subject to the 1947 National Security Act. Don't even think about repeating what I am about to tell you." He took in a deep breath and puffed it out.

"The President, being an astute politician, sees an opportunity here. By that I mean, an opportunity to raise his poll ratings. He has come up with the brilliant idea—and I put those words in quotes—to take personal credit for this whole affair. He wants me to spin it so that the 'alleged theft' of F-16s and subsequent shootdowns was his idea, a clandestine operation designed by him to fight back against the drug cartels. He didn't ask me for my opinion. If he had, I would have waved the bullshit flag and told him to lock you both up forever."

Hardwick stood up, went to the white board, and picked up an eraser. He wiped the board clean, except for the one big blue question mark at the bottom and sat back down. "So, listen carefully. As of this moment, you are to consider yourselves part of an undercover government operation." He looked over his shoulder at the blue question mark. "None of what I just erased ever happened. You will debrief us on how the hell you managed to do all this. You will sign a non-disclosure agreement. If you do these things, all charges against you will be dropped, to the great dismay, I am sure, of Agent Pompolatis out there."

He got to his feet and said, "Think it over. I'll go get the documents."

Chapter 49

"Well," Leslie said. "That was quite a surprise."

John nodded but didn't smile or look at her.

"What?" she said. "What's that look on your face? Surely, you're not thinking of refusing his offer?"

"Don't get me wrong," he said. "I don't want either of us to go to prison. No matter what happens, we won't. This situation is like a poker game. Hardwick thinks he holds all the cards, but he's wrong. There are some things you don't know, so let me explain. I've got to consider—"

The door opened, Hardwick walked in, sat down, and shoved some papers in front of them. "Grab a pen and get ready to sign. I'll explain the forms as we go along."

John said, "I don't think so, Lynwood." It was no accident that he had used Hardwick's first name. He wanted to put the guy on the defensive.

"What the hell!" Hardwick shouted. "Hear me and hear me well: Sign or go to prison."

John said, "Don't get all bent out of shape, Lynwood."

He had hoped for an extra minute to explain all this to Leslie. She'd just have to trust him, same as she had in the air.

He said, "Before we sign, I need to get a couple promises from you."

Hardwick recoiled as if he had been slapped in the face. Then he laughed. "You've got to be shitting me. You are in no position to dictate any conditions. I'll put it to your military mind like this. Think of yourself as the defeated Japanese Foreign Minister standing on the deck of the U.S.S. Missouri in 1945. Now, think of me as General MacArthur, who has set down on that famous table the surrender agreement that would end World War II in the Pacific. If you sign, it will end the killing and suffering. If you don't sign, I will drop a third nuke on one of your cities and incinerate hundreds of thousands more of your citizens. You are defeated. What's your choice?"

"Lynwood, there are two things wrong with your logic. First, from a historical perspective, you and I both know the United States did not have a third nuclear bomb. It was a bluff. Second, for our little, ah, situation, I have a nuclear option of my own. Do you remember those pictures I gave you? Did you ever wonder what I did with the actual piece of wreckage? And did you think those were the only copies of those pictures? If I disappear or go to jail, I have arranged for that piece of wreckage and the 23-millimeter bullet to be released to the press along with my written statement about our conversation in the White House during which, if you recall, you admitted there was a government cover-up of the shootdowns."

Hardwick leaned into him and said, "It's your word against mine, my friend. And who do you think everyone will believe? A renegade, disgraced, ex-fighter pilot or a trusted member of the President's cabinet?"

John said, "Well, *Lynwood*, back luck for you. It's not just your word against mine. You see, that renegade ex-fighter pilot also has an audio tape of our conversation in the White House. Everything word of it. It gets released to the press unless you agree to my conditions."

"Bullshit," Hardwick said. "You are the ultimate bullshitter. No one could get a tape recorder through security."

John said to Leslie, "See? Didn't I tell you this was like a poker game? One of us thinks he holds the winning cards. One of us, or both, may be bluffing."

He looked at Hardwick. "There is a flaw in White House security. Yes, they screen for recording devices. Yes, they take your cell phone. But they let me hold onto my laptop, because I told them you needed to see some data on there. That laptop has a voice recording feature. You can believe this or not. I don't give a shit. The question is, do you want to call my bluff?"

Hardwick sat down and stared at him for a good five seconds. "Let's say I'm undecided. What are your conditions?"

John said, "For us to participate in this coverup and promise our eternal silence, you must agree to the following: One: Leslie gets her Customs Service job back, if she wants it, with no black marks on her record. Two: Three other individuals, whom I will name later and who helped us, shall be exonerated of any wrongdoing. Three: The United States government will reimburse me for any expenses I have incurred in 'your' operation. That includes buying back my T-33 jet that I sold to finance this thing. If you agree to these three things . . ." He looked at Leslie. She nodded. "We will sign."

Hardwick chuckled. "So, you had help? Fascinating. Was someone in AWACS involved? It was too much of a coincidence that a $200 million asset would fail at that exact moment."

"I am waiting for a yes or a no," John said.

Hardwick's chest rose and fell. He narrowed his eyes, rubbed his chin, and stared at them. He closed his eyes for a long time, or what seemed like a long time to John. Long enough for him to watch Hardwick inhale and exhale, slowly, four times.

When he opened his eyes, Hardwick said, "I can't believe I'm doing this." His expression had changed to one of a football coach who had lost a close game and was walking across the field to shake hands with the winner. "I agree. Let's shake on it."

John kept his hands on the table. "General, I think it was you who once said, 'If it ain't in writing, it don't exist.' Would you be willing to sign a statement agreeing to what we just discussed?" He pushed a yellow legal pad across the table. "It doesn't have to be a formal typed document. A handwritten one will do."

Hardwick sat back and said, "How dare you imply that I might . . . shit! Well, never mind. Just know this, John. You have lost my respect."

John said, "Lynwood, the feeling is mutual."

While Hardwick wrote out his note, John looked over the non-disclosure agreement. Leslie did the same and picked up a pen. John put his hand over hers and shook his head.

"General, if we sign these, we both walk out of here, right now, free as birds?"

"Yes. As long as you agree to debrief at another time."

They agreed, set a date for the debriefing, and signed the papers. John slid them across the table. Hardwick signed his agreement. John read it over; it looked good.

"Well, I guess we're done here," John said. He pushed back his chair.

Hardwick said, "One more thing, John."

"There's always one more thing with you, isn't there?"

"What you did out there, how you got those jets, and how you kept it all under the radar, literally, shows a talent for, ah, unconventional thinking. Your country desperately needs someone like you. Are you *sure* I can't convince you to come work for me?"

"No thank you, General."

"Well, I had to ask. Again." Hardwick looked at Leslie. "How about you, Ms. Olsen? You seem to have many of these same talents. Are you interested in a career change?"

Leslie shoved her chair back, stood up, and said, "Right now, the only thing I am interested in is a cold beer. Come on, John, let's get out of here."

Acknowledgments

Four wonderful people did the copy editing for *Blue Bandits.* Three F-16 pilots, each of whom has significantly more experience than I in the Viper, provided invaluable technical expertise and advice on F-16A systems, tactics, and fighter pilot phraseology. They did more than that, though. They helped with the somewhat tedious job of identifying my (occasional?) grammar and syntax errors and plot inconsistencies. *Blue Bandits* would not be as readable or as accurate as it is without their contributions.

So, I offer sincere thanks to, in alphabetical order, Rex (*T. Rex*) Carpenter, Lt. Col. USAF (Ret), 5407.2 F-16 flight hours; Bob ("4 Qts") Gallon; and Kurt ("Lo Tek") Tek, 5803 F-16 flight hours, Fighter Weapons School Instructor.

The fourth copy editor is my soul mate, Linda. She encouraged me from the beginning and patiently endured the many hours I have spent on this book. She volunteered to be a copy editor, has read multiple drafts, and suggested many improvements. In fact, she is sitting next to me right now, reviewing what I hope is the final draft. I cringe every time she applies another sticky note to point out an error!

About the Author

Don Malatesta is a retired USAF fighter pilot with experience in six different jet fighters, including more than 1,800 flight hours in the F-16. He has retired from three other jobs: airline pilot, innkeeper and kayaking guide. He writes from his rural waterfront home near Olympia, Washington. After living in a great number of U.S. and foreign locations, Don is now happy ro write, garden and kayak in a place where wild animals, raptors and marine mammals vastly outnumber the human population.. Blue Bandits is his fourth book. Learn more about his current and future books at donmalatesta.weebly.com.

CPSIA information can be obtained
at www.ICGtesting.com
Printed in the USA
BVHW030245130722
641994BV00005B/198/J

9 781736 958230